D1590176

Critical Essays on
JULIO CORTÁZAR

CRITICAL ESSAYS
ON
WORLD LITERATURE

Robert Lecker, General Editor
McGill University

Critical Essays on

JULIO CORTÁZAR

edited by

JAIME ALAZRAKI

G. K. Hall & Co.
New York

G. K. Hall & Co.
1633 Broadway
New York, NY 10019

Library of Congress Cataloging-in-Publication Data

Critical essays on Julio Cortazar / edited by Jaime Alazraki.
        p.   cm.   — (Critical essays on world literature)
    Includes bibliographical references (p.   –   ) and index.
    ISBN 0-7838-0384-2 (alk. paper)
    1. Cortazar, Julio—Criticism and interpretation.   I. Alazraki,
Jaime.   II. Series.
    PQ7797.C7145 Z6265   1999
    863—dc21

                                            99-34318
                                            CIP

This paper meets the requirements of ANSI/NISO Z3948-1992 (Permanence of Paper).

10 9 8 7 6 5 4 3 2 1

Printed in the United States of America

Contents

◆

Publisher's Note

♦

Producing a volume that contains both newly commissioned and reprinted material presents the publisher with the challenge of balancing the desire to achieve stylistic consistency with the need to preserve the integrity of works first published elsewhere. In the Critical Essays series, essays commissioned especially for a particular volume are edited to be consistent with G. K. Hall's house style; reprinted essays appear in the style in which they were first published, with only typographical errors corrected. Consequently, shifts in style from one essay to another are the result of our efforts to be faithful to each text as it was originally published.

Introduction

JAIME ALAZRAKI

Julio Cortázar has been hailed as "one of the century's most gifted writers of short stories,"[1] and his novel *Hopscotch* has been described as "the most powerful encyclopedia of emotions and visions to emerge from the postwar generation of international writers."[2] Carlos Fuentes has described the language of *Hopscotch* with a lapidary phrase: "*Hopscotch* is to Spanish prose what *Ulysses* is to English prose."[3] Yet Cortázar was not only a consummate storyteller and the author of a masterpiece that has been praised as "the first great novel of Spanish America."[4] In addition to his 6 published novels and 10 collections of short stories, he wrote several books that defy generic compartmentalization. *Cronopios and Famas* (1969) is a hybrid that blends short fiction, sketch, humor, nonsense prose, poetry, and a surreal vision of objects and human behavior. *Around the Day in Eighty Worlds* (1986) contains selections from two volumes that Cortázar himself described as "almanac books," the first originally published in Spanish in 1967 under the same title and the second, *Último round* (Last round), in 1969. They are sort of collage books that include short fiction, essays, poetry, drawings, puzzles, pictures, photographs, criticism, engravings, quotations, and more. On the other hand, *A Certain Lucas* (1984) is a collection of vignettes of a character that voices Cortázar's habits, humor, feelings, anecdotes, tastes, and distates. A conventional writer would have chosen the autobiography or the memoir. Not Cortázar. He resisted tooth and nail telling the story of his life, perhaps because there is not a biographical tradition in Spanish literature but more probably because he believed in the imaginative and reflective powers of fiction as a more effective means of capturing human experience.

These unorthodox books point to the nonconformist side of Cortázar's art. His innovations transcend the sheer surface to focus on a different worldview and on its effects on the handling of form. His attempt to erase the

1

boundaries of genres in an effort to expand the perceptual capabilities of literature parallels his critique of language. "It seems to me absurd," he said in an interview, "to talk about transforming man if at the same time, or before, man doesn't transform his instruments of knowledge. How can we transform ourselves if we still use the same language Plato did?"[5] But his experiments with genre and his probings of language are not merely a feat at the level of form. They are part of a belief in the power of literature to change life, a power that Cortázar embraced early in his youth when he was spurred by surrealism and the examples of European poetry from romanticism on. As early as 1941, when he published an essay on Rimbaud, he distinguished two major directions in poetry: one that follows the example of Mallarmé and another that stems from Rimbaud. If both poets believed in the possibility of undermining the rational foundations of reality, Mallarmé represented for Cortázar the triumph of a dehumanized hermeticism that subordinates life to literature and views the book as the ultimate goal. Rimbaud, on the other hand, embodied life: "His problem was not," Cortázar writes, "a poetic one, but that of an ambitious human fulfillment for which the Poem must provide the clues." He concluded: "Mallarmé has left us an oeuvre; Rimbaud, the history of his blood. With all my devotion to the great poet, I feel that my being, as a whole, gravitates toward Rimbaud with an affection that is brotherhood and nostalgia."[6] Many years later, in a text included in *Último round*, he would summarize his evolution as a Latin American writer and intellectual with an allusion to Mallarmé's famous dictum "Tout aboutit à un livre" (the world exists for a book): "A writer for whom reality, as Mallarmé had it, existed in order to become a book left my country; in Paris a man for whom books become reality was born."[7]

These early preoccupations of Cortázar remained some of the pivotal concerns of his later work. His musings about poetry were not just academic, they were the probings of a poet in search of the expressive tools for shaping his visions and dreams. From his youthful collection of sonnets, *Presencia* (1938), up to his mature volume of poetry, *Salvo el crepúsculo* (*Save twilight* 1997), together with the scattered poems included in his two almanac books and the collection *Pameos y meopas* (1971), Cortázar wrote poetry throughout his life and liked to think of himself primarily as a poet. Several of his readers and critics see him as an authentic poet who wrote verse from childhood until shortly before his death and whose poetic work has been eclipsed by the early mastery and success of his stories and novels.

The undiscovered poet, the magician of the short story, the master of the novel, and the innovator of the essay form was also a trumpet player; a jazz connoisseur; a boxing fan; a secretive playwright; a prolific and intense letter writer; a devoted cinema goer; a tireless traveler; a exquisite music lover; a writer of tangos; an amateur photographer; a professional translator; a member of the Russell Tribunal; an activist for the "disappeared" in Argentina, Uruguay, and Chile during the military dictatorships of the seventies and eighties; a supporter of the Cuban and Nicaraguan revolutions; and a marvelous human being.

He started writing when he was barely nine years old, mainly poems that his proud mother showed to friends and relatives, who reacted with disbelief and retorted that the only way to explain their rare rhythmic perfection and ingenious use of rhyme was to conclude that the rascal had plagiarized them. This was the first critical blow Cortázar experienced in his career as a writer. He was still a child, and when his embarrassed mother went up to his room one night just before bedtime, ashamed because she respected and loved him very much but determined to find out whether he wrote those poems or took them from some book, she found a child in despair. Years later, Cortázar confessed: "I had an attack. I never cried so much. I must have been nine years old. I considered this an insult, as something that hurt my deepest feelings. I had written those sonnets with infinite love and they turned out well, even very well, and I was accused of plagiarism."[8]

Cortázar got used to the whims and whips of literary critics, and in the same way that he didn't let the unfairness of that early incident affect his lifetime dedication to poetry, he also didn't let the trends and conventions of criticism dictate or even influence the course of his writing. To the contrary, critics were compelled to forge new tools and approaches to interpret and understand his fiction effectively. This was a slow and complex process.

The most complete bibliography of Cortázar's works and of their critical commentary, compiled by Sara de Mundo Lo, was published by Albatross in 1985. It includes 2,619 items fitted into 274 large pages with three indices (one of Cortázar's works; one of critics', authors', translators', and illustrators' names; and one of cited journals and newspapers). In spite of its thoroughness, this exemplary bibliography has aged and needs updating. Since Alfaguara Publishers of Spain undertook the publication of Cortázar's complete works in 1985, at least a dozen new volumes of his writings have appeared: two previously unpublished novels, *Divertimento* (1988) and *El examen* (1987 The exam); three volumes of critical essays, *Obra crítica/1-2-3* (1994 Critical work, 3 vols.); a diary, *Diario de Andrés Fava* (1995); four theater pieces, published as *Adiós Robinson y otras piezas breves* (1995); a study of Keats, *Imagen de John Keats* (1995); an edition of his complete short stories, including the unpublished first collection, "La otra orilla" (The other shore), of 1945 (published as *Cuentos completos* in 1994); *Negro el 10* (1994), a facsimile edition of late and uncollected poetry; and more recently, in 1997, *Cuaderno de Zihuatenajo* (Zihuatenajo copybook). In addition, it is safe to surmise that between 1985 and 1999 the critical bibliography on Cortázar's works has at least doubled.

Critical recognition, however, has been slow in coming and controversial. His first published book was a collection of sonnets (*Presencia,* 1938). Then he wrote a short essay on Rimbaud, his first published prose, which appeared in the first issue of a literary journal, *Huella,* in 1941. The volume of poems and the essay placed Cortázar, who then used the pseudonym Julio Denis, in the Argentine literary generation of 1940, a group of poets who reacted fiercely against the playfulness and avantgarde prescriptions of the previous ultraist generation led by Jorge Luis Borges in the early twenties. In contrast to the lightness and verbal experiments of the latter generation, the poets of the forties assumed a certain gravity, saw poetry as epiphany, and adopted the sibylline tone of Rilke's *Duineser Elegien* and of Neruda's *Residence on Earth,* their literary gurus. But despite this early association with the spirit and aspirations of his generation, Cortázar from the outset followed his own intuitions and remained loyal to his own perceptions.

Before he published the volume of poems and the essay on Rimbaud, Cortázar earned a degree as an elementary and high school teacher, and in 1937 he left the University of Buenos Aires, where he was a first-year student in the Faculty of Arts and Sciences, to become a teacher first in Bolívar and later in Chivilcoy, two small towns in the province of Buenos Aires. (His father had left home when Cortázar was still a child, and as soon as he completed his teaching degree he was forced to work to support his mother.) For the next seven years he lived and worked in that provincial environment, but he also read there, literally, thousands of books. About those years, he reminisced: "I was always very ingrown. I lived in small towns where there were few interesting people, almost none. I used to spend the day in my room in my hotel or boardinghouse, reading and studying. That was very useful to me, and at the same time it was dangerous. It was useful in the sense that I consumed thousands of books. I certainly picked up a lot of book knowledge in those days. It was dangerous in that it probably deprived me of a good share of vital experience."9

The first and sole critic of *Presencia* (Presence) the book of sonnets published in 1938, was Cortázar himself. In spite of the rare perfection he achieved in these early sonnets, he dismissed them, years later, as "very Mallarméan," and the very fact that he never allowed its reprint or partial reproduction is a first indication that he saw this early peccadillo as the hasty step taken by a young man who rushed to the printed page out of sheer vanity. But he learned the lesson. Between 1937 and 1945, during the period he worked as a teacher in Bolívar and Chivilcoy, he wrote the stories that comprised his first collection of short fiction—"La otra orilla"—which was published posthumously in 1994 (as *Cuentos completos*) with the exception of "Bruja" (Witch), which appeared in the journal *Correo literario* in 1944. "I knew instinctively," Cortázar explained, "that my first stories shouldn't be published. I'd set myself a high literary standard and was determined to reach it before publishing anything. The stories were the best I could do at the time, but I didn't think they were good enough even though there were some good ideas in them" (Harss and Dohmann, 214). By 1947, he had written some of the stories that would be collected in his next volume, *Bestiario,* 1951 (Bestiary), but Cortázar was in no rush to publish them either. His commentary: "I was completely sure that from about, say, 1947, all the things I'd be putting away were good, some even very good. I am referring to some of the stories of *Bestiario*. I knew nobody had written stories like that before in Spanish, at least in my country. There were others. There were Borges' admirable stories, but I was doing something else."[10]

A few of the stories from *Bestiario* appeared in literary journals in Buenos Aires. The first one—"Casa tomada" (House taken over)—was published in 1946 in *Los anales de Buenos Aires,* a literary journal edited by Borges. Years later, Borges recounted the circumstances of the encounter: "I know very little about Cortázar's work, but the little I know, a few short stories, struck me as admirable. Besides, I am proud to be among the first to have published one of his works. . . . I remember that one day a very tall young man asked to see me. He left me a manuscript. I told him that I would read it. He returned a week later. The story was entitled 'House Taken Over.' I told him that I found it admirable. It was published in the journal and my sister Nora illustrated it."[11] Many years later, in 1985, Borges would edit and preface an anthology of Cortázar's short stories for the series Biblioteca Personal (A personal library), which Borges founded and edited with María Kodama in Buenos Aires.

In 1947, the title story—"Bestiario" (Bestiary)—was published in the same journal (August–September 1947), and a third story—"Lejana" (The distances)—appeared in *Cabalgata* in 1948. The next year he published *Los Reyes* (1949 The Kings), which appeared first in Borges's journal and subsequently in book form in a series entitled Gulab and Aldabahor, edited by Cortázar's friend the writer Daniel Devoto. It was published in an exquisite edition of 600 copies with a drawing by an Argentine artist named Oscar Capristo. The first 100 copies were numbered and printed on Ingres Fabriano paper, and the drawing was hand watercolored by the artist. The book was flatly ignored except for two reviews, one written for *Realidad* by Devoto, and the other by Cortázar's friend the poet Alberto Girri.[12] The public at large received the book in Cortázar's own words, with "absolute silence."

Although *Los Reyes* didn't elicit a greater critical reaction than his first published book, *Presencia,* it was a more mature work that reflected the 11 years separating the two. *Los Reyes* is a dramatic prose poem that reelaborates the myth of the Minotaur, but onto the old legend Cortázar packed additional layers of new and provocative ideas. The book was reissued in 1970 in a popular edition, reprinted in 1980, and then translated into French in 1983 in a bilingual edition. Cortázar commented in a 1967 interview on this early, sui generis book: "I am still very fond of *Los Reyes,* but it really has little or nothing to do with anything I have written since. It uses a very lofty language, a very polished and high-flown style, fine in its own way but basically very traditional. Something like a cross between Valéry and St. John Perse" (Harss and Dohmann, 217). When the second edition appeared in 1970, Cortázar's literary reputation was already established, and the slim volume received the critical attention it didn't get in its lavish first edition. Critics were divided. There were those who considered *Los Reyes* a sort of compendium of his entire oeuvre, or at least its embryo. Others, more cautiously, warned that the book was rather a mere exercise in style and should be seen as a closed chapter of his literary prehistory. According to this view, only with *Bestiario* does Cortázar's history begin. Yet this early book already anticipated some of his later interests and concerns, although he never repeated the use of its affected language.[13]

On 4 June 1943 a military coup brought to power General E. J. Farrell as president of Argentina and Colonel Juan D. Perón as its vice president. This event would have far-reaching effects on the history of the country for the next several decades, and its long-range consequences are still felt today. For Cortázar it marked the beginning of a personal hell. Chivilcoy, the small town in the province of Buenos Aires where he was teaching history and geography at the high school level, became a local mirror of what was happening in the rest of the country: political repression, authoritarian abuses, and academic favoritism. Local nationalists accused Cortázar of: (1) not showing enough enthusiasm for the new government (his three classes devoted to the "June 4th Revolution" that gave control of the country to Perón and the military were extremely cold, full of hesitations and reservations); (2) communism ("[I]f you were not an unconditional supporter of the Peronist Revolution you were a Communist," Cortázar commented tongue in cheek); and (3) atheism (during a bishop's visit to the school, Cortázar was the only teacher—out of 25—who didn't kiss the monsignor's ring). Cortázar commented on these accusations in a personal letter: "Next to me, John Dillinger was an angel."[14] These "charges" never turned into a formal legal suit, but for him the political climate at the school became unbearable.

Around that time, and as a most happy coincidence, he was offered a teaching position at the University of Cuyo in Mendoza, a western Argentine province bordering Chile. He accepted, and on 8 July 1944 he moved to Mendoza and soon after started teaching courses in French and English literatures. He enjoyed his students and university life. Mendoza is a very pleasant city, and Cortázar felt comfortable and happy there. In a letter to Mercedes Arias, a friend and colleague from his days in Bolívar, he wrote: "The university work is a pleasure: finally I can teach what I like! Mendoza is a lovely city crisscrossed by canals and high trees, with the mountains so near that one can go to study in their slopes. I plan to do that as soon as I organize my life and my work a bit better" (Domínguez, 268).

In 1946 Perón was elected president of Argentina, and his policies affected profoundly the life of the country and the administration of state universities. Cortázar was one of the many victims of the regime. He explains: "In 1945–1946, I participated in the political struggle against the Peronists, and since I knew I was going to lose my job because I'd been in the fight against Perón, when he won the presidential election, I resigned before I was backed against the wall, as so many colleagues who held on to their jobs were, and found work in Buenos Aires" (Harss and Dohmann, 214). He was called "a fascist," "a Nazi," and other names; there were political disagreements and arguments, the air was vitiated, and the university became a political battlefield. In a letter to Mercedes Arias dated 25 July 1945 he wrote: "I had violent clashes with the bosses of the university administration. The newspaper clipping I am enclosing will give you an idea of the conflict. . . . The root of the problem is that I was appointed during the Baldrich administration—a name that has become anathema in the present administration—and that makes me appear as sectarian and an unconditional of the old administration" (Domínguez, 273), in that political atmosphere and faced with the alternative of humiliation (similar to that suffered by Borges, who in 1946 was "promoted" out of a job as assistant librarian in a modest municipal library in the outskirts of Buenos Aires to "the inspectorship of poultry and rabbits in the public markets"), he resigned and moved to Buenos Aires. There, he started work as manager in the Cámara Argentina del Libro, an organization dedicated to the promotion and circulation of books.

That would do as a temporary job, but in 1947, the year after his return, Cortázar found himself working very hard to become a public translator. "I wanted to have a profession," he explained, "to be financially independent, already with the idea of moving to France. So I packed the three-year work required for the degree into eight or nine months. It was backbreaking" (Harss and Dohmann, 221). The following year, after obtaining his degree, he left the Cámara Argentina del Libro and began working as a translator. During this period he translated Louisa May Alcott's *Little Women*, Daniel Defoe's *Robinson Crusoe*, Walter John de la Mare's *Memoirs of a Midget*, G. K. Chesterton's *The Man Who Knew Too Much*, Henri Bremond's *La poésie pure*, Jean Giono's *Naissance de l'Odysée*, André Gide's *L'inmoraliste*, Alfred Stern's *Philosophie du rire et des pleurs*, and *Sartre: His Philosophy and Psychoanalysis*. Later, in the mid-fifties, he translated Edgar Allan Poe's *Complete Prose Works* and Marguerite Yourcenar's *Mémoirs d'Hadrian* with great success. In addition to these major works, he translated simple documents and letters.

Cortázar lived a solitary life and shunned the ceremonies and solemnities of the literary establishment, but he made sure he didn't miss the first series of public lectures Borges was giving in Buenos Aires at the time. Cortázar had a small circle of friends, from his high school days in the Colegio Mariano Acosta, and they met regularly in bars and cafés. He lived alone in a flat on the 12th floor of a building facing the harbor in the heart of downtown Buenos Aires. "I was able to see" he said of this time "the Río de la Plata and the ships coming and going. . . . I was writing a lot then."[16] Forty years later, he re-created this chapter of his life in one of his most striking stories, "Diario para un cuento" (A diary for a story), included in his last collection of short fiction, *Deshoras* (1982; published in English as *Unreasonable Hours* [1995]). Cortázar said of that story:

"Diario para un cuento" is rather autobiographical. I was in fact a public translator in Buenos Aires, where I had an office, and I used to translate to the pros-
titutes from the harbor area the letters sent to them by their sailors from all
over the world. The translations were from English into Spanish and the replies
to the addressers in English. As I explain in the story, I inherited that job from
my partner and I continued it out of pity, because those girls were totally
defenseless in epistolary and language matters. That is an episode of my life in
Buenos Aires that always seemed to me curious, out of the ordinary. And it is
also true, absolutely true, that through one of those letters I learned about a
murder. There was a woman who had been poisoned and had disappeared. I,
naturally, anticipating problems, didn't ask for details and stuck to my job, but
I always felt left with the concern of having been an epistolary witness of a
dark episode in that seedy environment. (Prego, 38)

In addition to working as a translator, Cortázar continued writing. During this period, until 1951, he completed his second collection of short stories, *Bestiario,* and also wrote two short novels (*Divertimento* and *El examen*), a
600-page monograph on John Keats (*Imagen de John Keats*), and a high number of articles and literary reviews published in journals and magazines. With
the exception of *Bestiario,* the other books, including the collected articles,
would be published posthumously. *Bestiario* appeared in Buenos Aires, on the
eve of Cortázar's trip to Paris, at the insistence of some of his friends who
were acquainted with his short fiction, thought highly of it, and encouraged
publication.

But by then Cortázar was not happy living in Argentina. The school he
had attended in Buenos Aires, Colegio Mariano Acosta, by some accounts one
of the best in the country, turned out to be a sham and would become the
subject of an engrossing story ("Escuela de noche" [Night school]) included in
Deshoras. The seven years he spent in provincial towns as a high school
teacher were profitable from the point of view of his vast readings, but they
were uneventful and empty in terms of human experience. When he finally
found in Mendoza a nearly ideal teaching position and a stimulating environment for working and living, the political manipulation of the university and
the advent of Perón had forced him to resign. He returned to Buenos Aires to
work and study under tremendous pressure to complete the degree requirements for public translating in just eight months. As a result of these exer-
tions, he developed a neurosis that he turned into two memorable stories—
"Circe" and "Letter to a Young Lady in Paris"—included in *Bestiario.* In spite
of this frantic literary activity, Cortázar said years later, referring to the political climate in Argentina and to the attitude of his generation regarding the
phenomenon of Perón: "We were very much disturbed by the loudspeakers
placed in the street corners, shouting relentlessly: 'Perón, Perón, how great
you are,' because the songs interfered with the last Alban Berg concerto we
were listening to. . . . Our condition of young petty bourgeois, who read sev-

eral languages, prevented us from understanding what was happening in Argentina. This led us to a great mistake, and many of us left the country."[17]

Actually, for Cortázar the political situation in Argentina was the last straw. Much earlier, when he was barely 18, "he and a group of friends made an abortive attempt to set sail to Europe in a cargo boat. . . . 'People dreamed of Paris and London. Buenos Aires was a sort of punishment. Living there was like being held in jail' " (Harss and Dohmann, 210). So when he was awarded a scholarship by the French government to study in Paris, he grabbed it. And when the scholarship ended in 1952, Cortázar remained in Paris, working odd jobs, such as wrapping packages in a department store, until he found a position as a freelance translator for UNESCO, a job he kept for a good part of his life. He established residence in Paris and married Aurora Bernárdez, returning to Argentina only for short visits, until his death in 1984.

Bestiario was published in 1951 the same month Cortázar left Argentina. Both events went unnoticed. In spite of the enthusiasm and support of his friends for the book, it was received with indifference, and other than one isolated review in *Sur,* the media ignored it completely. If the stories of "La otra orilla" were the literary endeavors of a talented apprentice, the fiction of *Bestiario* revealed the skills and maturity of a master. Cortázar must have been aware of that because he was undaunted by the silence of the critics. He kept writing stories, and in 1956 he published in México his second collection—*Final del juego* (End of the game)—which includes nine pieces in the first edition and double that number in the second, issued in Buenos Aires in 1964. Between the two editions of *Final del juego,* he published a third volume of short stories, *Las armas secretas* (The secret weapons, 1959); his first novel, *Los premios* (1960; published in English as *The Winners* [1965]); *Historias de cronopios y de famas* (1962; published in English as *Cronopios and Famas* [1969]); and *Rayuela* (1963; published in English as *Hopscotch* [1966]).

The very fact that *Final del juego* had to wait eight years before being reissued in a second, augmented edition indicates that the impact of this second collection was hardly felt. Even his third volume of short fiction, *Las armas secretas,* which includes "El perseguidor" (The pursuer), thought by some to be his most powerful story, was met with aloofness by commentators and critics. Cortázar himself said that "The Pursuer" represents, in his work, the closing of one chapter and the beginning of a new one with a different worldview:

> The discovery of my fellow man and woman . . . Many years later, I realized that had I not written "The Pursuer" I would have been unable to write *Hopscotch.* "The Pursuer" is like a little *Hopscotch.* Basically, the problems dealt with in *Hopscotch* are already discussed in "The Pursuer." The problem of a man, Johnny in one case, and Oliveira, in the other, who suddenly discovers that a biological fatality has caused him to be born and has brought him into a world he doesn't accept, Johnny for his reasons, and Oliveira for more intellectual, more elaborate, more metaphysical ones. But in essence they are very much

alike. Johnny and Oliveira are two individuals who question, criticize, and deny what the great majority accepts as a sort of historical and social fatalism.[18]

Cortázar believed that the publication of "The Pursuer" represented a turning point, not only in his development as a writer but also in the critical reception of his work. He has commented on the impact that this book had on his readers:

Las armas secretas rudely disturbed my readers with the story "The Pursuer." What followed was like those police reports in which a man returns home and finds his house turned upside down, the lamp table where the bathtub ought to be and all his shirts scattered among the geraniums on the patio. I do not know what readers were searching for in my house of paper and ink, but between 1958 and 1960 they stormed the libraries, and my books had to be reprinted to refurnish the empty house somewhat. To me in Paris this was unreal and amusing, but it was moving when so many letters began to arrive from young people wanting to discuss things or raise issues: gloomy letters, love letters, letters from people with a text for a thesis, and that sort of thing. (Guibert, 289)

"The Pursuer" is one of Cortázar's most widely read and frequently critiqued stories. Even before it was published, his readers were divided. When he showed the manuscript to a friend whose judgment he trusted very much— "a kind of private reader that often writers have"—the friend told him: "Throw it out. It is too long. It doesn't make any sense" (Prego, 69). Then Aurora Bernárdez, his first wife and a professional translator like himself, read it, and she liked it very much. Two or three more persons read the manuscript and shared his wife's enthusiasm.

No doubt that when the book was published in 1959 it elicited those letters to which Cortázar referred, but a scrutiny of the published criticism on this third volume of short fiction tells a different story about its reception. Of the 15 articles and reviews on Las armas secretas listed in Mundo Lo's *Bibliography,* only two reviews were written in 1960; all the others appeared after 1963, the year *Hopscotch* was published. And of 19 articles devoted to "The Pursuer," none was published earlier than 1967. The majority appeared in the seventies and eighties. If one adds that the first two collections (*Bestiario* and *Final del juego*) went virtually unnoticed in their first editions of 1951 and 1956 respectively, whereas the second editions of both collections in 1964 were followed by almost yearly reprints and sometimes two reprints in the same year, a clear pattern begins to emerge. Even his first published novel, *Los premios* (1960), which received six reviews one year after publication, would have to wait four years to be reprinted, but after 1964 a new reprint was released every year until the late seventies. The critical outpouring that followed was astounding. It is clear from these publishing data that between 1961 and 1964 something happened that changed the pace and degree of the reception of Cortázar's work in terms of readership (number of reprints of his books) and in terms of critical reaction (number of reviews, articles, and books published on his work). There is no mystery in the change of tide. In 1963, *Hopscotch* was published in Buenos Aires and became a watershed in the reception and critical evaluation of his entire oeuvre.

There were some lukewarm reviews, which were inevitable in the case of a novel that so radically changed the rules of the game and, one may say, the history of the genre, but the overwhelming majority acknowledged it as a masterpiece. It was after *Hopscotch* that readers stormed libraries and bookstores in search of Cortázar's earlier work, and publishers were compelled to reissue those three volumes of short stories that were ignored or received scant attention in their first editions. If, as Cortázar stated later, *Hopscotch* represented the philosophy of his short stories, the interest in his short fiction received a sudden boost with the publication of the novel. Readers were discovering, as Joyce Carol Oates put it years later, that some of his short stories "have the power to move us as Kafka's stories do."[19] Like Kafka's stories, Cortázar's tales have a realist surface and a fantastic twist. The presence of this fantastic element (a tiger that shares a country house with the family living there, a man who vomits bunnies, a dreamer who becomes his dream, an axolotl who switches place with the man who comes to see it at the zoo) has led some critics to define these stories as fantastic. Cortázar himself referred to them as "fantastic" adding, "for lack of a better name," "uncomfortable" with the label because he was well aware that the *fantastic,* as understood in the nineteenth century, when the genre was invented and produced its major works, responded to a different outlook and a different poetics. Gothic fiction appeals to the nocturnal side of life, and Cortázar was not interested in that side, that is, in assaulting the reader with the fears and horrors that have been defined as the attributes of the fantastic.

Yet it is clear that in his stories there is a fantastic side that runs against the grain of realist or psychological forms of fiction, allowing for uncanny events unthinkable within a realist code. This subject has received considerable attention by critics writing on Cortázar's short stories. To distinguish between the approach to the fantastic in Poe's stories and that found in Kafka's, I suggested the term *neofantastic* for defining the fiction of the latter.[20] It is not a matter of labels but of essence and generic definition. Rather than playing with the readers' fears, as the fantastic seeks to do, the neofantastic, as Cortázar put it in defining his own short stories, "seeks an alternative to that false realism which assumed that everything can be neatly described, as was upheld by the philosophic and scientific optimism of the eighteenth century, that is, within a world ruled more or less harmoniously by a system of laws, of principles, of causal relations, of well-defined psychologies, of well-mapped geographies." To conclude: "In my case, the suspicion of an other order, more secret and less communicable, and the fertile discovery of Alfred Jarry, for whom the true study of reality rested not on laws but on the exceptions to those laws, were some of the guiding principles of my personal search for a literature beyond overly naive forms of realism."[21]

Once this distinction has been made, we have not only a new label but a more effective critical tool for understanding these fictions that, as has been said of Kafka's stories, both accept and reject all interpretations. Sometimes these interpretations act as a Rorschach test: they tell us more about the interpreter than about the text being interpreted. The new code forged by the writer's imagination is translated into a realist code, the very code the narrative seeks to transcend, thus unconsciously undermining the author's endeavor. In Cortázar's fiction, this inherent difficulty of the story sometimes takes on the form of a metaphor (a tiger in "Bestiary," noises in "House Taken Over," rabbits in "Letter to a Lady in Paris"); in others, it becomes a mirror structure that organizes the narrative, as in most of the stories in *Final del juego.* In *Las armas secretas,* the metaphoric element disappears and so do the exact and playful structures. The focus is now on character, but the situations in which these characters are immersed and the conflicts they confront are far from responding to a realist perception. There is here a complexity that is of a piece with the metaphors and chiasmuslike structures of his earlier fiction.

This intrinsic complexity has led some critics to describe these stories as "difficult fiction."[22] It has also led to a number of different interpretations of the same story, as if we were dealing with a riddle that implies a preestablished solution or as if we were taking a Roschach test. This stems from the belief that the author has all the answers and has manipulated them through weird events to forge strange symbols or even to play with the reader, the way detective fiction does. This approach wrongly assumes that the fantastic, as it appears in Cortázar or Kafka, is translatable from one language (that of the fantastic) to the other (that of realism). But if realism has accustomed us to identify the explanations of fiction with our logical understanding of reality, because both accept a scientific perception of the world, the neofantastic seeks a new language with which to read the world, a new code with which to touch those areas of reality untouchable through the signs of the realist code. A meditation of this effort, its foundation, is found in the pages of *Hopscotch.*

The scope and circumstances underlying *Hopscotch* have been tightly summarized by Cortázar himself:

Hopscotch is a sort of synthesis of my 10 years in Paris, plus my earlier years. There I tried my best, at that moment, to deal, in novelistic terms, with what others, the philosophers, have dealt with in metaphysical terms: the great questions, the great problems. There is something else. In the same way that the book can be read at various levels—even the author suggests to the reader a double option—it is also divided (at least that was my intention) in a series of planes, sometimes definable, others diagonally and crisscrossing with each other. On the one hand, there is what could be called a total metaphysical critique. The main character, Oliveira—I think most readers have felt it clearly—refuses to accept the civilization of his time, the Judeo-Christian civilization. He doesn't accept it as a whole. He has the impression that there is a sort of error somewhere, and that there must be a way to either go back to where everything began in order to start again without making the same mistake, or else submit to a cosmic explosion from which a new road will open up. Paralleling this metaphysical level of the character, I was interested in undertaking a critique of language and a critique of the novel as a vehicle for those ideas.[23]

This may sound too abstract and hyperintellectual for a work of fiction, but Cortázar was fully aware of the risks and pitfalls of his undertaking. He points to the case of Thomas Mann as the countermodel for his novel:

> When Mann writes *The Magic Mountain* or *Doctor Faustus,* he always chooses hyperlearned characters. . . . He represents a humanism very respected in his time, but totally shattered and which doesn't hold any validity for me in this moment. . . . It seemed to me that the type of search in which Johnny [in "The Pursuer"] or Oliveira [in *Hopscotch*] are engaged not only did not require that class of intellectuals, but rather a kind of innocence, particularly in Johnny's case, a kind of naivité that appears in Rousseau, the customs clerk, when he paints masterworks without having the least idea of what he is doing, according to the critics' point of view, of course. (González Bermejo, 62)

This quest for the other side of reality, for a territory that rejects Aristotelian logic, or simply for an innocent view of the world partially explains the Zen quality that colors the narrative texture of *Hopscotch*.[24] The episodes that articulate the novel are not narrated in a cause-and-effect sequence but rather follow an irrational course that recalls the paradoxical approach of the Zen koan. Cortázar's statement confirms his proclivity to view the novel as a happening, as a mandala, as a narrative, which, like the Zen koan, seeks to modify the student's understanding of life following a path that contravenes Western reasoning. It is not a matter of disposing of one tradition of thought to adopt a new one. On the danger of misreading his effort, Cortázar warned: "I don't rely on Western tradition alone as a valid passport, and culturally I'm also totally disconnected from Eastern tradition, on which I don't see any particular compensatory reason to lean either. The truth is, each day I lose more confidence in myself, and I'm happy. I write worse and worse, from an aesthetic point of view. I'm glad, because I think I'm approaching the point where perhaps I'll be able to start writing as I think one ought to write in our time" (Harss and Dohmann, 245).

The impact of *Hopscotch* on readers and critics was as explosive as the book itself. Cortázar, for one, said of his novel, "Petrus Borel used to say: 'I'm a republican because I can't be a cannibal.' For my part, I should say I wrote *Hopscotch* because I could not dance it, spit it out, shout it, or project it as any form of spiritual or physical action through any conceivable medium of communication" (Guibert, 293). His readers, particularly the young, reacted with the same visceral attitude. Ana Basualdo, an exiled Argentine writer living now in Barcelona, summarized, in 1984, the reaction of her generation to *Hopscotch* at the time of its publication in Buenos Aires: "Today, it will be impossible for me to talk about my generation in Argentina without taking into account *Hopscotch* as a definitive influential factor. We reached the age of 20 reading that novel that expressed, formed, and projected us toward a future that was still in store for us. . . . We were seen with copies of *Hopscotch* in bars and streets, and at the same time, those bars and those streets and those people so much like ourselves were in a book written by a man that was 30 years our elder."[25] If that last comment stresses the strong affinity that the young had with the novel's characters and with their quest, the view of the older generation was not less enthusiastic. Mario Benedetti, a Uruguayan writer and Cortázar's contemporary, explains: "*Hopscotch* is, as all critics admit today, a key work, not only in Cortázar's fiction but in the twentieth-century Latin-American novel."[26] And Juan Gelman, the most powerful voice in Argentine poetry today, defines his debt with Cortázar's work in a letter addressed to him after his death: "In the streets of downtown Buenos Aires and at other times, I saw writers who never left the country and who wrote aping the French. I better understood Buenos Aires reading what you wrote in Paris. Such is your greatness, such is your love. Reading you, I also better understood the world. That is, I loved it more."[27]

But there were dissonant voices, too. For some readers the novel was too audacious and experimentalist. For others, it was a crude imitation of Joyce's *Ulysses* and as such a betrayal of Argentine sensibilities.[28] These were conservative voices that clung to the past and refused to recognize the forces of postmodernism leaving behind the last vestiges of an exhausted nineteenth century. Anything deflecting from the realist or psychological models was met with frowning and distrust. A few suspected in *Hopscotch*'s open structure and in its wealth of expressive devices a put-on, a way of pulling the reader's leg. Academicians criticized its language: it was too daring, too slangish, too free; it didn't have the beauty and the chiseled quality of his short stories. Cortázar defended his right to and necessity of a more lively and less conventional language. This undertaking was, in fact, at the very core of his search. He also engaged in a dialogue with those readers who contrasted his short stories with his novel, hailing the former and damning the latter:

> The reader has every right to prefer one or the other vehicle, to choose participation or reflection. Nonetheless, he shouldn't criticize the novel in the name of the story (or vice versa, if anyone is so inclined) because the central attitude remains one and the same, and the only thing different is the perspective from which the author multiplies his interstitial possibilities. *Hopscotch* is in a sense the philosophy of my stories, an investigation of what for many years determined their material and impulses. I reflect little or not at all when I write my

stories; as with my poems, I have the impression they write themselves. . . . The novels, on the other hand, have been more systematic enterprises in which poetical estrangement intervenes only intermittently to move forward action slowed by reflection. But has it been sufficiently recognized that those reflections are less concerned with logic than with prophecy, less dialectical than verbal or imaginative association?[29]

When the dust settled, *Hopscotch* emerged as a classic of contemporary fiction and became the turning point in Cortázar's work, the point of arrival of his early writings and a point of departure for his later fiction. A flood of printed commentary followed. On *Hopscotch* alone, Mundo Lo's *Bibliography* lists 187 items, including reviews, articles, and book chapters. By 1968, two book-length studies had appeared in Argentina. They constitute surveys that attempt to present an overview, the first assessments of his work as a whole. A year later, in 1969, the first Ph.D. dissertations on Cortázar were written in Europe and the United States, and 73 new ones followed suit during a 15-year period. This, in turn, set in motion the machinery of university as well as commercial presses. Dozens of books devoted to the study of Cortázar's fiction appeared in Latin America, Europe, and the United States. Academic conferences and symposia took place from Oklahoma to Manheim, from Barnard to Poitiers. The proceedings of these meetings were published in book form or in special issues of university journals. During the same period, 69 short, long, and book-length interviews appeared in newspapers, magazines, and literary journals. Fifty books and special volumes evinced the frenzy and fascination that his work triggered among readers and critics. The adjective "Cortázarian" was coined to define a vision through which an elusive dimension has been captured. This dimension rejects a monolithic and logical view of the world in favor of a version of reality that contains several versions, in favor of one identity that includes other identities, and in sum, in favor of a focus that is, in actuality, multifocal.

That is why the images presented in his stories are in constant motion, why they are what they are, and at the same time, are something else; the narrative situations are porous and accept more than one interpretation, and characters refuse to behave following the "current instrumental psychology." Cortázar believed, as he wrote in *Hopscotch,* that "man only is in that he searches to be, plans to be."[30] He also said in the same book: "Today fascinates me, but always from the point of view of yesterday, and that's how at my age the past becomes present and the present is a strange and confused future" (*Hopscotch,* 93). This liquid time that contains other times, this multifocal vision of reality, and this elastic perception of selfhood that resists a frozen self and a single identity are some of the foundations on which his literary universe is built.

Echoing the implications of this vision at the level of form, Cortázar forged a language that sounds colloquial but is intensely and essentially poetic. The naturalness with which his prose flows in his fiction is deceiving. Behind that apparent simplicity he mounted a complex verbal machinery, a system of rhythms and modulations that give to his prose the condition of a musical instrument. Borges was among the first to notice this quality. In his prologue to an anthology of Cortázar's short fiction, he writes: "Style seems careless, but each word has been carefully chosen. Nobody can tell the plot of a Cortázar story; each text includes certain words organized in a certain order. If we attempt to summarize it, we realize that something precious has been lost."[31]

Cortázar was fully aware of the presence of this musical quality in his prose. Musical, not in the exterior and sometimes ornamental way cultivated by French Parnassians and symbolists in the late nineteenth century and by their literary heirs in the Hispanic world, but as the natural pulsation of the story theme conveyed to the body of the written artifact as a rhythm, as a beat, and in sum, as music. He said on several occasions that he considered himself a frustrated musician: "If I had the talents of a musician, I would have been a musician. You find musical qualities in what I write? Yes; there is sublimation there or, better, consolation; because I couldn't play the piano well, because I couldn't sing, because I had no gift for composition, I made up for it by writing."[32] He was not exaggerating. One of the lectures he gave at the University of California, Berkeley, in 1980 was devoted entirely to this subject. In his musical pursuits, Cortázar might have been motivated by his frustration as an unfulfilled musician, but his efforts to endow his prose with a musical component resulted in a prose in which style supports and reinforces theme. The medium is partner to the message; it says through syntax what the message expresses at the semantic level. The text that perhaps best exemplifies this strategy is "The Pursuer," in which the story of a jazzman, Johnny Carter (modeled after Charlie Parker), is told in a prose that communicates through its tempo and cadence a jazz beat that is of a piece with the jazz music played by the main character and with some of his main concerns.

Although this is one of the least studied aspects of Cortázar's work, a perceptive reader can readily feel the musical power of his prose. And if one is to take seriously George Steiner's remark that "a great prose—Diderot's *Neveu de Rameau,* Kafka's *Metamorphosis*—has a music of its own, and one for which we do not, as yet, have adequate notation,"[33] it becomes sufficiently clear that even though we don't have a notation system for reading that music, we can still recognize a prose that sings from a prose that simply talks, a prose with a peculiar rhythm of its own from a prose that is forever frozen and motionless, a prose in which movement communicates an unwritten and yet audible reverse from a prose deaf and paralyzed by its own opacity. Cortázar's prose, it is self-evident, belongs to the first type. "He was one of the innovators of the Spanish prose," wrote the Mexican poet Octavio Paz about Cortázar. And he added: "He bestowed on it lightness, grace, freedom, and a certain defiance. An airy prose, weightless and disembodied, but one that blows with strength and raises in our minds flocks of images and visions. Julio revived many words and made them leap, dance, and fly."[34]

Notes

Unless otherwise noted all translations are my own.

1. Michael Wood, "The Not So Light Fantastic," *New York Review of Books* (12 October 1978): 61.

2. C. D. B. Bryan, "Cortázar's Masterpiece," *New Republic* 154 (23 April 1966): 19–23.

3. Carlos Fuentes, "*Hopscotch:* The Novel as Pandora's Box," *Review of Contemporary Fiction* 3, no. 3 (Fall 1983): 88.

4. "*On the Hop,*" *Times Literary Supplement,* 9 March 1967.

5. Luis Harss, *Los nuestros* (Buenos Aires: Sudamericana, 1968), 288. Hereafter cited in text.

6. Julio Cortázar, "Rimbaud," in *Huella* (Buenos Aires No. 1, 1941), 29–34. Also included in Jaime Alazraki ed., "Julio Cortázar," in *Obra Crítica* 2 (Maldrid: Alfaguara, 1994), 15–23.

7. Julio Cortázar, *Último round* (México: Siglo XXI Editores, 1969), 207.

8. Omar Prego, *La fascinación de las palabras: Conversaciones con Julio Cortázar* (Barcelona: Muchnik, 1985), 155–56; hereafter cited in text.

9. Luis Harss and Barbara Dohmann, *Into the Mainstream* (New York: Harper & Row, 1966), 215; hereafter cited in text.

10. Harss, 264. The last two sentences of this quotation are omitted in the published English translation (see Harss and Dohman, *Into the Mainstream,* 216).

11. Rita Guibert, *Seven Voices* (New York: Vintage Books, 1973), 108; hereafter cited in text.

12. Daniel Devoto, *Realidad* no. 6 (1949); Alberto Girri, *Sur* no. 183 (1950).

13. For a discussion of *Los Reyes* and its literary and historic contexts, see my essay "De mitos y tiranías: relectura de *Los Reyes,*" in J. Alazraki, *Hacia Cortázar: aproximaciones a su obra* (Barcelona: Anthropos, 1994), 43–55.

14. Mignon Domínguez, ed., *Cartas desconocidas de Julio Cortázar, 1939–1945* (Buenos Aires: Editorial Sudamericana, 1994), 266; hereafter cited in text.

15. Jorge Luis Borges, "An Autobiographical Essay," in Jaime Alazraki, ed., *Critical Essays on Jorge Luis Borges* (Boston: G. K. Hall & Co., 1987), 46.

16. Ana María Hernández, "Conversación con Julio Cortázar," *Nueva Narrativa Hispanoamericana* 3, no. 2 (September 1973): 31.

17. Ernesto González Bermejo, *Conversaciones con Cortázar* (Barcelona: Edhasa, 1978), 119; hereafter cited in text.

18. Evelyn Picon Garfield, *Cortázar por Cortázar* (México: Universidad Verocruzana, 1981), 20.

19. Joyce Carol Oates, "Triumphant Tales of Obsession," *New York Times Book Review* (9 November 1980): 9.

20. I have discussed this subject extensively in my book *En busca del unicornio: Los cuentos de Julio Cortázar (Elementos para una poética de lo neofantástico)* (Madrid: Gredos, 1983).

21. Julio Cortázar, "Algunos aspectos del cuento," in Jaime Alazraki, ed., *Obra crítica 12,* (Madrid: Alfaguara, 1994), 368.

22. I am referring to Seymour Chatman's long article "The Rhetoric of difficult Fiction: Cortázar's 'Blow-Up,' " *Poetics Today* 1, no. 4 (1980): 23–66.

23. Margarita García Flores, "Siete respuestas de Julio Cortázar," *Revista de la Universidad de México* 21, no. 7 (March 1967): 10.

24. I have studied this aspect of *Hopscotch* in my prologue to Cortázar, *Rayuela* (Caracas: Biblioteca Ayacucho, 1980), 60–75.

25. Ana Basualdo, *La Vanguardia* (Barcelona), 13 February 1984.

26. Mario Benedetti, "Un autor en busca de cómplices," in Hugo Niño, ed., *Queremos tanto a Julio,* (Managua: Nueva Nicaragua, 1984), 22–23.

27. Juan Gelman, "Carta a Julio," in Niño, ed., *Queremos tanto a Julio,* 19–20.

28. See, for example, Manuel Pedro González, "Reparos a ciertos aspectos de *Rayuela*" (Strictures to some aspects of *Hopscotch*), in Schulman et al., *Coloquio sobre la novela hispanoamericana* (México: Fondo de Cultura, 1967), 68–81.

29. Julio Cortázar, *Around the Day in Eighty Worlds,* trans. Thomas Christensen (San Francisco: North Point Press, 1986), 22–23.

30. Julio Cortázar, *Hopscotch,* trans. Gregory Rabassa (New York: Random House, 1966; New York: Signet/Plume Books, 1971), 363. Hereafter cited in text; all citations are from the signet/Plume Books edition.

31. Jorge Luis Borges, prologue to *Cuentos de Julio Cortázar,* Biblioteca Personal Jorge Luis Borges (Buenos Aires: Hyspamérica, 1985), 9.

32. François Hébert, "An Interview with Julio Cortázar," *Canadian Fiction Magazine* 61–62 (1987): 186–94.

33. George Steiner, *Extraterritorial: Papers on Literature and Language Revolution* (New York: Atheneum, 1976), 145.

34. Octavio Paz, "Laude: Julio Cortázar (1914–1984)," *Vuelta* (Mexico) 88, no. 8 (March 1984): 5.

TRIBUTES

Preface to Julio Cortázar's *Cuentos*

JORGE LUIS BORGES

In the late forties, I was the editor of a relatively unknown literary journal. One afternoon, one afternoon like all afternoons, a very tall young man, whose features I can't recall, brought me the manuscript of a story. I told him to return in ten days and I would then give him my answer. He came back a week later. I told him that I liked his story and that it was already in the printers' hands. Shortly there after, Julio Cortázar read in printed letters "Casa tomada" ("House Taken Over"), with two penciled illustrations by Nora Borges. Years passed by and one night, in Paris, Cortázar confided to me that "Casa tomada" was his first published story. I am honored to have been instrumental in its publication.

The theme of that story is the gradual occupation of a house by an invisible presence. In later pieces Julio Cortázar would try again this theme but in a more indirect way, and hence more effective.

When Dante Gabriel Rossetti read the novel *Wuthering Heights* he wrote to a friend: "The plot occurs in hell, but the places, I don't know why, have English names." Something similar happens with Cortázar's work. The characters of the story are deliberately trivial. They are ruled by a routine of incidental loves and incidental conflicts. They come and go amid trivia: brands of cigarretts, shopwindows, counters, whiskey, pharmacies, airports and platforms. They read newspapers and listen to the radio with resignation. The cityscape corresponds to that of Buenos Aires or Paris, and we might think in the beginning that we are dealing with simple chronicles. Little by little we feel that it is not so. Very subtly the narrator has attracted us to his terrible world in which happiness is impossible. It is a porous world in which human beings are interwoven with each other; the conscience of a man can enter into that of an animal or that of an animal into that of a human being. Cortázar delights in playing with the stuff we are made on, time. In some tales, two temporal series flow along and intermingle.

From "Prólogo" to Julio Cortázar, *Cuentos*. Biblioteca Personal Jorge Luis Borges (Series directed by J.L.B. with the collaboration of María Kodama). English translation by J.A. is published here for the first time by permission of María Kodama.

Style seems careless, but each word has been carefully chosen. Nobody can tell the plot of a Cortázar text; each text includes certain words organized in a certain order. If we attempt to summarize it, we realize that something precious has been lost.

"There but Where, How":
Saying Good-Bye to Julio Cortázar

LUISA VALENZUELA

Something in us has died. We are left maimed, one-eyed, lopsided, disjointed. I speak for myself, for all your friends, and we are legion—we must think of the readers who, in your case, can become the deepest of friends. I speak for Latin America and for the Argentina you loved and whose rebirth you fortunately got to see.

We need you now more than ever, Julio Cortázar, and you had to leave. But it's always now. We always needed you and we will keep on needing you, and in some way or other you will always remain among us. What is time, after all, what is it we call life, or reality, or any of those half-fatuous self-important words you used to make fun of. How you would have laughed at all this metaphysical babble! Let's have a good laugh together, Julio. Let's remember our good old 'Pataphysics and not take serious matters seriously. And death, being the most serious of matters, is the best not to take seriously. Your wife, Carol, died on you, and the book you two were writing together, living together, you had to finish alone. Summoning all your courage, accepting the pain for what it really was: the other face of your happiness.

The Autonauts of the Cosmohighway or An Atemporal Journey Paris-Marseille, an expedition of humor and writing which took 33 days, probing every parking area—just two a day—never leaving that no-man's land inscribed by France's Autoroute du Sud. A slow-moving, loving trip through marginality, as yours always were. A wink of recognition at poetry, always in wait even under layers and layers of asphaltic blindness.

Perhaps life *is* a highway, after all—you suggested it in one of your most memorable stories—but, not to be taken at full speed, desperately trying to get somewhere, that ever elusive, unreachable somewhere. No. The idea is to go sniffing around, questioning oneself in each and all of the possible parking areas. And, Julio, I must tell you that this parking area in which we are now frozen is one of the grayest, tinted by the hue of your absence. It's hard to get back to the highway, only you are pushing us from behind your own pages

From *The Village Voice Literary Supplement* (translated by Enrique-Fernández). New York, (March 1984); Reprinted here by permission of the author.

and we shall now keep on moving and look at life differently, with slanted vision. Even though a bubble has burst, a green balloon of fantasy, cronopio-color.

The causes you were fighting for are still around to keep us going. But give me a break! How I would like to run off, now, not even finish this page. A feeling you could understand well. Not three months have gone by since the day you told me that you too wanted to keep running. Sometimes I feel so comfortable in my easy chair, you said, a glass of Scotch in one hand, a good book in the other, listening to my favorite music, when suddenly out of nowhere this absolute need to be in Morocco hits me. Shoot, so much travel and never been to Morocco, you complained.

A shared dream. So we decided to go to Morocco together next summer. True, we both knew that next summer easily becomes utopian, that what we were trying to fight was this frequent desire to be elsewhere, always else-where—except, of course, when one learns to explore the highway, moving slowly into love. Julio, is there an elsewhere? Did you find it? Is it summer there? Shall we go?

Enough of this writing! I'm off to buy a bottle of vodka, or better still that book on Sacred Geometry I promised you (it was November, and you had come to New York to speak before the Independent Committee on Inter-national Humanitarian Issues) and never sent you. Last Saturday I went by the bookstore and again I thought I had to go back and get it for you. Sunday you didn't need it anymore. I'm the one who needs it; this book is now essen-tial to me.

A gloomy month, last November. You were tired and troubled. I deserve a sabbatical, you told me, I want to write a novel. I owe it to myself, you insisted as if in need of justification. I have done all I can for Nicaragua and Central America, for all the *compañeros* over there. Soon I will allow myself a sabbatical and write a new novel.

Do it now, Julio.

—No, I promised to be in Nicaragua for the New Year, and there is a writers' conference in Cuba, and then I have to go to Mexico for a while. And Argentina, of course; I'll be there in April, I want to celebrate democracy. After that I'll offer myself the sabbatical and plunge into the novel. So many years without writing a novel.

—Do it now, Julio, go on your sabbatical now. You deserve a rest and we deserve your novel, I pled in November. But not an eternal sabbatical, Julio, you really overdid it. It would have been much better for you to sit down and write instead of stepping out of life to take a look at the other side. It would have been much better if you kept on trying—no matter how desperately— to find the other side from this side, as in your other novels.

Do you know what the new novel will be about? Do you already have the beginning, the end, some clue to its plot? Those were my banal questions at the time.

And as usual your answer half-opened a secret door hidden behind everything we already knew: I hate talking about future work, the talk carries the work away from me. Then, I never know how a story or a novel will end, I just let myself be driven by the current. But in this particular case my ignorance is adamant, I know absolutely nothing about this novel, consciously. All I know is that it is complete and perfect somewhere in my head, and it will blossom as soon as I allow it to. For in my dreams I see it already published and it makes me immensely happy. I dream I am holding the book in my hands, turning the pages and understanding it clearly. Even though it's a book composed of pure geometric forms. Exact, balanced, elegant, coherent. That's, of course, in my dreams, for I don't know a damn thing about geometry or math. But there and then I read those forms as if they were words, and perhaps they are.

A novel that never managed to cross the bridge to this reality in which we are trapped without you, Julio. Your own private novel made to order for you who were always digging in that uncertain terrain where what we believe to be true unfolds and multiplies itself in search of another, larger truth. Geometric, Möbius strip dream book stuck in the eternity of your current dream with which you nourish a new dimension of our own ordinary, private dreams. I believe myself to be the repository of this dream book of yours and I regard it as a very precious present which I would like to share with others. In this nonexistent-existent novel you seemed to have reached knowledge and you have paid for it with your life. Your life is a price that grieves us all, Julio Cortázar. That's why I desperately look for some kind of explanation and only find dim clues:

> Geometry deals with pure form, and philosophical geometry re-enacts the unfolding of each form out of a preceding one. It is a way by which the essential creative mystery is rendered visible. The passage from creation to procreation, from unmanifest, pure, formal idea to the "here-below," the world that spins out from the original divine stroke can be mapped out by geometry . . .

You would have certainly omitted the word "divine," but it amounts to the same thing. To untie the knot, to render visible the invisible and above all to unveil the world that complements this one, these were your tasks, Julio. You observed them with all the rigor and folly and humor and despair and love you could give. Which was a hell of a lot. And with all the necessary courage to reach the heart of the unconfessable, the unspeakable, those horrors that torment us like the giant rats of Satarsa, in your last collection of short stories, *Deshoras*.

"Writing a story is for me like tearing a poisonous vermin off my skin," you once said. But the future novel might have been different. Perhaps, like geometry, it would have given us the exact measure of the Earth. Some order. It would have been your fifth novel, after *The Winners, Hopscotch, 62: A Model*

Kit, A Manual for Manuel. The Tetragrammaton, the Quadrivium? You would have laughed your head off at so much fatuity. You would have told me: Barely *the four,* remember? that one-legged flamingo stance our drinking buddies in Buenos Aires made us do to prove we could hold our liquor. The only thing worthy of a proof.

Tetragrammaton? No. Never take serious matters seriously. That is why you dismissed your working title *Mandala* and settled for *Hopscotch,* just a tormented children's game between heaven and hell.

At that time, geometric ideas were already haunting you, and later your collection of eight short stories was called *Octahedron.* That was 10 years ago, no geometric dreams yet, but always the search for "answers to death and nothingness . . . to establish rituals and passages against a disorder full of holes and stains." Of course disorder is stronger and more tempting than order, or perhaps what is tempting is the possibility of all those other orders, infinitely more complex, in which the octahedron (the double pyramid) is multiplied by eight and acquires the 64 facets of the diamond: all the lights.

Much like one of those Escher prints through which you could have roamed with ease, unique in knowing how to come and go at the same time, how to face the stairs that simultaneously climb and descend, leading to the exact point of departure, or everywhere, or . . . Much like that city of the mind known only to the characters of *62* and more intimately still to you, who confessed in a short story titled *There but Where, How:* " . . . the city I've mentioned sometimes, a city I dream of every now and then and which is the dwelling place of an indefinitely postponed death, of unavowable searches and impossible meetings."

Julio Cortázar, master, brother, my paredro, the-one-I-told-you: we are not going to look for you in that city where perhaps Polanco and Calac are still lingering, always a little behind, poor chaps, your displaced shadows. Nor in these cities where we live, feeling now more at a loss than ever, without your affection. Nor in the red threads la Maga searched as clues, neither *there but where, how.* We are not going to look for you because we shall go on discovering and treasuring and, above all, nurturing what you left glowing in all and each of us. Those embers.

Julio, Oh Buccaneer of the Remington

SAÚL YURKIEVICH

In reality, Julio Cortázar was a man partly child, a perpetual adolescent with big cat's eyes, particularly before he started wearing a thick beard, longed-for generous beard, that in the early seventies began to be streaked with gray giving him what he was after, not an air of venerable Brahman, but rather of a bearded alligator something like Che (whom he admired) and a bit like Walt Whitman and another bit like Orson Welles (whom he appreciated). Child for the always fresh look he turned on things to counteract all that habit licks down to smooth conformity, luminous look so as not to see the duck from the feathers but the feathers from the duck, to continue to be astounded before the marvels the world offers every day; and if it doesn't offer them, multiply the world by eighty, know how to turn it over and cut it up anyway at all and reassemble it like a model kit, put together a jigsaw puzzle of overlapping cities or make a continuous passage between the Galeria Güemes and the Galérie Vivienne or a hopscotch where two trios that are one without knowing it push the same stone in order to arrive at the heaven existing in each of them, it's just over there and a little more would be enough, a shove but they can't reach it and remain, with their rifts, their anguish, on the side of the earth in close camaraderie. Julio can light a fire long ago that flares up now within oneself or make resurge a distant incarnation that clamors for you that you cannot ignore and that possesses you and you transmigrate. And fish and man interchange their being through the look that goes through the glass of the aquarium, liquifies it, and the man, now natatory, undertakes his return ab ovo. And all this because of a desired destiny that now is not literature, that goes beyond profession and artifice, that is incandescent Tura-lura-lura where the imagination recognizes no other limit than that of the word constrained to enunciate the order that everything disturbs and perturbs. Because here the words, those bitches, those centipedes, those ants, are mediators, subject to the multiform vision that shapes them without giving ground to them and they fall like a garment made to order, fall exactly, like fate that leads to swimming underneath things. That's how you succeeded, Julio, oh buccaneer of the Remington, receiving outside full in the

From *Point of Contact* vol. 4, no. 1, Fall–Winter, 1994. (Translated from the Spanish by Cola Franzen). Reprinted by permission of the author.

face the wind that burns on the inside to carry us every time we read you to where we become more than we are capable of being, there where we accept, Julio interceding, the challenge of our innermost Phoenix, there where the supreme angels, the fly and the soul are all alike, there where Julio wished to lead us: "there where I was and where I wanted that which I was and it was that which I wanted."

I remember him when he was writing *Rayuela (Hopscotch)* (I did not know or barely knew about it, he did not like to talk about what he was writing); I saw him remaining outside of whatever might restrict him, outside of any institutional or official framework, outside of literary circles, with neither an acquired position nor secure earthly possessions, entirely ready to receive that mob that was coming: "on the floor or on the ceiling, under the bed or floating in a washbasin were stars and chunks of eternity, poems like suns and enormous faces of women and of cats where the fury of their species was fired up." And he had to write in that fission of the apparent real, in that fission of the crust of appearances only whatever came to him in chains of implosions and explosions, those refractives or obliteratives of the identity principle, that radical removal, the great turmoil, the timespace tempest that clamors at once for coagulation of being, unfolding suddenly, in sudden fits and starts with impetuous exaltation, the totality of man. And he yielded to himself, to that order of the gods that is cyclone or leukemia, cyclone that brings *Rayuela* or leukemia that strikes him with lightning. And he handed over to us *Rayuela,* earthtremor of letters that overturned not only the method of novel writing, but also and above all our existence in the world with the world jumbled, disarranged to make it possible (because everything is bridge from man to man, because it is born of a seed and not of a graft) to make it possible to leap from oneself into the one and into the other and from the one into the one and into oneself.

But I am letting myself be carried away by what I love, by the admirable man, by his gifts for which I am grateful. (If Julio could hear me he would say, But Saúl, don't glorify me, don't lay it on so thick.) Outwardly Julio was an unassuming man, always affable, solicitous, wholly dignified and amusing. He was dignified in a very affectionate way, so much so and so naturally that his behavior excluded everything crude, overfamiliar, or in poor taste. When with a person he was entirely present, entirely open and friendly but reserved, circumspect, little inclined to confidences of too private a nature, not at all prone to sentimental chronicles, absolutely averse to gossip. From the beginning he chose as his destiny to be a writer and devoted himself wholeheartedly to writing; he waged an all-out battle for a kind of writing that was neither escape nor instruction, where man might re-encounter his realm, where no limits to human possibilities would be recognized, where a story might be simultaneously living synthesis and synthesized living, something like a tremor of water inside a glass, transience contained in permanence.

In fact, Julio was a certain Lucas, that man who collects records, relaxes with Gesualdo and when near death asks to hear two pieces, Mozart's last quintet and a piano solo—"I Ain't Got Nobody"—by Earl Hines. (I hope that in his interworld he hears the fusing phrasing of "I ain't got nobody," those long nervous caresses of Earl Hines, that whirling dance of the spots Volaná and Valené.) Julio was the man who puts his pipe on the left side of the desk and the glass with pencils on the right a little further back, who has his black reading chair (which I now possess) beside the lamp and at his feet a select pile of books and magazines and who, every day at six-thirty, serves himself his Scotch with two ice cubes and a splash of soda, who likes English tobacco and Gothic novels, Chivas Regal and Woody Allen, Bessie Smith and Viera da Silva and who manages, with devotion, sincerity, without epistolary crutches, to reply like a suicide with a pen to all the letters he receives from incessant readers who due to the mere and foremost event of having read him consider themselves intimate friends of his.

Julio liked to reveal that unnameable thing that comes "from the center of life, from that other well (with cockroaches, with colored rags, with a face floating in dirty water?) to reveal on one side intimate pandemonium and on the other to play untrammeled, unabashed, delightedly with words: "volposado en la crosta del murelio se sentía balparamar perimos y márulos" ("volposited on the crest of a murelium, they felt themselves being balparammed, perline and marulous"), he wanted the bear and honey to be a ball of coaltar, coaltar hair paws, the honey of the sky on his snout tongue, in his joy hair paws, or that all of us co-participants in the game should greet each other by saying buenas salenas cronopio cronopio. On the one hand he brought to light again the appearance of mythical bestiality of Pasiphaë and the bull of Minos who couple frenetically in a dingy hotel room with dreadful flowered wallpaper, and on the other hand he liked playthings, mechanical toys that he brought back from his trips, such as the little piano from Saignon with the numbered keys on which he proudly played "Alexander's Ragtime Band," or the mobile of tiny sirens made with ladies' combs the color of pink candy, or the sinister bishop of Evreux who was a twisted vine root and also a mandrake and who in order to conjure up his evil powers had to remain closed in a meat chest hung from the ceiling of that room with a cement floor and a glass wall where Julio wrote. Workroom of the toy lover and the writer, that refuge with the large white mulberry tree on the side cave generator of masterworks it was.

Julio brings about miraculous meetings, makes his characters teeter on the edge of the abyss filled with echoes and premonitions, sees to it that the imperious immensity subsumes or exalts us and at the same time amuses himself with Gekrepten's silly language or with the stuffy conversations of Señora Cinamomo; and when the quivers of the undercurrents feel overwhelmed by the ontic mauls, he invents the distasteful Abdekunkus who is not a demon from a grimoire but rather a sort of neurotic silence, a concretion of emptiness, or Julio starts speaking in clever and witty lunfardo with us, with his friends, with those petiforros, those croncos, that pair of Buenos Aires wiseguys dressed like pimps who are Calac and Polanco, who pretend to fight tongue-in-cheek and everything, absolutely everything they say, they say as a joke, because they know, because of life, that tenuous and stubborn glimmer, because of existence (unraveling rag full of holes), of the throbbing antimatter within, of the wounds and the flowers of trembling lips we carry around they know all about it and like chatty Macedonios they allude to all that only with irony, to the whinevitable whinterpolation in the metaphysical hour only in jest they suggest it, what links this desk with a love of years ago, what struggles against a spongy wall, of smoke and cork, unseizable and offering itself, what for Calac and Polanco is unsayable or may be said only as Julio says it, is said through plague, through contagion, through instantaneous constellation, the world turned upside down.

INTERVIEWS
◆

Julio Cortázar, or the Slap in the Face

Luis Harss and Barbara Dohmann

Julio Cortázar, a true Argentine, is a many-sided man, culturally eclectic, elusive in person, mercurial in his ways. He is not a man who gives himself easily. There is something adamantly neat and precise about him that verges on punctiliousness. He received us two or three times and was always affable and straightforward with us, but perhaps a bit impersonal. There were areas that remained out of bounds. And those were the ones that counted. It was in his whimsical moments that we caught some hints of the true Cortázar, the man who imagines old aunts falling flat on their backs, families building gallows in their front gardens, governments collapsing on Leap Year, and mirrors clocking time on Easter Island. Behind these figments is a mind with as many facets as a diamond, as intricate as a spiderweb. Physically Cortázar is something of an anomaly for a Latin American. He cuts a considerable figure, well over six feet tall, lanky, long-legged, and freckled as a Scotsman. There is a child in his eyes. He looks much too young for his age. In fact, his generally boyish air is almost unsettling. An eternal child prodigy keeps winking at us from his work.

Cortázar has an intriguing background that makes him heir to an old dilemma. He was born in 1914, of Argentine parents—in Brussels. His ancestors were Basques, Frenchmen, and Germans. He has spent a lot of his time welding opposites. From the age of four he was brought up in the outskirts of Buenos Aires, a city whose instincts and attitudes run deep in his work. No one has stronger emotional ties with his land than Cortázar. But intellectually he has lived beyond it, in a broader context. There has been agony in his constant inward migration between physical roots and spiritual affinities. The displaced persons in his books testify to the length and depth of a conflict that has never been satisfactorily settled. Yet in some way it has been put to fruitful use. Cortázar has always managed to rise comfortably above the narrowness of our cultural outlook. Like Borges, he has always been something of an expatriate at heart. "My generation," he says, "was considerably at fault in its youth in that it lived, to a large degree, with its back turned to Argentina. We were great snobs, although many of us only realized

From *Into the Mainstream: Conversations with Latin-American Writers* by Luis Harss and Barbara Dohmann. Reprinted by permission of HarperCollins Publishers, Inc.

that later. We read very few Argentine writers and were almost exclusively interested in English and French literature, with a bit of Italian and American literature thrown in, and some German literature, which we read in translation. It wasn't until we were about thirty years old that suddenly many of my friends and I discovered our own tradition. People dreamed of Paris and London. Buenos Aires was a sort of punishment. Living there was being in jail." So unbearable was it, in fact, that at the age of eighteen he and a group of friends made an abortive attempt to set sail to Europe in a cargo boat. Yet when he finally made it there—he moved permanently to Paris in 1951— instead of breaking his attachments with his land he took it with him, and has been wrestling with its phantom shapes ever since.

Compared to that of some of our more prolific writers, Cortázar's production has been slim: three novels—one unpublished—a bit of poetry, a few dozen short stories. But almost every bit of it counts. Creative fatigue, that common ill of our authors toward middle age, when an early bloom is ruined by faulty plumbing, is unknown to him. An unflagging inventiveness and imagination, combined with sure marksmanship, have kept him steadily growing in stature through the years. Today, at the height of his powers, his restless and inquiring mind tells him his work is more unfinished than ever.

He was first heard from around 1941—the exact date is vague in his mind—with a small book of sonnets, published under the pseudonym of Julio Dénis, that he no longer cares to talk about. The sonnets were "very Mallarméan," he says succinctly. He had lofty aims at the time. There was a long silence, and then in 1949 he published *Los Reyes* (The Kings), a series of dialogues on the subject of the Cretan Minotaur, rather stately in style, abstract, intellectual, overrefined, reflecting his bookish addiction to classical mythology. There was nothing of particular note in those early works. But already in 1951, only two years after *Los Reyes,* he made what seems a complete about-face and came out with a stunning little volume called *Bestiario.* It was lean and luminous, and struck a keynote: the fantastic, suddenly revealing a master sorcerer. Cortázar had read his Poe, Hawthorne, and Ambrose Bierce, as well as his Saki, Jacobs, H. G. Wells, Kipling, Lord Dunsany, E. M. Forster, and, closer to home, Lugones, the old master Quiroga, and, of course— Borges. He was a skillful storyteller—too skillful, perhaps. Five years later, in *Final del juego* (End of the Game, 1956), he was still hard at work conjuring up his spells, a bit too scrupulously. Repeated exercises in an unchanging vein had given him an unfair advantage over himself, he says; he had begun to doubt his progress. There were already clear signs of a transition into new territory in his next collection of stories, *Las armas secretas* (Secret Weapons, 1959). Among them was "El perseguidor" (The Pursuer), which marked a break in his work. It issued in what we might call his Arltian phase. Without sacrificing the imaginary, he had begun to draw live characters taken from real life, with their feet on the ground. His style had also become more muscular, less "aesthetically" pleasing. Perhaps until then playing with literature had been his way of creating a fantasy world around himself to shield him against certain unpleasant realities. But now, more at home with himself, he took a closer look at the world. What he saw he described in 1960 in his first novel, *Los premios* (The Winners). It was the somewhat defective and shapeless book of an author fumbling toward a subject and new forms to go with it. It was followed, in 1962, by *Historias de cronopios y de famas,* an assortment of loose notes, sketches, brief insights into hidden dimensions that demonstrate the author's fondness for fruitful improvisation. The Cronopios and Famas, playful poltergeists with coined names and strange habits, were blobs in a bubble world in some ways not unlike the real one. With this book Cortázar seemed to pause and take a deep breath. What followed was a hurricane. It was called *Rayuela* (1963)—an "antinovel" that shows every sign of having represented a major breakthrough for him. *Rayuela* is a therapeutic book, intended as a complete course of treatment against the empty dialectics of Western civilization and the rationalist tradition. It is an ambitious work, at once a philosophical manifesto, a revolt against literary language, and the account of an extraordinary spiritual pilgrimage. The Cortázar of *Rayuela* is a deep-sea diver who comes up with a full net. He is a man of many means, contorted, contradictory, exuberant, paradoxical, polemic: not only a great wit and humorist, outshining all others in our literature, but also—as he shows in a pithy appendix somewhat detached from the main body of the narrative—a brilliantly aggressive, if slightly pedantic, literary theorist.

Cortázar is a married man. He and his wife, Aurora, who value their independence above all things, earn a living as free-lance translators for UNESCO, where their job, as he says somewhat wryly, is to help "maintain the purity of the Spanish language." They take it in stride for about six months a year, including an annual trip to Vienna for a meeting of the Atomic Energy Commission, then spend their holidays in retirement in their summer house in southern France or in Venice. They like to go gallivanting together, and their taste tends to the unusual. They frequent provincial museums, marginal literatures, lonely side streets. They resent intrusions on their privacy, avoid literary circles, and rarely grant interviews; they would just as well never meet anybody, Cortázar says. They admire the ready-made objects of Marcel Duchamp, cool jazz, and the scrap-metal sculptures of César. Cortázar once spent two years of his life translating the complete works of Poe; Aurora is an excellent translator of Sartre, Durrell and Italo Calvino. Cortázar visited the United States in 1960, principally Washington—and New York, where he spent most of his time in the Village, window-shopping in back alleyways. Something of what struck him there he pulled out of his bag of tricks later in portraying the American characters in *Rayuela.* He has always been a sort of intellectual pickpocket. To pick and choose—making an intelligent use of chance and coincidence—is also to create, he says. As proof of this he offers the long delirious insert in the appendix of *Rayuela* called "La Luz de la Paz del Mundo" (The Light of the Peace of the World), for the text

of which he is indebted to one Ceferino Piriz, a "mad genius" residing somewhere in Uruguay, who submitted it to a contest at UNESCO as his contribution to solving the problems of the world. It provides a Master Plan for divid-
ing our globe into color zones and distributing armaments according to
surface and population. Cortázar liked it because he saw it as a perfect example of the kind of raving madness that pure reason can lead to—the last thing
the mad lose is their reasoning power, Chesterton said—so he lifted it, without changing a word. And the truth is that it seems very much in place in a
fictional landscape where farce and metaphysics join hands to beat a path
across ultimate lines, among elements of apocalyptic scenery that seem to
have come out of some monstrous clearance sale in a flea market or a Turkish
bazaar.

By contrast, the Cortázar home, a three-floor pavilion overlooking a
quiet, shady courtyard, is a world of light and order. Our visit takes place on
a dark autumn night. A gust of wind sweeps us in the door. We shake a bony
hand, and a narrow spiral staircase leads us up into a spacious drawing room
with austere furnishings: a low central table, flat modern sofas, Venetian
blinds, abstract paintings on the walls. The Cortázars took over what must
have been an old barn or stable some years ago in a state of decrepitude and
completely remodeled it. Their thin years are over. A black crossbeam supports the ceiling. A tribal sculpture—a souvenir from a trip to Africa—looks
down on us with a beneficent smile. In *Rayuela* there is a circus tent with a
hole in the top, through which the protagonists catch a glimpse of Sirius.
Here, too, on clear nights, you can see the stars through the skylight. A
bookcase which spans a whole wall reflects Cortázar's somewhat uncon-
scionable preferences: 60 percent of the books are in French, 30 percent in
English, only a splenetic 10 percent in Spanish.

Cortázar sits with his long legs crossed, his hands clasped on his knees,
prim and prudent. He is a man of intellectual passions, reticent about himself. Yet where his work is concerned—he is unassuming, but without false
modesty—he speaks freely, and always to the point.

Although he made what one might call his official literary debut—with
Los Reyes—when he was thirty-five, he has been writing practically all his life,
he tells us. "Like all children who like to read, I soon tried to write. I finished
my first novel when I was nine years old. . . . And so on. And poetry inspired
by Poe, of course. When I was twelve, fourteen, I wrote love poems to a girl
in my class. . . . But after that it wasn't until I was thirty or thirty-two—
apart from a lot of poems that are lying about here and there, lost or
burned—that I started to write stories." But he did not publish them. There
was caution, and perhaps some arrogance, in his delay. "I knew instinctively
that my first stories shouldn't be published," he says. "I'd set myself a high
literary standard and was determined to reach it before publishing anything.
The stories were the best I could do at the time, but I didn't think they were
good enough though there were some good ideas in them." He reworked

some of the ideas later. But "I never took anything to a publisher. For a long time I lived far from Buenos Aires. . . . I'm a schoolteacher. I graduated from a normal school in Buenos Aires, completed the studies for a teacher's degree, and then entered the Liberal Arts School of the university. I passed my first-year exams, but then I was offered a job teaching some courses in a town in the province of Buenos Aires, and since there was very little money at home and I wanted to help my mother, who'd educated me at great cost and sacrifice—my father had left home when I was a very small child and had never done anything for the family—I gave up my university studies at the first chance I had to work, when I was twenty years old and moved to the country. There I spent five years as a high school teacher. And that was where I started to write stories, though I never dreamed of publishing them. A bit later I moved to Mendoza, to the University of Cuyo, where I was offered some courses, this time at the university level. In 1945–46, at the time of all the Peronista troubles, since I knew I was going to lose my job because I'd been in the fight against Perón, when Perón won the presidential election, I resigned before I was backed against the wall as so many colleagues were who held onto their jobs, and found work in Buenos Aires. And there I went on writing stories. But I was very doubtful about having a book published. In that sense I think I was always very clear sighted. I watched myself develop, and didn't force things. I knew that at a certain moment what I was writing was worth quite a bit more than what was being written by other people of my age in Argentina. But, because of the high idea I have of literature, I thought it was a stupid habit to publish just anything as people used to do in Argentina in those days when a twenty-year-old youngster who'd written a handful of sonnets used to run around trying to have them put in print. If he couldn't find a publisher, he'd pay for a personal edition himself. . . . So I held my fire."

The confidence and equanimity with which Cortázar confronted his literary prospects might suggest a particularly favorable atmosphere at home, but there was no such thing. He had to make it more or less on his own. His family, on both sides, were all white-collar workers. They belonged to that category of half-educated people "who, as Chesterton said, are the worst kind. Which has nothing to do with affection. These are strictly intellectual matters. . . . But I was lucky in one sense. In the normal school where I studied, an abysmally bad school, one of the worst schools imaginable, I nevertheless managed to make a few friends, four or five. Many of them have become brilliant poets, painters, or musicians. So, of course, we formed a sort of hard core of resistance against the horrible mediocrity of the teachers and the rest of our schoolmates. It's the only way to survive in Argentina. When I finished my studies I kept in close contact with those friends, but later, when I left for the country, I was completely isolated and cut off. I solved that problem, if you can call it solving it, thanks to a matter of temperament. I was always very ingrown. I lived in small towns where there were very few interesting people, almost none. I used to spend the day in my room in my hotel or boarding-house, reading and studying. That was very useful to me, and at the same time it was dangerous. It was useful in the sense that I consumed thousands of books. I certainly picked up a lot of book knowledge in those days. It was dangerous," he adds, looking back with indulgence on those years of encyclopedic erudition, "in that it probably deprived me of a good share of vital experience."

An illustration of this problem is *Los Reyes*—now out of print: a series of dialogues ("a dramatic poem," he calls it) on the subject of Theseus and the Minotaur. "There are dialogues between Theseus and the Minotaur, between Ariadne and Theseus, and between Theseus and King Minos. It's a curious approach to the subject, because it's a defense of the Minotaur. Theseus is portrayed as the standard hero, a typical unimaginative conventional individual rushing head on, sword in hand, to kill all the exceptional or unconventional monsters in sight. The Minotaur is the poet—the being who is different from others, a free spirit, who therefore has been locked up, because he's a threat to the established order. In the opening scene King Minos and Ariadne discuss the Minotaur and you learn that Ariadne is deeply in love with the Minotaur—her half brother, since they're both children of Pasiphaë. Then Theseus arrives from Athens to kill the Minotaur, and that's when Ariadne gives him the famous thread so he won't get lost when he winds his way into the labyrinth. But in my version the reason why she gives him the thread is that she hopes the Minotaur will kill him and then follow the thread out of the labyrinth to join her. In other words, my version is the exact opposite of the classical one."

Not that the switch made much of an impression on the Argentine literary public. *Los Reyes* was not exactly received by acclamation, says Cortázar. It was hardly noticed. Though Borges had liked it enough to preview it in a magazine he was in charge of at the time, when it appeared in book form there was "an absolute and total silence."

But he was not discouraged. By then he was looking well ahead. "I was completely sure that from about, say, 1947, all the things I'd been putting away were good, some even very good. I'm referring, for example, to some of the stories of *Bestiario*. I knew nobody had written stories like that before in Spanish, at least in my country." He was in no hurry. A short novel that he had finished at the time, which some friends had tried to get published for him, had been turned down for "its nasty words," a rejection that did not bother him in the least. Again, on the eve of his trip to Europe, in 1951, a few close friends who knew the stories of *Bestiario* in manuscript form snatched them from his hands to show to the Editorial Sudamericana, which published them immediately, but without any success. In the meantime, even when he was in Buenos Aires, he had been leading a very solitary life. He was satisfied to have a small but distinguished audience, which, aside from Borges, a staunch supporter to whom he acknowledges a special debt of gratitude, included his friends and the few readers of the little magazine (*Los Anales de Buenos Aires*) that had printed *Los Reyes.*

Los Reyes was originally published in a limited edition by a friend, Daniel Devoto. It was never sold commercially or reissued in any form. Which is something less than a tragedy, according to Cortázar, because "the truth is, I'm still very fond of *Los Reyes,* but it really has little or nothing to do with anything I've written since. It's done in a very lofty style, very polished and high-flown, fine in its own way, but basically very traditional. Something like a cross between Valéry and St. John Perse."

Nevertheless, the book introduces an image that makes a recurrent appearance in his work: the labyrinth. Here it is mere frontispiece and curlicue, but there is a Cortázar who attaches a deeper significance to this archetypal symbol. He says he is the last to know what obscure biographical sources—or literary reminiscences—may lie behind it. But in its web he discovers remnants of a childhood pattern. He remembers that "as a child, anything connected with a labyrinth was fascinating to me. I think this shows in a lot of my work. I used to construct labyrinths in my garden. I set them up everywhere. For instance, from my house in Banfield"—a suburb of Buenos Aires—"to the station there were about five blocks. When I was alone, I used to hop all the way. My labyrinth was a fixed road I'd laid out for myself. It consisted in going from sidewalk to sidewalk and jumping to land on certain stones I liked. If I miscalculated for any reason, or didn't land on the right spot, I had a feeling something was wrong, that I'd failed somewhere. For several years I was obsessed by that ceremony. Because that's what it was: a ceremony."

Ceremonial children's games are omnipresent in Cortázar's work, often with labyrinthian implications. The whole of *Bestiario* is like the title story, where the emotional problems of a sensitive little girl take on nightmarish proportions in the form of a ferocious tiger she imagines inhabiting the back room of a mansion full of interconnecting doors and criscrossing corridors. In "Casa Tomada" (House Taken Over), a brother and sister are gradually crowded out of house and home by the encroachment of unknown occupants (their ancestors?) who keep appropriating rooms and slamming doors in their faces. In "Los venenos" (Poisons) in *Final del juego,* the labyrinth is an anthole with mazes of underground passageways. Then, of course, there is the labyrinthian street game that gives its name to *Rayuela.*

Cortázar throws light on his intentions, remarking that *Rayuela* was originally to be entitled *Mandala.* "When I first got the idea for the book, I was very much taken with the notion of Mandala, because I'd been reading a lot of books of anthropology and above all of Tibetan religion. Besides, I'd been in India and I'd seen many reproductions of Japanese and Indian mandalas." A mandala, he recalls, is a sort of mystic labyrinth—"a design, like a hopscotch chart, divided into sections of compartments, on which the Buddhists concentrate their attention and in the course of which they perform a series of spiritual exercises. It's the graphic projection of a spiritual process. Hopscotch, as almost all children's games, is a ceremony with a mystic and religious origin. Its sacred value has been lost. But not entirely. Unconsciously some of it remains. For instance, the hopscotch played in Argentina—and France—has compartments for Heaven and Earth at opposite ends of the chart. Now, I suppose as children we all kept ourselves amused with these games. But I had a real passion for them."

There are also labyrinthian overtones in *Los premios,* where passengers on a mysterious boat attempt to gain access to the stern following a staircase down into the hold, into darkness and confusion. It is not easy to come out on the other side. The road is a long obstacle course—another sort of mandala that evolves as the plot unfolds. In an existential sense, says Cortázar, one might interpret the need the characters feel to reach the stern, to run a fore-set course, as a desire "to become realized as persons, as human beings. That's why some make it and others don't. It's a simpler notion, more rudimentary than in *Rayuela.*"

In *Rayuela* the mandala is a course that leads to a "beyond," to a "fall toward the center," into what Cortázar, who dreams of an Iggdrasil that will bind heaven and earth, describes as "a state of immanence" where opposites meet and one simply "is." *Rayuela* is an invitation to plunge through time in order to gain the far shore of eternity. It suggests a jump into the waters of selflessness, as well, says Cortázar, as what Musil called "the search for the millennium: that sort of final island where man would at last find himself, reconciling his inner differences and contradictions."

Oriental philosophy, in particular Zen Buddhism and Vedanta, offers "metaphysical positions" that have always appealed to Cortázar. Vedanta, for instance, is predicated on "denying reality as we understand it, in our partial view of it; for instance, mortality, even plurality. We are all illusions in each other's minds; the world is always a way of looking at things. Each of us, from his standpoint, is total reality. Everything else is an external, phenomenological manifestation that can be wiped out in a flash because it has no real existence; its reality exists only, one might say, at the expense of our unreality. It's all a question of inverting the formula, shifting the weights on the scale. For instance, the notions of time and space, as they were conceived by the Greeks and after them by the whole of the West, are flatly rejected by Vedanta. In a sense, man made a mistake when he invented time. That's why it would actually be enough for us to renounce mortality—I've spoken about that somewhere in *Rayuela*—to take a jump out of time, on a plane other than that of daily life, of course. I'm thinking of the phenomenon of death, which for Western thought has been a great scandal, as Kierkegaard and Unamuno realized so well; a phenomenon that is not in the least scandalous in the East where it is regarded not as an end but as a metamorphosis. The difference in the two outlooks is partly a difference of method: what we pursue discursively, philosophically, the Oriental resolves by leaping into it. The illumination of the Buddhist monk or the Master of Vedanta (not to speak, of course, of any number of Western mystics) is a bolt of lightning that releases him from himself and raises him to a higher plane where total freedom begins. The rationalist philosopher would say he is sick or hallucinated. But he has reached a state of total reconciliation that proves that by other than rational ways he has touched bottom."

In his own way, in *Rayuela*—via his protagonist, Oliveira, a man between two worlds, like his author—Cortázar has, too. Or at least he has tried to. "The attempt to find a center was, and still is, a personal problem of mine," he says. All his life he has been injecting it into his work without finding a concrete solution for it. Even the inexhaustible *Rayuela,* which provides a sort of unending catalogue of available alternatives, in the end can offer only partial subterfuges. "*Rayuela,*" says Cortázar, "shows to what extent the attempt is doomed to failure, in the sense that it isn't that easy for one to unburden oneself of the whole Judaeo-Christian tradition one has inherited and been shaped by."

Yet the search for alternatives started early in Cortázar. Perhaps the search, in ersatz form, is implicit in all fantastic literature. This would be the Quirogan, the Borgesean, lesson. In this sense, Cortázar's fantastic stories, with their mysteriously disjunctive patterns, seem premonitory. Their language, a kind of shorthand, full of whispered hints and coded signals, performs an almost ritual function. The stories are like incantations, psychic equivalents of magic formulas. One might compare them to charms that open doors, allowing the author a way out of himself. There is also what we might call a more practical side to them. Cortázar describes them as a sort of occupational therapy. "They're charms, they're a way out," he says, "but above all, they're exorcisms. Many of these stories, I can even single out a concrete example, are purgative, a sort of self-analysis." The case in point is "Circe," where a woman makes repulsive sweets with cockroaches inside, which she offers to her boyfriends. "When I wrote that story I was going through a time of exhaustion in Buenos Aires because I'd been studying to become a public translator and was taking a whole battery of exams, one on top of another. I wanted to have a profession, to be financially independent, already with the idea of eventually moving to France. So I packed all the work for my degree into eight or nine months. It was backbreaking. I was tired and I started to develop neurotic symptoms; nothing serious—I didn't have to see a doctor. But it was very unpleasant because I acquired a number of phobias which became more preposterous all the time. I noticed that when I ate I was constantly afraid of finding flies or bugs in my food, food prepared at home and which I trusted completely. But time and again I'd catch myself scratching with my fork before each mouthful. That gave me the idea for the story—the idea of something loathsome and inedible. And when I wrote the story, it really acted as an exorcism, because after I'd written it I was immediately cured. . . . I suppose other stories are in the same vein."

The stories leave a varied impression on the reader. Some are subtle word games—crossword puzzles. Others, like "Omnibus" (Bus Ride), one of the most speculative—and therefore most suggestive; which is why it has been interpreted as everything from a parable on death to a political allegory—seem to go crashing through barriers into unknown realms, to dip into orders of experience that are normally closed to us.

"The truth," says Cortázar, "is that though these stories, seen, let's say, from the angle of *Rayuela,* may seem like games, while I was writing them and when I wrote them I didn't think of them that way at all. They were glimpses, dimensions, or hints of possibilities that terrified or fascinated me and that I had to exhaust by working them off in the story."

Some were written at a sitting, spun out with almost supernatural force and intensity, says Cortázar—and the reader senses this. They were produced in a state of grace, which the author invites us to share with him. He is "on to" something, and points the way. Dramatic congruity or psychological verisimilitude is not important to him. The experience imposes its own terms. What counts is that we should be able to relive it—not as a vicarious experience, comfortably identifying with characters and situations, but in the flesh, as it were. We are in a closed circuit, armed with verbal formulas that, when invoked, will unleash the same sequence of events inside us as they did inside the author.

The source of a story's power, says Cortázar, is inner tension. The higher the tension the better it transmits the author's pulsations. "What the exact method for transmitting these pulsations is, I can't say, but in any case it depends on the ruthless execution of the story. The tense wiring permits a maximum freedom of action. In other words, I've watched myself writing at top speed—all in one breath, literally beside myself, without having to correct much afterwards; but that speed had nothing to do with the preparation of the story. I'd been concentrating my forces, bending backward to tighten my bow, and that increased my impetus when I sat down to write the story. The tension isn't in the execution of the story, though of course it remains trapped in the tissue from where it is later transmitted to the reader. The tension as such precedes the story. Sometimes it takes six months of tension to produce a long story that comes out in a single night. I think that shows in some of my stories. The best are packed full of a sort of explosive charge."

"Structures," he calls them. Words are mere touchstones in these stories; one finds oneself reading between the lines. The language is disarmingly simple and straightforward. There are no verbal flourishes, no tortured effects. The tone is conversational. The surface is crystal clear. But intangible forces are building up underneath. The clarity is made of shadowy undercurrents that gradually fuse in a climax with cathartic aftereffects. The reader, swept along, spills over the brim, delivered of himself.

An experience of this sort, no longer projected through fantasy but seen in the context of real life, becomes the actual theme and subject of a story somewhat later in the highly speculative "El perseguidor," which in a sense makes Cortázar's previous work obsolete by rendering its preoccupations explicit. The setting of the story—flagrant throughout—is Paris. When Cortázar wrote "El perseguidor," he had long liquidated his affairs in Buenos Aires. He seems to be making this point in every line. But Cortázar points are turnstiles, and tend to roll over on themselves. And so in "El perseguidor" we find ourselves in the numinous areas of Arltian lowlife. We are introduced to an underworld character, Johnny Carter—alias Charlie Parker—a Negro saxophonist, a man gifted by nature with metaphysical senses but of few intellectual resources, for whom music is not only a form of expression—a release into being—but an instrument in his search for an exit into godliness. Johnny, who walks the cemeteries of the earth, trying to revive the dead, hears echoes of divine voices in broken urns. He is a kind of blind seer—a starchaser, a man with a thirst for the absolute. He feels his true self mortgaged in space and time, a hostage waiting to be ransomed from the bondage of individuality. His talent is his strength, but also his undoing. Because basically he is a poor lost soul, ignorant of his powers, who lives in anguish and torment without ever knowing why. He has intimations of eternity, but cannot shape or grasp them. He thrashes about in hopeless confusion. The road leads downhill, through drug addiction into final madness. Like Oliveira—a man asphyxiated by intellectuality—and also Maga—a sort of embodiment of the poetic instinct in its pure form—in *Rayuela,* he has sudden intuitions, moments of inspiration, almost of mystic communion with the universe, but is too inept or, in his case, simple-minded, to form any sort of coherent strategy out of them. They remain unfulfilled, mere flashes in the dark.

Cortázar says of "El perseguidor": "In everything I'd written until that moment I'd been satisfied with inventing pure fantasies. In *Bestiario,* in *Final del juego,* the mere fact of imagining a fantastic situation that resolved itself in a way that was aesthetically satisfactory to me—I've always been demanding in that area—was enough for me. *Bestiario* is the book of a man whose inquiries don't carry beyond literature. The stories of *Final del juego* belong in the same cycle. But when I wrote 'El perseguidor,' I had reached a point where I felt I had to deal with something that was a lot closer to me. I wasn't sure of myself any more in that story. I took up an existential problem, a human problem which was later amplified in *Los premios,* and above all in *Rayuela.* Fantasy for its own sake had stopped interesting me. By then I was fully aware of the dangerous perfection of the storyteller who reaches a certain level of achievement and stays on that same level forever, without moving on. I was a bit sick and tired of seeing how well my stories turned out. In 'El perseguidor' I wanted to stop inventing and stand on my own ground, to look at myself a bit. And looking at myself meant looking at my neighbor, at man. I hadn't looked too closely at the human species until I wrote 'El perseguidor.' "

When he wrote *Los premios*—and the unpublished *El examen* (The Exam)—a bit later, he had already gone a long way toward remedying that deficiency. In *Los premios,* the search for a "way out"—playful at times, in spite of its underlying seriousness—has taken on an added dimension: now it is not only part of the subject matter but a procedural element. The characteristic Cortázar light touch is present, here put to work to make things happen—in the Nerudan phrase—"without obstinate form." Cortázar is a freer man than he was before, more conversant with social and psychological reality. The aesthete is never far away, but his workings take more devious forms. They might appear, for instance—as they do in *Rayuela*—in a lengthily erudite, and usually archly humorous, conversation on art, music, or literature, but casually, mixed with other components, sometimes almost irrelevantly, and never as anything more than means to an end. Cortázar says he started the book during a long boat trip—out of boredom, "to keep myself entertained"—letting it develop randomly, plotless. "I saw the situation as a whole, but in a very undefined and general way." He never knew for sure, from one chapter to the next, what to expect of himself. The result is rambling: a slow sprawl. It seems to be going nowhere. But it has pull. There are shrewd characterizations, some of them based on real people. Cortázar says: "I started to enjoy myself with the characterizations in the first chapters, which are too long, but I didn't have the faintest idea what was going to happen afterwards, though I'd already written quite a few pages. It was fascinating to me for a while to pretend I was also one of the characters of the book. It meant that I didn't have any advantage over them, I wasn't a demiurge deciding fates on a whim. I faithfully respected the rules of the game." They were complicated rules that sometimes remained on the drawing board. But toward the middle of the book the plot and themes suddenly coalesced and finally condensed in an adroitly handled resolution.

The subject, on the surface, is a holiday cruise—a tour offered to a number of otherwise generally unrelated people who have been thrown together on board by sheer coincidence, simply because they all happened to draw winning numbers in a lottery. On a primary symbolic level, it is an inner trip each passenger takes toward self-confrontation. But it is also the author's own inner trip toward himself. The obstacles are many. The end remains equivocal and unattainable. Its physical representation is the stern of the boat, which for some unknown reason has been closed to the passengers. No one has access to it. Not even the author. "I was in the same position as Lopez or Medrano or Raúl," he says. "I didn't know what was happening astern either. It's a mystery to me to this day."

Mystery is ever present in the book; the stern is shrouded in it. We do not know what to make of the situation. Certainly it must be very grave. But who knows? It may all be a funereal joke. In any case, there are many disturbing signs on board. The crew behaves strangely. There are inexplicable absences—for instance, that of the boat doctor. The atmosphere becomes sinister, then mutinous. We suspect an illegal traffic of some sort. But nothing is

revealed. We are probably in the hands of some mischievous underworld car-
tel ruled by an infernal overlord who may turn out to be our other self.

A seductive aspect of *Los premios*—and proof that Cortázar was looking
at the world when he wrote it—is the psychopathological portrait it gives of
the Porteño character. Cortázar is the furthest thing from a sociological-
minded novelist, but, though he has a tendency—as he admits—to overlap
instead of differentiating his characters, he draws their essential traits well. A
touch of satire adds spice to the narrative, particularly since it has the
poignant edge of self-satire. The satirical intent is secondary. "Whenever the
plot brought me face to face with ridiculous or disagreeable aspects of social
relations," says Cortázar, anxious to establish this fact, "I drew them as I saw
them. I had no reason not to. But the novel wasn't made for that purpose by
any means. The critics tended to see *Los premios* as an allegorical or satirical
novel. It's neither one nor the other." Nevertheless, these diverse ingredients
enrich the texture. We are shown a sort of cross section of Porteño types: two
circumspect and whimsical schoolteachers; a sedentary, fatuous old Galician
millionaire; a high-minded homosexual; a promiscuous woman of the world
with catholic tastes; an unbeautiful adolescent stranded in his doubtful sexuality; a representative from the Boca, the Genoese quarter in Buenos Aires,
which produces outstanding specimens of what is known as the "reo
porteño"—well-meaning, bighearted roughnecks, fanatic football fans,
"completely guileless, terribly dumb, but made of good stuff, basically genuine and worthy"; a young honeymooning couple distinguished mainly for
their smug self-satisfaction and rudeness. A large supporting cast—made up
mostly of colorful "popular" characters, among them the cantankerous per-
sonnel—provides an occasionally loudmouthed backdrop to the drama.

A mystifying character in *Los premios,* apparently something of a
holdover from Cortázar's Minotauran days, is Persio, a stationary, more or less
abstract, figure, a philosopher, a bit of an astrologer, who meditates the
length of the work, commenting on the action in oracular asides that appear
in the form of interior monologues. He has little stage presence; he gives a
sort of synthetic view of things, but in such abstruse language and so rarefied
a tone that he often obscures what he is meant to illuminate. There is a whole
literary clutter in Persio—the author's personal memorabilia—that suggests
the bookworm and sometimes the wastebasket. Persio, in the course of his
mediations, gives a symbol of the whole adventure on board the *Malcolm*
equating the image of the boat with the shape of a guitar in a Picasso painting. Cortázar says that here again he was playing by ear. "After the first two
chapters, one that takes place in the café on shore, the other showing the
arrival on board the ship, you have the first monologue of Persio. When I'd
written those first two chapters I suddenly felt—and when I say 'felt,' I mean
it literally—that the next thing had to be a different vision. And then Persio
automatically became the spokesman for that vision. That's why I numbered

his chapters differently and put them in italics. Besides the language there is completely different." The intention, the reader might think, may have been to create a sort of alter ego of the author. But there is more to it than that. "Persio," says Cortázar, "is not a spokesman for my ideas, even if he is in some sense, just as some of the other characters are, too. . . . Persio is the metaphysical vision of that everyday reality. Persio sees things from above, like a sea gull. He gives a kind of total and unifying vision of events. There, for the first time, I had an inkling of something that has been inhabiting me ever since, which I mention in *Rayuela* and which I'd now like to be able to develop fully in another book. It's the notion of what I call 'figures.' It's a feeling I have—which many of us have, but which is particularly intense in me—that apart from our individual lots we all inadvertently form part of larger figures. I think we all compose figures. For instance, we at this moment may be part of a structure that prolongs itself at a distance of perhaps two hundred meters from here, where there might be another corresponding group of people like us who are no more aware of us than we are of them. I'm constantly sensing the possibility of certain links, of circuits that close around us, interconnecting us in a way that defies all rational explanation and has nothing to do with the ordinary human bonds that join people." He recalls a phrase of Cocteau, to the effect that the individual stars that form a constellation have no idea that they are forming a constellation. "We see Ursa Major, but the stars that form Ursa Major don't know that they do. In the same way, we also may be forming Ursa Majors and Ursa Minors, without knowing it, because we're restricted within our individualities. Persio has some of that structural view of events. He always sees things as a whole, as figures, in compound forms, trying to take an over-all view of problems."

If Persio's abstract viewpoint seems a bit of an interference, it may be because we suspect it of being less metaphysical than aesthetic: a formal superstructure introduced artificially to satisfy the author's—and the reader's—instinct for order. But here we are on uncertain ground. The reproach has been held up to him more than once, says Cortázar. "But I have to say I've never held it up to myself. Because, in fact, Persio's monologues, though perhaps mainly aesthetic in effect, were born of an almost automatic writing, at great speed and without the control I deliberately kept over the rest of the novel. Instead of being conscious readjustments, they're like escape valves for a subconscious process. Besides they were written in the exact place where they stand. They weren't added afterwards as they might seem to have been. I'm sorry if they seem tacked on, but each fitted in exactly where it seemed to belong in the book. Something kept telling me there was a need to interrupt the sequence, to allow that other vision of things to take over for a while. Of course, the reproach may still hold, because what counts is the result, not the needs of the moment." Perhaps the real justification for Persio's synthesizing vision can be found in Cortázar's later work, where the aesthetic and the metaphysical chase each other tirelessly until at last they meet in *Rayuela,*

Persio in *Los premios* is the author's hand, still hesitant, for the first time attempting to make the two terms compatible.

More successful is the existential level of *Los premios*. There, vividly real to us, always fundamentally true in word and gesture, half a dozen human fates play themselves out under high pressure, as the author, in accordance with a secret scheme that gradually emerges from the shadows, realizes himself through them. Among them is Medrano, a dentist who has behaved like a heel, abandoning his mistress on shore, and finds the trip an occasion to do some soul-searching. A dramatic turn of events, masterfully travestied by the author, precipitates him into having "what the Zen Buddhists call Satori: a sort of explosive fall-in toward himself." Medrano is a man who never watched too closely where he stepped. Perhaps there is a parable here about an author who graced many pages before stopping to take stock of himself. The time had come for remedial action. Medrano realizes what a thin line he has been walking. So off he goes—and the author, figuratively speaking, with him—down the hatch, "on a headlong plunge which in the end he pays for dearly: with his skin."

Which is only as it should be. Because Medrano, like Johnny Carter, is a member of Cortázar's family of starstruck searchers, who know that the true road is a difficult one, often to be purchased at a high price, with life—or sanity. The latter—and perhaps the former—is the case with Oliveira in *Rayuela*. Oliveira, a triumphantly backboneless character, pursues a devious path down a blind alley to destruction. At the end of the book, past the point of no return, we are uncertain as to whether he has committed suicide or simply fallen into complete madness. But the question is immaterial. What we know is that he has made a concerted effort, the length of his unwholesome but edifying adventure, to undermine himself at every step, to subvert rational barriers and collapse logical categories, and that finally he has lost his footing and gone off the deep end into bottomless waters. There is something heroically Quixotic about his career. Within his abjectness, the uncompromising—and sometimes perverse—doggedness and dignity with which he pursues his search give him a kind of pseudo-tragic stature. Oliveira lives in extremities, a ruinous shadow of himself, going from stranglehold to deadlock. A chronic dreamer, his predicament is that of the man who, by means of sterile sophistries, empty paradoxes, synthetic rationalizations, has pushed himself to the point where he is incapable of finding a reason to live or to do anything. Everything is the same to him: love, abstract thought, art, causes. He can find irrefutable pretexts to justify—or negate—all of them. He has chosen "a course of inaction, instead of action"; his energies go to waste in "a purely dialectical movement." It is easier for him "to think than to be." In his battle to "be," his weapons are mockery, outlandish farce, absurdity, outrageous clownishness.

"I detest solemn searches," says Cortázar. Which is one reason why he admires Zen. "What I like above all about the masters of Zen is their complete lack of solemnity. The deepest insights sometimes emerge from a joke, a gag, or a slap in the face. In *Rayuela* there's a great influence of that attitude, I might even say of that technique."

As an example, he mentions the chapter about the wooden board toward the end of the book. Oliveira has returned to Buenos Aires after all his Parisian mishaps: his estrangement from Maga, the death of Maga's child, Rocamadour, his desperate and fruitless posturing. He runs into an old friend, Traveler, in whom he eventually begins to recognize a sort of double of himself—an avatar of one of his own previous, more enlightened, phases; and at a given moment in his confusion—which is compounded by acute bachelor pains—he starts to identify Traveler's wife, Talita, with his lost Maga. He has hotheaded dreams about her. Tensions mount and the problem comes to a head in an excruciatingly funny scene that has every external appearance of being completely insignificant. Oliveira and Traveler occupy rooms on opposite sides of the same street; their windows face each other. Oliveira, who has been setting up living quarters, asks Traveler for some necessary implements; Talita is charged with delivering them. To shorten her road, Oliveira spans the distance between the two windows with a long wooden board, inviting her to cross over it. She accepts, taking her life in her hands. As she confronts Oliveira, halfway between him and her husband, hovering in mid-air, forty feet above the street, masks drop, baring faces in separate solitary agony.

"The chapter of the wooden board," says Cortázar, "I think, is one of the deepest moments in the book. Because lives are in the balance. Yet, from beginning to end, it's treated as a wild joke."

In *Rayuela,* jokes, gags, are not only dramatic elements but stitches in the narrative fabric. Whole scenes are built on them. Cortázar is a great improviser. His humor can be harsh, hectic, grotesque, ironic, jeering. The episodic construction he uses favors his ends. He is a master of parody, jabberwocky, wordplay, non sequitur, obscenity, and even cliché, which he exploits with predatory relish. Farce alternates with fantasy, slang with erudition. Puns, hyperbole, innuendo, sudden shifts and dislocations, all the resources of comic art, including virtuoso nonsense passages, are put to work with inexhaustible versatility.

Cortázar explains that certain forms of Surrealism may throw light on his methods. Modern French literature in general has left a deep mark on his work. Though as a young man he had so little sense of values, he says, that he could hardly distinguish between Montaigne and Pierre Loti, "I changed radically as a result of reading certain French writers—for instance, Cocteau. One day when I was about eighteen I read Cocteau's *Opium.* It was a flash of lightning that opened a new world to me." He threw out half his library and "plunged headfirst into the world Cocteau was showing me. Cocteau put me on to Picasso, Radiguet, the music of the Group of the Six, Diaghilev, all that world between 1915 and 1925, and Surrealism: Breton, Eluard, Crevel. The

Surrealist movement has always fascinated me." He is one of those who think Surrealism was one of the great movements of the century, until it was ruined by the Surrealists themselves, among others, when it became a mere literary movement instead of an attitude toward life. Cortázar has also been a great reader of some of Surrealism's direct ancestors: Apollinaire, Lautréamont, Alfred Jarry. "Jarry," he says, "was a man who realized perfectly that the gravest matters can be explored through humor. That was just what he tried to do with his 'pataphysique'—to touch bottom via black humor. I think that notion had a great influence on my way of looking at the world. I've always thought humor is one of the most serious things there are." The respect for humor as a valid means of investigation is the sign of a high civilization, he believes. It indicates an ability to go prospecting for buried treasure without reaching for big phrases. "The English know that better than anybody. Much of great English literature is based on humor."

Humor, suggests Cortázar, can also be a useful defense mechanism in the more "surrealistic" circumstances of daily life. He remembers it served him well in Argentina in the forties when reality had become "a sort of waking nightmare" to him. Twenty years of social and political unrest came to a head with the advent of the Second World War, a difficult time in Argentina for anybody with a conscience. The country had bought neutrality—and an unprecedented surface prosperity—at the cost of self-respect. It was a period of hypocritical pacifism, of sham positions, false alliances, petty interests, and shabby betrayals. Then came the added foolishness of Peronism. Cortázar, like so many of his disillusioned contemporaries, after a brief brush with politics when he was on the faculty of the Liberal Arts School in Mendoza—he was actually imprisoned during a student mutiny—withdrew to the sidelines, into what he says frankly "may well have been nothing but escapism." The intellectual found himself in a somewhat ludicrous quandary in those days. Because resistance to the dictatorship had polarized public opinion at opposite ends of the spectrum, his problem was where and how to take a stand in a situation that allowed for no middle way. For those who, like Cortázar, believed there were underlying elements of genuine value in Peronism as a social movement but could not accept the leadership of Perón and his wife or, on the other hand, find any effective way to channel their opposition to the regime without playing into the hands of other political speculators and opportunists, a possible solution was to disconnect themselves rather guiltily from the scene, laughing it off as best they could.

Laughter, in all its dimensions, is the key to *Rayuela*. Its aim is to catch the reader off guard, penetrate his defenses, and set off uncontrollable reflexes. Cortázar tiptoes among weighty matters like a housebreaker. Part of the effect he achieves in his best scenes is a result of the enormous distance that exists between the narrative surface and the underlying reality it encloses and encompasses. At moments a meeting occurs: parallel lines intersect.

There is a burst of light. The multiple contrasting levels of a scene and the disproportions and incongruities existing between them often create a sense of high pathos.

"I think one of the moments in *Rayuela* where that works best is in the breakup scene between Oliveira and Maga. The scene is a long dialogue where a number of things come under discussion, none of which appear to have anything to do with the matter at hand. At one point they even burst out laughing and roll on the floor. There I really think I managed to get an effect that would have been impossible if I'd simply exploited the pathos in the situation. It would have been just one more breakup scene, like so many others in literature."

Another similar scene is the death of Rocamadour. The author plays it for laughs. It occurs in a dingy hotel room, during a smoky bull session, with jazz records in the background. Maga and Oliveira have gone on the rocks. The climate is one of despair. But all sorts of grotesque incidents distract from the scene: knocks on the ceiling, an irrelevant quarrel in the corridor. Rocamadour is agonizing. But nobody wants to rock the boat. Everybody, including, notably, the author, looks the other way.

Throughout all this—battered, bankrupt, demoralized—Oliveira continues his search for ultimates. In *Rayuela* the motif of the search is orchestrated at every possible level, including the level of language. Words are a process of elimination. We beat a path toward a distant shore, a sort of ulterior calm in the eye of the storm, a final turn in the thread leading to the center of the labyrinth. Language has a specific function in *Rayuela:* to talk the problem out until it has been exhausted or annulled—or exorcised.

"The whole of *Rayuela* is done through language," says Cortázar. "There's a direct attack on language to the extent, as it says explicitly in many parts of the book, that it deceives us practically at every word we say. The characters in *Rayuela* keep insisting on the fact that language is an obstacle between man and his own deeper being. We know the reason: we use a language that's entirely outside certain kinds of deeper realities we might gain access to if we didn't let ourselves be misled by the ease with which language explains, or purports to explain, everything." As for the "center" Oliveira touches at the end, "an end that remains undefined—don't know myself whether Oliveira really jumped out the window and killed himself or simply went completely mad, which wouldn't have been too great an inconvenience since he was already installed in an asylum; he kept switching roles, from nurse to patient, and back, like someone changing clothes—I think that was an attempt on my part to demonstrate from an Occidental viewpoint, with all the limitations and shortcomings this implies, a jump into the absolute like that of the Zen Buddhist monk or the Master of Vedanta."

For Oliveira common sense has led nowhere. Therefore, to break his mental block, abandoning words, he resorts to acts. But where does this leave the author? Oliveira's acts must be described in words.

"There we touch the heart of the matter," says Cortázar. "There's a terrible paradox in being a writer, a man of words, and fighting against words. It's a kind of suicide. But I want to stress that at bottom I don't fight against words as a whole or in essence. I fight against a certain usage, a language that I think has been falsified, debased, made to serve ignoble ends. It's a bit like the accusation—a mistaken accusation, it turned out to be finally—that was brought against the Sophists in their day. Of course, I have to fight by means of words themselves. That's why *Rayuela,* from a stylistic point of view, is very badly written. There's even a part (chapter 75) where the language starts to become very elegant. Oliveira remembers his past life in Buenos Aires, and does so in a polished and highly chiseled language. It's an episode that's written fussing over every word, until, after about half a page, suddenly Oliveira breaks out laughing. He's really been watching himself all the time in the mirror. So then he takes his shaving cream and starts to draw lines and shapes on the mirror, making fun of himself. I think this scene fairly well sums up what the book is trying to do."

Language must be of paramount concern to the writer, says Cortázar, in a literature which still demonstrates such glaring lacks in this area as ours does. Our difficulties he attributes in part to the bad influence of foreign translations. The apprentice writer is at their mercy. The language of translations is a landless abstraction, a sort of bloodless jargon that reduces every style to a common denominator. "In a country where there's a real literary tradition, where literature reflects the evolution of language, as might be the case in Spain, France, Germany or the United States, there evidently writers work with a sense of inherited responsibility. They have an acute sense of style, a well-trained ear, and high formal standards. In Argentina we have none of this." If pompous, labored styles still abound among us it is because writing, regarded as a performance, imposes a posture. The writer clears his throat, fans out his tail feathers, and "reproduces on the cultural plane the typical attitude of the ignorant, semiliterate man who, when he sits down to write a letter, finds it necessary to use a completely different language from the one he speaks with, as if he were struggling against some physical impediment, overcoming a series of taboos."

Cortázar's work denounces this false language. He works "against the grain," as he says. Just as he is anti- or parapsychological in his approach to character—that chip in the cosmic kaleidoscope—he is antiliterary in utterance. Morelli, a waggish professor he creates in the appendix of *Rayuela* to give voice to some of his ideas, is speaking for him when he proposes a novel that would not be "written" in the ordinary sense of the word, but "unwritten." We can take this bit of Morelliana as a point of departure for Cortázar, who for some time now has been struggling to devise a "counterlanguage" that will establish new circuits, dispensing with the conceptual baggage and other mental obstacles that hamper true communication.

"The book I want to write now," he tells us, "which I hope I can write, because it's going to be much more difficult than *Rayuela,* will carry this to its final consequences. It will be a book that will probably have very few readers, because the ordinary bridges of language that the reader logically expects will have been reduced to a minimum. In *Rayuela* there are many bridges left. In that sense *Rayuela* is a hybrid product, a first attack. If I manage to write this other book, it will be a positive contribution in the sense that, having concluded the attack I mounted against conventional language in *Rayuela*, I'm going to try to create my own language. I've already started to work at it, and it's no easy task. The ideal would be to arrive at a language that would reject all the crutches (not only the obvious ones but the others, the ones under cover) and other trappings of what is so cheerfully referred to as a literary style. I know it will be an antiliterary language, but it will be a language. The point is, I've always found it absurd to talk about transforming man if man doesn't simultaneously, or previously, transform his instruments of knowledge. How to transform oneself if one continues to use the same language Plato used? The essence of the problem hasn't changed; I mean the type of problems that were pondered in Athens in the fifth century before Christ are still basically the same today because our logical categories haven't changed. The question is: can one do something different, set out in another direction? Beyond logic, beyond Kantian categories, beyond the whole apparatus of Western thought—for instance, looking at the world as if it weren't an expression of Euclidean geometry—is it possible to push across a new border, to take a leap into something more authentic? Of course I don't know. But I think it is." The problem is not only to replace a whole set of images of the world but, as Morelli says, to go beyond imagery itself, to discover a new stellar geometry that will open new mental galaxies. Here is where the "figures" come in.

Says Cortázar: "The concept of 'figures' will be of use to me instrumentally, because it provides me with a focus very different from the usual one in a novel or narrative that tends to individualize the characters and equip them with personal traits and psychologies. I'd like to write in such a way that my writing would be full of life in the deepest sense, full of action and meaning, but a life, action, and meaning that would no longer rely exclusively on the interaction of individuals, but rather on a sort of superaction involving the 'figures' formed by a constellation of characters. I realize it isn't at all easy to explain this. . . . But as time goes by, I feel this notion of 'figures' more strongly every day. In other words, I feel daily more connected with other elements in the universe, I am less of an ego-ist and I'm more aware of the constant interactions taking place between other things or beings and myself. I have an impression that all that moves on a plane responding to other laws, other structures that lie outside the world of individuality. I would like to write a book that would show how these figures constitute a sort of break with, or denial of, individual reality, sometimes completely unknown to the characters themselves. One of the many problems that arise in this scheme, a problem already hinted at in *Rayuela*, is to know up to what point a character can serve a purpose that is fulfilling itself outside him, without his being in the least aware of it, without his realizing that he is one of the links in that superaction or superstructure?"

In attempting to answer this question, Cortázar will have to bear arms against conventional notions of time and space. Having already denied us ordinary identification with characters and situations, Morelli, in *Rayuela,* goes a step further. He points to the "error of postulating an absolute historical time" and suggests that the author should not "lean on circumstance." A principle Cortázar has already begun to put into practice in a new collection of stories called *Todos los fuegos el fuego* (The Fire of All Fires). He can point to a story in this collection that ignores stereotyped time. "A single character lives in Buenos Aires today and in Paris in 1870. One day he's strolling in downtown Buenos Aires and at a certain moment, without any break in the continuity, suddenly he's in Paris. The only person who may be surprised is the reader. A covered gallery—a sort of out-of-the-way territory I've always found very mysterious—symbolizes his passage from one place to the other. In France it's winter, in Argentina it's summer, but there's no clash in his mind. He finds it perfectly natural to live in two different worlds (but are they really two different worlds for him?)."

In a sense, this is the crucial point Cortázar has been trying to settle in all his work. No small part of Oliveira's problem in *Rayuela* is the fact that he is a rootless soul, inwardly divided between "two different worlds"—a "Frenchified Argentine," as he calls himself. And "nothing kills a man faster than being obliged to represent a country," the author quotes Jacques Vaché in the epigraph that introduces the first part of the book. Says Cortázar, a man who has learned that the problem is not to adapt to a country but to become acclimated in the universe: "I use the phrase ironically, because I think it's obvious from everything I've written that I've never considered myself an autochthonous writer. Like Borges and a few others, I seem to have understood that the best way to be an Argentine is not to run around broadcasting the fact all the time, especially not in the stentorian tones used by the so-called autochthonous writers. I remember when I moved to Paris, a young poet who is a very well-known critic and essayist in Argentina today bitterly reproached me for leaving and accused me of an act that sounded a lot like treason. I believe that all the books I've written from Paris have resoundingly disproved him, because my readers consider me an Argentine writer, even a very Argentine writer. So the quote is ironic in regard to that sort of flag-waving Argentinism. I think there's a deeper way of being an Argentine, which might make itself felt, for instance, in a book where Argentina is never mentioned. I don't see why an Argentine writer has to have Argentina as his subject. I think being an Argentine means to share in a set of spiritual and intellectual values, and nonvalues of all sorts, to assume or reject these values, to join in the game or blow the stop whistle; just as if one were Norwegian or Japanese. It has nothing to do with sophomoric notions of patriotism. In

Argentina there continues to be a grave confusion between national literature and literary nationalism, which are not exactly the same thing. In any case, the Argentina that appears in my later books is largely imaginary, at least where concrete references are concerned. In *Rayuela,* for example, the Porteño episodes, excluding the few topical references to streets and neighborhoods, are set against a completely invented background. In other words, I don't require the physical presence of Argentina to be able to write."

We might speak of the "metaphysical" presence of Buenos Aires in *Rayuela.* Perhaps that is the key to the whole thing. Buenos Aires in Cortázar— its gestures, its humor—is not a city but a skyline, a rooftop, a springboard into that longed-for "kibbutz" or nirvana, where differences vanish. Morelli, always useful in a tight spot, agitates for a race of writers who are "outside the superficial time of their era, and from that timeless point where everything is raised to the condition of a 'figure,' where it acts as a sign, not a subject for description, try to create works that may be alien or inimical to their age and their surrounding historical context, but which nevertheless include this age and context, explain them, and ultimately point them on a transcendent course that finally leads to an encounter with man."

"One must travel far while loving one's home," said Apollinaire in a phrase that supplies the epigraph for the second part of *Rayuela.* It gives the essence of the Cortázar adventure. It is one of the forms—perhaps the most personal—of this adventure that Oliveira lives in *Rayuela.* Oliveira is a split personality in pursuit of a multiple mirror-self that forever eludes him. Which is why his plight becomes acute as he wistfully confronts his double, Traveler. He touches parts of a lost self—a vanished unity—in others. The theme of the double, with its infinite variations, is a constant in Cortázar's work. It can take an oneiric form as in the story "La noche boca arriba" (The night face up) where a man in his sleep retreads ancestral paths, or again in "Lejana" (The distances), where a woman on a honeymoon trip in Hungary meets herself coming the other way on a misty bridge, just as she had previously dreamed she would; or serve as the basis for a meditation on immortality, as it does in the intellectually more stringent and exacting "Una flor amarilla" (A yellow flower). Doubles, says Cortázar, are like his "figures"—or, rather, reversing the equation, "the figures are a sort of apex of the theme of the double, to the extent that they would tend to illustrate connections, concatenations existing between different elements that, from a logical standpoint, would seem to be entirely unrelated."

Cortázar's illustrations, always bifocal at least, sometimes take us to odd places, not only mentally but also geographically. The mental fringes his characters inhabit are faithfully reflected in the marginal settings they frequent. In *Rayuela* we quickly lose our bearings as the scene shifts from a dark corner under a bridge to a mental hospital—in Cortázar a conference hall can suddenly become a urinal—to a circus with a shamanic hole in the tent.

"I like marginal situations of all kinds," he says. "I prefer back alleyways to main thoroughfares. I detest classic itineraries—at every level." An example of this attitude is his hobgoblinish *Historias de cronopios y de famas,* which is full of those serious jokes he is so fond of: instructions for mounting a staircase, for winding a clock; a sketch about a man who loses his head and learns to detect sounds, smells, and colors with his sense of touch; a section called "Ocupaciones raras" (Strange Occupations), which works its effects under the skin, on raw nerve ends. In *Cronopios* corpses grow nails, the bald drop their wigs. There is a warning against the dangers of zippers. The author is constantly emptying his pockets under the table. When the book appeared in Argentina, it was received with clacking dentures. Poets treated it with respect, says Cortázar, but the few critics who mentioned it were shocked. They deplored the fact that such a "serious writer" could stoop to such unimportance. "There," he says, "we touch on one of the worst things about Argentina: the stupid notion of importance. The idea of doing something just for the fun of it is practically nonexistent in our literature." Cortázar provides a cure for this ill. *Cronopios* came to him like a sudden twinge, a shot in the dark. "In 1951, the year I came to Paris," he tells us, "there was a concert one night in the Théâtre des Champs Elysées. Suddenly, sitting there, I thought of some characters that were going to be called Cronopios. They were somewhat extravagant creatures that I didn't see very clearly yet, a kind of microbes floating in the air, shapeless greenish blobs that gradually started to take on human traits. After that, in cafés, in the streets, in the subway, I started writing stories about the Cronopios and the Famas, and the Esperanzas, which came later. It was a pure game. . . . Another part of the book, 'The Manual of Instructions,' I wrote after I got married, when Aurora and I went to live in Italy for a while. You have Aurora to blame for these texts. One day, mounting an endless staircase in a museum, out of breath, she said suddenly: 'The trouble is that this is a staircase for going down.' I loved that phrase. So I said to Aurora: 'One ought to write some instructions about how to go up and down a staircase.' " He did. Similarly, in *Rayuela,* he composed a certain circus scene because it served "as a chance to include some elements of humor, of pure inventiveness: for instance, the mathematical cat, which I had a good laugh over."

Oliveira also has a good laugh over it—but it is a hollow laugh, the laugh of a man being led to the gallows. It has the ring of crisis.

Hilarity, in Cortázar, often becomes a sort of seizure. His comic pangs are like death throes. His comic scenes are really brink situations in an almost Dostoevskian sense. *Rayuela* is made up almost entirely of brink situations. Apart from their dramatic effectiveness, they provide the author with strong motor impulses. "For one thing, they heighten reader interest, which I always keep very much in mind. They're another form of inner tension in the book. Besides, I think these brink situations are a kind of displacement for the reader, a way of estranging him. They shake him up a bit, shift the ground under him. But, above all, they are the situations where the ordinary categories of understanding have either collapsed or are on the point of collapsing. Logical principles are in crisis; the principle of identity wavers. Brink situations are the best method I know for the author first, then the reader, to be able to dissociate, to take a leap out of himself. In other words, if the characters are stretched tight as bows, at the point of highest tension, then there's the possibility of something like an illumination. I think the chapter about the wooden board in *Rayuela* is the one that best illustrates that. There I'm violating all the laws of common sense. But precisely because I'm violating those laws by placing my characters and therefore also the reader in an almost unbearable position—it's as if I were receiving a friend sitting in a bathtub in tails and a top hat—at that moment I can really get across what I want to say. What I was trying to say in the chapter of the wooden board is that at that moment Traveler and Oliveira have a sudden complete meeting of minds. Perhaps this is where the notion of the double takes concrete form. Besides, they're gambling for the possession of Talita. What Oliveira sees in Talita is a kind of image of Maga." It recalls the first image in the book: Maga on a bridge—over a sacred element: water—in Paris. Bridges and boards are symbols of passage "from one dimension into another."

There are other means of passage in *Rayuela*, among them one that turns out to be a descent into Hell. There was already a staircase leading down into nether regions—the hold of the boat—in *Los premios*. Here the image is more chilling—and specific. Oliveira and Talita ride a dumbwaiter down into the madhouse morgue. Instead of hot coals we have a deep freeze. Oliveira stands clearly revealed in this scene. Toward the end of it he suddenly kisses Talita. Talita, who is no fool, rushes back up to tell Traveler what has happened, complaining: "I don't want to be somebody else's zombie." She has caught on, and "I think the descent into Hell was perhaps the way to create the necessary tension to permit that almost inconceivable moment. Under the circumstances, there could be no misunderstanding. Talita is terrified by what she has just seen in the morgue. She and Oliveira are in a situation of extreme tension, so extreme that right afterwards—the whole scene takes place literally on the borderline for Oliveira—he returns to his room and starts to set up his system of defenses, convinced that Traveler is going to come and kill him."

Extravagant as ever, Oliveira surrounds himself with a sort of huge spiderweb, made of networks of threads he extends all over the room, hoping Traveler will trip and tangle in them. Pans of water irregularly, but strategically, scattered on the floor fortify the stronghold with a moat. Thus buttressed, Oliveira props himself up to wait on the windowsill. And fate closes in. When Traveler opens the door, he finds Oliveira on the point of throwing himself out the window. Oliveira has just caught sight of Talita-Maga down below, in the courtyard, tromping on a hopscotch chart. He comes full circle. He has been an inveterate dabbler in deep waters, an "enlightened bum" for whom the first principle of self-respect was never to beg a question, to do it to death worthily instead. We see him for a moment congratulating himself over his downfall. Who knows what may happen? Breaking down may mean breaking through. His dead end may turn out to be the reverse side of a new beginning. On the other hand, his final loss may be in finding himself.

Oliveira is the creation of an author for whom literature—an act revolutionary by nature—has a high missionary purpose as an instrument for reform and renewal. Which is why, whereas "as a young man literature for me was the great classics—and also the best of the avant-garde, let's say the most established names: Valéry, St. John Perse, Eliot, Ezra Pound—the Goethian tradition, we might call it, now that literature interests me a lot less, because I find myself more or less at odds with it. Nobody can deny its remarkable achievements; but at the same time it's entirely circumscribed within the mainstream of the Western tradition. What interests me more and more nowadays is what I would call the literature of exception. A good page of Jarry stimulates me much more than the complete works of La Bruyère. This isn't an absolute judgment. I think classical literature continues to be what it is. But I agree with Jarry's great 'pataphysical' principle: 'The most interesting things are not laws but exceptions.' The poet must devote himself to hunting for the exceptions and leave the laws to the scientists and the serious writers." Exceptions, says Cortázar, "offer what I call an opening or a fracture, and also, in a sense, a hope. I'll go into my grave without having lost the hope that one morning the sun will rise in the west. It exasperates me with its obedience and obstinacy, things that wouldn't bother a classical writer all that much."

A problem Cortázar might have to wrestle with—if the sun did suddenly rise in the west for him one day—would be the communicability of this vision. How to transmit it? Would it be something that was "in the air"— that others also would see? One might perhaps assume that if he found the words to express it he would be telling us something we were already— though wordlessly, incoherently—telling ourselves. He would precede us, but only to make our realization, as it were, simultaneous with his. In *Rayuela* he speaks of an experience that would be latent in every page, waiting to be relived by the reader who would come prepared to discover it as his own.

In this sense, from the point of view of our literature, *Rayuela* is a confirmation. We could say it is our *Ulysses*. Like Joyce, Cortázar, by a sort of inner triangulation, measuring a personal magnitude, has fathomed our world in exile. From his solstice he has found our equator. It was partly a matter of pinpointing things, he says. A book like *Rayuela,* on the one hand, gives the reader a lot he was already prepared for. "Generally the books that a generation recognizes as its own," says Cortázar, "are those that haven't been written by the author alone but, in a sense, by the whole generation." *Rayuela* is one of those books. It raised blisters when it came out in Argentina. It sold out its first edition of 5,000 copies—editions of 10,000 being considered runaway best sellers—in a year. Since then the mailman has often been at the doorbell, usually with gratifying news. "The mail I've received on *Rayuela*," says Cortázar, "proves that this book was 'in the air' in Latin America. Many bittersweet letters say: 'You've stolen my novel,' or: 'Why go on writing when my book should have been like *Rayuela?*' Which goes to show the book was latent somehow, and imminent. I happened to be the one to write it, that's all. But that is only one side of the problem. The other side is that, obviously, a significant book also has to contribute something new. There must be a step forward."

And here is where *Rayuela* shines. The "step forward" it offers is a new concept of the literary experience that may come to live a long life in our literature. *Rayuela* is the first Latin-American novel which takes itself as its own central topic or, in other words, is essentially about the writing of itself. It lives in constant metamorphosis, as an unfinished process that invents itself as it goes, involving the reader in such a way as to make him a part of the creative impulse.

If there is any objection one can raise to *Rayuela,* it is that too much of it functions on the kind of intellectual premises the ordinary reader would be likely to break his teeth on. Its erudition, pursued at times to unnecessary lengths, is intimidating. Oliveira—we gather somewhere in the text—is a frustrated writer. His problems are formulated in what we might call a writer's terms, with a somewhat undigestible wealth of literary allusions. Effects depend heavily on the cultural backlog the reader can call on. None of this seems very intrinsic to the purpose of the book, unless we assume the premise implicit throughout that the writer's or the artist's problems, and even the terms in which they are expressed, can be equated with those of man in general. Cortázar argues that in Oliveira he created "a man of the street," as he says, "an intelligent and cultured man, but at the same time perfectly commonplace and even mediocre, so the reader could identify with him without any trouble, and even outdistance him in his own personal experience." Yet Oliveira may well seem out of reach to the ordinary reader. And here is the flaw. But is it that? Cortázar admits that "*Rayuela,* like so much of my work, suffers from hyperintellectuality. But," he adds, "I'm not willing or able to renounce that intellectuality, in so far as I can breathe life into it, make it pulse in every thought and word. I use it quite a bit as a freeshooter, firing always from the most unusual and unexpected angles. I can't and I shouldn't renounce what I know, out of a sort of prejudice in favor of what I merely live. The problem is to give it new intentions, new targets and points of departure."

In this labyrinthian enterprise he has succeeded beautifully. It has been his way of following the thousand different threads of self that lead toward the center of being. "I think no road is entirely closed to any man," he says. And certainly he has found more than one opening into the further reaches of experience. An achievement of no small moment for a man who confesses in

Rayuela to "the somewhat belated discovery" that "aesthetic orders are more a mirror than a passageway for metaphysical longing."

Anything, even to fall back, rather than remain static has been his motto throughout his career. He allows himself no false reconciliation with himself or the world. "The world is full of people living in false bliss," he says. He will continue to trip himself up as he goes along. The important thing for him is to keep his inner dialogue going. Learning to speak to himself has been his way of trying to talk to others. He has just begun to find his voice. "When all is said and done," he says, "I feel very much alone, and I think that's as it should be. In other words, I don't rely on Western tradition alone as a valid passport, and culturally I'm also totally disconnected from Eastern tradition, which I don't see any particular compensatory reason to lean on either. The truth is, each day I lose more confidence in myself, and I'm happy. I write worse and worse, from an aesthetic point of view. I'm glad, because I think I'm approaching the point where perhaps I'll be able to start writing as I think one ought to write in our time. It may seem a kind of suicide, in a sense, but it's better to be a suicide than a zombie. It may be absurd for a writer to insist on discarding his work instruments. But I think those instruments are false. I want to wipe my slate clean, start from scratch."

An Interview with Julio Cortázar

FRANÇOIS HÉBERT

Hébert

One thing that strikes me in your books is your distrust of "generalities," generalisations; firstly a distrust of conventions, but more profoundly your distrust of dialectic, daytime logic, and even of discourse; and on the other hand your affirmation of the "particular," of the irreducibly unique. Your work is therefore from the beginning, paradoxical, tense (and always on the verge of tearing), pulled by this (the unique, the enclosed, the unrepeatable) and the difficulty of speech, the efforts involved in expressing reality, in finding one's hidden figures that one has to believe in (the doors of heaven, for example, or the last hopscotch square), figures that are ever in hiding but sometimes seem to appear on privileged occasions, as if by chance.

Cortázar

No critic that I know of has mentioned that, and I appreciate your saying it because I believe that in all I have written, I have tried to avoid generalisations and conventions and to fight them. As an adolescent, indeed already as a child and even as a very young child, over the course of endless family meals, I would listen (without commenting, I would have got slapped!), I would listen, annoyed, sometimes disgusted, to the flood of generalities, commonplaces, things said in that authoritative tone that aunts, uncles, mothers adopt to say the most pathetically stupid things, like: "You shouldn't take too many showers, it'll weaken you" or: "If you have a drink of water after you've eaten a piece of watermelon, you can have a heart attack," and other assertions and second-hand ideas that seemed to me to be absolutely wrong; in other words, Flaubert's collection of ridiculous remarks adapted to Argentina. You can imagine!

First published in *Liberté* (no. 128, March–April 1980, pp. 37–51) and reprinted in *Canadian Fiction Magazine* (Vol. 61–62, 1987, pp. 186–94). Translated from the French by Luise Flotow-Evans. Reprinted by permission of the author.

What we call laws, species, types are often points of view, simplifications that only impoverish the real world. For me, everything was unique from the beginning. What you call my affirmation of the particular is not something I came up with yesterday, and when I started writing, this way of seeing things, of considering them as unique entities and of refusing to include them in a global definition, and of avoiding generalisations, this way of seeing things marked my writing. So, it will not surprise you that I quoted, I forget where, perhaps in *Hopscotch,* but with a very special pleasure, the idea that is central to pataphysics as Alfred Jarry expressed it: what interested him, as it did me, was not the laws, but the exceptions to those laws, in other words, the special cases, the unique cases. And I continue to defend this attitude. I need only go out into the street for everything I see and everything I hear to seem like complete units, carefully isolated moments that I refuse to include in the commonplaces. I reject the endless ideas of the type: "All conscierges are stupid" and: "Every mother is devoted," and similar idiocies.

Of course this attitude causes problems and perpetual suffering even in one's personal life. The notion of friendship, for instance, or the feeling of love: we tend to generalise these as well. In general you see a woman leave a man for another, or vice versa, as if someone left one cycle to enter another, these cycles in spite of their individual differences always remaining cycles, with a rise, a peak, a fall and an end. I myself have never believed that things happen this way. Each cycle seems to me absolutely separate and different from preceding cycles. Each time I have been in love, each time I have made a friend in my life, each time I have arrived in a city, I have not experienced these events as though they came out of a mold. I experienced them as totally new, virgin, so to speak, and that is what made them beautiful; but at the same time this did bring on certain catastrophes, because if that is how you look at reality, if that is how you live, you reject what is called experience, or anything you can extract from an experience, whatever its nature. No previous experience has ever helped me at the moment of tackling a new one. Obviously, I am not normal. But I have a clear understanding of my madness, and after all, if I am mad, so is everyone else, in his own way.

My madness makes me think of something I read (in Levi-Strauss, or Levy-Bruhl?) about certain primitive tribes, in Africa I believe, who have no understanding of or refuse the idea of species or global concepts. The "forest," for instance, is to us a collection of trees; in their language, in their thought, there is no forest; there is a tree, then another, then another, and then another, and so on. They never arrive at the total; they never transform a collection of trees into a "forest."

Well, my life has been a bit like that, although I am perfectly capable of understanding the idea of type and of accepting it for all practical purposes, because not to, would be suicide, extermination. You know very well that intelligence, what we call intelligence, does not allow this infinite multiplication of irreducible elements; that would really lead to madness, and the kind that is locked away. In literature, in the domain of emotion, and of my daily experience of the world, I continue to insist on the individual, which is why what I write sometimes astonishes those people who don't have this kind of understanding and who feel that what I do is rather paradoxical, and even constitutes a challenge to reality as we have understood it ever since old man Aristotle.

Hébert

In your library here, I see a lot of books on Dracula, on vampirism . . .

Cortázar

Yes, I didn't know I had quite that many books on the subject. I have been reading them over the last twenty-five or thirty years in a somewhat disorganised fashion. Oddly enough, vampirism is a sort of constant in my thought; I am attracted by the marginal aspects of reality, not only in literature but also in daily life. When I say "the marginal aspects of reality," I am talking about those somewhat exceptional moments when you suddenly discover, on turning a street corner, or simply on taking a shower, that the so-called normal things escape you, and you find yourself, just like that, without warning, in an area, in a domain of thought and feeling which no longer have anything to do either physically or spiritually with what surrounded you before. When I talk about the world of the vampires, I mean the world of all those creatures called supernatural. For me, Edgar Allan Poe's influence was decisive; when I secretly read his stories (my mother didn't want to let me read them, knowing I was too impressionable), I must have been eight or nine, and I literally got ill on them! Terror gripped me; I remember I slept in a small room at the top of the house, a house in the suburbs, very lonely, very dark; there was no electricity, my room was lit by a candle; and terror gripped me after I'd read Edgar Allan Poe, so great a terror that every evening before I went to bed, I would make a complete inspection of the room; I'd open and check the contents of every cupboard, even if I knew that in those cupboards there was no room for the creatures I imagined; I would look under the bed, and before blowing out the candle, I would make sure the window was hermetically sealed, and the door too. And even then, in the dark, I would take some time to fall asleep, feeling that the physical barriers (doors and windows) were precarious, insufficient against the Other, who could be a werewolf, a ghost, an apparition or even the king of the spectres—the vampire!

Later, as an adolescent, I saw the film by Dreyer, and that plunged me into terror again, a very shameful terror (I must have been nineteen or twenty) but an already critical terror because I knew it was irrational. Still it was terror!

Oddly enough I never knew physical fear, not as a child nor as an adolescent; I lived in an isolated suburb, with run-down, empty lots and dark nooks and crannies, and there were a lot of thieves, delinquents and criminals around; and still I wasn't afraid. I knew that when the moment came, I would always be able to get away, or even, who knows? defend myself.

Real terror came from the Other. Because I felt that against the omnipotence of the vampire I had no chance. Oh! I wasn't really the logical victim of a vampire, not being a young virgin, but that didn't make me any less afraid. Ever since, a fear of vampires has dominated me.

Of course these are fears where masochism plays a large part; I don't know if psychoanalysts have studied the phenomenon. In my case I know very well that this terror that was partly literary and inspired by Dreyer's great film, had profoundly masochistic roots; it is masochism that makes people go to see horror films, the difference being that the terror inspired by these films generally disappears within a few hours, whereas in my case it lasted and forced me to look up information and to read books on vampires. Which I did; and one day I came across *Dracula* by Bram Stoker, one of those books that marks you for life. Though well aware of the limitations of the story and its characters, it was thanks to Stoker's *Dracula* that I discovered something very profound in myself and in mankind in general, something I could not explore, that I simply had to endure. And that was what led me to extend my knowledge of vampires, of the origins of the legend, its development, its modifications and transformations. I never miss a film with a vampire in it, no matter how bad, and I must admit rather naively that I get angry every time I see a film like Polanski's where they make fun of vampires, because I have the impression that this is a very profound, very serious transgression, and that the consequences could be just as serious.

Nowadays, vampirism is fashionable; people talk quite naturally about vampires; they've become a topic of conversation. I listen to all that; I take part because one has to have some fun, but deep down, the terror is still there. Vampirism is a symbol, a very profound symbol of one of the, how can I put it? natures of man, one of the aspects of his nature.

I've also read a lot of books on criminology, and found that besides the fictitious vampires, the ones that rise from the dead, there are real vampires who make up a rather extraordinary section of criminology. There are people who kill in order to drink the blood of their victims; the case of Peter Kurten, the vampire of Dusseldorf is the most famous. It inspired the film *M* by Fritz Lang which was based loosely on the actual story. There is Heath too, the famous vampire of London. Now and again in criminology texts you hear of the appearance of another vampire on the earth. These vampires, who in most people's eyes are ordinary criminals, are in fact obeying a strange call, that is present in every human being. Where do they get this thirst for the blood of their own kind? The deep reasons escape me, but the fact unquestionably exists.

Another thing too: you know that in *62: A Model Kit* I was concerned with another type of vampirism that I know quite well, and that you probably know too, which can be called psychic vampirism. There are beings who don't actually drink the blood of their own kind, but who choose victims whose thoughts, strength, love, feelings they suck, until they have made them their slaves. This has nothing to do with the forms of domination or tyranny, or the hold that stronger people have over weaker ones: we are not concerned with that here. I knew a woman, a vampire of this sort, and when I talk about her I cross my fingers because I am so afraid of her (she is still alive) that I defend myself with this silly little superstition. I knew this female vampire who was apparently very weak and inoffensive, but who drained those around her of their blood—mentally, emotionally and psychologically. I was a personal witness to it. Ah! but I was able to escape from her . . . But you can see, even now, I am still afraid of her and I don't like to talk about it.

Hébert

Death is often present in your books; I am thinking particularly of the short story *The Pursuer,* one of the stories that impressed me the most, where Johnny dreams (that's not the right word, but let's say he dreams) that he is in an empty field, surrounded by nothing but urns, funeral urns of course; he is alone, all alone in this kind of cemetery, and he suddenly comes across his own urn, which to his great surprise is not empty! And also the love scene (if that's the right word for it) between Francine and Andrés, in *A Manual for Manuel:* the scene takes place in a hotel room that overlooks the Montmartre graveyard. One could say that the dead sometimes cry out to your characters, call them, that they have things to tell them, which are hard to hear, but that if you listen carefully . . .

Cortázar

What you say disturbs me a little. It is perfectly true that death runs through my stories and through my novels which are rather nocturnal, negative writings. However, I find it hard to answer you, because as a man, as a living being, I have always refused, blankly refused the idea of death as well as death itself. You may say that this is rather naive, but (for what it's worth): although I know that I am going to die like everyone else, I am absolutely convinced that I am immortal.

I am not referring to the simple fact that it is others who find you dead; you die without really being aware of it, I would want to in any case. No, I am not referring to that. It is just that for me the idea of death is absolutely inconceivable; not only inconceivable but absolutely scandalous. The greatest scandal for me is the fact that man has to die. He is the only animal who knows he will die; and knowing that, he is on the side of life and he loves life. That is how I feel. The idea of an unavoidable death seems to me utterly unacceptable and scandalous. I have to accept it, as I do many things in life, but it is my body that accepts it and that will endure it. Personally I persist in thinking that in some way or other, I am immortal. By that I don't mean to imply that I believe in the next world, a resurrection, far from it; I don't know, I don't know how things happen. It's just that I refuse to think that I will move from life to a void, that at a given moment, there will be a total cessation of life in me. I cannot imagine myself unconscious, even though I sleep for hours every night and when I wake up, if I haven't had a dream, I know very well that I was unconscious, and that for several hours I was dead. But this idea of eternal unconsciousness seems to me utterly inconceivable. So from that point of view, I am not all morbid. On the contrary, I was just talking about Poe—now there was an obvious necrophiliac—whereas I am a "biophile," if you'll allow that expression, I am an enthusiastic biophile!

Oddly enough, everything I write, through the system of opposites or by inversion of values, is somehow under the sign of death, and actually, the scene in *The Pursuer* that you mention and the love scene between Francine and Andrés in *A Manual for Manuel,* are two good examples of that. However, I would like to point out that Johnny, the character in *The Pursuer* is a man who despite his unhappiness, his obsession with death, his failures, drugs and all that has an intense desire to live, which comes out in his music. As for the love scene between Francine and Andrés, the fact that it takes place overlooking Montmartre cemetery corresponds, if you like, to what was developing in the earlier part of the book: it is a scene of exorcism. Andrés is going to take a stand; he is going to try to get involved, and is finally going to break out of his isolation. He will thus have experienced death, by making love at the edge of death and in conditions that are particularly horrible for both him and his companion.

I lost interest in the fate of the girl; I was getting to the end of the book, and I couldn't follow her any further. You know, once you have abandoned your characters, you still think about them: What is happening to them? What will they do? I think that for Francine this would have been a positive experience, this night of love where she touched the limits of horror, suffering and disgust. I think that she may have discovered herself, recognized herself, separated from Andrés forever, but perhaps for the first time facing a more authentic life, a less petit-bourgeois life than the one she was leading up to that point.

In fact, experiences of death are quite plentiful in my books, but these are extreme experiences as a result of which, perhaps, other things begin, which lead toward life and not toward death.

Hébert

In reading your work, one sometimes has the impression that music interests you as much as, if not more than literature; there are frequent allusions, especially to jazz, and one might say that for you music is a better way of reaching what you call the metaphysical domain, and also your lyric style offers more to hear than to see or understand, at least in certain passages where poetry is no longer far off . . .

Cortázar

You are right, especially in that you say music interests me as much as, if not more than literature. Over the last years I have listened to more records than I have read books. Very often when I am reading a book, I am in a hurry to get to the end of the chapter, so that I can put on a record. I am a failed musician. Ever since my childhood, music has been something almost sacred for me. Another aspect of the ridiculous attitudes of my family was that people would listen to music as an agreeable noise and their comments were always sadly trivial. Later when I read Erik Satie on what he called music that blinds, I understand that my family listened to music like someone who puts a piece of furniture in its place and looks at it without seeing it! In spite of all that, I very soon began to play the piano and buy records, and I learnt quite a lot about music, classical music, the music of the Middle Ages, but also modern music—and of course our national music, the tango, which I like very much, as you can imagine.

And then one day, jazz arrived. I was fifteen or sixteen. It arrived on the radio. For the first time I heard Jelly Roll Morton, Benny Moten, Louis Armstrong and then Duke Ellington: a totally fantastic universe opened before me, and it has never stopped growing.

If I had had the talents of a musician, I would have been a musician. You find musical qualities in what I write? Yes; there is sublimation there or better, consolation; because I couldn't play the piano well, because I couldn't sing, because I had no gift for composition, I made up for it by writing. Just as in the history of man we start with poetry, I at first wrote poems; poems that recounted the rather inane banalities that come to a young man, but that were already quite accomplished from the auditive aspect. Even though they are utterly mediocre, you find in them hardly any errors of rhythm, of tempo; the rhymes are beautiful, sometimes quite exquisite. When I started to write prose, these values shifted. But the problem of rhythm always interested me. In my short stories, particularly at the end of them, the concluding sentences are written without any intellectual control, so as to give the sentences a rhythmic movement which for me is what contains the essential, let's say, intellectual elements of the story. Very often translators do not notice this and miss what is essential, neglecting the musical content of the prose, when it is just this music that gives the story its value; in general, the readers do not notice this either and are gripped by the dramatic content. But I believe that if the words didn't have this "swing," this beat, this rhythm, my stories would be less successful.

Hébert

Unfortunately I read your books in a rather erratic way, pell-mell, (that I am not very proud of), which is why I wouldn't want to make any blanket statements, but it seems to me that there is a development in your work, a progression that moves basically from fantasy to realism, to use somewhat vague terms, or from the story to the history, from the Cronopios to the newspaper clippings in *A Manual for Manuel*, as though reality were becoming more and more apparent, and by that I mean political reality, or what is called daily reality, which of course does not exclude a certain amount of fantasy.

Cortázar

You are absolutely right. There has been what you call development, progression in my work, that is true. It has been a long journey from the first stories like *Bestiary* or *End of the Game* to *A Manual for Manuel*. I should say in passing that I have just completed a collection of ten stories, some of which are determinedly and even dizzily fantastic. But it is true that on the whole there has been a progression which has distanced me from pure fantasy, from fantasy as an end in itself, and has brought me nearer to an idea of literature based on history, on experience; and so my characters have become intimately linked to what is happening in our world at the present.

To explain that would take a long time; I will try to do it in a few words. As a young man I was totally indifferent to history and to its daily and local manifestation, politics. Reality for me was aesthetic reality, and I firmly believed with Mallarmé that reality existed to end in a book. Now I believe the opposite: I think that every book should be written to lead to reality. And that is what I try to do.

But it is terribly difficult, because reality is not just the actual reality perceived by people; reality also includes fantasy. So we have the problem of dosage, of balance; reality and fantasy are sometimes heterogeneous areas that are mutually exclusive if you don't have the (if you'll excuse the expression) inspiration to blend these elements, as I tried to do in *62,* for instance, and to arrive at an understanding where reality and fantasy can exist side by side, mingling their waters, without becoming one and the same, but in a harmony that in my opinion reveals the beauty of life, its prestige, its mystery and also its terrifying aspect.

Nowadays, as you know, I am very concerned with Latin America, and I have been writing very little because my time is taken up with concerns over Chile, Argentina, Uruguay. In Nicaragua, I was amazed by what this small nation has done and I give all my time and all my effort to help them. One can do so little as an individual, as an intellectual. Still I believe in it.

Hébert

At first sight, religion is not important to you, or to your characters, but on a closer look (at *Hopscotch* for example: the search for the centre), and if you take the word "religion" in its etymological sense of bridge, passage, link, then you can almost make "religious" the synonym of "metaphysical" and as such the centre of your search, wouldn't you agree?

Cortázar

That's hard to answer. Was I influenced by my family, my environment? Officially, they were all Catholic, but in reality they were indifferent. From the start any notion of religion was foreign to me. I never felt a curiosity that might have swept me away, or led me to look for an explanation of the mysteries, as happens to many children. I had friends at school who were worried by religious problems, who tried to find guidance and to understand. I was indifferent, and I stayed that way. I think that the intuitive feeling for the divine from which all religion stems, is a category of being, just as for Kant there are time and space and the other categories of understanding. I believe that some people are born with this intuition, and others are not; I belong to the latter category. I have no notion of the sacred, no feeling for what is sacred. That escapes me completely.

On the other hand, I am a profoundly metaphysical being and have always been so. The mystery of what is beyond things, "on the other side of things" as Federico García Lorca said, has struck and fascinated me since my childhood. I felt a mystery behind everything: a fork, a dog, a person. Everything was mysterious. And that is what made a little metaphysical animal of me. I remember that when I was very young I began to read things that were difficult for my age, metaphysical texts. All the dialogues of Plato, for example, I read at the age of sixteen or seventeen; I don't know what I understood of them, but I was deeply moved by Plato's metaphysical flights. Add to that other readings of this sort and long conversations with schoolmates who were as interested in metaphysics as I was, and you have *Hopscotch,* which is a metaphysical book, an ontological search, the search for a true centre beyond all the mistakes we have made since the pithecanthropus.

This has always been a metaphysical concern for me, with no feeling for the sacred, and excluding God. The metaphysical mind, without being materialist, which I am not, manages without God, without the feeling for the sacred, and at the same time demands and has an intuition for whatever is beyond the physical. Perhaps the metaphysical and the sacred intersect? I don't know. Perhaps God is present and I don't know it . . .

In any case I have never had the slightest revelation. Divinity, in that sense, makes no sense to me. However, what is beyond our daily reality, beyond what our senses and our intelligence can perceive and grasp, that for me is fundamental. I am convinced that we are at the point of a first hesitant understanding and sensitivity, and that we will go far. And perhaps what we call religion and metaphysics will at that moment join up in final wisdom. Has Eastern thought arrived at this point? Again I don't know.

In the middle of February, a few days before my arrival in Paris, my friend Julio Cortázar died. It had to come—leukemia is unrelenting. But it is difficult to resign myself. Edison Simons and I went to put a red rose on his grave, just to make a gesture. I did it for myself, of course. As his wife Carol Dunlop, buried close by, used to say, "it is never death one mourns." There were a lot of flowers, already wilted, from Nicaragua and elsewhere. A black cat came out from under one of the bouquets. The sun broke through the clouds—a good sign, I said to myself. In the face of death one is reduced to suppositions and superstitions. At Carol's funeral, a black and white cat was prowling around the grave. And then Julio's cat disappeared, nonchalantly: it's seen it all before. The gravestone white marble, topped by small discs like suns stolen from a spring morning. A stylized face whose smile reminds one of Alice's cat decorates the uppermost disc. Cortázar had just completed the book he had written with Carol, *Los autonautas de la cosmopista,* a report on a rather special journey in 30 days from Paris to Marseille, without once leaving the freeway. The book contains all the photos of the heroes and the monsters they encountered. In the *New York Times Book Review* (March 4, 1984) Carlos Fuentes notes that shortly after Cortázar's death, the French highways were jammed—doubtless machinated by the Cronopios, in homage to their departed author.

Writing at Risk: Interview with Julio Cortázar

JASON WEISS

*W*hen *Julio Cortázar died of cancer in February 1984 at the age of sixty-nine, the Madrid newspaper* El País *hailed him as one of the Hispanic world's great writers and over two days carried eleven full pages of tributes, reminiscences, and farewells.*

Though Cortázar had lived in Paris since 1951, he visited his native Argentina regularly until he was officially exiled in the early 1970s by the military junta, which had taken exception to several of his short stories. With the victory in late 1983 of the democratically elected Alfonsín government, Cortázar was able to make one last visit to his home country and to see his mother. Alfonsín's minister of culture chose to give him no official welcome, afraid that his political views were too far to the left, but the writer was nonetheless greeted as a returning hero. One night in Buenos Aires, coming out of a movie theater after seeing the new film based on Osvaldo Soriano's novel, No habrá más pena ni olvido *(A Funny, Dirty Little War), Cortázar and his friends ran into a student demonstration coming toward them, which instantly broke file on glimpsing the writer and crowded around him. The bookstores on the boulevards still being open, the students hurriedly bought up copies of Cortázar's books so that he could sign them. A kiosk salesman, apologizing that he had no more of Cortázar's books, held out a Carlos Fuentes novel for him to sign. . . .*

Throughout his years in Paris, Cortázar lived in various neighborhoods. In the last decade of his life, royalties from his books enabled him to buy his own apartment. It might have been the setting for one of his stories. The building, in a district of whole-salers and chinaware shops, stands removed from the street by several rows of similar buildings, which have residences only on the top floors. Successions of light and shadow, in and out of the several archways, led to his staircase. Somehow the apartment seemed unexpectedly spacious, despite the thousands upon thousands of books spilling from every wall. A short, winding corridor led to other book-filled rooms, the walls lined with paintings by friends, each room suggesting a greater depth than its walls would allow.

Cortázar was a tall man, six foot four, though he had grown thinner than pho-tographs revealed. The months before this interview had been particularly difficult for him, since his last wife, Carol, thirty years his junior, had recently died of cancer. In addition, his extensive travels, especially to Latin America where his political commit-ments took up much of his time, had obviously exhausted him. This interview took place

Reprinted from *Writing at Risk: Interviews in Paris with Uncommon Writers* (1991) by permission of University of Iowa Press.

on July 8, 1983, while he was home for barely a week. He was sitting in his favorite chair, smoking his pipe, near the thousands of records that filled the shelves from floor to ceiling.

JW: In some of the stories in your most recent book, *Deshoras,* it seems the fantastic is entering into the real world more than ever. Have you yourself felt that? As if the fantastic and the commonplace are becoming one almost?

JC: Yes, in these recent stories I have the feeling that there is less distance between what we call the fantastic and what we call the real. In my older stories the distance was greater because the fantastic was really very fantastic, and sometimes it touched on the supernatural. Well, I am glad to have written those older stories, because I think the fantastic has that quality to always take on metamorphoses, it changes, it can change with time. The notion of the fantastic we had in the epoch of the gothic novels in England, for example, has absolutely nothing to do with our notion of it today. Now we laugh when we read about *The Castle of Otranto*—the ghosts dressed in white, the skeletons that walk around making noises with their chains. And yet that was the notion of the fantastic at the time. It's changed a lot. I think my notion of the fantastic, now, more and more approaches what we call reality. Perhaps because for me reality also approaches the fantastic more and more.

JW: Much more of your time in recent years has gone to the support of various liberation struggles in Latin America. Hasn't that also helped bring the real and the fantastic closer for you? As if it's made you more serious?

JC: Well, I don't like the idea of "serious." Because I don't think I am serious, in that sense at any rate, where one speaks of a serious man or a serious woman. These last few years all my efforts concerning certain Latin American regimes—Argentina, Chile, Uruguay, and now above all Nicaragua—have absorbed me to such a point that even the fantastic in certain stories dealing with this subject is a fantastic that's very close to reality, in my opinion. So, I feel less free than before. That is, thirty years ago I was writing things that came into my head and I judged them only by aesthetic criteria. Now, I continue to judge them by aesthetic criteria, because first of all I'm a writer, but I'm a writer who is very tormented, preoccupied by the situation in Latin America. Very often that slips into my writing, in a conscious or in an unconscious way. But in *Deshoras,* despite the stories where there are very precise references to ideological and political questions, I think my stories haven't changed. They're still stories of the fantastic.

The problem for an engagé writer, as they call it now, is to continue being a writer. If what he writes becomes simply literature with a political content, it can be very mediocre. That's what has happened to a number of writers. So, the problem is one of balance. For me, what I do must always be literature, the highest I can do. To go beyond the possible, even. But, at the same time, very often to try to put in a charge of contemporary reality. And that's a very difficult balance.

JW: But are you looking to mix the two?

JC: No. Before, the ideas that came to me for stories were purely fantastic, while now many ideas are based on the reality of Latin America. In *Deshoras,* for example, the story about the rats, "Satarsa," is an episode based on the reality of the fight against the Argentine guerrilleros. The problem is to put it in writing, because one is tempted all the time to let oneself keep going on the political level alone.

JW: What has been the response to such stories? Was there much difference in the response you got from literary people as from political people?

JC: Of course. The bourgeois readers in Latin America who are indifferent to politics or else who even align themselves with the right wing, well, they don't worry about the problems that worry me—the problems of exploitation, of oppression, and so on. Those people regret that my stories often take a political turn. Other readers—above all the young, who share these feelings with me, this need to struggle, and who love literature—love these stories. For example, "Apocalypse at Solentiname" is a story that Nicaraguans read and reread with great pleasure. And the Cubans read "Meeting" with lots of pleasure as well.

JW: What has determined your increased political involvement in recent years?

JC: The military in Latin America, they're the ones who make me work harder. If they get out, if there were a change, then I could rest a little and work on poems and stories that are exclusively literary. But they're the ones who give me work to do. The more they are there, the more I must be against them.

JW: You have said many times that for you literature is like a game. In what ways?

JC: For me literature is a form of play. It makes up part of what they call the ludic side of man, *Homo ludens.* But I've always added that one must be careful, because there are two forms of play. There's soccer, for example, which is a game. And there are games that are very profound and very serious, while still being games. You must consider that when children play, you only have to look at them, they take it very seriously. They're having fun, but playing is important for them, it's their main activity. Just as when they're older, for example, it will be their erotic activity. When they're little, playing is as serious as love will be ten years later. I remember when I was little, when my parents came to say, "Okay, you've played enough, come take a bath now," I found that completely idiotic, because for me the bath was a silly matter. It had no importance whatsoever, while playing with my friends, that was something serious. And for me literature is like that, it's a game but a game where one can stake one's life, one can do everything for that game.

JW: What interested you about the fantastic in the beginning? Were you very young?
JC: Oh yes. It began with my childhood. I was very surprised, when I was going to grade school, that most of my young classmates had no sense of the fantastic. They were very realistic. They took things as they were . . . that's a plant, that's an armchair. And I was already seeing the world in a way that was very changeable. For me things were not so well defined in that way, there were no labels. My mother, who is a very imaginative woman, helped me a lot. Instead of telling me, "No, no, you should be serious," she was pleased that I was very imaginative, and when I turned toward the world of the fantastic, she helped me because she gave me books to read. That's how at the age of nine I read Edgar Allan Poe for the first time. That book I stole to read because my mother didn't want me to read it, she thought I was too young and she was right. The book scared me and I was ill for three months, because I believed in it . . . *dur comme fer,* as the French say. For me the fantastic was perfectly natural. When I read a story of the fantastic, I had no doubts at all. That's the way things were. When I gave them to my friends, they'd say, "No thanks, I prefer to read cowboy stories." Cowboys especially at the time. I didn't understand that. I preferred the world of the supernatural, of the fantastic.

JW: When you translated Poe's complete works many years later, did you discover new things for yourself from such a close reading?
JC: Many, many things. To begin with, I explored his language, which is highly criticized by the English and the Americans because they find it too baroque, in short they've found all sorts of things wrong with it. Well, since I'm neither English nor American, I see it with another perspective. I know there are aspects which have aged a lot, that are exaggerated, but that hasn't the slightest importance next to his genius. To write, in those times, "The Fall of the House of Usher"—that takes an extraordinary genius. To write "Ligeia" or "Berenice," or "The Black Cat," any of them, shows a true genius for the fantastic and the supernatural. I should say, in passing, that yesterday I went to a friend's house on the rue Edgar Allan Poe. There is a plaque where it says, "Edgar Poe, English writer." He wasn't English at all! I wanted to point that out because they should change the plaque. We'll both protest!

JW: In your own writing, besides the fantastic, there is a real warmth and affection for your characters as well.
JC: Certain readers and certain critics have told me that too. That when my characters are children and adolescents, I have a lot of tenderness for them, which is true. I treat them with a lot of love. I think they are very alive in my

novels and stories. When I write a story where the character is an adolescent, I am the adolescent while I write it.

JW: Are many of your characters based on people whom you've known?
JC: I wouldn't say many, but there are a few. Very often there are characters who are a mixture of two or three people. I have put together female characters from two women I had known. It gave the character in the story or the book a personality that was more complex, more difficult, because she had different ways of being that came from two women.

JW: As with La Maga in *Hopscotch?*
JC: Well, she is based on one woman, with a lot of psychological characteristics that are completely imaginary. I don't need to depend on reality to write real things. I invent them, and they become real in the writing. Very often I'm amused because literary critics, especially those who are a bit academic, think that writers don't have any imagination. They think a writer has always been influenced by this, this, and this. They retrace the whole chain of influences. Influences do exist, but these critics forget one thing: the pleasure of inventing, pure invention. I know my influences. Edgar Allan Poe is an influence that is very present in certain of my stories. But the rest, I'm the one who invents it.

JW: Is it when you feel the need to give a character more substance that you mix two together? How does that happen?
JC: Things don't work like that. It's the characters who direct me. That is, I see a character, he's there, and I recognize someone I knew or occasionally two who are a bit mixed together, but that stops there. After that, the character acts on his own account. He says things . . . I never know what they're going to say when I'm writing dialogues. Really, it's all between them. I'm just typing out what they're saying. And sometimes I burst out laughing, or I throw out a page because I say, "There you've said silly things. Out." And I put in another page and start again with the dialogue, but there is no fabrication on my part. Really, I don't fabricate anything.

JW: So it's not the characters you've known who impel you to write?
JC: Not at all, no. Often I have the idea for a story where there aren't any characters yet. I'll have a strange idea: something's going to happen in a house in the country. I'm very visual when I write, I see everything. So, I see this house in the country and then abruptly I begin to situate the characters. It's at that point that one of the characters might be someone I knew. But it's not for sure. In the end, most of my characters are invented. Well, there is myself, there are many autobiographical references in the character of Oliveira in *Hopscotch*. It's not me, but there's a lot of me. Of me here in Paris, in my bohemian days, my first years here. But the readers who read Oliveira as Cortázar in Paris would be mistaken. No, no, I was very different.

JW: Does what you write ever get too close to being autobiographical?
JC: I don't like autobiography. I will never write my memoirs. Autobiograph-ics of others interest me, but not my own. Very often, though, when I have ideas for a novel or a story, there are moments of my life, situations, that come very naturally to place themselves there. In the story "Deshoras," the boy who is in love with his pal's sister who is older than him, I lived that. There is a small part of it that's autobiographical, but from there on, it's the fantastic or the imaginary which dominates.

JW: You have even written of the need for memoirs by Latin American writ-ers. Why is it you don't want to write your own?
JC: If I wrote my autobiography, I would have to be truthful and honest. I can't tell an imaginary autobiography. And so, I would be doing a historian's job, self-historian, and that *bores* me. Because I prefer to invent, to imagine.

JW: José Lezama Lima in *Paradiso* has Cemí saying that "the baroque . . . is what has real interest in Spain and Hispanic America." Why do you think that is so?
JC: I cannot reply as an expert. The baroque has been very important in Latin America, in the arts and in literature as well. The baroque can offer a great richness; it lets the imagination soar in all its spiraling directions, as in a baroque church with its decorative angels and all that or in baroque music. But I distrust the baroque a little in Latin America. Very often the baroque writers let themselves go too easily in writing. They write in five pages what one could very well write in one page, which would be better. I too must have fallen into the baroque because I am Latin American, but I have always had a mistrust of it. I don't like turgid, voluminous sentences, full of adjectives and descriptions, purring and purring into the reader's ear. I know it's very charming, of course, very beautiful, but it's not me. I'm more on the side of Jorge Luis Borges in that sense. He has always been an enemy of the baroque; he tightened his writing, as though he used pliers. Well, I write in a very dif-ferent way from Borges, but the great lesson he gave me is one of economy. He taught me when I began to read him, being very young, that it wasn't necessary to write these long sentences at the end of which there was some vague thought. That one had to try to say what one wanted to with economy, but with a beautiful economy. It's the difference perhaps between a plant, which would be the baroque with its multiplicity of leaves, it's very beautiful, and a precious stone, a crystal—*that* for me is more beautiful still.

JW: The lines are very musical in your writing. Do you usually hear the words as you're writing them?
JC: Oh yes, I hear them, and I know that in writing—if I'm launched on a story, I write very quickly, because I can revise later—I will never put down a word that is disagreeable to me. There are words I don't like—not just crude

words, those I use when I have to—the sound, the structure of the word displeases me. For example, all the words in juridicial and administrative language, they are frequently present in literature. And I hardly ever use those words because I don't like them.

JW: No, I can't imagine them in the spirit of your writing.
JC: It's a question of music, finally. I like music more than literature, I've said it many times, I repeat it again, and for me writing corresponds to a rhythm, a heartbeat, a musical pulsation. That's my problem with translations, because translators of my books sometimes don't realize that there is a rhythm, they translate the meaning of the words. And I need this swing, this movement that my lines have. Otherwise, the story doesn't sound right. Above all certain moments in the stories must be directed musically, because that's how they give their true meaning. It's not what they say but how they say it.

JW: But it's difficult to be at the same time rhythmically musical and economical like a crystal.
JC: Yes, it's very difficult, of course. But then I think especially of certain musics that have succeeded in being like that. The best works of Johann Sebastian Bach have economy with the greatest musical richness. And in a jazz solo, a real jazz solo, a Lester Young solo, for example, at that point there is all the freedom, all the invention, but there is the precise economy that starts and finishes. Not like the mediocre jazz musicians who play for three-quarters of an hour because they have nothing to say. That's why I'm very critical of certain forms of contemporary jazz. Because they have nothing more to say, they keep filling up the space. Armstrong, or Ellington, or Charlie Parker only needed two or three minutes to do like Bach, exactly like Johann Sebastian Bach, and Mozart. Writing must be like that for me, a moment from a story must be a beautiful solo. It's an improvisation, but improvisation involves invention and beauty.

JW: How do you start with your stories? At any particular point of entry? An image?
JC: With me stories and novels can start anywhere. But on the level of writing, when I begin to write, the story has been turning around in me a long time, sometimes for weeks. But not in a way that's clear; it's a sort of general idea of the story. A house where there's a red plant in one corner, and then I know that there's an old man who walks around in this house, and that's all I know. It happens like that. And then there are the dreams, because during that time my dreams are full of references and allusions to what is going to be in the story. Sometimes the whole story is in a dream. One of my first stories—it's been very popular, "House Taken Over"—that was a nightmare I had. I got up like that and wrote it. But in general they are fragments of ref-

erences. That is, my subconscious is in the process of working through a story. The story is being written inside there. So when I say that I begin anywhere, it's because I don't know what is the beginning or the end. I start to write and that is the beginning, finally, but I haven't decided that the story has to start like that. It starts there and it continues. Very often I have no clear idea of the ending, I don't know what's going to happen. It's only gradually, as the story goes on, that things become clearer and abruptly I see the ending.

JW: So you are discovering the story *while* you are writing it?

JC: That's right. I discover it a bit while I am writing. There too is an analogy, I think, with improvisation in jazz. You don't ask a jazz musician, "But what are you going to play?" He'll laugh at you. He simply has a theme, a series of chords he has to respect, and then he takes his trumpet or his saxophone and he begins. But he hasn't the slightest idea . . . it's not a question of an *idea*. They're different internal pulsations. Sometimes it comes out well, sometimes it doesn't. Me, I'm a bit embarrassed to sign my stories. The novels, no, because the novels I worked on a lot; there's a whole architecture. My stories, it's as if they were dictated to me a little, by something that is in me, but it's not me who's responsible. But then it appears they are mine after all, I should accept them!

JW: Are there certain aspects of writing a story that always pose a problem for you?

JC: In general, no, because as I was explaining, the story is already made somewhere inside me. So, it has its dimension, its structure, it's going to be a very short story or a fairly long story, all that seems to be decided in advance. But in recent years I've started to sense some problems. I reflect more in front of the page. I write more slowly. And I write in a way that's more spare. Certain critics have reproached me for that, they've told me that little by little I'm losing that suppleness in my stories. I say what I want to, but with a greater economy of means. I don't know if it's for better or worse. In any case, it's my way of writing now.

JW: You were saying that with the novels there is a whole architecture. Does that mean working very differently?

JC: The first thing I wrote in *Hopscotch* was a chapter that is found in the middle now. It's the chapter where the characters put out a board to get from one window to another. Well, I wrote that without knowing why I was writing it. I saw the characters, I saw the situation, it was in Buenos Aires. It was very hot, I remember, and I was next to the window with my typewriter. I saw this situation of a guy who's trying to make his wife go across, because he's not going himself, to go get some silly thing, some nails. It was totally ridiculous in appearance. I wrote all that, which is long, forty pages, and when I finished I said to myself, "All right, but what have I done? Because that's not a story.

What is it?" And then I understood that I was launched on a novel but couldn't continue. I had to stop there and write the whole section in Paris before. That is, the whole background of Oliveira, because when I wrote the chapter with the board, I was thinking of myself a little at that point. I saw myself as the character, Oliveira was very much me at that point. But to do a novel with that, I had to go backward before I could continue.

JW: You were in Buenos Aires at that point.
JC: At that point, because afterward the whole book was written here. That chapter I wrote in Buenos Aires.

JW: And you sensed right away that it was a novel.
JC: I sensed right away that it would be the novel of a city. I wanted to put in the Paris I knew and loved there, in the first part. It would also be a novel about the relations among several characters, but above all the problems, the metaphysical searches of Oliveira, which were mine at the time. Because at that period I was totally immersed in aesthetics, philosophy, and metaphysics. I was completely outside of history and politics. In *Hopscotch* there is no reference to questions of Latin America and its problems. It's later that I discovered that.

JW: You've often said it was the Cuban revolution that awakened you to that.
JC: And I say it again.

JW: Do you revise much when you write?
JC: Very little. That comes from the fact that the thing has already been at work inside me. When I see the rough drafts of some of my friends, where everything is revised, everything's changed, moved around, there are arrows all over the place . . . no no no. My manuscripts are very clean.

JW: What are your writing habits? Have certain things changed?
JC: There's one thing that hasn't changed, that will never change, that is the total anarchy and the disorder. I have absolutely no method. When I feel like writing a story I let everything drop, I write the story. And sometimes when I write a story, in the month or two that follows I will write two or three stories. In general, it comes in series. Writing one leaves me in a receptive state, and then I catch another story. You see the sort of image I use, but it's like that, where the story drops inside of me. But later, a year can go by where I write nothing literary, nothing. I should say too that these last few years I have spent a good deal of my time at the typewriter writing political articles. The texts I've written about Nicaragua that are distributed through the syndicated press agencies, everything I've written about Argentina, they have nothing to do with literature, they're militant things.

JW: Do you have preferred places for writing?

JC: In fact, no. At the beginning, when I was younger and physically more resistant, here in Paris for example a large part of *Hopscotch* I wrote in cafés. Because the noise didn't bother me and, on the contrary, it was a congenial place. I worked a lot there, I read or I wrote. But with age I've become more complicated. I write when I'm sure of having some silence. I can't write if there's music, that's absolutely out of the question. Music is one thing and writing is another. I need a certain calm; but, this said, a hotel, an airplane sometimes, a friend's house, and here at home are places where I can write.

JW: About Paris. What gave you the courage to pick up and move off to Paris when you did, more than thirty years ago?

JC: Courage? No, it didn't take much courage. I simply had to accept the idea that coming to Paris, and cutting ties with Argentina at that time, meant being very poor and having problems making a living. But that didn't worry me. I knew in one way or another I was going to manage. Primarily I came because Paris, French culture on the whole, held a lot of attraction for me. I had read French literature with a passion in Argentina. So, I wanted to be here and get to know the streets and the places one finds in the books, in the novels. To go through the streets of Balzac or of Baudelaire. It was a very romantic journey. I was, I am, very romantic. I have to be rather careful when I write, because very often I could let myself fall into . . . I wouldn't say bad taste, perhaps not, but a bit in the direction of an exaggerated romanticism. So, there's a necessary control there, but in my private life I don't need to control myself. I really am very sentimental, very romantic. I'm a tender person, I have a lot of tenderness to give. What I give now to Nicaragua is tenderness. It is also the political conviction that the Sandinistas are right in what they're doing and that they're leading an admirable struggle. But it's not only the political idea. There's an enormous tenderness because it's a people I love. As I love the Cubans, and I love the Argentines. Well, all that makes up part of my character, and in my writing I have had to watch myself. Above all when I was young, I wrote things that were tearjerkers. That was really romanticism, the *roman rose*. My mother would read them and cry.

JW: Nearly all your writing that people know dates from your arrival in Paris. But you were writing a lot before that, weren't you? A few things had already been published.

JC: I've been writing since the age of nine, right up through my whole adolescence and early youth. In my early youth I was already capable of writing stories and novels, which showed me that I was on the right path. But I didn't want to publish. I was very severe with myself, and I continue to be. I remember that my peers, when they had written some poems or a small novel, searched for a publisher right away. And it was bad, mediocre stuff, because it lacked maturity. I would tell myself, "No, you're not publishing. You hang onto that." I kept certain things, and others I threw out. When I did publish for the first time I was over thirty years old; it was a little before my departure for France. That was my first book of stories, *Bestiario,* which came out in '51, the same month I took the boat to come here. Before, I had published a little text called *Los Reyes,* which is a dialogue. A friend who had a lot of money, who did small editions for himself and his friends, had done a private edition. And that's all. No, there's another thing—a sin of youth—a book of sonnets. I published it myself, but with a pseudonym.

JW: You are the lyricist of a recent album of tangos, "Trottoirs de Buenos Aires." What got you started writing tangos?
JC: Well, I am a good Argentine and above all a *porteño*—that is, a resident of Buenos Aires, because it's the port. The tango was our music, I grew up in an atmosphere of tangos. We listened to them on the radio, because the radio started when I was little, and right away it was tangos and tangos. There were people in my family, my mother and an aunt, who played tangos on the piano and sang them. Through the radio we began to listen to Carlos Gardel and the great singers of the time. The tango became like a part of my consciousness and it's the music that sends me back to my youth again and to Buenos Aires. So, I'm quite caught up in the tango. At the same time being very critical, because I'm not one of those Argentines who believe the tango is the wonder of wonders. I think that the tango on the whole, especially next to jazz, is very poor music. It is poor but it is beautiful. It's like those plants that are very simple, that one can't compare to an orchid or a rosebush, but that have an extraordinary beauty in themselves. In recent years, as I have friends who play tangos here—the Cuarteto Cedrón are great friends, and a fine bandoneón player named Juan José Mosalini—we've listened to tangos, talked about tangos. Then one day a poem came to me like that, which perhaps could be set to music, I didn't really know. And then, looking among unpublished poems—most of my poems are unpublished—I found some short poems which those fellows could set to music, and they did. But we've done the opposite experience as well. Cedrón gave me a musical theme, I listened to it, and I wrote the words. So I've done it both ways.

JW: In the biographical notes in your books, it says you are also an amateur trumpet player. Did you play with any groups?
JC: No. That's a bit of a legend that was invented by my very dear friend Paul Blackburn, who died quite young, unfortunately. He knew that I played the trumpet a little, for myself at home. So he would always tell me, "But you should meet some musicians to play with." I'd say, "No," as the Americans say, "I lack equipment." I didn't have the abilities; I was playing for myself. I would put on a Jelly Roll Morton record, or Armstrong, or early Ellington, where the melody is easier to follow, especially the blues which has a given

scheme. I would have fun hearing them play and adding my trumpet. I played along with them . . . but it sure wasn't *with* them! I never dared approach jazz musicians; now my trumpet is lost somewhere in the other room there. Blackburn put that in one of the blurbs. And because there is a photo of me playing the trumpet, people thought I really could play well. Just as I didn't want to publish without being sure, it was the same thing with the trumpet. And that day never arrived.

JW: Have you worked on any novels since *A Manual for Manuel*?
JC: Alas no, for reasons that are very clear: it's because of political work. For me a novel requires a concentration and a quantity of time, at least a year, to work tranquilly and not abandon it. And now, I cannot. A week ago I didn't know I would be leaving for Nicaragua in three days. When I return I won't know what's going to happen next. But this novel is already written. It's there, it's in my dreams. I dream all the time of this novel. I don't know what happens in the novel, but I have an idea. As in the stories, I know that it will be something fairly long that will have elements of the fantastic, but not so much. It will be, say, in the genre of *A Manual for Manuel,* where the fantastic elements are mixed in, but it won't be a political book either. It will be a book of pure literature. I hope that life will give me a sort of desert island, even if the desert island is this room, and a year, I ask for a year. But when these bastards—the Hondurans, the Somocistas and Reagan—are in the act of destroying Nicaragua, I don't have my island. I couldn't begin to write, because I would be obsessed by that all the time. That demands top priority.

JW: And it can be difficult enough as it is with the priorities of life versus literature.
JC: Yes and no. It depends on what kind of priorities. If the priorities are like those I just spoke about, touching on the moral responsibility of an individual, I would agree. But I know many people who are always crying, "Oh, I'd like to write my novel, but I have to sell the house, and then there are the taxes, what am I going to do?" Reasons like, "I work in the office all day, how do you expect me to write?" Me, I worked all day at UNESCO and then I came home and wrote *Hopscotch*. When one wants to write, one writes. If one is condemned to write, one writes.

JW: Do you work anymore as a translator or interpreter?
JC: No, that's over. I lead a very simple life. I don't need much money for the things I like: records, books, tobacco. So now I can live from my royalties. They've translated me into so many languages that I receive enough money to live on. I have to be a little careful; I can't go out and buy myself a yacht, but since I have absolutely no intention of buying a yacht . . .

JW: Have you enjoyed your fame and success?

JC: Ah, listen, I'll say something I shouldn't say because no one will believe it, but success is not a pleasure for me. I'm glad to be able to live from what I write, so I have to put up with the popular and critical side of success. But I was happier as a man when I was unknown, much happier. Now I can't go to Latin America or to Spain without being recognized every ten yards, and the autographs, the embraces . . . It's very moving, because they're readers who are frequently quite young. I'm happy they like what I do, but it's terribly distressing for me on the level of privacy. I can't go to a beach in Europe; in five minutes there's a photographer. I have a physical appearance that I can't disguise; if I were small I could shave and put on sunglasses, but with my height, my long arms and all that, they recognize me from afar.

On the other hand, there are very beautiful things: I was in Barcelona a month ago, walking around the gothic quarter one evening, and there was an American girl, very pretty, playing the guitar very well and singing. She was seated on the ground earning her living. She sang a bit like Joan Baez, a very pure, clear voice. There was a group of young people from Barcelona listening. I stopped to listen to her, but I stayed in the shadows. At a certain point, one of these young men who was about twenty, very young, very handsome, approached me. He had a cake in his hand. He said, "Julio, take a piece." So I took a piece and ate it, and I told him, "Thanks a lot for coming up and giving that to me." And he said to me, "Listen, I'm giving you so little compared to what you've given me." I said, "Don't say that, don't say that," and we embraced and he went away. Well, things like that, that's the best compensation for my work as a writer. That a boy or a girl come up to speak to you and to offer you a piece of cake, it's wonderful. It's worth the trouble of writing.

ARTICLES AND REVIEWS
◆

Lying to Athena:
Cortázar and the Art of Fiction

GREGORY RABASSA

In Book 13 of the *Odyssey,* when Odysseus has been put ashore on Ithaca at last, he encounters his patroness Athena, who is disguised as a shepherd. Almost at once he goes into the well-honed tale of his Cretan origins and all the great deeds to his credit. This stock-in-trade of his was useful for conceal-ment, but the verve with which he tells the story and embellishes upon it betrays the joy of the bard, the creator. Finally the goddess is so pleased with him that she smiles and gives him a caress, shedding her mask and assuming female shape, as she reveals herself to him and says:

> "Whoever gets around you must be sharp
> and guileful as a snake; even a god
> might bow to you in ways of dissimulation.
> You! You chameleon!
> Bottomless bag of tricks! Here in your own country
> would you not give your stratagems a rest
> or stop spellbinding for an instant?
>
> You play a part as if it were your own tough skin.
>
> No more of this, though. Two of a kind, we are,
> contrivers, both. Of all men now alive
> you are the best in plots and story telling.
> My own fame is for wisdom among the gods—
> deceptions, too. . . ."[1]

Thus it is that fiction is a tool of wisdom and, indeed, one which is used with great joy, even by Athena herself. So that if our philosophic search for truth is to go on, we must cease to gather the shreds we take to be particles of the ultimate truth and, instead, fashion our own bits and pieces in the shape of

First published in *Books Abroad* 50:3 (Summer 1976), pp. 542–47; reissued in *The Final Island: The Fiction of Julio Cortázar.* Ivar Ivask & Jaime Alazraki, eds. (Norman: University of Oklahoma Press, 1978). Reprinted by permission of the publishers.

that vague reality which Plato has described to us. This is precisely what the philosopher does at the end of the *Republic* with his myth of Er.

The Brazilian novelist Érico Veríssimo once said that his old *gaúcho* grandfather in Rio Grande do Sul was quite proud of the fame his grandson had acquired but that he had some serious reservations nonetheless because Érico was telling lies after all. This attitude is the heritage of the joyless nineteenth century, which tried to seek the truth directly, ignoring Plato's strictures concerning our incomplete grasp of reality. As thousands wheeze themselves to death, tobacconists say, "It hasn't been proven"; when someone says, "We must be realistic," another set of morals has gone down the drain. Myth may indeed be the closest we have come to truth, and if we put it to the mean and niggling test of realism, we retreat even deeper into Plato's cave, where so many of our critics deserve to be with their chopping blocks and single-edged cleavers. We think that the invention of devices improves upon our surroundings, and of late we even go on endlessly about life-style instead of life. Yet, if we turn our invention to words and concepts, we are given the lie. In his *Naufragios* the intrepid proto-anthropologist Alvar Núñez Cabeza de Vaca tells of how he had great difficulties in extracting facts from one certain tribe of Indians because they loved to novelize so much ("porque son grandes amigos de novelar"). This is certainly in the Odyssean spirit and that of tale-telling (even this last wonderful word has the connotation of something dirty), but it can also be the basis of Disneyland and other enforced hallucinations.

Julio Cortázar is a writer who has thrown off the restrictions of mental Calvinism imposed by the past century and still so much with us. Going along with Jarry, he finds that life imitates art and that homo ludens must precede homo faber ("homo faber & faber," as he calls him in *Libro de Manuel*.) This is most evident in his conception of structure. A form is of its own making, an object is defined by its use, as Ortega y Gasset has said, and the reader really creates his own novel as he goes forward. This is the starting point of *Hopscotch,* where Cortázar gives us a carefully ordered alternate version and also invites us to go to work and bring forth further variations. We have before us a rich lode of chiastic possibilities. When the novel was first published in the United States, a great many critics did not know that along with the interesting possibilities put forth to them they were also being had. Cortázar shook his head in dismay at this straitlaced interpretation and agreed that it would be awful to have to read any novel through twice, this one above all. What he did do, however, was to point out the possibilities of reality, and this can best be done and perhaps only be done by recourse to fiction, to the lie. Our wisdom is still so limited that it most often needs to be primed with a cupful of untruth in order to start pumping up new ideas and concepts. Before we can begin to write, we must unwrite, as the mononymous Morelli says in *Hopscotch* (a fine and complex pun can be essayed in Spanish with the words *escribir* and *describir*).

As we put the pieces of *Hopscotch* together we find that the puzzle is the novel itself, that we are in a sense writing it as we read it, much in the way that Aureliano Babilonia in *One Hundred Years of Solitude* lives his life to the end and can only do so as he reads the manuscript of Melquíades, which is the book we are reading too. This is also the structure of *Don Quixote,* accepted as the first novel, although Homer and, indeed, Odysseus himself have some claim through the narrative techniques of the *Odyssey.* The Duchess recognizes Don Quixote because she has read the first part, just as we have, putting character and reader on the same level, giving the characters of the novel a real existence and making the reader a member of the cast.

Cortázar's art as seen in *Hopscotch* and its sequel *62: A Model Kit* is essentially indehiscent. The conclusion is vague, real rather than factual. Life cannot end so neatly and so precisely. When Allen R. Foley's Vermonter is asked, "Have you lived here all your life?" he answers, "Not yet."[2] Oliveira seeks truth and meaning in the accepted sense and finally comes to realize that they are elusive, that his illusions are closer to his goal. The very name of his friend Traveler is evidence that our words and labels in their assigned usage are apt ultimately to be a mockery of the very thing they are meant to represent. Oliveira's *nostos* is tragic, more like Agamemnon's than that of Odysseus, perhaps because, like the former, he is prone to accept standard definitions in spite of himself and only becomes a contriver when his mind begins to slip. Although he has traces of the grace entailed, Oliveira is not the thoroughgoing cronopio that Odysseus was.

Toward the end of the novel, in the madhouse already even though because of devious circumstances which ultimately prove meet, Oliveira finally has his katabasis as he descends into the refrigerated morgue, an image quite in keeping with the utter depths of Dante's Inferno rather than with the subsequent impression the world has come to give it. This would imply that Oliveira has plumbed the very bottom, where those punished as betrayers of benefactors are lodged. Here his revelation is negative. He loses his Eurydice as he kisses Talita, in whom he sees the lost Maga. He has looked back, but this time there is a reversal and it is the future which has disappeared; it is not the past reborn. Juno, counter-fate, has won out over Jupiter; fate, *furor* over *ratio,* and Oliveira goes mad in his labyrinth of string, basins and ball-bearings, or is it Agamemnon's net self-assumed?

The tragedy is that Oliveira had been following a process of rigidity until he became as cold and stiff and lifeless as the idems in the mortuary drawers, each of whom once had a life, a life befitting a nineteenth-century novel of the kind we call realistic. Oliveira had been lying to himself by following what he thought was true and reasonable instead of lying to Athena so that she would reveal herself and impart her wisdom. Suicide is rarely tragic, however, and if this is what Oliveira has done at the end of part two, the result is more pathetic. Cortázar in his scheme of things, however, in his reliance on the concept of quantum, has offered an alternative version in the dispensable chapters of part three. Oliveira is broken but saved. His body rather than his mind has cracked. This salvatory recourse brings to mind the treatment accorded the Hungarian suicide song of the late thirties, "Gloomy Sunday," which had ever so many people leaping into the Danube off the bridges between Buda and Pest. I recall that when Billie Holiday recorded the song here, lines were added to mitigate the urge and show that it was all a dream, that we could rest assured.

In Cortázar's perception of the truth the use of dreams and dreamlike states leads us in important directions. Much of this in *Hopscotch* is hallucinatory or a ribald caricature of surface reality, like the Berthe Trépat episode. (This section has the stuff of a happening about it and must be staged someday, replete with original music.) In *62* we meet the City, a vision shared by the characters and not really a dream. It is, rather, an epiphany which has a collective mise-en-scène. The City is, of course, a labyrinth and the hotel a labyrinth within a labyrinth. Here the direction of the elevator leads to anabasis before it turns horizontal. The coming up is frustrated, then, and the revelation incomplete, leading into difficulties on a higher level. This would bear out what has subsequently been discovered in mathematics regarding the so-called "Traveling Salesman Problem," a sort of maze puzzle which can be solved when it is in limited form but becomes insoluble when enlarged, showing that microcosmic solutions do not always obtain in the macrocosm. Returning to the Dis imagery of *Hopscotch,* we must wonder if the last scene in the City in *62* might not be Stygian in import, with the canal at the north end serving as the underground river.

It is also in *62* that the other self acquires more cohesion. In *Hopscotch* Traveler is seen as a kind of doppelgänger for Oliveira (the irony of names again: Traveler who has never left Buenos Aires, and Oliveira with the connotations of roots and staff of life, the trunk upon which the bed of Odysseus and Penelope was anchored). The idea of the double is broadened in *62,* and we have the notion of the *paredros,* the Egyptian concept of a guiding spirit, a fellow traveler, but one which here is shared and which possesses different people at different times, when that character, without being identified, is referred to simply as "my paredros." Able as she is to appear to or to influence the minds of whomsoever she chooses according to her will, Athena might well be called Odysseus's paredros. In his last novel, *Libro de Manuel,* Cortázar has a figure called "the one I told you," quite similar in concept to the paredros, but given an added dimension by the satanic suggestion of his title, so close to many Latin American euphemisms for the Prince of Darkness; and, of course, the name of God is never spoken in Hell except by the foul-mouthed Vanni Fucci. In classical mythology Hermes/Mercury, the messenger (*angelos*) of the gods, was given many of the mischief-making attributes later assigned to the Christian devil—Candanga, as he is known in some Asturian parts. Indeed, in Brazilian *candomblé* Exu, the messenger in the Yoruban pantheon, has often and mistakenly been coordinated with the devil.

Of all the Spanish American writers who have been said to practice a style called "magic realism," Cortázar is the one who might be closest to the mark. Straight fantasy is found more often in the short stories and is never explained. In the novels the case is more often one of creating fantasy out of the raw material of the reality at hand, as in the case of the Berthe Trépat episode in *Hopscotch* and Frau Marta in *62*. The most striking example of the creation of fantasy out of the stuff of reality is also in *62,* and it is most apt that the one who fashions this fantasy and turns it into reality (so that the real situation then ceases to exist and becomes fantasy) is the sculptor Marrast. His intervention perverts the aims of incongruent groups to such a degree that reality becomes what otherwise would be an absurd fantasy at the Courtauld Institute in London. Marrast here is being a cronopio, the figure Cortázar has invented and explained in *Cronopios and Famas* but who appears almost unobtrusively at times in the novels, where the cronopio is more often a spirit, like the paredros, who will overwhelm a character to make him reverse reality and fantasy. The only overt appearance of the battle between cronopio and fama is in *62* with Polanco and Calac. The two types are really well established in the brothers Shem (the Penman) and Shaun in Joyce's *Finnegans Wake:*

> Shem (Jerry), the introvert, rejected of man, is the explorer and discoverer of the forbidden. He is an embodiment of dangerously brooding, inturned energy. He is the uncoverer of secret springs, and, as such, the possessor of terrific, lightning powers. The books he writes are so mortifying that they are spontaneously rejected by the decent; they threaten, they dissolve the protecting boundary lines of good and evil. Provoked to action (and he must be provoked before he will act), he is not restrained by normal human laws, for they have been dissolved within him by the two powerful elixirs of the elemental depths; he may let loose a hot spray of acid; but, on the other hand, he can release such a magical balm of forgiveness that the battle lines themselves become melted in a bacchanal of general love. Such absolute love is as dangerous to the efficient working of society as absolute hate. The possessor of the secrets, therefore, is constrained to hold his fire. . . .
>
> Shem's business is not to create a higher life, but merely to find and utter the Word. Shaun, on the other hand, whose function is to make the Word become flesh, misreads it, fundamentally rejects it, limits himself to a kind of stupid concretism, and, while winning all the skirmishes, loses the eternal city.[3]

As is the case with Joyce, Cortázar and many of his Latin American contemporaries delve deeply into the real and the unreal and try to separate or conjoin them according to less traditional standards. Those who have been most successful in this penman's quest have been the ones who have undertaken cronopian means.

Another holdover from realism that Cortázar has been forced to grapple with is the element of time. His approach has not been as patently self-conscious as that of another neoteric Spanish American novelist, Mario Vargas Llosa, and it is therefore much more effective and "real." Although temporal changes are more clearly discerned in some of his stories, the stuff of time has also been manipulated in the novels. The pathetic and bitter death scene of Rocamadour shows how the time of going hence differs from the banal time roundabout, which seems static in comparison with the *hora de la verdad,* all too well reflected in Tirso de Molina's magnificently mediocre figure of Don Juan Tenorio and his shallow "tan largo me lo fiáis."

The time of the City becomes the time of Rocamadour's agony, brief and intense and existing amidst the superficiality of the other world or dimension, the one we see or see the shadows of. The infant Manuel, in some ways a Rocamadour redivivus, still exists in cradle time, still wet from the Lethe as well as other waters, as his parents devise a sort of scrapbook for him so that he will be aware of that other time in which he lives but which he has not fully entered as he pushes the memory of Limbo deeper into his unconscious. In *62* it is the residue of time past in the Blutgasse of Vienna which brings Tell and Juan to relive a vampiric episode in Mozart's room. This is another version of reality which Cortázar brings out and follows much in the spirit of a recent breakthrough in mathematics which has revealed that any infinite series of numbers contains within itself an infinite quantity of other series of infinite numbers. This was the basis of Borges's story "El libro de arena" in his latest collection of the same name. The paradoxical problem is that the universe (macrocosm) is finite and speckled with quanta, adding to the difficulties of finding reality or truth, if such there is. Pontius Pilate, a noble Roman who tarried too long in the Hellenistic world, has yet to receive a proper answer to his question.

Julio Cortázar is wise enough to know that there is no answer; for it is a question that can only be put to the gods, and ever since Eden and after Babel we are hard put enough to communicate with our fellows. While life as we see it in our daily rapidity has the feel of the flow of a *carmen perpetuum* about it, it is really made up of individual frames. As in the story "Blow-Up" and the subsequent film, when we examine these frames at our leisure, we see another reality, one which has come out of our own purview, however. Both aspects, then, are true, both are real; but as they are so different, can they both be such? Is Athena lying to us instead? Is our very wisdom, what we have of it, the culprit which leads us into conceptual error? The seemingly absurd becomes possible through words, but always with a mystery remaining as regards the fruition of our verbal notion. Cortázar has given us the wherewithal at least to move closer to the mouth of the cave and shake off the effects of the lottery of Babylonia.

The Cortazarian hero is, like all of us, schizophrenic in that he too is the heir to two distinct though superficially similar heroisms. Like Aeneas he is seeking his dutiful dose of *pietas* so that Rome can be built, the promised land, the *civis,* civilization; but the Odyssean element is too strong, the best he can do is preserve Ithaca and then go forth again in search of people who do not know what oars are for, much in the manner of the seeking narrator in Alejo Carpentier's *The Lost Steps,* trying to begin over again, to be Jung and unaFreud.[4] The origins of music as depicted in Carpentier's novel correspond to the Babelic universal sounds of Gliglish in *Hopscotch,* as basic elements are given a new structure but with the same implied meanings, just as concrete poetry attempts to become the mortar used to build another tower. In *One Hundred Years of Solitude,* again, José Arcadio Buendía, during the insomnia plague, wisely or unwisely, perhaps, labels things so that we will remember, thus cheating us out of the grace of an Adamic lexical renovation. From Gliglish and from the speech of Polanco and Calac in *62* or Lonstein in *Libro de Manuel* we can see that words are the real liars, that the truth is found in what is left unsaid, even though in English we cover those gaps with grunts while Spanish Americans use *éste* and Spaniards a rather more scabrous bit of putty. Borges has also shown us that the unsaid, the unwritten has as much significance as what has been articulated, perhaps even more, and the page of *blens* in Cabrera Infante's *Three Trapped Tigers* has more extensive meaning than can be found in the whole of *Fortunata y Jacinta.* (When will we purveyors of Spanish literature join Buñuel and celebrate *Nazarín?*) It is due time that our critical Perseuses turned and looked at the heads they have severed and shared with us the petrification we have suffered at their instance. If they are lucky, they might even turn to oilcloth stone.[5]

The approach to Cortázar's works, then, must be carried on in the same spirit as that with which they are written. We must prevaricate, we must lie to our wisdom, just as our wisdom itself lies to her peers on the Olympian level, elevated and beyond our ken. Then we will be proper readers, the kind that Cortázar pleads for and the kind that he does not always receive. I have found that my work with Julio has made me a better reader, and I have enough hubris to believe that I may have fooled Athena once or twice; in any case, I have felt her caress on occasion, and this is because, like Dante, I have been well guided by Julio and his paredroi.

Notes

1.   Homer, *Odyssey,* Robert Fitzgerald, tr., Garden City, N.J., Doubleday, 1963, p. 239.
2.   Allen R. Foley, *What the Old-Timer Said,* Brattleboro, Vt., Greene, 1971.
3.   Joseph Campbell, Henry Morton Robinson, *A Skeleton Key to* Finnegans Wake, New York, Viking, 1961, pp. 12, 13.
4.   William York Tindall has used this play on words in his classroom lectures at Columbia University.
5.   This is the stone that Marrast has come to England to buy. No definition or further description is given.

Art and Revolution in the Fiction of Julio Cortázar

LOIS PARKINSON ZAMORA

Art is the community's medicine for the worst disease of mind, the corruption of consciousness.

R. G. Collingwood

The use of the myth of apocalypse by writers as different as García Márquez and Pynchon reaffirms its wide artistic appeal. In considering its appeal to the Argentine writer Julio Cortázar, we will not look at the fictional potential inherent in the historiographic patterns of the myth, but rather at its esthetic and political implications. Cortázar is attracted to the visionary energy of the myth of apocalypse, to its revitalizing power: Its transformative vision becomes for Cortázar the central metaphor for the artistic imagination operating under extreme conditions of personal and/or political crisis.[1] The apocalyptic imagination is subversive in its recognition that present forms of thought and action are inadequate, and revolutionary in its impulse to create a new synthesis out of psychic or social dislocation. The apocalyptic artist seeks to relocate his or her creative synthesis within a revitalized community, to connect an individual vision to a shared future. Literature is for Cortázar a revolutionary act, an instrument of esthetic and political renewal.

There is no shortage of critical commentary on the nature and processes of the apocalyptic imagination. Austin Farrer, in his seminal study of poesis in the Book of Revelation, discusses apocalyptic images and "the process of inspiration by which they are born in the mind";[2] Kenneth Burke, in his introduction to the reprinted edition of Farrer's study, also emphasizes the insights provided by Revelation into the psychology of creativity. D. H. Lawrence anticipates Farrer's study in his own extended commentary on the Book of Revelation, published in 1931. In this very personal exegesis, Lawrence dismisses the temporal projections and historical explanations of

From *Writing the Apocalypse: Historical Vision in Contemporary U.S. and Latin American Fiction* (Cambridge, England: Cambridge University Press, 1989) 76–96. Reprinted with the permission of Cambridge University Press.

apocalypse in favor of the imaginative activity that it both describes and inspires.[3] He recognized his own affinity (and that of the modern artist generally) to the biblical apocalyptist, struggling against repression and fragmentation to achieve spiritual and symbolic wholeness. Lawrence is particularly attracted to the expansive spatial form and content of the apocalyptic vision. Addressing the open form which the apocalyptic artist is likely to create in his rejection of the constraints of social and literary convention, he argues that the apocalyptic work of art resists completion, that it is constantly struggling to say something that it does not know how to say, something that cannot be said.[4] In Julio Cortázar's fiction, a creative impulse operates that is apocalyptic in these Lawrencian terms. His visions of apocalypse inspire spatial symbols and open narrative structures which challenge the accepted conventions of both artistic and political forms.[5]

In an homage to Julio Cortázar at the time of his death in 1984, Carlos Fuentes praised the Argentine writer's dedication to a dual revolution, internal and external. Fuentes develops this characteristic of Cortázar's by referring not only to the Argentine writer, but also to Octavio Paz. He writes that Cortázar and Paz were both born in 1914 and, for the next generation of writers, they "gave a sense to our modernity and allowed us to believe a bit longer in the adventure of the new. . . . Both Cortázar and Paz spoke of something more than novelty or progress—they spoke of the radically new and joyful nature of every instant, of the body, the memory and the imagination of men and women."[6] Though Cortázar's political commitment differed greatly from that of Paz, their esthetics are, as Fuentes suggests, closely linked. In the following discussion, I will refer to essays by Paz to illuminate the creative process which Cortázar dramatizes in his early fiction on art and artists. Furthermore, we will find that Paz's essays on the nature of revolution are very applicable to Cortázar's later political fiction, the ideological differences of these writers notwithstanding.

Until the mid-1960s, Cortázar was primarily concerned with the portrayal of characters, often artists, who are struggling to bring about revolutionary change in their art and their lives. However, reflecting his growing commitment to liberal political reform in Latin America, Cortázar began to create characters who were not confronting psychic or esthetic limitations, but rather political repression. Cortázar has commented on this transition, saying that at this time, "I realized that as an author, though maintaining my interest in literature, in aesthetics, I could not skirt a very elementary, simple, and important thing: I am Latin American."[7] Cortázar had lived in France since 1951, so this realization was more than a manner of speaking. It represented his increasing support of Latin American political solutions to what he insisted were peculiarly Latin American political situations, namely Castro's Cuba and, more recently, the Sandinista regime in Nicaragua. During the 1970s, the worsening political repression in Argentina made Cortázar aware that his exile in France could no longer be considered voluntary. Much of his late fiction deals with political violence such as that documented in Argentina, and with exile, a condition he portrays as existing under a repressive regime, even when his characters do not leave their country. Thus, the emphasis of Cortázar's revolutionary concerns shifts from art to politics, though never are the two completely separated. Because the apocalyptic imagination addresses both individual and communal ends, we may trace its workings throughout his fiction, underlying and integrating his esthetic and political idealism.

I

Cortázar's most explicit early portrayal of the artist as apocalyptist is in his story, "The Pursuer" (1964). Johnny Carter is a jazz saxophonist, and it is with his music that he attempts the apocalyptic "explosion" which Cortázar believes to be the artist's function.[8] Jazz provides for Johnny a means of transcending the limitations of time and space, the means of freeing himself from the rational, analytical tendency of Western thought. He seeks to synthesize rather than analyze, to use the chaos of human experience as the substance of his vision, for he conceives of art as created from, not in spite of, chaos. He is aware of the creative work that he must perform, internally, in order to find the holes, as he puts it, through which to project his expansive art.

The apocalyptic movement of Johnny's art is described in spatial terms. It is centrifugal, spinning upward and outward, sending flying fragments into space. His best music is produced in a dreamlike state which is referred to as a spin. His style is "like an explosion in music . . . the crust of habit splintered into a million pieces."[9] This spatial expansion seems limitless: "Incapable of satisfying itself, useful as a continual spur, an infinite construction, the pleasure of which is not in its highest pinnacle but in the exploratory repetitions, in the use of faculties which leave the suddenly human behind without losing humanity" (208). Here, Cortázar describes the open form to which his artist/characters aspire, as he does in his own fiction. This form is never final or definitive because it is neither linear nor stable. The narrator describes Johnny's art as a structure of desire, always searching for "ultimate possibilities" in its continuous creation. And it is both highly individualized and at the same time a source of universal symbols.

The epigraphs of "The Pursuer" address the apocalyptic impulse underlying Johnny's art. The first is from Rev. 2:10: "Be thou faithful unto death."[10] Johnny lives in the presence of death, dreaming of walking the cemeteries of the earth and finding burial urns in the fields. He renounces the limitation of death as he does the limitations of time and space, considering death not an end but a metamorphosis, a means of regeneration. Johnny rejects the notion of life as moving progressively toward a given end, and embraces instead the intimations of eternity, the moments of mystic communion with the universe, that his art provides. Through his music, Johnny attempts to encompass all things in their totality, to reveal a world beyond the reach of rational analysis, a world gained only through the intuitive powers of the mind.

The epigraph is not the only reference in this story to Revelation: Johnny refers to himself in terms of John's imagery, quoting Rev. 8:10, which describes one of the seven trumpet woes: "The name of the star is called wormwood" (234). Wormwood, or absinthe, is associated with bitterness and drunkenness. The star, "burning as it were a lamp," falls into the rivers and fountains, and "Many men died of the water" (Rev. 8:10–11). In apocalyptic writings, angels and stars are often linked. In this case, the star—an angelic being—unlocks the fearful judgment but remains under the control of God. Johnny identifies both with the victims of the star and with the star itself: "they see that you belong a little to the star called wormwood" (235). In this passage, Johnny mixes his verb tenses. Like the biblical apocalyptist, who alternately speaks in the prophetic future, the accomplished past, and the timeless present, Johnny also attempts to overcome the incongruity between the temporal limitations of language and his own encompassing vision. The character's choice of astrological images from Revelation is instructive. The author of Revelation, a political prisoner when he wrote his visionary text, describes expansive celestial vistas which are in inverse proportion to his actual situation and testify metaphorically to his desire to break the bonds that hold him captive. Cortázar's character adds esthetic and psychological levels to the original content of these images. Johnny reminds us that human existence always involves bondage, and that artistic assaults upon that bondage, even if they are short lived, are necessary to sustain our fictions of freedom and our belief in worlds beyond the mind's enclosure. So Cortázar uses the myth of apocalypse to create his own myth of the artist.

It is appropriate that jazz should be Johnny's artistic medium, for jazz is based not only on melodic sequence and synchronized rhythmic patterns, as is most classical and popular music, but also on syncopation and the superimposition of conflicting rhythms. Its structure depends on the apprehension of many unstable elements simultaneously. The connection made between Johnny's art and the myth of apocalypse confirms my assertion that Cortázar, in his early fiction, is interested not in the historical implications of the myth but in its spatial imagery as a metaphor for the imaginative activity of the artist. The affinity of Cortázar's musician for myth is perhaps more completely understood in the general terms suggested by Claude Lévi-Strauss in his "Overture" to *The Raw and the Cooked*. Here Lévi-Strauss compares the temporal structures of myth and music, asserting that both transcend articulate expression and yet require, like speech, a temporal dimension in which to unfold. Myth, like music, exists in tension between experienced time and a "permanent constant" realm, between external, serial time and internal, psychophysiological time.[11] Cortázar emphasizes this paradoxical temporality by having his musician refer to apocalypse, a myth which describes time's movement toward a timeless end.

The second epigraph of this story is Dylan Thomas's phrase: "O make me a mask."[12] Johnny refers several times to Dylan Thomas in the story, and to his own search for a mask which will allow him to transcend his limited point of view, extend his consciousness into space, and surrender himself to cosmic process. His identification with universal truths explains Johnny's vatic intensity, and it also approaches an explanation of his alternation between abjection and euphoria. The authority of the individual vision is often problematic in expression that is presented as inspired. Susan M. Bachmann, in her study of the narrative strategies of Revelation, points to John's vacillation between self-emergence and self-depreciation, and to his shifting narrative motivations, from individual expression to communal imperative, and ultimately, of course, to divine revelation.[13] John speaks of the "annhilating wonder" of his vision (Rev. 1:17), repeatedly asserting that he is merely a vehicle of cosmic truth, a revealer of God's plot rather than a creator of his own. Yet, at the same time, he frequently asserts his own authority as seer and hearer of the text which he himself has written. This narrative ambivalence reflects the ambivalent origin of his revelation—divine and therefore universal, yet also poetic and therefore personal. For Cortázar's artist/characters too, the problem is how to approach the unfathomable source of their vision, and how to find the medium by which to express it.

I do not mean to imply that Johnny Carter's artistic inspiration is in any way ascribed to God, or that his purpose is the same as the biblical apocalyptist's. Nevertheless, the search of Cortázar's visionary artists for an expressive medium is related to the narrative ambivalence of Revelation. Octavio Paz explores the relation between religious utterance and artistic expression in *The Bow and the Lyre,* and his understanding of the psychology of creativity coincides in a number of ways with Cortázar's. Though Paz's primary interest is in poetry, his comments on poetic inspiration are, as he insists at the outset, generally applicable to the many languages of art, including music. In chapters titled "The Poetic Revelation," "Inspiration," and "The Other Shore" (a phrase also used by Cortázar to suggest the movement of the artistic consciousness, both in "The Pursuer" and in his 1963 novel, *Hopscotch*), Paz develops his argument for the congruence of poetic inspiration and religious revelation: "Poetry is knowledge, salvation, power, abandonment. An operation capable of changing the world, poetic activity is revolutionary by nature; a spiritual exercise, it is a means of interior liberation. Poetry reveals this world; it creates another."[14] Paz follows this assertion with an almost breathless incantation of words suggesting the special nature of the new world created by the artist: prayer, litany, epiphany, presence, madness, ecstasy, logos, nostalgia for paradise. Similarly, Johnny Carter, referring to his music, says that he makes his own God, and the narrator of the story confirms the analogy, avowing that when he listens to Johnny's music, he understands why prayer demands that one fall instinctively to one's knees.

Like Cortázar, Paz emphasizes not the temporal progression which a poetic or religious vision may describe, but the timelessness of the visionary experience itself. Though Paz acknowledges that without history and community, poetry would have no meaning, he nonetheless insists that the poem "consecrates" the timeless instant of the poet's revelation: "chronological time—the common word, the social or individual circumstance—suffers a decisive transformation: it ceases to flow, it stops being succession . . ." (169). Paz recognizes what Cortázar dramatizes in his fiction, that this transformation is more problematic for the modern artist than for the religious visionary, because the possibility of inspired revelation contradicts our current conception of the world. Like Cortázar, Paz wishes to counterbalance the emphasis of Western culture on scientific rationalism, and he finds in religious revelation the analogy which he needs to do so. As García Márquez finds in the myth of apocalypse the means to structure his magical histories, Paz and Cortázar find in it the means to usher the idea of inspiration back into the world.

Paz again describes what Cortázar dramatizes in his assertion that artistic revelation is never final or circumscribed. Both authors locate the basis of "the open work" in the universalizing function of poetic inspiration. The artist's search for adequate expression of his or her vision transcends the self and opens up the work of art—both structurally and substantively—to a multitude of meanings. Paz writes: "[Poetry] re-creates man and makes him assume his true condition, which is not the dilemma: life or death, but a totality: life and death in a single instant of incandescence" (139). In Paz's statement, the significance of the two epigraphs of "The Pursuer" may be integrated. Johnny Carter is faithful unto death in this apocalyptic sense of the simultaneous death and rebirth inherent in the moment of vision; his artist's mask, the self-transcendence represented in the universality of his art, is the product of that faith. Here, the "annihilating wonder" of religious vision and artistic inspiration coincide.

Cortázar's artists share the apocalyptist's search for the medium to express his vision, and they share as well an acute sense of the dangers of their undertaking. In Revelation, the power of language is constantly symbolized, but so is its potential perversion. God's word is figured as a double-edged sword, both redemptive and destructive, and also double-edged in the sense that God's enemies may use it to subvert his text. The narrator of Revelation is obsessed by the possibility that he himself may bear false witness, and he repeatedly symbolizes evil as monsters who speak blasphemous words and dragons who devour truth and spew lies. Language also proves to be double edged in "The Pursuer." The story is narrated by Bruno, a jazz critic whose reputation rests on his definitive verbal analysis of Johnny's jazz style. Bruno wants to make controllable, closed structures of both Johnny's life and art, the same impulse that motivates García Márquez's first-person narrator to recount Santiago's murder in *Chronicle of a Death Foretold.* But unlike that narrator or Johnny Carter, Bruno is not interested in death because it will open up possibilities for rebirth and renewal, but because it will close them off. He hopes Johnny will die so that his analysis will not be undermined by new directions in Johnny's art. So the apocalyptic esthetic Johnny represents in "The Pursuer" is not embodied in the structure of the story itself, for multiplicity and fluidity are threats to the narrator's analytic control. Rather, it is thematized in the description of Johnny's esthetic medium and aspirations, and dramatized ironically in the simultaneous development of the narrator's opposing attitude toward the language of art.

The irony implicit in this story conveys the fact that Johnny's vision is not tenable for long in a culture where reason, rather than passionate transcendence, is the rule. The art critic, the voyeur, easily outlasts Johnny, the voyant. Johnny dies, the book on Johnny's art is published to popular acclaim. That Johnny fails to sustain his unbounded vision does not invalidate it, however, for continual aspiration rather than the finality of achievement is what characterizes Cortázar's apocalyptic esthetic. Although the critic tells us he is sure that Johnny will continue searching after death, he admits that he is delighted not to have to try to understand that search. The story ends with a play on the ambivalence between sealing and unsealing which we have observed in apocalyptic texts. The critic boasts about his "ultimate analysis" of an artist whose art is characterized by its resistance to closure and, hence, to final definition.

There are in Cortázar's fiction a number of artist/characters who confront their limited points of view; like Johnny, each manages momentarily, in a conscious apocalyptic act, to deny the limits of his individual perspective and project himself into an expanded spatial dimension.[15] In "Blow-up" (1964), the photographer Robert Michel finds that his unbounded vision is not accompanied with unbounded powers of expression. The visual language of his blow-up, like the verbal language with which he struggles to write his story, is ultimately inadequate. For Horacio Oliveira, the Argentine intellectual and novelist manqué in *Hopscotch* (1963), apocalyptic visions again serve to focus artistic desire rather than fulfillment. The novel is a graphic spatial projection of a spiritual process. The geometrical pattern of the game of hopscotch—a chalk grid, a small stone, the words "heaven" and "earth" in the boxes at the ends of the grid in the Argentine version of the game—becomes a figure for the elusive transcendental reality that Horacio pursues. It symbolizes his intermittent moments of esthetic transcendence, and his ultimate esthetic failure. It is, furthermore, a figure for the structure of the novel itself, and reflects Cortázar's own apocalyptic impulse to abolish the boundaries of narrative genres and conventions. In place of linear narrative progression, spatial relativity becomes the novel's basic structural principle. Cortázar offers a quantity of temporally disconnected narrative fragments which depend for their significance and their synthesis upon the reader's perception of their relationships. If his characters, Johnny Carter, Roberto Michel, and Horacio Oliveira, manage momentarily to create an expanded spatial dimension in their art. Cortázar's multitiered text, *Hopscotch,* offers itself as a lasting example of such art.

Cortázar refers generally to spatial patterns like his hopscotch grid as *figuras.* Whereas John Barth uses geometrical figures to create closed narrative structures, Cortázar's *figuras* are, on the contrary, central to his conception of the open narrative structure. *Figuras* represent systems of relations, intuitive constellations of meaning in which people, events, places relate to each other across time and space in patterns that transcend discursive, diachronic reason. In these patterns of relation, the artist may transcend at least momentarily the limitations of the self to discover an integrated vision—a "crystallization," as Cortázar calls it —such as is symbolized for Johnny Carter by the astrological skies of Revelation. Morelli, the mature novelist in *Hopscotch,* explains that by means of a crystallization, the artist attempts to create "a work which may seem alien or antagonistic to the time and history surrounding them, and which nonetheless includes it, explains it, and in the last analysis orients it towards a transcendence within whose limits man is waiting."[16] This is also the paradox that exists at the heart of apocalyptic narration. The apocalyptic order opposes the historical moment and yet encompasses it, is limited by it yet transcends it. Though Horacio Oliveria does not achieve his artistic crystallization, his failure is presented in a novel which is itself an example of such a creation. The open structure of Cortázar's novel itself remains dynamic, never reaching a point of temporal or spatial stasis, never making a definitive whole out of the fragments. In this novel, and again in *A Manual for Manuel* (1974), Cortázar masters the paradox with which his characters struggle, creating verbal structures that challenge the linear enclosures of diachronic discourse.

I have said that Johnny Carter's situation is analogous to the imprisoned apocalyptist's, and I would extend my assertion to include Roberto Michel and Horacio Oliveria. Cortázar's artist/protagonists occupy an analogous epistemological stance. Each feels imprisoned within a hostile environment which he seeks to transcend by imaginative flight. His transcendence depends upon the mind's mediation, which promises to transform time and place into a timeless, limitless realm. The artist's vision, however, requires language, whether words or another artistic vocabulary, and language, when required to express the inexpressible, inevitably falls short, for it can evoke such a realm only in images which are temporal and in forms which are of necessity limited and specific. Thus, Roberto's animated blow-up becomes a self-reflexive window, Johnny's music is reduced to his critic's verbal summary, and the "heaven" of Horacio's hopscotch pattern is necessarily drawn on the ground. By means of these characters and their experiences, Cortázar integrates into his fiction a rhetoric of self-criticism, a commentary on the problematic endeavor of creating expansive apocalyptic structures in a time-bound world.

In his characters' failures, Cortázar demonstrates his awareness of the limitations as well as the possibilities of the artist's shaping mind. These works remind us that transcendent artistic structures lead back to a world of language where bondage is the rule, but they are nonetheless apocalyptic in their assault on the limitations of consciousness and artistic form. Their visionary and narrative energy is directed to overcoming those limitations, to creating new realms of consciousness and new forms in which to express them.

II

In his essay of eulogy in 1984, Carlos Fuentes wrote of Cortázar that he had more than one dream, that he believed in more than one paradise.[17] Coming from Fuentes, praise for utopian visions is rare, because he knows that such visions may be exclusive, hierarchical, and veer easily toward totalitarianism. However, Fuentes recognizes that Cortázar's idealism is plural and relative. It is not the potential perfection (hence singularity) of utopia his characters seek, but its multiple freedoms—artistic, political, social. The freedom to discover new forms of expression and action is what motivates Cortázar's characters. In fact, Cortázar insists upon the connection between artistic invention and political change: "by revolutionary we must understand not only those who fight for revolution but also those who have inaugurated it in themselves and transmit it through words or sounds or pigment, not to mention those who combine those activities, those assassinated in the Bolivian jungle with a copy of Pablo Neruda's *Canto general* in their pocket till the end."[18] In Cortázar's implicit reference to his countryman Che Guevara, and in his explicit reference to Latin America's great poetic epic of cultural self-definition, he joins the goals of revolution and literature. As in the fiction of García Márquez and Fuentes, visions of apocalypse in Latin American are likely, sooner or later, to be construed as communal mandates.

In the last fifteen years of his life, Cortázar came to insist upon the interconnectedness of artistic and political renewal in ways that he had not before. Specific political aims and activities are not an issue in his early work. Indeed, his character Horacio Oliveira explicitly rejects political engagement. Recall his soliloquy in Chapter 2 of *Hopscotch* on his unwillingness to participate in communal activity, and his quotable commitment to noncommitment: "I'm not renouncing anything. I simply do what I can so that things renounce me" (193). Cortázar, in an interview the year before his death, commented upon his own apolitical stance during the 1950s and early 1960s in Paris, the time of *Hopscotch,* and the change that occurred when he began to sense the significance of the Cuban revolution.[19] Not surprisingly, one of his first stories to embody this change is about the Cuban revolution. In "Reunion" and the other short fiction I will discuss in this section, Cortázar's apocalyptic vision acquires a new sense of revolutionary purpose.

As its title suggests, "Reunion" is about a community—in this case, a community that is alienated from the existing social and political system, and that shares a vision of a better future. The narrator of the story is a member of a guerrilla group fighting to enact the ideals of the revolution; though the characters are never explicitly identified, we are given the evidence to deduce that among them is Che Guevara himself. These characters are concerned primarily with survival and strategy, not with artistic expression, as we have seen Cortázar's earlier characters to be. Octavio Paz's distinction between the rebel and the revolutionary is useful in tracing this shift in Cortázar's characters, and in defining their different though related desires. Paz defines the rebel as "the accursed hero, the solitary poet, lovers who trample social conventions underfoot," a definition that easily applies to Johnny Carter or Horacio Oliveira.[20] It is, however, Paz's definition of the revolutionary that applies to Cortázar's characters in "Reunion." Revolutionaries object to the existing social order and believe in the possibility of changing it by means of communal action. The revolutionary, not the rebel, attacks tyranny and envisions sudden leaps forward for society as a whole. Paz concludes: "Art and love are rebels; politics and philosophy revolutionaries" (142).

The narrator of "Reunion" is clearly a revolutionary in Paz's terms, and yet he often reverts to the metaphor of art to describe the collective consciousness and historical aims of the revolution. It is music to which he refers—not jazz this time, but the structural order of the classical sonata. He says, "We have wanted to transform a torpid war into an order which makes sense, justifies it, and ultimately carries it to a victory which will be like the reinstatement of a melody after so many years of hoarse hunting horns, will be a final allegro which follows the adagio like an encounter with light."[21] The order, progression, and resolution of the classical sonata form, rather than the open and improvised structure of jazz, better evokes the revolutionaries' more defined social and political future. The final paragraph of the story reiterates the image of the culminating allegro of history, to which the narrator adds the description of "a star in the middle of the design" (86). This luminous point, "small and very blue," seems calculated to reinforce the vision of the ideal end toward which Marxist history moves.[22]

Like Cortázar's earlier artist/characters, his revolutionaries are aware of historical potential, but much more than the artist, it is the revolutionary's particular compulsion to choose a future and then play out the consequences of this choice. So we detect a changing conception of the goals of both history and narration as Cortázar begins to focus on actual social and political ends. It is Marxist ideology which provides the author with the philosophical means to transpose his early interest in the alienated visionary artist to his subsequent revolutionary political concerns.

As Cortázar knew well, Marxism explicitly connects alienation and revolution. Georg Lukács was the first to call attention to the importance of the Hegelian conception of alienation in Marxist philosophy. In his preface to the reprinted edition of *History and Class Consciousness,* Lukács quoted Hegel to show that the philosopher regarded alienation not as a mental construct or a "reprehensible reality" but "as the immediately given form in which the present exists on the way to overcoming itself in the historical process."[23] Marx follows the thread of this Hegelian argument, Lukács tells us, basing his theory of class-struggle on the tenet that those alienated from existing society—the proletariat—could call into question old forms, create new ones. In humanity's alienation lay the potential to transform the whole of society.

For Cortázar, this is not a utopian ideology in the sense of proposing an unrealizable ideal. Marx understood the human mind as a reflection of the material world, and human history as a dialectical process based on the exigencies of economic and social relations—a model that Cortázar believed to be essential in approaching the political and social realities of contemporary Latin America. But of course Cortázar is also attracted to the utopian idealism inherent in Marxism. He recognized that Marxism *is* idealist in its understanding of history as progressing toward world revolution and world renovation: The goal of history is an egalitarian society which will be instituted by revolution. Marxist historiography is thus allied to apocalyptic eschatology in its emphasis on the teleological nature of temporal movement: Despite Marx's criticism of religion, his vision of the eventual reconstitution of society by the disenfranchised carries the clear traces of biblical apocalypticism.[24] Cortázar makes use of this complementarity of apocalypticism and Marxist idealism in his story "Apocalypse at Solentiname."

The narrator of "Apocalypse at Solentiname" is meant to conjure up Cortázar himself; among the autobiographical details provided to establish the narrator's identity are a reference to his story "Blow-up," his friendship with the Nicaraguan poet Ernesto Cardenal, his permanent residence in France. He tells of his visit to Solentiname, Ernesto Cardenal's commune on an island in Lake Nicaragua. While there, the narrator sees some paintings by the peasants who form part of the community, and is so impressed that he takes slides of a number of them. They are naive representations of the activities and natural surroundings of the community: The childlike innocence of their Edenic vision is made explicit by the narrator's observation that the paintings are "once more the first vision of the world."[25]

When the narrator returns to his apartment in Paris, he projects the slides he has taken of the paintings, only to have them change before his eyes into scenes of torture and murder. The sudden, irrational explosion of horrifying images from behind the pastoral surface of the paintings seems to burst forth from the narrator's unconscious; they represent the fears, and perhaps the realities, that the narrator has entertained during his visit to Nicaragua. The intensity of the collision between the images of the ideal community of Solentiname and their opposite, the hellish landscape of political repression, reiterates the structures of the opposing images of heaven and hell in traditional apocalyptic narration. The moral tension inherent in the photographs has the effect of suggesting the inevitability of violence in Central America, just as the moral opposites in Revelation—Christ and Antichrist, Whore and Bride, Babylon and New Jerusalem—point to Armageddon.

This story provides a useful pivot for tracing Cortázar's shifting fictional concerns, because its plot is parallel to that of "Blow-up," but the narrators' concerns in the two stories are markedly different.[26] Both narrators are artists, but the essential problem of the narrator in "Blow-up" is how to *tell* his story, whereas how to *tolerate* his story is what torments the narrator of "Apocalypse at Solentiname." The earlier story describes a single potential crime which is averted by the narrator's action, the later story describes accomplished acts of political terrorism. The narrator's action in "Blow-up" results in the rescue of the intended victim, whereas the narrator of "Apocalypse at Solentiname" can only watch passively as the paradise of his photographs assumes the shape of totalitarian hell.

Yet there is nonetheless a hopeful element in the apocalyptic vision of the later story, and that is in its homage to the political and artistic activity of the Nicaraguan poet Ernesto Cardenal. Cardenal has inherited Neruda's place as the foremost Latin American poet speaking for the ideological left; his poetry is known for its social criticism and its advocacy of radical political change. If Cortázar's use of apocalyptic elements in his story is secular, Cardenal's apocalyptic poetry is deeply rooted in the Catholic tradition. Cardenal studied under Thomas Merton at the Trappist novitiate at Gethsemani Abbey in Kentucky during the late 1950s, and eventually completed his studies for the priesthood in Mexico and Colombia. His community of Solentiname was founded on his revolutionary interpretation of Pauline Christianity and on contemporary "theologies of liberation"; before it was destroyed by Samoza, it was a part of the movement of *concienciación* which promotes social and religious awareness on the lowest economic levels of Latin American society.[27] Cardenal's poetic versions of biblical material convey his political and social vision of renewal: His Psalm 21 ends, "A banquet will be set before the poor / Our people will celebrate a great feast / A new people will be born."[28] His poem, "Apocalypse," to which Cortázar specifically alludes in his story, describes the end of the world through political unreason. The poem's narrator uses the images and cadences of Revelation to describe a technological Armageddon but, true to the biblical genre, he concludes by envisioning the regeneration that apocalyptic cataclysm implies.[29] Cardenal insists that in Latin America, spiritual attitudes toward time (hence, salvation) cannot be dissociated from political and social realities; his poetry embodies his desire to overcome the separation between individual hope and collective fulfillment. That the autobiographical narrator of "Apocalypse at Solentiname" sees the realities of violence and death behind the Edenic paintings from Solentiname suggests the extent to which Cortázar has come to conceive of art as serving a political function in Latin America.

"Apocalypse at Solentiname" was published in Spain in 1977; the political content of this story and others in the same collection explains its publications outside of Argentina. The two volumes of short stories which follow it (the author's last)—*We Love Glenda So Much* (1980) and the as-yet untranslated collection, *Deshoras* (1983)—were published in Mexico, and they also contain examples of what one critic has labeled Cortázar's "literature de denuncia."[30] Though many of the stories in these collections can be fruitfully read on a psychological or esthetic level, they also yield political insights; private relations unmask the realities of politics, and vice versa. Cortázar's stated aim, to demonstrate the common ground of literature and politics, impels the fiction in each of these volumes.

The torture and public violence which irrupt into the Solentiname paintings are the subject of a number of Cortázar's recent stories. "Second Time Around" suggests the politics of torture but never calls it by its name. The author presents a scenario in which a young man simply disappears, thus evoking the horrible reality of thousands of "desaparecidos," people who were arrested in the late 1970s by the military regime in Argentina and were not heard from again.[31] The story is presented from the viewpoints of both victimizers and victims. The victimizers sanitize their language into vague euphemisms in order to deny the moral responsibility—indeed, the reality—of what they are doing, and the language of the victims is equally vague through ignorance and/or fear. Arrest and torture become "procedures," the sites of such activities "offices," and the people summoned to those offices likened to patients sitting in doctors' waiting rooms. Abuses are sanctioned by yet other deformations of language, like "governmental efficiency" and "the good of the country." But if language is the mechanism behind which evil hides, it is also a means of uncovering evil. These stories communicate the unspeakable with dreadful clarity. As I have said, narration, to be properly considered apocalyptic, must entertain the notion of amelioration as well as damnation; it must denounce injustice as it describes it. Like the Solentiname paintings, Cortázar's late stories present images of paradise irretrievably lost and utopias yet to be established. Beneath the descriptions of wrong, the right is always implicit, always potential.

Such is also the case in "We Love Glenda So Much," which addresses totalitarianism in the realms of both art and politics. I have cited Carlos Fuentes's statement that Cortázar believed in more than one paradise. "We Love Glenda So Much" presents characters who believe in only one, and would impose it upon the world. It is as if Cortázar wished to examine the dangers inherent in his own idealism and in the utopian ideology to which he committed his hopes for renewal in Latin America. The first-person narrator of this story describes a group of admirers of the movie actress Glenda Garson. So devoted are they to her work that when she retires they go quietly about the business of collecting all the copies of all of her films and editing them to conform to their conception of her art. They cut scenes that they consider to be inferior, substitute sequences, change their order. Through these activities, which the narrator refers to as their "mission," the fans seek the illusory promise of static perfection: "Glenda's last image in the last scene of the last movie."[32] Their goal is a changeless and hence totally controllable ideal.

The finality of their image of Glenda is threatened, however, when the actress announces that she will come out of retirement to make more films. The narrator, one of her most devout fans, sighs, "a poet had said under Glenda's same skies that eternity is in love with the works of time" (15). Although murder is not mentioned, the reader is given to understand that her disciples will not tolerate any disruption of the static image they have created. Their only means of assuring perfection is to stop time, or at least the life-time of Glenda: "We loved Glenda so much that we would offer her one last inviolable perfection" (16). So they tell themselves that they have no choice. The narrator's insinuation is insidiously indirect, but clear enough. The distinction between "fan" and "fanatic" begins to blur. The implications of their blind devotion and uncritical commitment are social and political as well as esthetic.

Because of their desire to suppress divergences from their own unanimously held ideal, Glenda's fans and their spokesperson (who narrates in the first-person plural) inevitably assume an ideological stance. The achievement of their single, unchanging ideal depends upon absolute obedience to that ideal, and upon the suppression of any possible alternative. The ideological unison of the group's activities is stylistically embodied in their rhythmic repetition of the phrase "we love Glenda so much." The narrator speaks derisively of differences of opinion or moral objections within the group itself ("analytical voices contaminated by political philosophies"), but he assures the reader that such "heresy" has been eradicated. And when certain moviegoers protest that they remember Glenda's films differently, the narrator dismisses public memory as fickle and transitory: "people are fickle and forget or accept or are in search of what's new, the movie world is ephemeral, like the historical present, except for those of us who love Glenda so much" (13).

A seemingly casual narrative juxtaposition—the movie world and historical reality—is significant, for the group's cinematic revisionism and the historical revisionism practiced by repressive political regimes is closely related. As the fans modify cinematic images and hence the public memory of Glenda's art to conform to their requirements, so dictatorship attempts to revise reality by depriving people of their relationship to the remembered past and to the "ephemeral" temporal continuum of human history. The group's editing seems calculated to suggest governmental censorship, and their vision of esthetic totality to suggest political totalitarianism.

It is interesting that another exiled artist, the Czech writer Milan Kundera, indicts political censorship with an image similar to Cortázar's. Kundera begins *The Book of Laughter and Forgetting* with the description of a photograph from which the figure of a discredited Czech leader has been airbrushed into oblivion by the revisionist historians of the Communist Party. Of the agents of this revisionism, Kundera's narrator says, "They are fighting for access to the laboratories where photographs are retouched and biographies and histories are re-written."[33] For Kundera, the images of memory are the essence of individual and communal identity, reference points in the flow of time which differentiate among human beings and cultures. The self is constituted by what we remember, so when the past is intentionally distorted or destroyed, when its names and faces are changed to suit the present, then distinctions among people and nations are lost. Not only would Cortázar's characters in "We Love Glenda So Much" change the face of the past: They are themselves nameless and faceless. Their lack of individualized features and names suggests both the unanimity and the anonymity required by their repressive methods. Of course one might argue that the characters in Cortázar's stories are often nameless, so cerebral and psychological is the fictive interaction among many of them that the sociological identification, the name, is irrelevant. Here, however, the characters seem willfully to have assumed faces without features in order to dissemble their defacing of the past. Their facelessness is a principal source of the malignity that pervades the story.

The retouched image of reality which Glenda's fans create is called by quite another name in the story. The narrator refers repeatedly to the "perfection" that the group seeks. Revision, falsification, intolerance, even murder, are justified in the present for the sake of future "perfection." The narrator explains that "we loved Glenda so much that above and beyond ethical or historical disagreements the feeling that would always unite us remained, the certainty that perfecting Glenda was perfecting us and perfecting the world" (14). What event or idea or person cannot be dismissed as an "ethical or historical discrepancy" if it should happen to conflict with the group's definition of perfection, jostle their static ideal?

Again, Milan Kundera's literary vision resembles Cortázar's, for Kundera describes in similar terms the abuses spawned by an idealized conception of the future which overrides the reality of the present. In an interview with Philip Roth published at the end of *The Book of Laughter and Forgetting,* Kundera says, "Totalitarianism is not only hell, but also the dream of paradise— the age-old dream of a world where everybody would live in harmony, united by a single common will and faith, without secrets from one another. . . . If totalitarianism did not exploit these archetypes [of paradise], which are deep inside us all and rooted deep in all religions, it could never attract so many people, especially during the early phases of its existence. Once the dream of paradise starts to turn into reality, however, here and there people begin to crop up who stand in its way, and so the rulers of paradise must build a little gulag on the side of Eden" (233). Whether it is the "rulers of paradise," as Kundera calls the contemporary Czech leaders about whom he writes, or

Glenda's fans who attempt to impose their own absolute definition of the perfection onto the past and the future, they do violence to the multiplicity and variability—the "discrepancies"—of present experience. Cortázar, whose celebration of artistic revelation and political idealism has been a constant theme, dramatizes here the tragic countertruth that visionaries are often blind to all but their own version of the end.

The word "perfection" by definition contains the notion of unanimity and temporal stasis. Words that suggest change over a period of time— progress, growth, development, decay—are in some sense its opposite. Such definition is implicit in Judeo-Christian myth, which proposes that perfect worlds are necessarily outside of time altogether. On either side of history lie the eternal realms of Eden and Israel, or the New Jerusalem. ("Eternal" in this context does not mean "endless" or "forever," but rather "atemporal," "timeless.") Nevertheless, I have said that the biblical apocalyptist, for all his concern with the next world, is passionately engaged in this world—describing its injustices and interpreting God's activity to end injustice. But when the apocalyptic vision shifts from an engagement with the present to focus on a future realm of absolute and unchanging unanimity, there are likely to be abuses such as those perpetrated by Kundera's dictators and Glenda's fans, and, as we will see, by Walker Percy's character, Lancelot. The abuses of dogmatic utopianism are also a central concern in the fiction of Carlos Fuentes.

Those who would impose their vision of perfection on the political or esthetic realm are particularly interested in the consummation of their ideal, in the terminal point of time or form. Throughout "We Love Glenda So Much," the narrator emphasizes "the completed work," "the last, inviolable perfection." In his last sentence, ending and end, form and content seem to coincide, for the finality of his image, placed in the final structural position of the narration, reinforces the group's search for timeless ultimacy: "On the untouchable heights to which we had raised her in exaltation, we would save her from the fall, her faithful could go on adoring her without any decrease; one does not come down from a cross alive" (16). The image justifies the mythic interpretive context in which I have placed the group's fanatic idealism. That the crucifixion image is applied to a contemporary movie star emphasizes the inversions and perversions of such fanaticism; that it is used to conclude the story serves as ironic commentary on the group's intentions to put a stop to time, for the crucifixion is, in its usual Christian context, a symbol not of death but of rebirth. If the cross traditionally represents the subversion of finality, here Cortázar manipulates the meaning of the symbol to imply its opposite. The forceful closure of his account is calculated by the narrator to deny any illusion of temporal continuance or development beyond the ideal which the group has imposed.

It is for this reason that the epilogue to the story, published three years after the story itself, comes as an interesting surprise. "Epilogue to a Story" takes the form of a letter to Glenda Jackson, the model, Cortázar tells us, for his character Glenda Garson, and is labeled with place and date, Berkeley, California, September 29, 1980, where in fact Cortázar was teaching at the time. The author, in an ironic return to his own story, considers the problematic enterprise of detaining a moving medium, whether film, narration, or human history.

In his letter, Cortázar retells the plot of "We Love Glenda So Much" to Glenda Jackson, emphasizing the dialectic in the story between temporal movement and stasis. He reiterates his character's retirement in terms of the group's ideal of arrested movement, her retirement "bringing to a close and perfecting without knowing it a labor which repetition and time would have finally sullied."[34] He describes the group's opposition to Glenda's return in similar terms, explaining that the group is determined to maintain the image they have created, "closed, definitive." But, writes Cortázar to Glenda Jackson, the continuity of life undermines the finality of fiction. A film called *Hopscotch,* in which she stars, has appeared just after the publication of "We Love Glenda So Much," as if to defy the absolute end which the story proposes. That the new film should have the same title as his best-known novel seems to Cortázar to add force to the defiance. As Glenda Jackson's film undoes the fictional seal on Glenda Garson's art, so Cortázar's epilogue reverses the finality of his story and challenges the very possibility of complete closure in any esthetic structure. The epilogue ends with a reference to Glenda Jackson's next movie.

<h1 style="text-align:center">III</h1>

The ending of Cortázar's novel about revolution, *A Manual for Manuel* (1974), contains elements comparable to the ending of "We Love Glenda So Much," and it is with a brief discussion of those elements that I will conclude this chapter. The novel describes a revolutionary group, several of whom are Argentines, in Paris. We read of their political and their personal relations, in particular those of a character named Andrés, who begins as an observer but during the course of the novel makes a commitment to the activities and goals of the revolution. Andrés keeps a record of the group and of contemporary events to give someday to the baby son of one of the members of the group. The record is in the form of a scrapbook, with short entries comprising an open narrative structure like that which Morelli describes in *Hopscotch.* Interspersed among the short narrative sections that describe the characters' revolutionary activities are actual, dated newspaper clippings, reproduced government records and diagrams, interviews of cases of torture as reported in the Forum for Human Rights. This factual material locates the novel at the intersection of history and fiction, a self-conscious narrative positioning, as Cortázar's introduction to the novel makes clear.

I have cited Octavio Paz's statement that art and love are "rebels," politics and philosophy "revolutionaries"; in this novel, however, Paz's distinction does not apply. The roles of rebel and revolutionary in fact converge, for erotic liberation and political liberation are closely identified by Cortázar and his character Andrés; furthermore, in this novel, Cortázar's esthetic concerns consciously reflect his political philosophy. The atmosphere that Cortázar creates here is related to the theory of revolution proposed by Norman O. Brown.[35] Brown's use of apocalypse as a metaphor for political and sexual liberation is well known, and his insistence on the interdependence of repression in these areas coincides with Cortázar's understanding of the nature and necessity of revolution. If Brown's writing now seems hyperbolic and somewhat dated, too much a product of the prevailing romanticism of his time, Cortázar's novel escapes that fate by virtue of its inventive narrative techniques, its particular brand of Cortázarian humor, and its dramatization of the complexity of human relations, whether political or sexual or both.

The novel ends after the revolutionaries' violent confrontation with government forces: The scene shifts to the silent stillness of a morgue, where a corpse, presumably one of the revolutionaries, is lying. The description of the scene recalls the famous photograph of Che Guevara lying dead in a stark room in the Bolivian jungle. If the indirect reference to a corpse at the end of "We Love Glenda So Much" is meant to figure the fanatic narrator's desire to negate potentiality, here the corpse, alluding as it does to revolutionary involvement, suggests a far more complex relation to the historical future. Of course a dead body is an obvious and irrevocable terminal point. We are told that in the morgue "all marks of history" will be washed away. However, the novel is not the closed temporal structure that the concluding scene in the morgue would seem to imply. The member of the revolutionary group who attends the body says: "Rest easy, there's time,"[36] as if to assure his companion (and himself) that he hasn't died for nothing, that the revolutionary struggle will continue. This final scene of individual death implies collective continuance, collective betterment.

The reader has known all along that the novel he or she is reading implies another: *A Manual for Manuel* is a book about the preparation for a book which will be undertaken after this one ends, and which will to a large degree reiterate its contents. Thus the temporal context of the novel explicitly extends beyond its own ending, not only into a political future but also into a literary one. At the beginning of the novel, the narrator addresses this process, commenting on Andrés's accumulation of narrative fragments: "he had gathered together a considerable amount of notes and clippings, waiting, it would seem, for them to end up all falling into place without too much loss. He waited longer than was prudent, evidently . . . that neutrality had led him from the beginning to hold himself as if in profile, an operation that is always risky in narrative matters—and let us not call it historical which is the same thing. . . . All this, of course, so that all those notes and scraps of paper would end up falling into an intelligible order . . ." (6). Andrés has not, at the beginning of the novel, committed himself to the revolution, and therefore he can only wait: The "neutrality" of his stance, it is implied, initially prevents him from creating the literary order which his subsequent involvement in revolutionary activity will allow. Cortázar's novel describes the political engagement that permits artistic engagement. The existence of Manuel's book depends upon Andrés's commitment to history, as the existence of *A Manual for Manuel* depends upon Cortázar's.

The book that Andrés will begin after the end of Cortázar's novel will preserve a record of the past for the baby Manuel in the future, and is thus a gesture of historical affirmation. Much as a family photo album or scrapbook is assembled to preserve a record of the past for the future, fixing on its pages the visual and verbal images of moments of familiar history, so Andrés wishes to fix in Manuel's book a historical record of a more public sort. The fact that Andrés will include *verbatim* documentary evidence of the past suggests his wish to impede the kind of revisionism, the retouching of history, practiced by Glenda's fans and Kundera's rulers of paradise. The newspaper clippings and government reports that will be integrated into his book are meant to be authoritative, objective: Political and social abuses must be remembered and recorded precisely. Regard for the past and visions of a better future fuse in the revolutionary order, an order symbolized for Andrés by the book he will yet create.

Andrés's literary intention conveys his understanding of revolution as far more than a total break with the past or the initiation of a unanimous future. Here again, I return to Octavio Paz's observations on revolution. Paz has commented on the concept of time contained in the word as it was originally conceived, as opposed to its modern usage. "Revolution is a word that implies the notion of cyclical time and therefore that of regular and recurrent change. But the modern meaning of the word does not refer to an eternal return, the circular movement of worlds and stars, but rather to a sudden and *definitive* change in direction of public affairs."[37] Whereas the original etymology of the word implies the primacy of the past, its modern usage postulates the primacy of the future; the known past has been replaced by the unknown future as the object of modern revolutionary desire. It is clear, however, that Cortázar, in his description of Andrés's literary project, wishes to combine the two meanings of the word, and thus to undermine the contemporary conception of revolution as instituting a singular future. So we understand that Andrés is both a relativist and a revolutionary. Like Cortázar, he knows that there is more than one paradise, more than one means of working toward the fulfillment of historical desire.

In order that the fragments of Manuel's book may "end up falling into an intelligible order," as Andrés intends them to, Cortázar's narrator tells us that Andrés must find a narrative stance outside of time, "an hour outside the clock so that all of a sudden fate and will can immobilize the crystals in the kaleidoscope. Etc." (7). Like the apocalyptist, the novelist Andrés is aware that he must place himself beyond the end of the history he recounts and impose his narrative vision upon it (as have the characters Quentin and Aureliano and Stencil). If Cortázar's characters in his early fiction reflect their author's esthetic concerns, here Andrés reflects Cortázar's concern with revolutionary process and how to narrate it. The image of the kaleidoscope, and the "Etc." which ends the phrase quoted above, suggest that Andrés will create an open structure like the one in which he has himself been placed. We are given to believe that his manual will, like the fiction of Cortázar, self-consciously embody the truth of Henry James's assertion in his preface to *Roderick Hudson:* "relations stop nowhere and the exquisite problem of the artist is eternally but to draw, by a geometry of his own, the circle within which they shall happily appear to do so."[38] I have already cited Henri Bergson's analogous insistence that, in the absence of historical ends, our need to create fictional endings makes us all geometricians.

Notes

1. In this respect, Cortázar is in the modern tradition that begins with William Blake. The importance of the metaphor of apocalypse for the Romantic poets has been discussed by M. H. Abrams in *Natural Supernaturalism: Tradition and Revolution in Romantic Literature* (New York: W. W. Norton, 1975), and by Mario Praz in *The Romantic Agony* (London: Oxford University Press, 1951). See also Eleanor Wilner, *Gathering the Winds: Visionary Imagination and Radical Transformation of Self and Society* (Baltimore: Johns Hopkins University Press, 1975), a study of William Blake, Thomas Lovell Beddoes, and Karl Marx.

2. Austin Farrer, *A Rebirth of Images: The Making of St. John's Apocalypse* (1949; reprint, Boston: Beacon Press, 1963), pp. 17–18.

3. D. H. Lawrence, "Apocalypse," in *Phoenix: The Posthumous Papers of D. H. Lawrence,* ed. Edward D. McDonald (1931; New York: The Viking Press, 1964). The complete writings of Lawrence on apocalypse are contained in *Apocalypse and the Writings on Revelation,* ed. Mara Kalnins (Cambridge: Cambridge University Press, 1980).

4. Earl Rovit discusses apocalyptic myth in terms of its spatial nature, arguing, as does Lawrence, that it "is most revolutionary in that it provides a fully 'openended' form, circumferential without being what we normally think of as circular and spherical." "On the Contemporary Apocalyptic Imagination," *The American Scholar,* 37, *iii* (1968), 464–5.

5. Cortázar's narrative structures are organized according to techniques of juxtaposition, montage, interpolation, rather than linear progression, creating structures that have been termed *spatial* after an influential essay by Joseph Frank; more recently, literary analysis based on semiotic theory has focused attention on the text as a spatial model in which time is a function of space, event a function of the spatial perspectives from which it is perceived and rendered. See Joseph Frank, "Spatial Form in Modern Literature," *Sewanee Review,* 53 (Spring, Summer, Fall, 1945), 221–40, 433–56, 643–53: reprinted in condensed form in *The Widening Gyre: Crisis and Mastery in Modern Literature* (New Brunswick, New Jersey: Rutgers University Press, 1963); and Jurij M. Lotman's discussion of spatial modeling in "On the Metalanguage of a Typological Description of Culture," *Semiotica,* 14, *ii* (1975), 97–123.

6. Carlos Fuentes, "Julio Cortázar, 1914–1984: The Simón Bolívar of the Novel," *New York Times Book Review,* 4 March 1984, p. 10.

7. Interview with Antonio Marimon and Braulio Peralta in the Mexico City newspaper, *Uno más uno,* 3 marzo 1983, p. 15.

8. Using spatial metaphors, Cortázar describes the artist's responsibility—and compulsion—to cause "an explosion that opens wide a much larger reality," to find the "opening" through which to project his or her dynamic vision. See Cortázar's essay, "Algunos aspectos del cuento," *Cuademos Hispanoamericanos,* 255 (1973), 406–7.

9. Julio Cortázar, "The Pursuer," in *End of the Game,* trans. Paul Blackburn (1964; New York: Pantheon Books, 1967), p. 199. Subsequent references to "Blow-up" and "The Pursuer" are from this edition.

10. Cortázar's use of this phrase may be construed ironically, because John in the Book of Revelation exhorts his contemporaries to be faithful to Christ in that time of persecution, even if they must suffer martyrdom. Johnny Carter is not faithful to a religious ideal but to his art, and to death itself, hoping to find answers in death that he has found only incompletely in life. The full passage from Revelation 2:10 is: "Fear none of those things which thou shalt suffer: behold, the devil shall cast some of you into prison, that ye may be tried; and ye shall have tribulation ten days: be thou faithful unto death, and I will give thee a crown of life."

11. Claude Lévi-Strauss, *The Raw and the Cooked,* trans. John and Doreen Weightman (1964; New York: Harper & Row, 1969), pp. 15–16.

12. The comparative connection between Dylan Thomas and Cortázar has been explored by Hugo J. Verani, "Las máscaras de la nada: *Apocalipsis* de Dylan Thomas y 'El perseguidor' de Julio Cortázar," *Cuadernos Americanos,* 227 (1979), 234–47.

13. See Susan M. Bachmann, "Narrative Strategy in the Book of Revelation and D. H. Lawrence's *Apocalypse,*" Dissertation, SUNY Buffalo, 1984.

14. Octavio Paz, *The Bow and the Lyre: The Poem. The Poetic Revelation, Poetry and History,* trans. Ruth L. C. Simms (1956; New York: McGraw-Hill, 1975), p. 121. Subsequent references are noted in the text.

15. I have discussed a number of Cortázar's artist/protagonists in "Voyeur/Voyant: Julio Cortázar's Spatial Esthetic," *Mosaic,* 14, *iv* (1981), 45–68.

16. Cortázar, *Hopscotch,* trans. Gregory Rabassa (1963; New York: Avon Books, 1966), p. 489. Subsequent page references are noted in the text.

17. Fuentes, "Julio Cortázar, 1914–1984: The Simón Bolivar of the Novel." p. 10.

18. Cortázar, *Territorios* (México, D.F.: Siglo Veintiuno Editores, 1978), p. 96, my translation.

19. Cortázar states, "You know well that in *Hopscotch* there are very few, or practically no allusions of a historical or political sort. . . . I was completely consumed by literary and esthetic concerns, and my interest in historical process did not go beyond a theoretical sympathy or a knowledge which came from reading the classics. . . . I had absolutely no personal commitment. . . . The change which would necessarily be reflected in my writing occurred when I became aware of the Cuban revolution." *Uno más uno,* 3 marzo 1983, p. 15, my translation.

20. Paz, "Revolt, Revolution, Rebellion," in *Alternating Current,* trans. Helen R. Lane (1967; New York: Seaver Books, 1967), p. 142.

21. Cortázar, "Reunión," in *Todos los fuegos el fuego* (Buenos Aires: Editorial Sudamericana, 1974), pp. 74–5. Some of the stories from this collection were published in *End of the Game,* but this one has not been published in English. The translations in the text are mine.

22. I do not mean to suggest that the structure of the story is itself closed off or circumscribed by that ideal end: The "design" to which the narrator refers may be considered a Cortázarian *figura,* conditioning the text's openness to multiple and shifting perspectives. Cortázar's growing commitment to Marxist socialism never implied a shift to the techniques of social realism. He rejected writing that was dictated by revolutionary theory, saying that he wished to be among the revolutionaries of literature, not the literary men of the revolution. Steven Boldy addresses the tension between political commitment and serious literary experi-

mentation in Cortázar's fiction and in his statements about his fiction: *The Novels of Julio Cortázar* (Cambridge: Cambridge University Press, 1980), pp. 161–5.

For Cortázar's discussion of socialism and literature, see, "La literatura en la revolución y revolución en la literatura," in a collection of related articles under that title by Oscar Collazos, Julio Cortázar, and Mario Vargas Llosa (México, D.F.: Siglo Veintiuno Editores, 1971), and *Viaje alrededor de una mesa* (Buenos Aires: Editorial Rayuela, 1970).

23. Georg Lukács, *History and Class Consciousness: Studies in Marxist Dialectics*, trans. Rodney Livingston (1923; Cambridge: MIT Press, 1971), p. *xxxv*. The "Preface to the New Edition," from which I cite, was written in 1967 to introduce the reprinted German edition.

24. This connection between Judeo-Christian eschatology and Marxism has been influentially asserted by Karl Löwith in *Meaning in History* (Chicago: University of Chicago Press, 1949), Chapter 2, "Marx," pp. 33–51; and by Walter Schmithals, *The Apocalyptic Movement, Introduction and Interpretation,* trans. John E. Steely (Nashville: Abingdon Press, 1975), who asserts: "Marx himself occupied the position of apocalyptist. His missionary consciousness has a prophetic format, his vision the character of revelation, which, to be sure, in harmony with the secular point of view, is worked out as a science" (p. 238).

25. Cortázar, "Apocalypse at Solentiname," in *A Change of Light and Other Stories,* trans. Gregory Rabassa (New York: Knopf, 1980), p. 121. The stories in this collection were originally published in two separate collections, *Alguien que anda por ahí* (1977) and *Octaedro* (1974). "Apocalypse at Solentiname" is from the former.

26. Saul Sosnowski compares "Blow-up" to "Apocalypse at Solentiname" in "Imágenes del deseo: El testigo ante su mutación," *INTI,* Nos. 9–10 (1980), pp. 93–7.

27. This biographical information is taken from Jose Promis Ojeda et al., *Ernesto Cardenal: Poeta de la liberación latinoamericana* (Buenos Aires: Fernando García Cambeiro, 1975).

28. Ernesto Cardenal, *Nueva antología poética: Ernesto Cardenal* (México, D.F.: Siglo Veintiuno Editores, 1978), p. 94, my translation.

29. Cardenal, "Apocalypse," in *Apocalypse and Other Poems,* eds. Robert Pring-Mill and Donald D. Walsh, trans. Thomas Merton, Kenneth Rexroth, et al. (New York: New Directions, 1977), pp. 33–7. "Apocalypse" is translated by Robert Pring-Mill; it was originally published in *Oración por Marilyn Monroe y otros poemas* (1965).

30. Eric Nepomuceno, *Uno más uno,* 3 marzo 1983, p. 7. An anthology of Cortázar's "denunciatory literature" has been collected under the title *Textos políticos* (Barcelona: Plaza & Janés, 1984).

The volumes published in 1980 and 1983 are Cortázar's final collections of short stories, but a collection of miscellaneous writings, primarily poems and short nonfiction prose pieces, has been published posthumously under the title of *Salvo el crepúsculo* (México, D.F.: Editoral Nueva Imagen, 1984). One of the poems, "Los vitrales de Bourges," takes its epigraph from Revelation.

31. The violations of human rights by the military government in Argentina in the late 1970s are being fully exposed. See, for example, John Simpson and Jana Bennett, *The Disappeared: Voices from a Secret War* (London: Robson Books, 1985).

32. Cortázar, "We Love Glenda So Much," in *We Love Glenda So Much,* trans. Gregory Rabassa (1980; New York: Knopf, 1983), p. 10. Subsequent page references are noted in the text.

33. Milan Kundera, *The Book of Laughter and Forgetting,* trans. Michael Henry Heim (1979; New York: Knopf, 1980), p. 22.

34. Cortázar, "Epílogo a un cuento," in *Deshoras* (México, D.F.: Siglo Veintiuno Editores, 1983), p. 14, my translation.

35. See, for example, Norman O. Brown, "Apocalypse: The Place of Mystery in the Life of the Mind," *Harpers,* May 1961, 46–9; this essay is translated into Spanish in a collection which includes translations of Eric Fromm, Herbert Marcuse, Daniel and Gabriel Cohn-Bendit, entitled *Ensayos sobre el apocalipsis,* ed. Luis Racionero (Barcelona: Editorial Karios, 1973).

See also Brown's *Life against Death: The Psychoanalytic Meaning of History* (Middletown, Connecticut: Wesleyan University Press, 1959).

36.   Cortázar, *A Manual for Manuel,* trans. Gregory Rabassa (1974; New York: Pantheon, 1978), p. 389.

37.   Paz, "Revolt, Revolution, Rebellion," in *Alternating Current,* pp. 143–4, Paz's emphasis.

38.   Henry James, "Preface to *Roderick Hudson,*" in *The Art of the Novel,* ed. R. P. Blackmur (1907; reprint, New York: Charles Scribner's Sons, 1962), p. 6.

Julio Cortázar: The Fantastic Child

SARAH E. KING

"What—is—this?" he said at last.
"This is a child!" Haigha replied eagerly, coming in front of Alice to introduce
her . . .
"We only found it today. It's as large as life, and twice as natural!"
"I always thought they were fabulous monsters!" said the Unicorn.
　　　　　　　　　　　　　　　—Lewis Carroll, *Through the Looking Glass*

"It is perhaps childhood which comes closest to 'true life.' "[1] This statement, made by André Bretón in his *First Manifesto of Surrealism,* is echoed by Medrano, the fatally adventuresome protagonist of Julio Cortázar's first novel, *The Winners,* when he confesses that childhood remains for him "the most profound part" of his life.[2] Given Cortázar's consistent quest to gain access to some "truer life," one which he glimpsed, or intuited lay beyond the realm of our ordinary, everyday awareness, this statement by one of his first protagonists is highly significant. For Medrano, like Horacio Oliveira in *Hopscotch,* like Johnny Carter in "The Pursuer," and like Alina Reyes in "The Distances" (and the list could be extended) are all typical of a type of character found throughout Cortázar's writings—both his novels and his short stories—characters who are insatiable seekers, each compatible with the following well-known self-description offered by Oliveira:

> It was about that time I realized that searching was my symbol, the emblem of those who go out at night with nothing in mind, the motives of a destroyer of compasses.[3]

Judging from the frequent appearance of children throughout Cortázar's writings, many of whom share basic characteristics with their adult counterparts listed above (or perhaps vice versa), it would seem that Cortázar concurs with Franz Kafka's assessment of the child as "the only incorruptible searcher

From *The Magical and the Monstrous: Two Faces of the Child-Figure in the Fiction of Julio Cortázar and José Donoso* (New York & London: Garland Publishing Inc., 1992). Reprinted by permission of the author.

after truth."[4] In establishing the association between the employment of the figure of the child and the major concerns of Cortázar's writings, Luís Harss goes so far as to say:

> All themes in Cortázar, in one way or another, constitute a transit, a passage—frequently explicit—to the heaven of childhood.[5]

If this might be said to be exaggerating the case somewhat, it is not entirely farfetched to say that children, in various guises and to varying degrees of prominence, occupy a central place in Cortázar's fiction.

For the most part, it is in the short stories that Cortázar fully ventures into the territory of the child. In the earlier collections (*Bestiario, Final del juego*) the voices of children are heard directly in those stories which employ a child-narrator: "Después del almuerzo" (After Lunch), "Los venenos" (The Poison), "End of the Game." In the story "Bestiary," although told in the third person, events are seen largely from the naive perspective of the child Isabel, and the narrative is interspersed with her fragmented, elliptical letters to her mother. Other stories, such as "A Yellow Flower" and, from various later collections, "Silvia," "In the Name of Bobby," and "Summer," all employ mature narrators, but each focuses on some type of adult fascination or obsession with the childhood world. And, in Cortázar's final collection of short stories (*Unreasonable Hours*), the title piece is at once a last retrospective look at childhood through the writer's eyes, as well as a meta-account of the act of recalling and reliving childhood events.

Of considerably less interest in the examination of the childhood theme are those few short stories in which children appear more as recurring motifs than as realized personalities—stories such as "La puerta condenada" (The Blocked Door) "Return Trip Tango" and "Las fases de Severo" (The Phases of Severo). What is significant about these last examples, however, is that the less prominent child-figures in each share their passive category with the majority of their novelistic siblings. That is, with the notable exception of Jorge in *The Winners,* who plays a pivotal, albeit unconscious role in the life and death occurrences on board the *Malcolm,* most of the juvenile figures who appear in Cortázar's novels are minor characters in the extreme. In this category belong the still-infant Manuel of *A Manual for Manuel,* and la Maga's Rocamadour, who plays more the role of an inconvenience than of a character in *Hopscotch.* These silent novelistic children, then, are the antitheses of their outspoken short-story counterparts. Not unexpectedly, it is among this latter group of children who appear in the more autonomous settings of the short stories that we will find certain fundamental traits which place his fictional children among the major emissaries of Cortázar art.

In a 1978 interview with Ernesto Bermejo, Cortázar talks about his affinity to children and his fascination with the childhood period of existence.[6] This discussion goes a great way toward explaining, at one level, the frequent occurrence of presumably naive characters in the Argentine's writings. There are two separate, but related, aspects of Cortázar's predilection for childhood themes which emerge from this conversation. First, from various autobiographical anecdotes which he has revealed in this and other interviews, it is clear that the writer still recalls, with astonishing clarity, even the minutest details and seemingly trivial specifics of events which took place in his own childhood days in Banfield. It is an epoch which he evokes with apparent ease despite many elapsed years, one which he has referred to as a unique territory, a privileged time out of time.[7] But, in addition to being close to his memories of childhood, Cortázar seems also to have remained close to the child he was as well. In fact, it is not without a certain amount of boyish pride that Cortázar confesses a kindredness to J. M. Barrie's Peter Pan, that other child of fiction who never grew up. In commenting on his own much-remarked youthfulness of both appearance and outlook, he recalls how:

> In my earliest years . . . I read that classic of English literature, Peter Pan . . . and I identified to a certain extent with him. Once a woman in Buenos Aires told me: "you should have been called Peter Pan," and it struck me, because it coincided with that very assimilation of the character that I had already noted definitively. (Bermejo 48)

In addition, Cortázar also professed a certain rapport with children:

> I communicate well with children. I have a good relationship with their world because I don't try to impose my own structures to gain entry. And a child understands that perfectly. (52)

A well-known photograph of Cortázar surrounded by youthful admirers (while one intractable pre-cronopio "tootles" the camera-man) would seem to corroborate this statement. But by and large, there seems to be little doubt that for the most part the numerous children who inhabit the territories of Cortázar's fiction are the product of the self-exploration of the author's own seemingly ever-present past. Cortázar acknowledges this without equivocation in that same interview:

> In general, the children who circulate throughout my stories represent me in some way. (51)

That there is a considerable autobiographical element to be found in the childhood events recounted in such stories as "Bestiary," "Los venenos," and "Unreasonable Hours," is a fact readily attested to by Cortázar on more than one occasion. As he goes on to tell Bermejo, "The depth of sensibility of the little girl Isabel of 'Bestiary' is mine, just as the boy of 'Los venenos' is me." Just as in another interview, this time with Evelyn Garfield, he dutifully details the real-life infantile attraction and subsequent disillusionment which comprised the premise of the latter of those two stories.[8] And clearly, the recurrence of Banfield as the setting for a number of the child-narrated or childhood related evocations shows that the writer is not at all loath to include, undisguised, this or other well-known or easily identifiable elements of his own childhood days. Another minor example of this might be the frequency of fatherless or female-run households in these stories. Yet, despite these rather blatant autobiographical interjections, it is clear that autobiography, *per se,* even of the hybridized, fictionalized type so popular in recent childhood memoirs, is not a central concern or motivating purpose in Cortázar's art. Rather, these elements seem to be present in the majority of cases to lend an authenticity to the children who are, as Rousseau and others maintained they ought to be, the heroes of their own stories—considered not as "incomplete adults" but in their own right.[9] Nevertheless, without insisting on a necessarily autobiographical reading of Cortázar's childhood related stories, it is interesting to note the extent to which they share characteristics with the non-fiction Childhood genre—as will be seen shortly in discussing the child's perspective of time and space.

In the meantime, it is important to note that for the most part it is in the stories of the earlier collections that the childhood world is most often portrayed as an autonomous region which, while it inevitably intersects with the adult world, appears to be of interest in and of itself. In this category belong all of the child-narrated stories, as well as the bits and pieces of childhood recollections to be found in Cortázar's essays and poetry. And even in those later stories which involve adults in some way "possessed" by children, the focus ultimately falls on the secret, unfathomable closed order of the child's world. Inevitably, it is this second, alternate world which proves to be the more powerful of the two, and which works a type of irresistible reversed Pied Piper charm over the adults, whose own reality becomes controverted by the more compelling reality of the child. It is important to emphasize here that thus far no distinction has been made between the positive and negative portrayals of children by Cortázar. This is due to the fact that the writer himself appears to draw no such rigid distinctions in his exploration of the early period of life. Angelic or demonic, what marks Cortázar's fictional children is an authenticity, a trueness to self that comes closer to the heart of Cortázar's art than any mere fairy tale version of good and evil might have.

A great deal more could be said concerning Cortázar's quest for authenticity via the childhood motif, along with such themes as the importance of play and ritual and the conception of childhood as "a time outside of time." But such broad categorization robs much of the enchantment from the universe of the child as Cortázar presents it. It is a universe of primordial *cronopios,* which simultaneously taps into a number of the universal archetypes traditionally associated with the figure of the literary child, but at the same time is full of idiosyncrasies and nuances that indelibly stamp each portrayal of the child with Cortázar's unmistakable mark. Through the combined forces of memory, imagination, humor (and, inevitably, the influence of vast readings) Cortázar arrives at the representations which comprise what he himself has called "the museum of childhood" (*Territorios*). Only after examining—and enjoying—the contents of this museum can or will any attempt be made to justify its existence as central to Cortázar's work as a whole, or to identify in the omnipresent figure of the child an almost inevitable manifestation of what Luis Harss reminds us is a constant in Cortázar's fiction, "the nostalgia for a lost kingdom."[10]

BANFIELD

If, as Cortázar intimated in the essay just cited from *Territorios*, his childhood recollections constitute a type of museum to which he returns periodically, attracted by the "enthusiasm and wonder" of his former self, the return to childhood via his fiction can be said to provide the reader with a similarly refreshing anti-intellectualized—which is not to say always idealized or necessarily light-hearted—departure. And while the time of childhood for Cortázar remains, as we have said, a type of non-specific *illo tempore* which defies a definitive position in history, the place of childhood in the Argentine's fiction has become, by antonomasia, the town of Banfield.

The explicit setting for Cortázar's "childhood stories" is not always Banfield, nor in those stories in which the town *is* specified is it always the case that it is described in any detail or given any special attention or significance. But, paradoxically, it is perhaps this very lack of insistence on place which lends verisimilitude to the child's limited perspective. This is especially true in two stories which specifically name Banfield in a single off-handed line, and never again refer to the town by name in the text. These two stories are "Bestiary" and "Los venenos."[11] In the opening paragraph of the latter, the excited young protagonist, preoccupied with the new machine and the art of ant-killing, knowingly mentions "the ants of Banfield," the only direct naming of the place which will provide the setting for the narrator's first amorous disillusionment. Even more cursory is the literal "reference-in-passing" made to Banfield in "Bestiary" as the town left behind as little Isabel sets out on her adventure into the country:

they were passing through Banfield at top speed, vavoom! (79)

These scant references, for all that they may seem trivial to the point of insignificance, capture an essential facet of the limited juvenile perspective through which the story is projected. There is no need for the young protagonists to further elaborate on Banfield any more than an adult narrator would feel any need to specify in what solar system the events he was describing took place. That is, for the child, the home town—here Banfield—in effect comprises his or her entire universe. The idea of Banfield as the safe, all-encompassing haven of childhood is borne out in the first of these stories by the fact that the event that will signal the turning point in the protagonist's childhood, in effect, the first abrupt introduction of betrayal into his universe, occurs simultaneously with the outside intrusion into the closed world of Banfield by the arrival of cousin Hugo. This outsider from the capital descends on the suburb like the proverbial City Mouse with accouterments that inspire both jealousy and disdain in his young cousin:

> It was plain to see that he was from Buenos Aires, with his clothes came books by Salgari and one on botany, because he had to prepare for his first year exams. (26)

Again in "Bestiary," Banfield will be associated with the secure world of the child, and this time it is the native protagonist's excursion away from the town which will coincide with the disruptive event destined to alter the previous state of innocence and tranquility. The reference is scant but suffices to establish the dichotomy between Banfield and adventure. For Isabel, Banfield represents security, Mamá and the dull Inés, knitting, boredom, or simply the bland everyday reality ("rice pudding with milk, very little cinnamon, a shame") while Los Horneros, the Funes' home, is adventure, the unknown, the tiger, Nino "hunter of cockroaches"and "country intermingled with the taste of Milky Way and . . . menthol drops" (79). These two early examples, which situate the time of childhood in the space of Banfield, are only a fore-shadowing of the extent to which Banfield becomes almost synonymous with childhood in Cortázar's writings. Clearly, in strictly biographical terms, it is not remarkable that Banfield should be associated irrevocably with the writer's past. But the method of recollection of the town in the strictly biographical context of the essays, as compared to the similar evocations of Banfield in the short stories, serves to demonstrate the large extent to which the latter depend upon the element of memory rather than of pure invention. There is little appreciable difference between the "phosphorescent summer sky of Banfield" evoked in *Territorios* as compared to a similar scene described in "Unreasonable Hours." Just as the gleeful acts of infantile rebellion recalled in a footnote in *A Certain Lucas* do not differ greatly from the prepubescent insurrections mounted in "End of the Game."[12]

Regardless of the genre in which they appear, in fact, such scenes—whether in the stories or the essays—tend to adhere almost to the letter to the archetype of the evocation of the place of childhood as described by Richard Coe in *When the Grass Was Taller,* wherein he points out "the significance of the insignificant" when examining the childhood world.[13] As we have said, the presence of Banfield is only one indication of the extent to which Cortázar relies on his own childhood recollections in creating his fictional children. So it is not surprising that what is applicable to the factual portrayals of childhood in the essays should apply likewise to the short stories which employ a child's perspective. Although set in Buenos Aires instead of Banfield, the method of evoking the child's environment in "Después del almuerzo" (After Lunch) is similar to that employed by other writers of the Childhood genre, according to Coe's assessment of the latter:

> The child's world is a small world. Obvious as this statement may sound, it has implications which affect the literary reconstruction of that world, and which may not be so immediately apparent. The child's world is confined to a few streets or to a few fields; it is a path down to the beach along which every fence and every stile is known intimately by name, and the names remain as incantations; it is a "private domain," a "little world apart," a "small but very personal world," in which the names of streets were like the names of continents on a map of the world. (139)

The observations made in this statement could easily have been made regarding the following passage from the Cortázar story:

> . . . Besides, I was accustomed to walking through the streets with my hands in my pants pockets, whistling or chewing gum, or reading comic books while watching with the bottom part of my eyes the sidewalk blocks that I know by heart from my house to the streetcar, so that I can tell when I pass in front of Tita's house or when I'm about to arrive at the corner of Carabobo.[14]

Still another autobiographical aspect enters into the slightly different presentation of Banfield—although still connected with the childhood motif—which occurs in Cortázar's later writings. In at least two notable instances, Banfield ceases to be merely the setting for the child and becomes, via the recollective processes of adult characters, synonymous with the lost age of childhood. This equation appears both in the scenes of recollection by Andrés in *A Manual for Manuel* and finds what is perhaps its most blatant expression in the short story "Unreasonable Hours" from the author's last collection, which will end the cycle of child-related narratives on a note of deep nostalgia.[15]

In both cases, the immediacy of the Banfield of the child-narrated accounts—both briefer and more matter-of-fact in tone—is replaced by the hazy, somewhat romanticized versions of the town filtered through the nostalgia-laden perspective of the adult memory process. For Andrés, an exiled Argentine in Europe (hence the alluded-to autobiographical aspect), Banfield becomes almost the symbol of his irrecuperable, you-can't-go-home-again past. Childhood in that setting is presented as a safe garden in contrast to the adult's disenfranchised Parisian existence. Thus the past, full of a soporific kind of familial security, "My grandmother talking to me in a garden in Banfield/a sleepy suburb of Buenos Aires" is contrasted with the dispossessed, orphan-like uncertainty of a stranger in a strange land: "What a strange thing/being an Argentine on this night/knowing I'm going to an appointment with no one . . ." (357).

This passage constitutes a type of *deja vu* of an earlier scene minutely recalled by the character known as "the one I told you" who, through what he calls a mechanism of memory, is able to describe in great detail

> the smell of jasmines . . . in a town in Buenos Aires province a long time back when his grandmother would get out the white tablecloth . . . and someone lighted the lamp and there was a sound of silverware and plates on trays, talking in the kitchen, the aunt who would go to the alley with the white gate to call the children who were playing with their friends in the garden next door or on the sidewalk and there was the heat of a January evening, [his] grandmother had watered the garden before it grew dark and you could get the smell of the wet earth . . . the honeysuckle covered with translucent drops that multiplied the lamp for a child with eyes born to see things like that. (18)

Clearly, in this passage the writer has moved beyond the mere concrete reality of Banfield as backdrop to arrive at Banfield as subject, almost analogous to childhood itself. Again, Coe's observations regarding the phenomenon of childhood recollection bear some striking similarities with how Cortázar portrays this same process via his fictional characters. In discussing the relationship between mobility and memory, Coe asserts the following:

> The child who was born, grew up, lived, and died in the same village or hamlet was less able to distance his adult from his immature self than the child who, having passed his early years on some remote farm, estate or sheep-station unidentifiable from the atlas, came later to roam among the great cities and capitals of the world. Even the childhood experience itself becomes more vivid when it contains not one but two clearly distinct modes of being: the one commonplace and familiar, the other abnormal and ecstatic, a "summer-holiday self," moving in a magic dimension, far away amid the dunes and the forests, the towering grasses and the multicolored panoply of butterflies and unfamiliar birds. (17)

Andrés, looking back at Banfield from exile in no less a "capital of the world" than Paris, is a clear example of the distancing effect of nostalgia, and it is not difficult to see in the scene depicted earlier—with its jasmine-perfumed air, white table-cloth, children playing in balmy temperatures and dewy honeysuckle—the very epitome of the "magic dimension" to which Coe alludes.

Without a doubt, however, the short story which most echoes this "summer-holiday self" conception of childhood, in contrast to the commonplace and familiar atmosphere which pervades stories such as "Los venenos,"

is "Unreasonable Hours." The paean to Banfield in this story establishes the
memory of the town as being inseparable from that of childhood itself:

> And along with all that there was, of course, Banfield, because that's where
> everything had taken place; neither Doro nor Aníbal could have imagined
> himself in any other town except Banfield in which the houses and the play-
> grounds were then vaster than the world itself. (102)

The reference to the size of the houses is a first indication of the subjective
"inaccuracies" of the child's perspective, to which the story gradually reverts.
And while the following description may at first appear to be realistic, there is
an "otherness" about it that converts this small insignificant town into a type
of Shangri-La of childhood:

> Banfield, a town with its dirt roads and its Southern Railway station, with its
> vacant lots that in summer, during the siesta, crawled with many-coloured
> locusts and, at night, seemed to congregate timorously around the few street
> lamps . . . with a vertiginous halo of flying insects around each glowing bulb.
> Doro and Aníbal's houses were so close to each other that the street was like
> one more room, a place that kept them together day and night . . . And sum-
> mer, always; the summer of holidays, the freedom of playing games, time
> theirs alone, without school timetables or bells calling them to class, the scent
> of summer in the hot air of the afternoon and night, in the faces, sweaty after
> winning or losing, fighting or running, laughing and sometimes crying but
> always together, always free, masters of a world of kites and soccer balls and
> street corners and sidewalks. (103)

From the emphasis on Banfield as distant in space we move in this short story
to an emphasis on its distance in time, and if the place is now colored even
more deeply by nostalgia, it is because the description is intended to paint a
more faithful portrait of memory than of Banfield *per se*. So it is that the character will recall with perfect inaccuracy a Banfield which existed in eternal
summer, in what is almost an exact translation of the "summer-holiday self"
perspective of childhood typical of the genre. Luís Harss has noted that a
number of Cortázar's "childhood stories" occur in summer, citing as examples
"Los venenos," "Bestiary," and of course, "Summer" itself.[16] Not only should
"Unreasonable Hours" be added to this list, but moreover, it can be seen as
almost the "metatext" of the entire "childhood cycle" of stories in Cortázar's
fiction. That is, here the very *modus operandi* of the story is the process of recollection and the writing of one's childhood experiences. So it is not the actual
suburb of Banfield any more than it is merely the events of childhood that are
the real subject here; rather, it is the recollection of Banfield tinged with nostalgia, the process of reliving the past via another process, that of writing,
which preoccupies the writer.

A considerable amount of space has been devoted thus far to situating Banfield as the quintessential "place of childhood" in Cortázar's fiction. This is because while Banfield does not figure in all of the childhood stories, it is a recognizable recurring motif in what is largely a pattern of shifting, sometimes contradictory, images of the child. Most of the alternating perspectives of the enigmatic child-figure which appear in Cortázar's work center around ideas already hinted at in the earlier discussion. As was noted, aside from the dichotomy we have seen between those stories which are narrated from the child's own perspective and those in which the child is seen through the eyes of an adult character, another important distinction arises if the child being viewed by the adult is his own former self. Other important aspects to consider in relationship to Cortázar's ever-dynamic portrayal of the child-figure is the way that the writer plays with the boundaries between autobiography and fiction, the limits of the mundane vs. the magic (some of these stories, such as "Bestiary" or "Silvia" have a neofantastic element—the tiger, the ephemeral Silvia herself—while the surrounding anecdote remains largely quotidian).

Viewing these stories as a group will make possible a discussion of these themes as well as of one final significant dichotomy which figures considerably in our overall perception of Cortázar's fictional children: the Blakean opposition between innocence and experience. For as we shall see, Cortázar's fascination with the young does not preclude the portrayal in his art of the darker side of innocence.

Precocious Children and Peter Pan Adults

Having begun by looking at the "where" of childhood, it is time now to turn to the "who," that is, to examine more closely the question of the various voices through which Cortázar will narrate the events of childhood. Looking first at the general nature of the children portrayed in Cortázar's fiction, once again the autobiographical would seem to provide insight into the fictional. A look at two of the non-fictional incursions into Cortázar's own past, one the already mentioned essay from *Territorios,* the other an introductory note in the poetry collection *Salvo el crepúsculo (Save Twilight),* provides a partial portrait of Cortázar the child (at least as he is perceived by Cortázar the adult).[17] The first of these essays recalls a precocious, sensitive boy who takes delight in the surrounding universe but who also experiences the dawning realization that this very enthusiasm will in some way set him apart, not only from the adult world, but from his less inquisitive playmates as well. It is a sensation of being "different" which Cortázar recalls experiencing more than once, and which he sums up in *Around the Day in Eighty Worlds* with a quote from Edgar Allen Poe's "Alone":

From childhood's hour I have not been
As others were; I have not seen
As others saw; I could not bring
My passions from a common spring—[18]

In the two Cortázar stories we have seen which are narrated entirely in the child's voice, "Los venenos" and "Después del almuerzo," the young child narrator in each case shares this remembered category of the child as loner. The betrayal by Lila of the protagonist of "Los venenos" is exacerbated by the fact that she was in effect the only person whose company he had preferred over solitude. And secretly, he had even thought of her as in some way sharing his aloneness:

> After Lila left, I began to get bored with Hugo and my sister who were talking about typical orchestras. . . . I went to my room to look for my stamp album and all the time I was thinking about how Lila's mother was going to scold her and how she was probably crying or else that her sore was going to get infected the way they do so often. . . Probably Lila was thinking of us, alone in her house there (that was so dark, and her parents were so strict) while I was playing with my pen and my stamp collection. . . Better to put everything away and just think of poor brave Lila. (30)

Except for "poor Lila," the young narrator seems to shun the company of his peers. He openly spurns his sister, not only for the unforgivable shortcomings of being both younger and a girl, but also for her unabashed adoration of their cousin Hugo. And he apparently thinks only slightly more highly of the latter, partially because he knew so many stories by heart, but mainly because Hugo, too, disdains the sister: "Hugo laughed at her in secret, and at those moments I could have hugged him" (33).

In the story just mentioned, the preference for solitude on the part of the child could well be attributed to a type of pre-machismo-cum-sibling-rivalry. This tendency toward solitude is magnified to the point of pathology in "Después del almuerzo," wherein the narrator's introversion is exacerbated by the embarrassingly noticeable, although undisclosed impairment of the brother. As does the boy in the previous story, the child here will also try to take refuge in the solitude of his room, amid his books:

> After lunch I would have liked to stay in my room and read, but Mama and Papa came almost immediately to tell me that this afternoon I had to take him for a walk. . . The first thing I said was no, let someone else take him, could I please stay in my room and study. (137)

But unlike the child in "Los venenos" who has companions and rejects them—who is a loner by choice—here we have a glimpse of the far more pathetic figure of the lonely child. (Luc, the sickly and timid avatar of a failed life in "A Yellow Flower" is another example.) To a much greater extent than the child in "Los Venenos" the narrator of "Después del almuerzo" seems to be all alone against an alternately hostile and hypercritical adult world (with the exception of the sympathetic but ineffectual tía Encarnación).

The third example in Cortázar's repertoire of child-loners is probably the most enigmatic of all the child-figures to be found in the Argentine's stories. Unlike the two preceding examples, in "Summer" it is a girl-child who seems even initially almost disquietingly self-possessed, polite, but as if removed from the world of her mildly perplexed baby-sitters. Upon arriving at the summer cabin, she tacitly establishes a distance that gives her a subtle form of control over the two non-nonplused adults:

> Florencio had left his car in the village square, he had to take off right away; he thanked them and kissed his little girl, who had already spotted the stack of magazines on the bench. When the door closed, Zulma and Mariano looked at each other almost questioningly, as if everything had happened too fast.[19]

Shortly thereafter, Zulma, portrayed as a tentative, childless-mother type, seems all but superfluous as she attempts to interact with the little girl, only to meet with rote manners but little success, as the child seems totally absorbed with her magazines:

> Zulma asked the little girl if she was hungry, she suggested she play with the magazines, in the closet there was a ball and net for catching butterflies; the little girl said thank you and began to look at the magazines; Zulma watched her for a moment as she prepared the artichokes for dinner that evening and thought she could let her play by herself. (4)

It is as if the child's solitude here is a weapon, repeating, but with greater success, the withdrawal into books as an attempt to combat the adults' intrusions which was seen in the previous story.

Closely related to this concept of the child as loner—a measure of the extent to which the child interacts with his or her peers, with well-meaning adult intrusions, or declares his independence from others—is that of the precocious child, who, from an early age exhibits the maturity, wisdom, or simply the autonomy usually associated with the adult world. The predilection Cortázar seems to have for creating this type of child marks yet another common trait shared by his fictional projections and the complex child he remembers as his former self. The enigmatic "nena" of "Summer," like the two young narrator-protagonists of "Los venenos" and "Después del almuerzo" all exemplify the youthful version of the hybrid between the child and the adult which so pervades Cortázar's art. The essay "On Feeling Not All There" deals precisely with this intermediary state, beginning with the following admission/boast:

I will always be a child in many ways, but one of those children who from the beginning carries with him an adult, so when the little monster becomes an adult, he carries in turn a child inside and, *nel mezzo del camin* yields to the seldom peaceful coexistence of at least two outlooks onto the world. (17)

The precocious child, then, for Cortázar, is merely an early stage—as opposed to an inversion—of the type of adult character the writer typically employs as protagonist; one who, like the writer himself, has the capacity to be adult and yet maintain a child-like attitude towards things, one that is "positive, enthusiastic, with a sense of playfulness, of the gratuitous . . ."[20] As children, the three figures we have been discussing all possess, *de facto,* the capacities listed here. At the same time, the precociousness of each places him/her among the ranks of the aforementioned children who carry the adult with them. This becomes of particular significance in those stories narrated by children, for without this "double aperture"—the mixture of the ingenuous and the sophisticated—a forced choice would have to be made between the complexity and the maturity of the mode of discourse and the authenticity and believability of the child's voice which is presumably being employed.

Clearly, the use of the oxymoronic precocious child as narrator constitutes one ingenious solution to this dilemma. Another method of overcoming this inherent contradiction is to employ the other end of the analogy outlined by Cortázar,—the grown-up narrator who, as the writer has described, "has not renounced the child's vision as the price of becoming an adult." (*Around the Day* 21) Such adults who, it would appear, occupy yet another of the well-known Cortázarian interstices—this time between childhood and adulthood—heavily populate the otherwise largely all-adult worlds of the Argentine's novels. Horacio Oliveira, Medrano, Andrés, Johnny Carter, not to mention the list of their female counterparts, headed by la Maga, Paula, Alina Reyes and even Talita, all can be said to exhibit what has come to be known in popular psychology as "The Peter Pan Syndrome."[21]

In the short stories involving "actual" children who come face to face with these children-at-heart, the results of such a confrontation often involve an element of fantasy somewhat reminiscent of the bittersweet atmosphere surrounding childhood which J. M. Barrie's original "boy who refused to grow up" conjures in the mind. This is especially the case in the story "Silvia" whose writer-narrator, almost certainly a Cortázar *persona,* is fascinated by the children's games and rituals (which are seen as an annoyance or distraction by the other adults) and who is rewarded by glimpses of the phantasm they have invented. A more disquieting example of an adult who enters into the fantasy world of the child is seen in the eerily ambiguous "In the Name of Bobby."[22] As in "Silvia," the ability of the grownup to enter into the child's perspective, however fleetingly, creates a propitious opportunity for the adult's secret fantasies and repressed desires to be expressed indirectly.

Nor is it incidental that it is the aunt in the story "In the Name of Bobby" who sympathizes with the child's fantasy world. She is in fact only one of a fairly considerable number of aunts and sometimes uncles who exist as adult accomplices to the child in Cortázar's stories. In "Después del almuerzo" as was already mentioned briefly, it is also the aunt who is the only sympathetic adult in the story. There is something almost childish in the conspiratorial way that she offers the young narrator comfort:

> Aunt Encarnación must have noticed that I was upset about having to go out with him, because she stroked my hair and then she bent and gave me a kiss on the forehead. I felt her slip something into my pocket. "So you can buy yourself a little something," she said into my ear, "And don't forget to give him a little—it's preferable." (138)

In "Los Venenos" it is the uncle who seems to be as excited as the child is by the new "toy," a fact which Cortázar conveys with ironic humor:

> "They're all going to die," said my uncle, who was very pleased with the way the machine was working, I stood alongside him with dirt up to my elbows, and it was plain to see that this was a man's job. (24)

In "Bestiary," too, there is a similar relationship of complicity between Isabel and the "adoptive aunt" figure of Rema, the two becoming literal accomplices by the story's end.

Again, an amusing autobiographical anecdote in *Around the Day in Eighty Worlds* indicates that this type of secret alliance between nephew and aunt occurred in the writer's own past. The essay "On the Sense of the Fantastic" offers the following confession:

> One obtains a more complete notion of my abominable realism during this period [childhood] when I confess that I often found coins in the street—coins that I stole at home and casually dropped while my aunt studied a store window, in order to pick them up afterwards and claim the right to buy candy. My aunt, on the other hand, must have been quite accustomed to the fantastic, for she never found this too frequent occurrence strange, but actually shared my excitement, as well as an occasional caramel. (28)

The conspiratorial role between child and aunt or uncle which we see in each of these examples is something of an extension of the somewhat bland but nevertheless applicable archetype of these marginal relatives and their relationship to the child which Coe outlines in his study of the childhood genre. He describes the archetypal "avuncular" relationship as one which supplies warmth and affection without the demands and complexities which accompany parental love. Coe then describes the common portrayal of aunts and uncles as the "bringers of gifts" and makes reference to the all-important characteristic of "trustworthiness," which he claims is their "essential quality, at any event in the eyes of the still-young child" (160).

Similarly, in "Silvia," the fact that the narrator, who identifies more with the children than with the other adults at the gathering, is a writer by profession is not accidental. In the absence of a sympathetic aunt or uncle, the artist becomes a second type of (frequently eccentric) adult figure who will be deemed trustworthy by the child. The well-established literary convention which associates the mind of the poet with the child's mentality does not appear for the first time in Cortázar's writings with this story. In *The Winners,* it is Persio, the erratic poet-translator, who enjoys a secret communication with the eight-year-old Jorge who, the former insists, "knows things that . . . he'll later forget" (87).

In "Silvia," while the child-poet affinity is more obliquely presented, the mutual attraction between the narrator and Graciela, the little girl who instructs him in the rudiments of the children's fantasy-world, is evident. She plays a type of coy Alice to his Charles Dodgson, sitting fleetingly on his lap, rushing off again to rejoin her playmates and generally treating him with an off-handed sort of affectionate tolerance. There is a whimsical irony to the role reversal which has her patiently explaining the details of Silvia's appearances to the narrator, an obligation she feels, as he wryly notes, "based on her notion that I am a little dim" (187). Both this relationship and that of Persio and Jorge, secret alliances formed between poets and children, seem closely related to Cortázar's belief in the innate poetic capabilities of the latter. In his conversation with Bermejo, he humorously cites Cocteau's somewhat petulant statement on the subject: "all children are poets except Minou Drouet." Who, Cortázar goes on to explain:

> was that little monster who had written a book of poems at eight years of age, a bit prefabricated by the mother, and who all of France admired.

And he goes on to note that

> it's true that if you leave children alone with their games they do marvelous things . . . With writing it's the same. The very first things that children tell, or that they like having told to them, are pure poetry; the child lives in a world of metaphors . . . of permeability. 16–17

This last description, that of the child's world as one of "metaphor, acceptance and permeability," explains not only those stories by Cortázar which depict an affinity between children and writers literally, but also explains why in other stories it is most often that character who is a writer who retains the closest ties with the child who was his former self. We have already seen how it is Andrés, the self-appointed chronicler of the activities of la Joda in *A Manual for Manuel,* who slips most easily into "a past that becomes more present every day" (19). But it is not only such fictional characters as Andrés or the narrator of "Silvia" who experience this phenomenon, for Cortázar himself has attested to an equally extraordinary memory:

I remember many details, a quantity of things that have happened . . . , in short: *une recherche de temps perdu;* I am lost in that, in an interminable and detailed recollection. (Bermejo 16–17)

We have already noted that "Unreasonable Hours," the last Cortázar short story to embrace the childhood theme, deals more with the process of remembering childhood—through writing—than it does with children or childhood, *per se.* In light of the above quote, the narrator seems almost to be speaking for Cortázar when he contrasts his own recollective abilities with those of others:

I never knew quite why, but time and again I returned to things that others had learned to forget so as not to slouch through life carrying all that past on their shoulders. I was certain that among my friends there were few who remembered their childhood playmates the way I remembered Doro . . . (101)

In addition, the story seems to come very close to explicitly defining Cortázar's lifelong fascination with remembering and writing events from his childhood, to which he apparently assigns a value similar to that assigned to his past by the character, Aníbal, when he speaks of childhood as

things that could not be relived but that became somehow present, as if a third dimension opened up within the memories themselves, lending them a frequently bitter but much longed for proximity. (101)

As we have seen, Cortázar has employed various narrative perspectives in his attempt to regain access to this "third dimension." The voices he has employed in this pursuit range from that of the child to that of "child-like" adults and even to thinly veiled *personae* who represent the writer himself communing with children. But regardless of the narrative voice employed in these stories, it is clear that in presenting the complex figure of the child, Cortázar has never completely abandoned that one child's voice which he seems to hear very clearly despite distance in time and space: his own. It is on this voice that he seems to rely most heavily in re-creating the *vox puerilis* of the child-narrated stories, just as it is largely memory which supplies the details of the childhood realm in those tales in which it occurs.

The child's role in the writer's lifelong quest for a secular millennium has been twofold. The child himself is perceived by the Argentine as a quintessential seeker in his own right, while childhood, as a contiguous territory through which we have all passed, is presented in Cortázar's works as a metaphorical destination, another name for a time and space which is lost but which we may again encounter: the kibbutz of childhood.

Cortázar's preoccupation with nostalgia, both personal and collective, however, is more a longing for the future than for the past. And if the child becomes a favorite emissary/metaphor for Cortázar's message of a barely glimpsed alternate reality, it is no doubt for one quality, above all others, which is valued by the writer: the child's greater degree of authenticity.

When Cortázar envisions "rescuing" the child who exists, sometimes buried beneath layers of social conditioning, in every adult, it is to this authentic, ideal child-self that he refers. It is for this reason that the majority of his adult protagonists, each embarked upon his or her own form of a quest toward greater authenticity, must prerequisitely exist as an interstitial being, a hybrid between the child and the adult states. At the same time, the abstract values assigned to the childhood phase of existence do not blind Cortázar to the assets (or the short-comings) of the flesh-and-blood variety of child: spontaneity, enthusiasm, passion, imagination, creativity, rebelliousness and humor. It is by accessing all of these qualities, as well as the more mysterious, darker aspects of the child as enigma or transgressor, that Cortázar finds the adequate voice via which he projects himself through the complex, kaleidoscopic prism of the child-narrator.

It is not difficult to comprehend the allure of the child for a man who once proclaimed, "I detest solemn searches" (see Harss, *Into the Mainstream*). Nor do we need Cortázar's confession of a life-long affinity with the character Peter Pan to convince us that in many ways, in the best sense of the phrase, the Argentine, like Barrie's prototype, never entirely grew up. The curiosity and humor which naturally, unaffectedly mark the child's perspective, seem never to have abandoned Cortázar. He in turn, never forgot how to listen to that child-like voice—long dormant in many adults—which remains skeptical toward the limited arguments of the purely rational, suspicious of all that is not genuine.

Seemingly, much that delights us in Cortázar's art can be attributed to that thriving inner child, who remained a friend and an accomplice to the writer throughout his lifetime. Perhaps it was this childish alter ego, peeking over Julio's shoulder, who whispered those conversations in "glíglico" recorded in *Hopscotch* into the writer's ear; the same "paredro" who dictated the child-like antics of that other infantile pair in *62: A Model Kit* or recalled the childhood trauma of putting on a sweater for "No se culpe a nadie" (Don't You Blame Anybody); who puckishly named the group of merry pranksters in *A Manual for Manuel* la Joda; or, who could doubt it, helped compile that humorous catalogue of misfits and iconoclasts called *Historia de cronopios y famas* (Cronopios and Fames). In all of these cases, Cortázar, listening to his child-like muse, traded solemnity for humor, without sacrificing seriousness. It was and is a serious business, this rescuing of the child. As the body of works which are his legacy attests to, Cortázar was seemingly successful in rescuing his own inner child. Just as he remained faithful until the end to his larger quest of rescuing the dormant child in all of humankind.

Notes

1. André Bretón, *First Manifesto of Surrealism* as quoted in Reinhard Kuhn, *Corruption in Paradise* (Hanover: University Press of New England, 1982), 229.
2. Julio Cortázar, *The Winners,* trans. Elaine Kerrigan (New York: Pantheon, 1965), 182.
3. Cortázar, *Hopscotch* (New York: Random House, 1963), 7.
4. Franz Kafka in a letter to his sister Elli, Autumn 1921, as quoted by Reinhard Kuhn in his *Corruption in Paradise; The Child in Western Literature* (Hanover: University Press of New England, 1982), 36.
5. Luís Harss, "Infancia y cielo en Cortázar," in *Julio Cortázar.* ed. Pedro Lastra (Madrid: Taurus Ediciones, 1981). (My translation.)
6. Ernesto González Bermejo, *Conversaciones con Cortázar* (Barcelona: EDHASA, 1978), 48. Subsequent references appear in the text. (All translations mine.)
7. "Esa hora fuera del tiempo . . . Una condición privilegiada . . . un instante de temblorosa maravilla . . . ," in Cortázar, "Las grandes transparencias" (The Great Transparencies), in *Territorios* (México: Siglo XXI Editores, 1978), 81.
8. Evelyn Picon Garfield, *Cortázar por Cortázar* (México: Universidad Veracruzana, 1981), 81.
9. As quoted by Richard Coe, *When the Grass Was Taller: Autobiography and the Experience of Childhood* (New Haven & London: Yale University Press, 1984), 27.
10. Harss, "Infancia," 267.
11. Cortázar, "Bestiary," in the collection *End of the Game and Other Stories,* trans. Paul Blackburn (New York: Harper and Row, 1967); "Los venenos" (Poisons) appears in *Final del juego* (Buenos Aires: Ediciones Sudamericanas 1978). (For "Los venenos": my translation; subsequent references to "Bestiary" appear in text.)
12. Cortázar, *A Certain Lucas,* trans. Gregory Rabassa (New York: Knopf, 1984).
13. Coe, *When the Grass Was Taller,* 127.
14. Cortázar, "Después del almuerzo," in *Final del juego* (v. note 11), 139. (All subsequent translations mine.)
15. Cortázar, *A Manual for Manuel,* trans. Gregory Rabassa (New York: Pantheon, 1978), 353. The passage cited here was previously discussed in this context by Harss—see above. The story "Unreasonable Hours" appears in the collection of the same name (Toronto: Coach House Press, 1983), 102. Subsequent references in text.
16. Harss, "Infancia," 264.
17. Cortázar, "De edades y tiempos," *Salvo el crepúsculo* (México: Editorial Nueva Imagen, 1984), 39–40.
18. Cortázar, "On Feeling Not All There," in *Around the Day in Eighty Worlds,* trans. Thomas Christensen (San Francisco: North Point Press, 1986), 19.
19. Cortázar, "Summer," in *A Change of Light and Other Stories,* trans. Gregory Rabassa (New York: Alfred A. Knopf, 1980), 4. Subsequent references in text.
20. Garfield, *Cortázar por Cortázar,* 67.
21. Dan Kiley, *The Peter Pan Syndrome: Men Who Have Never Grown Up* (New York: Dodd, Mead, 1983).
22. Cortázar, "In the Name of Bobby," in *A Change of Light* (see above); "Silvia" first appeared in *Ultimo round* (Last Round) and is translated in *Around the Day in Eighty Worlds.*

From *Bestiary* to *Glenda:*
Pushing the Short Story to Its Limits

In *We Love Glenda So Much* (1980) one can recognize themes and motifs found in previous collections. "Orientation of Cats" brings to mind Cortázar's fondness of cats purring and pawing throughout his writings. "We Love Glenda So Much" reenacts the paroxismal admiration for an artist that borders on the collective hysteria treated earlier in "The Maenads." The unexpected twist that closes "Story with Spiders" reminds one of a similar situation and ending in "Condemned Door." Cortázar's attraction to subways as the scene of bizarre encounters and dramas, previously explored in "Throat of a Black Kitten" and "Manuscript Found in a Pocket," is once again probed in "Text in a Notebook." "Press Clippings" deals with violence in terms reminiscent of his famous story "Blow-Up." His penchant for plots about triangular relationships—most memorably treated in "The Idol of the Cyclades," "The Motive," and "All Fires the Fire"—is evinced here in "Return Trip Tango." The exquisite structure of "Clone," based on that of Bach's *Musical Offering,* reveals a close affinity with *Hopscotch*'s intricate patterning, and at the level of theme, it restates Cortázar's fascination for groups as the framework of his novels: all of them resort to this constellational coterie for the development of situations and characters. "Stories I Tell Myself" pivots around that twilight zone where reality yields to dream, so characteristic of a good segment of his short fiction and so brilliantly captured in "The Night Face Up." "Moebius Strip" is less a motif than a "state of mind": Cortázar's intuition of an uncharted order where opposites coalesce and harmony follows.

That a writer writes and rewrites those few obsessions that form the backbone of his/her creation is neither new nor uncommon. One begins to be suspicious of a writer whose range of themes is unlimited since what determines the limits to his craft is the same limitation that underlies his human experience. . . . If a subject is too complex, it requires by necessity not one but several formulations, as if its intensity overflows the capacity of a single version and calls for new ones. Successive variations on a given theme aim at cap-

From *Review of Contemporary Fiction.* 3, no. 3 (Fall 1983.) Reprinted here by permission of the publisher.

turing new angles of the same face. If "Blow-Up" is an exploration of evil and violence, "Press Clippings" ventures into the same area, but the difference in treatment between the first story and the second is the same difference that separates Cortázar's art when he wrote *Secret Weapons* (which includes "Blow-Up" in the original edition of 1959) and this last collection twenty years later.

Cortázar's handling of the short story has gone a long way. Although the stories of his first collection—*Bestiary* (1951)—display a rare perfection for an author who was making his first strides in the genre, his subsequent collections have been a relentless endeavor to push the medium's power to its utmost limits. Cortázar has refused to capitalize on what he calls, quoting Gide, the acquired "élan." Instead of relying on previous success, he has sought new roads, new challenges, new peaks to climb, reaching unsuspected heights. Since his beginning as a writer, he distrusted realism. He felt that realism and reality had little to do with each other. Realism had to do with convention, with an accepted code that acted as a surrogate of reality. One may say that all art forms are conventions seeking to represent reality; realism, on the other hand, posed as the embodiment of reality. Cortázar endorsed, instead, a motto written on one of Artaud's drawings: "Jamais réel et toujours vrai." He was subscribing, of course, to the surrealist effort "to discover and explore the more real than real world behind the real." But if he recognized in its philosophy his own outlook on art, he never joined the verbal experimentalism of its magus and iconoclasts. His stories invariably present a world we recognize as our own, a world that seemingly does not depart from that of realism: the same routines, duties, ceremonies and institutionalized games; the same problems and situations, stereotypes and conflicts. Yet, his stories do not point at those surfaces we associate with realism, but rather at cracking them, at forcing them to yield to a hidden face. It is as if we mistakenly took the mask for the face, and the story proceeds to subtly remove that mask so that for a fleeting second the true face can be glimpsed. Another way to describe his approach is contained in a passage from Clarice Lispector's *Close to the Savage Heart* quoted as the epigraph for "Moebius Strip": "Impossible to explain. She was leaving that zone where things have a fixed form and edges, where everything has a solid and immutable name. She was sinking deeper and deeper into the liquid, quiet, and unfathomable region where vague and cool mists like those of morning hovered." Although the passage fits more accurately the situation of the story where it has been inserted, it is also applicable to most of his stories. Most of them struggle to explain what "is impossible to explain" by means of language's conceptualizations, simply because language deals with those surfaces we habitually identify with reality. When language faces those cracks in its own makeup, it naturally closes them in the way skin heals its wounds. Why not peep through those cracks? How to make language enter that zone where things no longer "have a fixed form and edges," to become, instead, "a liquid and unfathomable region"? That is the province where most of his stories travel to. Of course the question is *how* to get there. If language, as the master tool of reason, has constructed the world we inhabit, it follows that to abandon the logic of language entails abandoning also the logic of our world. Confronted with this alternative, Cortázar broke with surrealism. In *Hopscotch,* one of the characters retorts: "The surrealists hung from words instead of brutally disengaging themselves from them. . . . Language means residence in reality, living in a reality. Even if it's true that the language we use betrays us, wanting to free it from its taboos isn't enough. We have to relive it, not reanimate it." Reliving language meant for him what it has always meant to literary art: converting the signs of its code into means of expression of a new code, that of literature. A notion or situation inconceivable in the language of communication—a person turned into an insect—becomes possible through the language of fiction. Fiction speaks where language remains silent. Furthermore, fiction dares to enter that *region* which is out of language's reach: a space irreducible to physical scales, a time outside the clock's domain, emotions not yet recorded in psychology manuals.

To explore that region, Cortázar resorted first to a fantastic event (a man who vomits rabbits, noises that evict homeowners from their house, a tiger roaming freely through the rooms of a middle-class home, etc.). I am referring to the stories collected in *Bestiary.* In all of them, the conflict presented through their plots comes to a resolution by means of this fantastic "crack" on the realist surface of the story. This is far from being fantastic fiction as understood in the nineteenth century, since their ultimate effect is not to assault the reader with those fears and horrors that have been defined as the attributes of the fantastic. In addition, the technique of mounting suspense gradually leading to a sudden break in our rational order—someone dead who is alive—characteristic of the fantastic tale, does not operate here. Instead, the fantastic event can appear at the very beginning of the story, purporting not to frighten or horrify the reader but rather to offer a metaphor. A metaphor is a sign, or group of signs, that stands for a meaning other than the normative one represented in that sign. The rabbits vomited by the character in "Letter to a Young Lady in Paris" stand for something else, pointing to a tenor contextualized in the story but never quite named or openly disclosed. Metaphors assist the poet in naming what conventional language cannot name, at least not quite in the same way. For Cortázar, these stories were a form of describing those perceptions which, coming from "an unfathomable region," defy conventional language. Their irrational images transcend realism to explore a territory loosely labeled as the fantastic.

Without totally abandoning this literary artifice, most of the stories in his next collection—*End of the Game* (1956)—respond to a different narrative strategy. The fantastic element reappears in the form of a classical Greek myth—"The Maenads" and "The Idol of the Cyclades"—through a metamorphosis of sorts ("Axolotl"), or by means of an unyielding silence ("After Lunch"), but the rest of them abandoned altogether the weird side manifested in the fantastic break. Not that the fantastic ceases to act in these stories; it does act, but in a different way. We have no longer uncanny metaphors, as in the first collection. The fantastic dimension of the story must be sought now at the level of its organization; not so much in its theme as in the way that theme has been treated. In each one of these stories there are two stories that have been craftily integrated. In "Continuity of Parks," one story deals with an estate owner, and the other with two lovers plotting to murder the estate owner. In "The River," there is a narrative about a middle-class couple and a second one about the wife's suicide. In "After Dinner" ("Sobremesa"), there are two juxtaposed versions as to what happened during a reunion of friends. A similar juxtaposition of two versions of the same event occurs in "The Friends." There is a third juxtaposition; yet in "The Motive," one triangular love affair, which ends in a killing, is understood and solved in the context of a second mirroring triangle. In "Axolotl," the narrator's vision of the axolotl overlaps the axolotl's vision of the narrator. "End of the Game" has also this contrapuntal quality: the perception three girls have of an outsider collides with the outsider's perception of the three girls. This technique attains to virtuosity in "The Night Face Up" where the story of a motorcycle accident interlocks with the story of a Moteca Indian sacrificed by the Aztecs.

If there is a fantastic side to these stories, it does not depend on any fantastic event, but rather on the way the two stories or points of view have been amalgamated. There is nothing uncanny or particularly disturbing in each of the two stories if they are taken separately. But by coupling them in one single narrative where one bears a close adjacency with the other, the two stories can generate a meaning absent in each of the two individually. It goes without saying that braiding the two stories is not a haphazard or mechanical operation. It is precisely in this interweaving where Cortázar's art lies. By creating a net of intrinsic interrelations between the two stories, he has forced them to say something denied to each one in isolation. There is nothing appealing or appalling in the story of a motorcyclist having an accident, being rushed to a hospital, and undergoing surgery. Nor is there anything unusual in the second story of a Moteca Indian fleeing hunting Aztecs during the "war of the blossom" and brought finally to a pyramid's altar to be sacrificed. Both stories are narrated in that compelling and liquid style that has become Cortázar's trademark, but what makes the story a narrative feat is the masterful articulation of the two stories in a single structure. By cunningly presenting the second story as a dream of the character in the first story, and by gradually reversing the condition of dream from the second to the first character, this short story achieves a magic that challenges causality. Its impact lies somewhere between the two stories: in that space or interstice that their interlacing has created. The fantastic aura that the story may have stems from that point of intersection where one tale is cleverly linked with the other: what was a dream becomes reality and what was reality becomes a dream. For the motorcyclist, the sacrificed Indian is a dream caused by his own delirium after the accident; for the Moteca Indian, the motorcyclist and his accident in a Paris street is a dream caused by his own delirium before the Aztec priest lowers his arm with a stone knife in his hand to open his chest. We readers shall never know who is the dream and who is the dreamer. There is here a reverberation of that old piece of wisdom uttered by Shakespeare— "Life is a dream." There is also an echo of that dilemma that has troubled generations of Chinese readers: Was it Chuang Tzu who dreamed that he was a butterfly or was he a butterfly dreaming that it was Chuang Tzu? A third reading points to the confrontation of two civilizations, one attempting to understand the other, one unfailingly appearing as a dream of the other. Jacques Soustelle expressed this idea in a lapidary and intense sentence: "The reality of one civilization is the dream of another." These interpretations and many others constitute a multiplicity of meanings embodied in the story and underline its nature of metaphor capable of manifold tenors. If in the previous collection only the fantastic event bears the metaphorical weight, in *End of the Game* the entire story has become, by virtue of its narrative organization, a metaphor. Cortázar has moved from reliance on fantastic events interpolated in the plots in *Bestiary,* to situations that depend no longer on *what happens* at the level of plot but on *how* the story has been structured in this second collection. In the first case, he resorted to a fantastic resolution; in the second, to a compositional solution. The second choice required, beyond any doubt, a greater skill in the handling of the genre.

In his next collection, *Las armas secretas (Secret Weapons)*, 1959, he avoided cashing in on the accomplishments of his previous volumes. Instead, he left behind the fantastic metaphors of the first and the structural virtuosity of the second, to seek new possibilities, new questions, and new answers. Of that period, he said:

> When I wrote "The Pursuer," I had reached a point where I felt I had to deal with something that was a lot closer to me. I wasn't sure of myself any more in that story. I took an existential problem, a human problem which was later amplified in *The Winners,* and above all in *Hopscotch.* Fantasy for its own sake had stopped interesting me. By then I was fully aware of the dangerous perfection of the storyteller who reaches a certain level of achievement and stays on that same level forever, without moving on. I was a bit sick and tired of seeing how well my stories turned out. In "The Pursuer" I wanted to stop inventing and stand on my own ground, to look at myself a bit.

With *Secret Weapons,* Cortázar found new tones and inflections for his voice, new preoccupations and themes for his fiction, and new forms of expression to tackle more effectively those new concerns. His stories became longer—an average of 30 to 40 pages as opposed to the 3 to 10 page story in the earlier collections—less focused on the exactly structured plot and closer to the breadth of the novel, less geared to situations and more concentrated on characters, more vital and less dependent on plot. All this should suffice to prove the constant process of renovation in his art, his tireless search for new forms and narrative modes, his commitment to the short story as a genre capable of inexhaustible regeneration. What we have seen thus far brings us also to the question of his most recent collection, *We Love Glenda So Much,* and to its place in Cortázar's production as a short-story teller.

A good point of departure is his view of the short story as a sister genre to poetry. In an essay devoted to the former and included in his book-collage *Ultimo round (Last Round,* 1969), he stated that "there is no genetic difference between the brief short story and poetry as we understand it since Baudelaire." . . . Cortázar alludes to the nature of literary artifact of the short story or poem: autonomous and precise organisms capable of breathing on their own, and of communicating their charge of experience thanks to their sensitive and delicate machinery. The narratives of this new collection share with earlier ones the same effort addressed to capturing an experience or perception or feeling incommunicable by means of ordinary language. They also share the condition of extended metaphors in the sense that while they tell a well-crafted story, they also open in the body of the narrative a double bottom, a second meaning awaiting to be detected in the same way that a poem offers a message that goes beyond its immediate text. We cannot have an exact translation for the rabbits vomited by the narrator in "A Letter to a Young Lady in Paris," just as the ultimate message conveyed by the two merged stories in "The Night Face Up" escapes a single and rigid interpretation. In the end, the reader of these stories is confronted with a silence which represents its most powerful message. In reading them, one has the distinct feeling that the narrative has been woven around that silence, as its habitat, as the only way of transmitting its implications and resonances. The whistling wind one hears in the nautilus shell is not the shell, but without its spiral shape and its air-filled chambers there would not be that sea whistle one hears. This is not a mystic silence; it is a literary silence similar to the one elicited by poetry, hence the brotherhood between the two genres Cortázar referred to. The new in the stories from *Glenda* is the way that silence has of existing. Like poems, which convey their meaning through the interplay of images and through the music-filled lines of their linguistic patterns, these stories too emit messages through narrative patterns of imagery, rhythm and fictional diction.

The first three stories have in common an elliptic quality that accentuates their kinship with poetry. What do cats see when their look is lost in an invisible point? What does a woman see when she looks at the images of a painting? How to explain that the admiration for an artist could be so strong as to destroy the very object of admiration? Is there a point where a rapist and his victim could have reversed their times and turned the heinous crime into a human experience? Are dreams and reality just different manifestations of the same substance? How to answer these questions without falling into the traps of common sense and correct syllogisms? What *Glenda's* stories seek is not to provide answers but simply to explore questions, and they do that in the same way a piece of music explores an emotion and a poem encodes a charged silence. Yet the medium of fiction is not music or verse. Its task is to tell a story, but Cortázar tells it in the way a poem exudes poetry and a musician plays music. So much so that "Clone" was patterned following the model of Bach's *Musical Offering,* and "Orientation of Cats" reads like a prose poem. What approximates these stories to other art forms, however, is not their dress but their substance. Powerful short stories loyal to their medium, they share with other art forms the same matter that becomes music at one point, painting, at another, and poetry, at a third: messages devoid of rational meaning.

What we have said thus far might give the impression that *Glenda's* stories suffer from an excessively aesthetic proclivity. This will be, of course, a wrong impression. They are, quite the opposite, deeply rooted in the most immediate experiences of everyday life, but they avoid the triteness and the stereotype of its mechanics to focus on what we suspect lies underneath that ocean of practicalities: not what a truck driver does, but what he dreams; not what a cat eats or breaks, but what she sees with her eyes lost in some invisible sight; not a rape as reported by a newspaper, but as examined from within; not the entries of a couple's diary vacationing on an island, but the only entry omitted in that hypothetical diary. Cortázar is a wizard of those ellusive spaces, unrecorded experiences, unmeasurable times. The butterflies caught in his fictional net are either rara avis or extinguished species.

At the same time, and paradoxically, he is one of the most courageous writers to have emerged from Latin America. He comes from a country where military torture and murder have become the only laws. Argentina under the military rule has been turned into a prison, a slaughterhouse, a swindled, deceived and frightened nation. . . . "Press Clippings" is one of the most powerful literary texts written about that form of crime that Amnesty International has called "political killings by governments." The 30,000 people who have "disappeared" in Argentina can no longer be dismissed: they are public information. We haven't been able yet to measure the human suffering and horrors implied in that abstract figure. Their story is beginning to unfold painfully. How to deal with such an explosive subject without turning literature into a political pamphlet? How to approach this horrible tragedy without trivializing it? How to shout the horrors and stay at the same time within the bounds of art? Julio Cortázar has performed this tour de force with skill, verve, and integrity. In "Press Clippings" we recognize all the marks of his craft: mastery over his medium; the exactness, vivacity, and dignity of his language; the text folding over itself to say the unsayable. At the same time, he has confronted with unusual courage not only the murderers, but also himself as a human consciousness witnessing those murders. Should violence be met with violence? The story's answer is neither passionate nor legalistic, neither intellectual nor rhetorical. It is an existential one that chooses to elucidate the question rather than provide answers. The narrator is swept away by violence, and she herself falls into its vortex before she can reflect: "How could I know how long it lasted, how could I understand that I too, I too even though I thought I was on the right side, I too, how could I accept that I too there on the other side from the cut-off hands and the common graves, I too on the other side from the girls tortured and shot that same Christmas night. . . ." Facing violence, the narrator is forced to act, and yet, by acting, she falls herself into the nightmare of violence. There are no blacks and whites: white turns black and vice versa. The reader is confronted with the inevitability of violence on the face of violence: evil cannot be witnessed impassively. At the same time, reacting to violence with violence puts us on the side of the criminal. The criminal has succeeded in turning us into criminals. Human values and human rights have disappeared, force has replaced laws and institutions, the stronger destroys the weaker and the weaker seeks to defend himself with the only weapon his oppressor understands: more violence. Savagery. Jungle. People turning into beasts.

Although Cortázar does not present a clear-cut answer, in poignantly enlightening the question, he has given his reader all the insights needed for a human response. This has always been art's task: not to dictate answers but to illuminate the question, not to solve the presented problem but to unveil its ins and outs. Catharsis still remains the only answer to which art accedes. To go any further amounts to distorting it and, consequently, to its denial. Cortázar understands too well this dangerous borderline. He knows that literature's power lies not in transgressing its boundaries, but in accepting them and pushing against them until those limits become the hidden source of its own strength and the secret fulcrum of its leverage. In *We Love Glenda So Much,* he put into practice his wisdom and craftsmanship as a storyteller. These stories prove, once again, that he can break his own record. It matters not if the story ponders on what a cat sees, or if it dares to venture into the hells of political killings; if it traces a literary counterpart to Bach's *Musical Offering,* or if it depicts the city subways as our modern purgatory. In all of them we sense the hand of a master telling us what perhaps we once knew and forgot. (pp. 94–9)

A Change of Light:
Triumphant Tales of Obsession

JOYCE CAROL OATES

A Change of Light is Cortázar's eighth book of fiction to appear in English, and it is in many ways a change: of tone, of manner, of style, of emphasis, of "light" itself.

Here one does not find the lush and motile openness of *Hopscotch,* or the risky, funny, ceaselessly inventive predicaments of *End of the Game* (1967). The penchant for exploring obsessions—the more futile, the more fertile for the ravenous imagination—that was a thematic undercurrent in *All Fires the Fire* (1973) is given in these 20 stories an unexpected delicacy, a surprising Jamesian dignity, by the elegiac tone of Cortázar's language and a less hurried (and more dramatic) pace.

"You who read me," one of Cortázar's typical narrator-protagonists says, "will think that I'm inventing; it doesn't matter much, for a long time now people have credited my imagination for what I've really lived or vice versa." In "The Faces of the Medal" the narrator Javier—a man who "doesn't know how to cry"—attempts to free himself from nightmares of loss and impotence by "writing texts that try to be like nightmares . . . but, of course, they're only texts."

Throughout *A Change of Light* one is always aware that a story, an artifact, is being created. The political context is sometimes in the foreground, sometimes an ominous assumption, but at all times we are aware of the words that constitute the story as words, for the most part judiciously chosen. "He" frequently shifts to "I" and back again to "he" and then again to "I." The narrator may suddenly announce his own befuddlement. One of the more self-consciously literary of the stories, "Footsteps in the Footprints," is prefaced, not altogether unfairly, by the author's terse summary, as a "rather tedious chronicle, more in the style of an exercise than in the exercise of a style, say that of a Henry James who might have sipped maté in some Buenos Aires or Mar del Plata courtyard in the twenties"; the least satisfactory story, "The Ferry, or Another Trip to Venice," written in 1954, is

From *The New York Times Book Review,* 9 November 1980. Copyright © Joyce Carol Oates. Reprinted by permission of John Hawkins & Associates, Inc.

"revised" here in a high-spirited gesture of defiance—the author, acknowl-
edging the story's inferiority, is nevertheless intrigued by it and cannot let it
go: "I like it, and it's so bad." (Cortázar, following the possibly infelicitous
examples of Nabokov, is intermittently tempted to take himself very seriously indeed—as a literary phenomenon, a cultural figure whose every utterance, "bad" or not, is of value. Or is the pomposity really playful? Are the
prefaces themselves jokes? Cortázar says: "Ever since I was young I've been
tempted by the idea of rewriting literary texts that have moved me but the
making of which seemed to me inferior to their internal possibilities. . . .
What might have been attempted [however] through love would only be
received as insolent pedantry." But even the most willfully self-conscious stories, even the "bad" story, are so finely written, sentence by sentence, and the
author's melancholy intelligence so evident in every line, that the actual
reading of *A Change of Light* is an invariable pleasure. And the incursions of
fantasy, of improbability and nightmare, do not deflect from the stories'
"realist" emotional authority: Several stories in this collection have the
power to move us as Kafka's stories do.

In "Summer" . . . the pleasurable monotonous marriage of a quite ordinary couple is interrupted, perhaps fatally, by the overnight visit of a young
daughter of a friend. The girl is innocent enough, a mere child, yet she
appears to be accompanied by an enormous white horse who gallops snorting
around the house, a ferocious white blur, a "rabid" creature, or anyway one
maddened enough to want to enter a house. The white horse has stepped
magnificently out of a dream recorded in Kafka's diary for 1914 (the year of
Cortázar's birth, incidentally), and in this eerie parable of ritual monotony
and ritual violence he acquires a new menacing authority: "In the window the
horse rubbed his head against the large pane, not too forcefully, the white
blotch appeared transparent in the darkness; they sensed the horse looking
inside, as though searching for something. . . . He wants to come in, Zulma
said feebly." In fact the horse does not enter the house, though the little
girl—accidentally or deliberately—leaves the front door open for him. But
the marriage has been altered, the "new day that had nothing new about it"
has been irrevocably lost. Cortázar's most sympathetic people are those who
believe in compulsions (which they call rituals or games) as a response to
death and nothingness—"fixing things and times, establishing rituals and
passages in opposition to chaos, which was full of holes and smudges." But no
ritual can accommodate the snorting white horse, or even the overnight visit
of a friend's child (p. 9).

This collection's most compelling stories are unambiguous elegies. The
narrator of "Liliana Weeping" imagines not only his own poignant death but
a future for his wife that guarantees her survival; the narrator of "The Faces of
the Medal" addresses a woman he has loved but to whom he cannot, inexplic-
ably, make love—

We didn't know what to do or what else to say, we didn't even know how to be silent . . . find each other in some look. It was as if Mireille were waiting for something from Javier that he was waiting for from Mireille, a question of initiatives or priorities, of the gestures of a man and the compliance of a woman, the immutability of sequences decided by others, received from without. . . . It would have been preferable to repeat together: we lose our life because of niceties; the poet would have pardoned us if we were also talking for ourselves.

And in the volume's title story two "lovers" are victims of their own self-absorbed fantasies about love: They are real enough people, but not so real as their obsessive dreams.

There are one or two stories here that seem out of place in the volume—fairly conventional "suspense" stories that dissolve to sheer plot, despite the fastidious writing. And no story is so irresistible, so immediately engaging as the classic "Axolotl" of *End of the Game*—my favorite Cortázar tale. But the risks of psychological realism, of genuine emotion, of the evocation of human beings enmeshed in plausible cobwebs of friendship and enmity make this volume all the more valuable. "I know that what I'm writing can't be written," one of Cortázar's narrators says in despair, and in any case, as the unhappy protagonist of "Footsteps in the Footprints" learns, one is always writing autobiography, however disguised; and the autobiography is always distorted. Perhaps writing is "social revenge" of a sort? Or an attempt, necessarily doomed, to compensate for the fact that one doesn't know how to cry? Nevertheless the writing is triumphant, and Cortázar's text survives tears or the lack of tears. It transcends both game and ritual to become art. (pp. 34–5)

Blow-Up: The Forms of an Esthetic Itinerary

DAVID I. GROSSVOGEL

The essays contained in *Focus on Blow-up* (Ed. Roy Huss. Englewood Cliffs: Prentice-Hall, 1971) confirm much of what one might have concluded already about the film itself and about film criticism as it is generally practiced. The sheer amount of ink that flowed because of *Blow-up* establishes it as one of the most important and enduring motion pictures of the sixties.

Collectively, these essays demonstrate how inadequately even trained eyes see a motion picture (the accounts of what Vanessa Redgrave does or does not do with the roll of film she has come to retrieve from David Hemmings are sufficiently diverse to cast serious doubt on the value of eye-witnesses in a court of law. They also show with what haste the so-called film critics rush to their typewriters and their effortless words. The essay by John Freccero, "From the Word to the Image," saves us the trouble of dwelling on this point: in addition to a masterful analysis of Antonioni's work, he lays to rest the petulant, narrow-minded and self-seeking pronouncements of the "professional" movie critics whose culture begins and ends with the cinematic experience).

There might have been fewer words wasted if critics had first gone to the work of Julio Cortázar—as did Antonioni himself. (References to the short story which suggested the motion picture are scant in *Focus;* one especially benighted critic goes so far as to write, "Small wonder that Hollywood's film makers, still wedded to the written script derived from a literary source, find *Blow-up* so difficult to accept" p. 69). The oversight is unfortunate: most clues to Antonioni's movie were not to be found under the hero's magnifying glass but within the pages of the Argentinian writer.

"Las babas del diablo" (which is closer to "Skin of the Teeth" than to Antonioni's more salable title under which Cortázar's short stories are being marketed in this country) tells the story of Michel, an amateur photographer (actually a translator by trade), who discovers, during one of his walks through Paris, a woman seducing a young boy on the Ile Saint-Louis. Michel takes a picture of the scene. The woman notices him and comes up to demand the incriminating film while the young boy flees. An older and ugly

From *Diacritics* 11, no. 3 (Fall 1972) 49–54. Reprinted by permission of the author.

man, to whom the photographer had paid only scant attention, gets out of a parked car and walks towards them. Michel refuses to give up the film and leaves. He believes that his action has saved the young boy from the woman's clutches.

Some time later, Michel develops the roll of film. He enlarges the frame of the Ile Saint-Louis to life size. As he does so, the scene is reenacted for him in such a way as to divulge its truth: the boy is once again within the woman's embrace, but she is not seducing him for her own sake; she is doing so for the benefit of the ugly old man who has now moved into the picture. Even though the boy escapes again, Michel is powerless to alter the event and is, in fact, sucked into its happening. The old man moves closer to the center of the picture, occupying more and more space, until he becomes its out-of-focus and blurring totality. Michel covers his eyes and begins to sob. When he opens them, he is a prisoner of the huge and empty blow-up across which a cloud or a stray bird occasionally drift.

There is of course more to Cortázar's story than this science-fiction synopsis. Like most of Cortázar's short stories, it is primarily a tale about the impossibility of *telling* and about the frustration of *seeing*—twin expressions of the ontological dilemma that defines man, for Cortázar, as an irreducible separateness that recognizes similarly hermetic presences, without ever being able to establish more than a surface contact with them, without being able to *assimilate* them through either perception (sight) or definition (telling). The dramatic tension of Cortázar's stories derives from the exacerbation of their people's attempts to cancel and transcend their ontological sentence. They fail, but their efforts are sometimes of such magnitude as to alter forever the order of the natural world in which they previously dwelled.

Michel is a translator: his job is to understand *telling* and to make it *intelligible* to others. Hitherto, he has performed his task mechanically: it was merely a matter of finding "the way to say in good French what José Norberto Allende was saying in very good Spanish" (*Blow-up and Other Stories*. New York: Collier Books, 1971. Third ed.; p. 111). But as a consequence of his unearthly adventure Michel will sense that his plight resulted from a desperation to see beyond the surfaces that limit human sight, and that even beyond existence (for the people of Cortázar are afficted with the same curse as Beckett's people: death does not still their metaphysical questioning) the problem remains one of *telling*.

Michel's dilemma is that however he focuses on the objects of his world, those objects remain separate from him and alien; his focusing instrument—the camera, the typewriter, the word—cannot *bite* on those objects, is irremediably inert: "if I go, this Remington will sit turned to stone on top of the table" (p. 100). His camera is no better. The "stupid" lifelessness of the photograph is the most signal subversion of the *live* scene it intends to record. Even as an amateur photographer, and prior to his conscious questioning, Michel has had qualms about the ability of his camera to *comprehend* a "life that is rhythmed by movement but which a stiff image destroys" (p. 108). "Michel knew that the photographer always worked as a permutation of his personal way of seeing the world as other than the camera insidiously imposed upon it" (p. 103). But the camera which Michel carried with him in his walks through Paris was, even then, evidence that his questioning of *othernesses* had already begun—an indication of pre-conscious stirrings, a first effort to escape from his ontological bondage by penetrating an existence other than his own, while at the same time maintaining his ontological awareness by *describing* this process of self-transcendency (the paradox of understanding noted by Camus in *The Myth of Sisyphus* which would require him to be himself *and* the tree in order for him to *know* that tree): "I think that I know how to look, if it's something I know, and also that every looking oozes with mendacity, because it's that which expels us furthest outside ourselves" (*Blow-up*, p. 104). But "furthest" is not far enough; ultimately, the word and the act do no more than express the frustration of remaining hopelessly locked within the limits of the self, knowing how unknowable are the objects and the people beyond.

As the virulence of the ontological sickness intensifies, the victim's urge to escape into, and posses, his vision increases his need to voice the sense of his proximity to this vision and the sense of his frustration at not being able to cancel the forever remaining distance. He must *tell* his state of being: "if you take a breath and feel like a broken window, then you have to tell what's happening, tell it to the guys at the office or to the doctor. Oh, doctor, every time I take a breath . . . Always tell it, always get rid of that tickle in the stomach that bothers you" (p. 101). But the attempt to tell becomes a frustration commensurate with the frustration that the telling was to have conveyed: this second attempt to break out of the ontological prison is as ineffectual as the first: "nobody really knows who is telling it, if I am I or what actually occurred or what I'm seeing" (p. 101). Just as the still photograph subverts the life it intends to reproduce, the very act of telling subverts the substance of what is to be told: "Right now (what a word, *now,* what a dumb lie)" (p. 103). But in Michel, as in so many of Cortázar's protagonists, the ontological exacerbation is sufficient to affect the fourth dimension of his universe; like that of a latter-day Pygmalion, Michel's relentless desire to possess the object of his sight informs the photographic blow-up with the life of that desire and that life is sufficiently powerful to draw him into its own truth. He crosses over to another ontological dimension (retracing, in a sense, the steps of the surrealists drawn into their metaphysical mirror) and, in so doing, forever affects the natural balance of his universe without allaying the need that precipitated the metaphysical calamity.

Whatever else the parable may convey about the human condition, Cortázar's fable comments upon the Mallarmean need and frustration of the writer whose work is tensed between his unbounded vision and his unequal capacity to express it. Cortázar makes a literary point from the very first: "It'll never be known how this has to be told, in the first person or the second, using the third person plural or continually inventing modes that will serve for nothing" (p. 100). Like Michel, the artist can neither tell as he knows he must, nor can he accept *not* to tell, or tell inadequately. He must possess through words (if he is a writer) the objects of his world (and his sense of those objects), but the words have an opacity equal to his own ontological encapsulation: he cannot *be* the other and therefore he cannot *tell* what that other is, and the failure of telling extends to his inability to tell in its fullest the failure of telling. His attempts end in fiction. The writer is doomed to live out the double anxiety of his failure to achieve or voice the intensity of his questioning, but through a process of world reversal, his anxiety becomes the parafictional substance of his character. Michel's hunger and his agony are those of Cortázar—the writer attempting to deliver himself of that "tickle" in his own stomach and of which Michel is only an irremediable fiction. Michel's hopeless journey is the desperate groping of his creator.

The frustration of the writer begins with the ambiguity of the word. Except as *sound,* the word is only a stimulus for *something else.* The ultimate truth of any word as *sign* is in the experiential assimilation of a reader. In addition to his frustration at never being able to sate his desire to *know* the world (to *understand* it and to *possess* it), the writer experiences the added frustration of never being able to know the exact resonance of his words within the intimate consciousness of another. His reader is at all times the opacity of an *otherness,* but one which, in its assimilation of the author's words, puts those words likewise out of the author's reach.

It is that same "tickle"—the itch of all modern art to understand and outreach itself—that must have brought Antonioni to consider the work of Cortázar with special care. That and the additional dimension that remained to be analyzed: the self-defining awareness of a significant difference between the artist who uses words and the one who uses images: "The idea for *Blow-up* came to me while reading a short story by Julio Cortázar. I was not so much interested in the events as in the technical aspects of photography. I discarded the plot and wrote a new one in which the equipment itself assumed a different weight and significance."[1]

One assumes that Antonioni did not need Cortázar to experience the opacity of the artifact. Like Cortázar, he must have felt that his creation could never be more than a mediating object, imperfectly suggesting a truth of which he would never be fully enough possessed. He had previously said, "The greatest danger for the film maker consists in the extraordinary means the medium provides in order to lie" (*Focus,* p. 120)—an especially serious danger for the artist who, as Antonioni had noted about himself, "does nothing more than search for himself in his films. The films are not the record of a completed thought, but rather that very thought in the making" (*Focus,* pp. 122–23). One can safely assume that the ontological itch was within Antonioni before he read Cortázar—both being products of a time that has seen so much of its art become a reflection upon itself and grappling for esthetic absolutes that measure the distance between the artist's inner eye and what he feels to be the inadequacy of his artistic reach. Pictures like Bergman's *Persona* and Fellini's *8½*, were comments about the nature of the motion picture and its making, by motion picture makers who had progressed beyond autobiography.

Antonioni is likewise an analyst rather than a translator: he needed Cortázar in order to explain their differences—once their common esthetic quandary had been stated. Cortázar's Michel is an amateur photographer because, for Cortázar, photography is an analogue for the translating word. Antonioni, concerned essentially with the visual statement, knows that the analogue is hasty. Instead, his hero is a professional photographer, a cool product of London's youth and mod cultures—for reasons that have little to do with either London or culture: each protagonist is a maker of art forms and each evidences a similar need to *possess* the world around him through the form he constructs. Thomas has fewer metaphysical questions and, at first, fewer anxieties because he is seen in his former life while Michel is a troubled voice that addresses the reader *after* the event. Also, Thomas does not use words: his world has always been his instantly, through his view-finder. When, in the course of this effortless world-appropriation, each hero is involved in a drama that is too intense for such automatic assimilation, the first reaction of each is identical—and identically wrong. Each believes that his appropriative control persists: on the basis of inadequate evidence, each believes that he has saved a human life. And each must slowly lose his self-assurance through the progressively more urgent questioning of an art object that has now become irremediably *separate* from its maker.

In fact, the two analyses are as different as the different modes that are being analyzed: only the initial posit of absolute possession through the art form, and the failure of that absolute endeavor, are identical. Not having experienced the ambiguous world of words, Thomas is a less complex character than Michel. He is simply his camera: his eye is its lens, his life-rhythm (disjunctive, episodic, made of instants that are neither judged nor related to any other) is the rhythm of his picture taking;[2] it is significant that the only sexual encounter which he follows through to its climax is the one he shares with the model he is photographing. (His attempted intercourse with Jane aborts: it is only prior to their going to bed, when he sees her as a photographer's model, that he is actually *with* her.) His intrusion upon the park scene is not his but his camera's and he will first turn to his camera for the answers to his questions.

Such questions as Thomas will eventually ask derive from his particular phenomenology: he is an esthetic creature, supremely intuitive in his response to shapes, colors and the shades of light and darkness. His studio is visible proof of the fact that he lives in a world of exquisite and unusual colors that are harmonized and contrasted with consummate skill. His eye (in this case,

Antonioni's camera) endows the face of London with the same rich, metallic hues. In *Red Desert* (1964), Antonioni had similarly repainted his natural settings but with less logic: in that film, the chromatic expression of the heroine's inner world inhibited the statement of the crude industrial city that had contributed to induce her frame of mind. Thomas' eye may make of London something which it is not: he is not dependent, as a character, on the image of London as it is. In his first incarnation, he is largely defined by the fact that his eye is a superficial and esthetic caress. The propeller which he buys (and into which nearly every critic read dreams of escape and flight) is a *pleasing* object because of the harmonious lines of the helix. Thomas also spends much of his time in antique shops for the same reason—on a quest for shapes that are interesting and new because they are obsolete. Thomas has yet to go from esthetic intuition to artistic questioning, but he is necessarily moving in that direction. Already, he is in the process of turning a discontinuous artistic intuition (as might be, for example, the publicity or fashion shots of commercial art, limited to a contrived and fraudulent world—that of the synthetic studio and the artificial model—a world reduced to estheticism) into a structured artifact that attempts to interpret and represent a defining world—the world of the *book* about London which he is in the process of *putting together.* It is this inevitable process that must draw him into the same vortex that absorbs Michel and must give him a first resemblance to Cortázar and Antonioni.

Michel, however much he is informed and displaced by Cortázar, remains a fictional creature to be accepted or rejected by the reader, and he uses words whose final meaning is not his but that of the same reader. But when Thomas takes a picture of an identical world (or, more accurately, when Antonioni takes a picture of Thomas' picture), that *sight* is unequivocally the spectator's: there need be no mediation to prevent the immediacy of the spectator's perception and no fictional distancing. Fiction enters into the motion picture world through stimuli that are more equivocal than those of sight—its *voice* (especially its dialogue, but also its music, or as in *Blow-up,* specifically cognitive sounds) or its mood-inducing tones—color, light, shade, etc., all of which Antonioni has generally downgraded, if one thinks of such pictures as *The Cry* (1957), *The Adventure* (1960), *The Eclipse* (1961), etc. But through Antonioni's camera lens, the eye of Thomas (which is his own camera lens) becomes directly the spectator's. The surface sexuality of Thomas is the spectator's who stands in Thomas' position over the model and has approximately the same *contact* with her as does the photographer (scarcely more than a voyeur's). The artist's studio is a *real* studio, inasmuch as both the (fictional) photographer and the (non-fictional) spectator see it through the same lens. As long as Thomas does not *interpret* the transients whom he photographs at the Camberwell Reception Center for his book on London, Antonioni's spectator sees them as superficially, but as immediately, as does his fictional character. When Thomas turns Jane into a model, it is a parafictional model whom the spectator sees—not an actress playing the role of a fictional model—since at that moment she is only *modeling* before a camera. And since there is in fact no fictional photographer, but only Antonioni's camera, the image-maker's statement is instantly his spectator's. It is this unequivocal immediacy of his own eye and the spectator's, and the identity of the surfaces seen by both, that Antonioni will use to analyze and convey the distance that exists for him between his vision and the image that expresses it.

This distance begins with the necessary failure of the artifact to satisfy the artist's intent, an intent for which the modern artist has come to substitute more and more his statement and assessment of that failure, making of his art object the exemplar and the cause of his reflection. The modern art object is double as a result, being both what it is (a statement of the artist's failure) and what it is not (with reference to the parafictional commentary of the artist that is embodied in it). In the Cortázar story, Michel so desires his inadequate artifact to be more than its inadequacy that the artifact is ultimately loosed from the bonds that normally keep it within the phenomenal world and becomes, ironically, the object that *possesses* him. (In a similar way, the hero of Cortázar's "Axolotl" is so fascinated by the salamanders in the aquarium that his exacerbated need to *know* them projects him within the object of his desire: it is as an axolotl that he can finally see the desireless part of him losing interest in, and leaving, the aquarium.) When this intensity to know turns the characters into the representation of the one who conceived them (and the reason for that conception), the characters can no longer tolerate the artifact that has come to stand as an opacity between them and their artistic sense of the world. But they must also be the evidence of the unbridgeable distance that persists between artistic desire and expression: they must enter, without ever penetrating it, the object of their creation (Cortázar's protagonists upset the natural balance of the universe without ever alleviating their artistic dilemma). No critic, to my knowledge, has shown to what extent the blow-ups of Thomas *come alive* in their stillness: the first series yields no clue, showing only a man and a woman walking through a park. For reasons that are more acceptable at the symbolic level and at the level of the story being told, Thomas wants to *know* Jane better than he was able to in his bedroom and he starts enlarging the enlargements. A movement of her head away from her lover directs the attention of Thomas towards the bushes to her left. He begins enlarging the portion that her glance has indicated until the grainy pattern of the tremendous magnification discloses the spectral suggestion of a human figure. From this moment on, Thomas remains within the ambiguity of his own mind: he is no longer his camera but a private consciousness questioning a hitherto unquestioned statement. What happens from now on happens in a realm of unclear statements and tenuous answers.

As answers come less readily, Thomas' fever to know increases: it is he who must now suggest answers. His inner world is mustered frantically to compensate for an exteriority that is gradually separating itself from him (the wind that rustled through the park trees of the original scene is heard once again). Thomas continues to blow up the prints to ever larger dimensions. As he does so, the grain of the prints reveals less and less but affords, proportionally, an ever freer interpretation. The last blow-up is Antonioni's—an extreme close-up of the absurdly magnified print: Thomas believes that it shows a gun held by the figure in the bushes. He thinks he has *penetrated* the photograph: "*The wind's rustling has stopped.* [He phones his friend.] 'Ron? . . . Something fantastic's happened! Those photos in the park! Fantastic! Somebody was trying to kill somebody else. I saved his life . . .' " (*Focus,* p. 139).

He is wrong: that much at least is clear—he was not able to save a life. A little later, by accident, he discovers in the over-enlarged print the grainy suggestion of a corpse partly hidden by the bushes: the prints keep offering suggestions in order to show the tenuousness of any affirmation. At the point where reviewers (and the spectators) should have separated themselves from Thomas and accepted at least the ambiguity of the enlarged photographs, even respectable critics chose to *see* Thomas' interpretation and fell back on positivistic affirmations. None noted how little evidence there is for *any* affirmation, such as would suppose, for example, that the presumed murderer comes out of the bushes after Jane moves towards Thomas (Jane's lover is still alive—the prints show this—until that moment). For a subsequent picture to show the corpse, it is necessary to assume that the man in the bushes shot the older man and dragged the corpse towards partial cover (in broad daylight) during the interval in which Jane attempted to recover the film (fifteen camera shots) and within sight of Thomas, since Jane was able to see Thomas from the spot of the presumed murder.[3] But that is precisely the point: we are no longer in the realm of an absolute statement and an unmediated artifact, but at the core of the problem as Antonioni sees it. In the article previously cited, Freccero describes that problem as a latter-day form of the medieval journey *intra nos,* a self quest no longer accomplished through the spiritual odyssey of morality texts but through the questioning of the artifact for a revelation of the same final truth. Freccero quotes Antonioni on the subject: "We know that beneath the revealed image there is another more faithful to reality, and beneath this still another, and once more another. Up to the true image of reality itself, absolute, mysterious, which no one will ever see. Or perhaps up to the decomposition of any image at all, of any reality at all" (p. 123).

Through the exacerbated eye of the artist, Antonioni is able to place his spectator directly within this Platonic journey towards the Idea by offering that spectator stimuli identical to those that move his fictional hero and are very precisely of Antonioni's making: the picture can be as intense a mystery for the spectator as for Antonioni inasmuch as that picture is the same for both.

The interposed fiction of characters provides the level of commentary. It is Bill, the abstract painter, who says of his own canvases, "While I'm doing them, they don't say anything to me—just one big mess. After a while I find something to hang onto. Like that leg there. Then it comes through by itself. It's like finding the key in a mystery story." The fallacy of Bill's esthetics is that they require his surfaces to yield a meaning. He does not understand that if that "leg" were indeed the "key" to the artistic mystery, he would be required, as a painter, to seek it out in the phenomenal world and paint it. Bill is a fraud: his painting is the haphazard occurrence that allows him, interpretationally, to discover something that he neither discerned in the phenomenal world nor wrought in the artistic one. Bill, the painter, exists only in a verbal and non-painterly dimension.

Bill's is the false path along which Thomas is first led:[4] he is looking for a truth to "hang onto" in an artifact which every succeeding analysis destroys a little more. He is moving away from Antonioni's speculation (which would lead him from the shallowness of representational images to the truth of unintelligible ones): like Bill, Thomas first attempts to move from the opacity of representation to the revelation of an analysis based on that given representation. His error extends his previous mode—the belief in effortless assimilation; he is not yet purged of his former hubris. At this point, Thomas has forgotten the lessons of his estheticism: he liked the propeller because of its *shape*, not because of its function or its symbolism. But a process of growth compensates for this temporary loss; he has begun to question the surfaces which he intuited before (cf. Rimbaud's visionary trajectory as he described it in his "Alchimie du verbe"): Thomas has begun to experience the defining anxiety of the artist.

It is at this point that the spectator should separate himself from Thomas (until he encounters him again at the moment of his final epiphany): the stimuli that affect both Thomas and the spectator are identical, but the spectator does not have the same reasons as Thomas for interpreting what he sees. It should be possible for that spectator to measure the extent of the character's error and, in so doing, to speculate on the reasons for, the form and the consequences of that error. Thomas, the superficial creature of a superficial culture, but one with the affluence and the training at least to *possess* those surfaces, is the right sort of hero to be placed at such a crossroads: it is only a question of time until, having mastered the technical aspects of his craft, he must begin to question the craft itself; and, reinforcing this process, it is likewise only a question of time until his attention to surfaces begins to draw him to a truth concealed beyond those surfaces (once again, cf. Rimbaud). Just as his questioning of the prints represents a first level of growth, the emergence of Jane as a reality beyond the pictorial surface represents an acknowledgement of the phenomenal world that inverts the previous impositions of his esthetic eye (within the contrivances of his studio or upon the brilliant surfaces of his selective London—the "brutality" of which emerged presumably in the moments when the brilliance unexpectedly limed without offering ready reasons or eliciting questions). It is this acknowledgment that takes Thomas away from his prints at last and into the park to see the corpse in its phenomenal unequivocalness. It is interesting that he is interrupted in his new way of seeing by what sounds like the click of a camera shutter.

Having taken these first steps away from his camera, Thomas will not be able to return to its mediating protection. When he comes back to his studio, the prints are no longer there. It is here that Antonioni introduces another parable in his continuing commentary on the nature of the esthetic process. In search of Jane, Thomas reenters a part of his former world, a rock hall where the Yardbirds are performing. The large crowd filling the hall is presumably there for the music. But when one of the performers who is displeased with the working of his electric guitar smashes it and throws the pieces out to the audience, it is apparent that the crowd is part of a cult— their scrambling for the pieces shows that the fragments of the dead guitar are at least as valuable as the music it performed. By accident, Thomas leaves the night spot in possession of a sizable piece of the cultist instrument. His belonging to this mod and swinging world, as well as his special attention to *objects trouvés,* should make the fragment valuable for him. But he is now in a different moment of his journey. He throws the broken instrument away. A passer-by picks it up, but he too belongs to a different world (the world *outside* the rock hall—the night spot being, like the studio, the encapsulated world of a limited number of imposed acceptances): the passer-by is unable to read any significance into the broken guitar which is now discarded for good.

One by one, the unidimensional voices of the closed world in which Thomas dwelled must be stilled. After the uselessness of his camera, he must experience the uselessness of his friends. Late that night, the pot party, at which he tries to talk about the corpse in the park, turns into the same kind of *separateness* as the enlarged prints. Nor is this the end. Since every spiritual journey is essentially a process of denudation, Thomas must lose even the evidence of his phenomenal world. When he returns to the park the following day, the corpse which he had seen by night is no longer there. Thomas is now ready to enact and demonstrate the final parable. As he walks towards the tennis courts, he finds the same Rag Week students (whose presence opens and closes the picture): they are miming a tennis game. There are no rackets, there is no ball: many of the critics who sensed the importance of this final scene assumed that when the mimes direct their attention to Thomas by casting an imaginary tennis ball at his feet and inviting him to return it, Thomas' acceptance signifies his final and irremediable sinking into the world of illusion. This interpretation would not seem to conform either to the previous evolution of Thomas or to the kind of illusion which the mimes represent.

The illusion which the Rag Week students indulge momentarily is of their own making; it is not the passive acceptance of someone else's imposition. They are not *victims* of a set of circumstances (like Bill) but the creators of those circumstances (possibly, even serious creators: they are students and they have been seen previously mingling with a group of peace demonstrators): their illusion is a game, not a truth born of a camera or a cultist guitar.

In the exclusive world of the mod swinger, the neo-individualist establishes his identity through the isolation of induced forms of inwardness—the deafening pitch of his music that encloses him within a world of sound, the narcissism of his dancing that refuses touch, the solitariness of his drug-attained states, the asexual nature of his episodic promiscuity (all of which *Blow-up* examines). And he performs these attempts at individuality in the midst of large and identical groups, accepting a number of given illusions as the emblem of his difference. In contrast with these groups, the small cluster of Rag Week students creates for a moment a willed act of illusion (its gaily outlandish dress and masking) of which the mimed tennis game is symbolic. We may well assume that when Thomas returns the imaginary ball to the mimes, in a *participatory* gesture, he has understood that the self-hypnosis of looking for a leg in a non-objective painting or a gun within the black and white blots of a blow-up is sterile. His gesture is an affirmation of life that rejects both the unquestioning acceptance of surfaces and the imposition of answers dictated by those surfaces. Within an expanded, existential consciousness, the artifact will henceforth require anxious questioning (since it will be *the artist's* expression), but it will no longer be expected to yield the ready answers that still questioning.

Other than being a photographic term, a blow-up is also the explosion that destroys what formerly was. Like Fellini's movies, this one ends in the morning, when the light of day exposes the illusions and the lies of the night (here the actual night and the permanent night of the photographer's studio that is only artificially lit). As Thomas walks away, the sound of a ball being struck by tennis rackets is heard, as once was heard the rustling of the park trees within Thomas' studio. It remains for the spectator to determine whether the sounds are now part of his own reality or part of a rejected image.

Notes

1.   Translated by Roy Huss (*Focus,* p. 5). However thoughtful the statements of a movie maker, they are no match for the instant pronouncements of his reviewers. Antonioni also said: "I do not really intend to make a film about London. The same story could be shot in New York, perhaps also in Stockholm, and certainly in Paris." "As for knowing if it tells a story about our time, or, on the contrary, a story without any relevance to our world, I am incapable of deciding" (*Focus* pp. 10, 11). Nevertheless, the film was generally regarded as a disquisition on the swinging London youth scene—if the reviewer was of a swinging turn of mind—or as a social comment when the reviewer was possessed of a social consciousness. Etc.

2.   Leading socially-conscious critics to logical developments about the hero's alienation in a mercantile world.

3.   Nor is there absolute proof that Jane, after her first outburst in the park, is particularly desperate to recover the film. In Thomas' studio, her attention certainly strays from her purpose and she does not treat the spurious roll, when she has it, as an object of special concern.

4.   When he will show Bill's woman what might be the corpse in one of the magnified prints, she will look at it with unseeing eyes and tell him, "Looks like one of Bill's paintings."

Cortázar's Masterpiece [On *Hopscotch*]

C. D. B. BRYAN

Julio Cortázar was born in Brussels in 1914, is Argentinian, and has lived and worked in Paris since 1952. He is the author of three volumes of short stories and his first novel, *The Winners,* was published in this country last year. He is also a poet, a translator, and an amateur jazz musician. His new novel, *Hopscotch,* has already been hailed by the prestigious *Times Literary Supplement* as "Cortázar's masterpiece. This is the first great novel of Spanish America." However, *Hopscotch* will be in grave trouble here unless the American reader can overcome his innate apathy toward (1) a South American novel (2) about a forty-plus-year-old bohemian's (3) search for meaning in life (4) in Paris and Buenos Aires. Even should this be possible, the reader must still cope with a giddily written Table of Instructions which explains that *Hopscotch* consists of two books:

> "The second should be read by beginning with Chapter 73 and then following the sequence indicated at the end of each chapter. In case of confusion or forgetfulness, one need only consult the following list: 71 - 1 - 116 - 3 - 84 - 4 - 71 - 5 - 81 - 74 - 6 - 7 - 8 - 93 -

and so on for one-hundred-and-forty more chapters. It is not difficult to imagine the glaze now descending over the reader's eyes. And yet, if he succumbs to apathy with this foreknowledge of *Hopscotch,* he will deny himself the opportunity to read the most brilliant novel in years.

Hopscotch is hard going. Deliberately. It is a spiraling, convulsive, exploding universe of a novel. It is the most powerful encyclopedia of emotions and visions to emerge from the postwar generation of international writers. And if it does not render every other novel written about a search for meaning obsolete, *Hopscotch* certainly emphasizes their inadequacy.

The significance of this book's title is explained by the major character in this novel, Horacio Oliveira, as follows:

> "Hopscotch is played with a pebble that you move with the tip of your toe. The things you need: a sidewalk, a pebble, a toe, and a pretty chalk drawing,

From *The New Republic* 154 (23 April 1966):19–23. Reprinted by permission of the author.

preferably in colors. On top is Heaven, on the bottom is Earth, it's very hard to get the pebble up to Heaven, you almost always miscalculate and the stone goes off the drawing. But little by little you start to get the knack of how to jump over the different squares (spiral hopscotch, rectangular hopscotch, fantasy hopscotch, not played very often) and then one day you learn how to leave Earth and make the pebble climb up into Heaven, the worst part of it is that precisely at that moment, when practically no one has learned how to make the pebble climb up into Heaven, childhood is over all of a sudden and you're into novels, into the anguish of the senseless divine trajectory, into the speculation about another Heaven that you have to learn to reach too. And since you have come out of childhood you forget that in order to get to Heaven you have to have a pebble and a toe. . . . A pebble and a toe . . . yes, reach Heaven with kicks, get there with the pebble (carry your cross? Not a very portable object) and with one last kick send the stone up against *l'azur l'azur l'azur l'azur,* crash, a broken pane, the final bed, naughty child, and what difference did it make if behind the broken pane there was the kibbutz, since Heaven was nothing but a childish name for his kibbutz."

Horacio's search assumes just such a random pattern.

There are four major male characters: Horacio Oliveira, the forty-plus-year-old Argentinian living in Paris who realizes that "searching was [his] symbol, the emblem of those who go out at night with nothing in mind, the motives of a destroyer of compasses"; Traveler, Horacio's childhood friend in Buenos Aires, the keeper of a counting cat for the Estrellas Circus, who "hated the name Traveler because he had never been outside Argentina except for trips over to Montevideo and once up to Asunción in Paraguay, centers that he remembered with sovereign indifference"; Morelli, an old man, a philosopher-author, who best understands the meaning, the need for Horacio's search, whom Horacio believes might provide the key; and, last, the author of *Hopscotch* whose presence, whose manipulative restraint is felt throughout. Horacio, Traveler, Morelli and Cortázar are four different men; and yet, each bears a progressive relationship to the other. Traveler is what Horacio would have been, had Horacio not left Argentina. Horacio is what Morelli would have been had Morelli succumbed to the joy of the search for the sake of searching, the search without direction, the "destroyer of compasses"; and Morelli is what Cortázar might have become, had not Cortázar written *Hopscotch*—a theorist, a cataloguer of customs, an accumulator of clippings, notebooks and incomplete novels. The relationship between Cortázar and Morelli is the most tenuous since one blurs into the other. Cortázar, of course, does not actually appear in the novel. And yet he is there, for he has accomplished what the older author, Morelli, merely proposes.

There are two major female characters: La Maga and Talita. Horacio lived with La Maga in Paris until, in a shocking episode in their apartment, La Maga's young son, Rocamadour, died unattended a few feet from where Horacio, La Maga and their friends were intensely discussing the meaning of life. Because of her son's death La Maga left Paris and perhaps returned to Argentina (where she went is never explicit). Horacio goes back to Argentina to find her. But does he? Yes and no. He finds Traveler's wife, Talita, who isn't *really* La Maga, but looks like her, thinks like her, and Horacio even addresses her as La Maga.

Therefore, the characteristics and thoughts of the men and women in *Hopscotch* are superimposed one upon the other until there emerge different levels and currents of perception which, in turn, serve as catalysts affecting the perception of the reader. The reader becomes drawn into the processes of the book, Julio Cortázar somehow—and it is difficult to determine how, or even when this happens—establishes contact with the reader, a contact so personal that the reader becomes physically involved. There *is* a physical involvement, or how else does one explain the reader's willingness to play hopscotch with those back chapters of the book?

What is Horacio searching for? Gregorovius, a minor male character who serves in the dual role of Devil's Advocate and straight man to Horacio asks him:

"But what are you after with all that, Horacio?"

"The freedom of the city. . . . It's a metaphor. And since Paris is another metaphor (I've heard you say so sometimes) it seems perfectly natural that I came here for that reason."

"You," insisted Gregorovius, "have an imperial notion in the back of your head. Freedom of the city? Rule of the city. Your resentment: a half-cured ambition. You came here to find a statue of yourself waiting on the edge of the Place Dauphine. What I don't understand is your method. Ambition, why not? You're outstanding enough in some ways. But up till now all that I've seen you do has been just the opposite of what other ambitious people would have done . . . but without denying ambition. And that's what I don't understand."

"Oh, understanding, you know. . . . It's all very mixed up. Take the bit that what you call ambition can only be productive if it's denied. Do you like that formula? That's not it, but what I want to say is something really unexplainable. You've got to turn round and round like a dog chasing his tail. . . ."

" . . . It's not a path, like Vedanta or things like that, I hope."

"No, no."

"A lay renunciation, could we call it that?"

"Not that either. I'm not renouncing anything. I simply do what I can so that things renounce me. Didn't you know that if you want to dig a little hole, you've got to shovel up the ground and toss it far away?"

"An ambition to clear the table and start all over again, is that it?"

"A little bit, a touch of that, just a hair, a drop. . . ."

What Horacio is searching for really is unexplainable. Each time he attempts to explain *what it is,* he ends up explaining *how to find it.* Throughout the novel the object of Horacio's search appears under various guises: "Freedom of the city"; "an ideal of purity"; a "Millenary Kingdom"; "that conciliation without which life doesn't go beyond being an obscure joke"; "a nonreligious sainthood, a state *without differentiation,* without saints"; "some grasshopper of peace, some cricket of contentment"; "the forgotten kingdom"; and, his best defined, "kibbutz of desire."

> "Kibbutz of desire, a way of summing up closed in tight this wandering from promenade to promenade. Kibbutz: colony, settlement, taking root, the chosen place in which to raise the final tent, where you can walk out into the night and have your face washed by time, and join up with the world, with the Great Madness, with the Grand Stupidity. . . . Kibbutz of desire, not of the soul, not of the spirit . . . that vehement nostalgia for a land where life could be babbled out according to other compasses and other names. . . ."

Horacio's search does not follow compass directions. He is not searching for himself as an individual, "as a supposedly timeless individual," as a "historical entity," because he knows to do so would be a waste of time. Gregorovius was close when he asked Horacio whether his ambition was to start all over again. Horacio's search necessitates his attempts to isolate—never alienate—himself from others. He tries to reach "the dog or the original fish as a starting point for the march towards himself. . . . Search is just what it is *not*. . . . It's not a search because he has already found himself. Just that the finding has not taken any shape." Therefore, since it is not a search, it cannot be "a question of perfecting, of decanting, of redeeming, of choosing, of free-wheeling, of going from the alpha to the omega. *One is already there.* Anybody is already there. The shot is in the pistol; but a trigger has to be squeezed and it so happens that the finger is making motions to stop a bus, or something similar." The problem is, of course, that although Horacio does not intend to alienate himself from others, it does in fact occur because he is so totally absorbed in this search (or non-search) that he cannot enjoy an emotion without first examining it. "We could really have become friends," Gregorovius tells him, "If you had had something human about you." Babs, an unrestrained American contemporary of Horacio and Gregorovius, said about Horacio: "in all her lousy days she'd never met anyone as low, cold-blooded, bastardly, sadistic, evil, butcher, racist, incapable of the smallest kindness, trash. . . ." La Maga tells Horacio "You're like a witness. You're the one who goes to the museum and looks at the paintings. I mean the paintings are there and you're in the museum too, near and far away at the same time. I'm a painting . . . this room is a painting. You think that you're in this room, but you're not. You're looking at the room, you're not in the room." This is one of the symptoms of Horacio's isolation. He calls them "paravisions" and cultivates them. He strives for "an instantaneous aptitude for going out, so that suddenly I can grasp myself from outside, or from inside but on a different plane, as if I were somebody who was looking at me (better still—because in reality I cannot see myself—like someone who is living me). It doesn't last, two steps along the street, the time needed for taking a deep breath (sometimes when I wake up it lasts a little longer . . .) and in that instant I know *what I am* because I know exactly *what I am not.*"

Well, Horacio eventually does discover his kibbutz. He finds it in an insane asylum in Argentina where he, Traveler, and Talita work because it was bought by the manager of the circus. Horacio understands that Traveler is his *doppel-gaenger* and that Talita is La Maga's. Horacio sets a trap for Traveler by leaning out of an upper story window. He is certain that Traveler will be sent to dissuade him from jumping. Horacio then forces an eerie psychological and physical confrontation with Traveler, because he knows that through Traveler he can reach his kibbutz, even though he isn't quite sure how. Afterward, Traveler seeing that Horacio never had any intention of killing himself, rejoins his wife, Talita, in the courtyard below. The asylum director's wife still attempts to lure Horacio away from the window by tempting him with a hot breakfast with nice, hot croissants, and says, "Shall we go make some coffee, Talita?"

> "Don't be an ass," Talita said. And in the extraordinary silence that followed her admonition, the meeting of the looks of Traveler and Horacio was as if two birds had collided in flight and all mixed up together had fallen into square nine, or at least that was how it was enjoyed by those involved. . . . The harmony lasted incredibly long, there were no words that could answer the goodness of those two down there below, looking at him and talking to him from the hopscotch, because Talita had stopped in square three without realizing it, and Traveler had one foot in six, so that the only thing left to do was to move his right hand a little in a timid salute and stay there looking at La Maga, at Traveler, telling himself that there was some meeting after all, even though it might last just for that terribly sweet instant in which the best thing without any doubt at all would be to lean over just a little bit farther . . . and let himself go, paff the end."

Hopscotch is divided into three sections: "From the Other Side," which covers the lives of Horacio and La Maga in Paris; "From This Side," Horacio's life with Traveler and Talita in Argentina; and "From Diverse Sides," the final section composed of the so-called "Expendable Chapters." It is this section which, according to the Table of Instructions, "the reader may ignore with a clean conscience." To do so would be a mistake; it is through these chapters that the reader's sense of personal involvement is accomplished. There are 98 "Expendable Chapters" but the majority of them are no more than a page long, some of them just a few lines from a newspaper clipping, a reference source, or one of Morelli's notebooks. The 98 chapters are inserted between the 56 chapters which make up book one. A reader could begin with book two (book two includes book one), but this will lessen the multidimensional effect gained by covering the material again. To ignore book two entirely, would involve missing the sequences with Morelli and his notes.

Julio Cortázar has absolute control of the craft. He is the master of the simile: "Oh, Maga, whenever I saw a woman who looked like you a clear sharp pause would close in like a deafening silence, collapsing like a wet umbrella being closed." He has delightful eye for detail: "[Horacio] spotted the posters of the Salle de Geographie and took refuge (from the rainstorm) in the doorway. A lecture about Australia, the unknown continent. A meeting of the disciples of the Christ of Montfavet, a piano concert by Madame Berthe Trépat. Open registration for a course on meteors. Win a black belt in judo in five months. A lecture on the urbanization of Lyons." (Horacio attended the concert by Berthe Trépat, and the account of the concert and what follows is perhaps the most brilliant and poignant writing to appear in this novel.) Cortázar can lend grace to the simplest acts as in this excerpt from Morelli's notebook on "forgotten gestures":

> "Tonight I found a candle on a table, and as a game I lit it and walked along the corridor with it. The breeze stirred up by my motion was about to put it out, then I saw my right hand come up all by itself, cup itself, protect the flame with a living lampshade that kept the breeze away. While the flame climbed up again alert, I thought that the gesture had belonged to all of us for thousands of years, during the Age of Fire, until they changed it on us to electric lights."

His descriptive passages are clean and evocative: "Up above, under the lead gutters, the pigeons must have been sleeping, also lead, wrapped up in themselves, perfect antigargoyles." And when languages fail Cortázar (Latin, French, Spanish, Italian, and German words and phrases slip easily into and out of the narrative) he invents his own: Gligish, a cross between double-talk and the Official Sex Manual: ". . . suddenly it was the clinon, the sterfurous convulcant of matericks, the slobberdigging raimouth of the orgumion, the sproemes of the merpasm in one superhumitic agopause." Cortázar uses a few other literary devices to augment his style. Most of them are successful. He occasionally writes in free verse, or he employs parenthetical asides, and even a shorthand reference to literature such as: "and a basic generalization had carried him off, etc. Retrospective jealousy, cf. Proust subtle torture and so on." At one point Cortázar uses numbered paragraphs to indicate degree of understanding between two men who are discussing La Maga. The numbers increase the more they attempt to understand La Maga which only carries them farther away. Another device is the use of wh before a word which makes the narrator self-conscious: " 'Whunity,' whrote Whoracio. 'The whego and the whother.' He used this wh the way other people used penicillin. 'The whimportant thing is not to become whinflated.' " Don't worry, Cortázar does not use it too often.

One device was not successful, and it was not the author's fault but the fault of whoever at Pantheon designed the book. In an attempt to provide an insight into Horacio's mind as he reads a book left behind by La Maga, the author alternates lines from the book with what Horacio is thinking:

> In September of 1880, a few months
> AND the things she reads, a
> after the demise of my father, I de-
> clumsy novel, in a cheap edition
> cided to give up my business activi-
> besides, but you wonder how she
> ties trans-
> can get interested in

and so on. If the designer had used two different type faces (perhaps the novel Horacio is reading in the regular face and Horacio's thoughts in italics or boldface) there would have been no difficulty in reading this section the way the author intended.

An enormous share of the credit for this book must be given its translator, Gregory Rabassa. He may be forgiven for occasional lapses such as "Take the bit that what you call ambition" and "from the word go" because he has succeeded somehow in conveying Cortázar's exuberant style.

Hopscotch cannot be read through in a few sittings. The prose is far too rich. But it is worth it. It is worth it! Cortázar does succeed in making, as Morelli instructs, "an accomplice of the reader, a traveling companion."

Bon Voyage.

Vampires and Vampiresses: A Reading of 62

ANA MARÍA HERNÁNDEZ

Cortázar has always shown a keen interest in the Gothic aspects of vampirism. He is thoroughly acquainted with the numerous *nosferati* preceding and following Bram Stoker's darkly illustrious Count and jokingly refers to himself as one of the "undead," since he is allergic to garlic and preserves an oddly youthful appearance at sixty-two years of age. His interest in vampirism might have been reawakened by the many publications on the theme immediately preceding the writing of *62: A Model Kit;* Valentin Penrose's *Erszebet Báthory, la comtesse sanglante* (Paris, 1962); Roger Vadim, Ornella Volta and Valeria Riva's *The Vampire: An Anthology* (London, 1963); Tony Faivre's *Les vampires* (Paris, 1963); and Ornella Volta's *Le vampire, la mort, le sang, la peur* (Paris, 1962).

    62 works with a very complex system of cross-references and allusions, functioning on different levels but with the central theme of vampirism as a common basis. The novel's major "keys" are presented in the first paragraph. The words spoken by the fat client ("Je voudrais un chateau saignant") refer to a raw Chateaubriand, but also to the "blood castle" at Csejthe (near the town of Fagaras in Romanian Transylvania) where Erszebet Báthory (the "Blood Countess") performed the deeds that made her famous in the early seventeenth century. The restaurant Polidor alludes to Juan's namesake, Dr. John William Polidori (private physician to Lord Byron), who conceived his novel *The Vampyre* during the memorable soirée at the Villa Diodati in Switzerland (15 June 1816) at which Mary Shelley's *Frankenstein* was born. The Byron circle, inspired by Byron's own dramatic recitation of Coleridge's "Christabel," had gathered to create horror stories. At one point in the reading Shelley ran away shrieking; later, they found him, pale as death, leaning against a fireplace. After Polidori revived him with ether, he confessed he had envisioned a woman with eyes in place of nipples.[1] "Vision," as we shall see, is one of the main motifs in *62*.

First published in *Books Abroad*. 50:3 (Summer 1976): 570–76; reissued in *The Final Island: The Fiction of Julio Cortázar*. Ivar Ivask & Jaime Alazraki, eds. (Norman: University of Oklahoma Press, 1978). Reprinted by permission of the publishers.

Polidori's own novel deals with the destructive effects of an uncontrolled, boundless egoism. Lord Ruthven, the vampire in question, is a transparent allusion to Byron. "Christabel," on the other hand, deals with *female* vampirism and has distinct lesbian overtones. The book Juan bought, as we are told later in the paragraph, is by Michel Butor, whose last name is partially homophonous to the Countess's. It also sounds like *vautour* (vulture), a traditionally sinister bird of prey which feeds on the young and the weak, like Lord Ruthven, Christabel, Juan and Hélène—and, of course, the Countess.

Upon entering the restaurant Polidor, Juan decides to sit facing a mirror; immediately we are reminded that vampires, according to folklore, have no reflection. Even though we are not told whether Juan sees his reflection or not, his mental confusion at this point shows that he lacks mental "reflection." Loss of reflection or of the "shadow" is a rather common occurrence in tales of supernatural horror; in most cases, this phenomenon is associated with some kind of diabolical pact or ceremony performed in one of the magical vespers. In "A New Year's Eve Adventure" E. T. A. Hoffmann presented Adalbert von Chamisso's character Peter Schlemihl, who had sold his "shadow" to the devil. The loss of the shadow—Jungian symbol for the repressed, true self—implies a loss of the soul or a loss of virility. Most importantly, it implies the loss of the capacity to establish lasting human relations.[2] A man without a "shadow" is, like Melmoth, a wanderer. Like the hero in Hoffmann's tale, Juan performs his ritual (entering the restaurant Polidor, buying the book, sitting in front of the mirror) on a magical vesper, Christmas Eve. Christmas Eve marks the birth of a Divine Child, likewise a Jungian symbol for the true self. But this child will be condemned to death by men's spiritual "blindness." Similarly, the young patient who represents Juan's true self is condemned to death by Juan's own spiritual blindness and egoism. Juan deliberately looks for loneliness and degradation in the magical vesper associated with love and hope; and as a result of his diabolical rite, he will lose his soul at the end of the novel. The mirror also alludes to the incantatory spells celebrated by Countess Báthory in order to preserve her youthful appearance. She celebrated these rituals at dawn, facing a mirror.

Another "key" is provided by the bottle of Sylvaner that Juan orders. The first letters of its name contain a reference to "the middle syllables of the word in which there beat in turn the geographic center of an obscure ancestral terror."(*62: A Model Kit,* 21)—that is, Transylvania, Cradle of Vampires. Throughout the novel Cortázar alludes to "the Countess" in connection with the Hotel of the King of Hungary but does not mention her by name. Countess Báthory, a native of Hungarian Transylvania, was walled in as a punishment for her crimes. However, neither the crimes nor the punishment took place in Vienna. Critics who have traced the allusions to the Blood Countess have skipped a second set of mirror images: those associating the Viennese Frau Marta with Erszebet Báthory's Aunt Klara, who initiated her niece in the sadistic practices that made her famous. Erszebet's "amusements" had started when her husband, Count Nadasdy, left her for long periods of time to fight the Turks:

> During his [Count Nadasdy's, Erszebet's husband] long absences his bride paid frequent visits to her aunt, the Countess Klara Báthory, a well-known lesbian, who raped most of her ladies-in-waiting, and whose amorous advances to soldiers on guard duty and washerwomen at her castle had made her the talk of Vienna. Her procuress, well provided with funds, had provided a steady stream of attractive and easy-going girls for her lesbian orgies. Countess Elizabeth must have been very much attracted to the sexual perversions devised by her aunt's fertile mind, to judge by her frequent visits.[3]

As Juan and Tell wander around the Blutgasse (a street named after a Mayor Blut, but interpreted by Juan as "the street of blood") expecting to find the spirit of Countess. Erszebet the narrator says "knowing quite well that we weren't going to find her at that hour, although it was probably only because the countess must have been wandering through other ruins" (*A Model Kit*, 82). They know Erszebet's ghost is not there. Is it, then, Klara's ghost they are searching for? Significantly, Clara is the name of the heroine of Cortázar's first, unpublished novel, "El examen." She was married *to a character named Juan.* Does Cortázar include Klara Báthory (Frau Marta) in the novel because he sees her as his own sweet Clara twenty years later? Does he blame Juan for her metamorphosis?

A further key is provided by Tell, who reads a novel by Joseph Sheridan Le Fanu. The novel is, most probably, "Carmilla," reputedly the best vampire story ever written. In this novel, as in "Christabel," the vampire is a woman and a lesbian. She is also eternal, successively reincarnated under anagrams of the same name: Millarca, Mircalla, Carmilla. The novel provided the theme for Carl Theodor Dreyer's movie masterpiece, *Vampyr,* well known to Cortázar. In the novel we find a play of mirrors involving an older, sinister vampiress (Countess Mircalla Karnstein) and a younger, seductive one (Carmilla) who captivates the young heroine with her fatal charms. The theme of lesbianism plays a central role in Cortázar's works. This aberration, openly admitted in the case of Hélène, is subtly suggested in most other feminine characters. Paula forms a strange liaison with the homosexual Raúl; Paula/Raúl, as their names indicate, seem to be two sides of the same personality. During Horacio's conversation with the *clocharde* the latter hints at a possible relationship between herself and La Maga. Ludmilla, Andrés Fava's mistress in *A Manual for Manuel* has a lesbian past as well. Gabriel Ronay observes that in exploring the psychology of lesbian aberrations—one of which is vampirism—the link between love and pain, the most fundamental in the whole range of sexual psychology, is of crucial importance. Women have a natural penchant for rituals involving blood, since the shedding of blood is inseparable from the female's rites of passage (menstruation, defloration, childbirth, et cetera). The lesbian aberrations are often accompanied by a regression to "primitive" courtship rituals wherein the shedding of blood occupies a central place.[5]

Cortázar's male characters often express the primitive's dread for those "women's societies" in which strange rituals beyond the comprehension of men are performed ("The Idol of the Cyclades", "The Maenads", Oscar's dream of the moonstruck girls in *A Manual for Manuel*, Dina [Diana] the black Artemis in "Throat of a Black Kitten.") But the theme has other implications as well. Homosexuality involves a failure to grow beyond the early narcissistic stage and come to terms with the "otherness" of the opposite sex.[6] Cortázar's self-centered, narcissistic heroes are bound to look for women who resemble them as much as possible, so that in loving them they would still be loving themselves. Likewise, in possessing them they would really be possessing themselves. Juan and Hélène are two manifestations of the same personality. A relationship which originates in a failure to deal with "the Other" and in a desire to "recover oneself" must be, in essence, vampiristic.

By dealing with its psychological implications we discover the very essence of Cortázar's vampirism, which is—in spite of the many references to Gothic novels—essentially psychological, like Poe's. Rather than Sheridan Le Fanu's "locked room" situation (briefly parodied in the episode of Frau Marta and the English girl), what we have here is a set of relationships like those uniting Ligeia to her husband or Madeline Usher to her brother. Juan's obsession with the remote, cold and cruel Hélène is as metaphysical as that of the typical Poe hero. For Juan, as for Morella's or Ligeia's husband, "the fires were not of Eros." He really wants to possess Hélène's essence, not her body. He cannot even approach her, and when he does, he does not "see" her. He makes love to "Hélène Arp, Hélène Brancusi, Hélène dama de Elche." Nor does he "see" Tell, on whom he projects his ideal vision of Hélène, too ("lad of Elche, cold astute indifferent courteous cruelty," p. 78). Tell is cast in the role of the physical Lady Rowena whom Ligeia's husband employs in order to bring back his celestial, defunct wife. Tell is indeed nothing more than a "thing" on which Juan "feeds" ("te cosifico," p. 67). The rest of the characters, too, are vampires or are vampirized in their turn: Nicole and Marrast by each other, Celia and Austin by their respective parents, Austin by Nicole, Nicole by Calac (aspiring), "la gorda" by Polanco.

Hélène, the most evident vampiress, is branded by the pin she wears, which has the form of a basilisk: "The basilisk has such a dreadful stare that birds at which it merely glances fall down and are devoured."[7] The vampire, likewise, fixes and petrifies its victim with its stare. "Vision" is Hélène's terrible attribute. Her vision, however, is no different from Juan's "blindness." Hélène does not look at the other in order to see him; she looks at him in order to immobilize and devour him. Neither she nor Juan will be able to break the spell that hangs over them, for they are incapable of understanding the symbolic events of which they are part.

These events start when Hélène's patient dies. From the moment she sees him, Hélène will identify her young patient with Juan. After he dies, she falls into a trance during which she associates him with past memories and vague anticipations regarding herself and Juan. The patient becomes a link between her past and her future. While thinking of him, she centers her attention on the advertisement of "the girl who loves Babybel cheese"; her eyes appear like tunnels leading to something she needs to discover—or recover. Then, as if by chance, she meets Celia, the exact opposite of the young man who has died. Celia has just broken away from *las escolopendras,* her family, and confronts life like a young mythological heroine, a Psyche. To Hélène, she appears as overwhelming as the girl in the ad. Hélène, rather than breaking away from her own *escolopendras,* misunderstands the message and tries to reach "the other side of the tunnel" through Celia, whom she associates with the doll she has just received from Tell. The doll is Hélène herself: a petrified figure hiding an undefined or perverted sexuality. Celia, on the other hand, appears as the promise of deliverance. But like the hero in Hoffmann's "The Sandman," Hélène must *see* through the doll. She does not. Instead, she tries to "fix" Celia, to absorb her life and turn her, too, into a doll or a vampiress. She loses her first chance of deliverance when she kills the young patient. He was Juan's soul and, as such, the reckless young hero who could have killed "the basilisk" and delivered the maiden hidden inside herself. She misses her second chance when, having failed to recover her own soul and live her own life, she tries to absorb Celia's. She reenacts the fate of Countess Erszebet, who, having wasted her life waiting for a perennially absent husband, attempted, after his death, to steal from others the youth she had lost forever:

> The death of her husband in 1604 had a shattering effect on Countess Eliza-beth, and played an important role in the loosening of the last vestiges of con-trol over her bloodlust . . . she resolved to bathe regularly in virgins' blood. She took these baths at the magic hour of 4 a.m., when the dark forces of night were already powerless and the first nascent rays of light heralded the birth of a new day.[8]

Celia, however, understands the ceremony when she breaks the doll by acci-dent. The doll was her own motionless and lifeless existence as an undefined adolescent; she breaks the bisexual doll, thereby breaking the homosexual spell Hélène had tried to place on her.

Hélène seems somehow to hold Juan responsible for the course the events have taken. Indeed, if she had to decipher the doll's and the patient's message, he had to decipher at the same time the meaning of the scene between Frau Marta and the English girl. Yet at the decisive point, when Frau Marta is about to possess the girl, Juan fails to understand what these actions mean: "Things have taken place in a different way, maybe because of us, because of something I was on the point of understanding and didn't understand" (187). When Parsifal fails to ask about the mysteries in the Grail Castle, castle, king, Grail and attendants all disappear and the Waste Lands remain sterile. Only the eye of consciousness can break the spell. Likewise, Juan fails to ask the meaning of the scene he witnesses. As the result of this failure Hélène's life remains waste.

In their studies of the theme of vampirism in Poe's works Allen Tate and D. H. Lawrence agree that Poe's heroines are turned into vampires through a man's inability to awaken them to womanhood: "D. H. Lawrence was no doubt right in describing as vampires [Poe's] women characters; the men, soon to join them as 'undead,' have, by some defect of the moral will, made them so.[9] The same can be said of Hélène. When Juan finally visits her apartment, he fails to kill the Gorgon in her by symbolically piercing her with his sword (phallus), because he has not subjugated her first with the eye of consciousness. She retaliates by "petrifying" him, symbolically castrating him. After a night of love, she mocks his very manhood, laughing in his face and telling him "Celia meant the same as you" (273). Indeed, there is no difference between him and Celia, except that Celia succeeds in outgrowing her adolescent vagueness after she leaves Hélène's apartment. Juan chooses not to: "I lost myself in analogies and bottles of white wine. I got to the brink and preferred not to know. I consented to not knowing, even though I could have"(273–74). He does not want to know because he does not want her reality to interfere with his own selfish vision of her. But by petrifying her, he becomes, paradoxically, her victim. As Esther Harding observes, love for an ideal vision is a sin against the Moon Goddess, against life.[10] Juan sees Hélène as Diana, himself as Acteon (235); he is right when he fears, in his nightmare, "el Perro's" revenge. Diana's dogs (34, 238) represent her "terrible" side, unleashed in order to destroy and dismember Acteon, who looked at her body without *seeing* her. His inability to see Hélène makes Juan cling to her, vampire-fashion—or like a child to its mother—expecting her to satisfy his needs and conform to his ideal of her. But this expectation robs him of his manhood: "It is, as the ancient myth puts it, a castration to the mother . . . not the initiation ordeal voluntarily taken with a religious motive. It is an involuntary sacrifice to the mother, which brings no renewal."[11]

Austin's meeting and falling in love with Celia stands out as one of the most idyllic love scenes in the whole of Cortázar's writings. In this scene Austin and Celia "look"—literally and symbolically—at one another. Open, honest love between man and woman breaks the spell of the vampire. Through their act of love Austin and Celia, now free, are cleansed from their former "perverse" entanglements; they take the "bath" Juan and Hélène were always unable to take in their nightmare. Juan and Hélène, on the other hand, experience a blind, negative and mutually destructive encounter. Imprisoned in their respective egos, they act out a grotesque parody of the act of love.

Austin, described as "Parsifal" and later as "Gallahad" and "Saint George," acts the part of the mythological hero, slaying the Dragon he has first "seen." But Juan, who has lost his shadow, will be cursed with the repetition of that one event he did not understand in the Hotel of the King of Hungary. In the scene where Austin kills Hélène we read that "Someone, perhaps a woman, cried out in the bed, one single time." Later, after Hélène has been killed, we read that "Someone cried out again, fleeing through a door in the back of the room. Face up, Hélène's eyes were open" (278). That "someone" is Nicole, in whom the slain vampiress's spirit becomes reincarnated in order to haunt Juan. When he leaves the apartment after finding Hélène's corpse, he sees Nicole on a boat, sailing toward the sunset, about to jump into the water. He prepares to jump after her, but it is too late—Frau Marta (Klara Báthory) takes her by the arm, whispers in her ear, takes her to a certain hotel. Nicole is, in reality, a mirror image of Hélène, just as Marrast and Calac are mirror images of Juan. The latter's spiritual impotence is reflected in Marrast's statue (sculpted on an "oilcloth stone" and, as such, "soft") and in Calac's "failure." Juan/Marrast/Calac fail Hélène/Nicole through their deliberate blindness and softness, and the latter retaliate by turning into vampires and haunting them. At the end of the novel Juan cannot participate in Feuille Morte's "rescue." He is a victim of his own monster.

Notes

1. E. F. Bleiler, ed., *Three Gothic Novels,* New York, Dover, 1966, p. xxxv.
2. E. F. Bleiler, ed., *The Best Tales of Hoffmann,* New York, Dover, 1968, p. xxiii. The vampire in Hoffmann's story is called Julia.
3. Gabriel Ronay, *The Truth About Dracula,* New York, Stein & Day, 1970, p. 102.
4. Page numbers refer to *62: A Model Kit,* Gregory Rabassa, tr., New York, Pantheon, 1972.
5. Ronay, p. 106.
6. "The stage of development from which paranoids regress to their original narcissism is sublimated homosexuality . . . they reduce the chief pursuer to the ego itself, the person formerly loved most of all . . . the homosexual love object was originally chosen with a narcissistic attitude towards one's own image." Otto Rank, *The Double: A Psychoanalytic Study,* Chapel Hill, N.C., University of North Carolina Press, 1970, p. 74. Also R. D. Laing, *The Divided Self,* New York, Pantheon, 1969, pp. 146–47.
7. Bram Stoker, *The Annotated Dracula,* Leonard Wolf, ed., New York, Potter, 1975, p. 54, note 16.
8. Ronay, pp. 116–18.
9. Allen Tate, "Our Cousin, Mr. Poe," *Poe: A Collection of Critical Essays,* Robert Regan, ed., Englewood Cliffs, N.J., Prentice-Hall, 1967, p. 42; D. H. Lawrence, "Edgar Allan Poe," *Selected Literary Criticism,* Anthony Beal, ed., New York, Viking, 1956, pp. 330–46.
10. M. Esther Harding, *Woman's Mysteries: Ancient & Modern,* New York, Putnam, 1970, pp. 196–97.
11. Ibid., p. 202.

The Deluxe Model [on *62: A Model Kit*]

C. D. B. Bryan

I can no longer tell you what *62: A Model Kit,* this most recent of Cortázar's works of fiction, is about. I did know at the moment I finished it: and later on I still *thought* I knew. But now, having returned to the book to read certain passages again, I discover that those "certain passages" never existed, or that they don't exist quite the way I remember them, or that what I had been searching for was said by someone quite different from whom I thought had said it, that the incident occurred not between character "A" and character "B" but between "A" and "C" (although "B" said something very similar to "D" as well) and that it all took place *before,* not after the murder which may or may not have been committed at all. And disquieting as this reading experience might seem to be, it was absolutely satisfying and enlightening and exactly what Julio Cortázar intended.

The "62" in the title refers to Chapter 62 of Cortázar's masterpiece, *Hopscotch,* in which the character Morelli (a character, I would think, based partly on Cortázar, partly on Borges—part Master and part Impatient Pupil) proposes writing a novel in which

> . . . standard behavior (including the most unusual, its deluxe category) would be inexplicable by means of current instrumental psychology. The actors would appear to be unhealthy or complete idiots. Not that they would show themselves incapable of current *challenges and responses:* love, jealousy, pity, and so on down the line, but in them something which Homo sapiens keeps subliminal would laboriously open up a road as if a third eye were blinking out with effort from under the frontal bone.

"The subtitle *A Model Kit,*" the author explains in the opening to this new book

> . . . might lead one to believe that the different parts of the tale, separated by blank spaces, are put forth as interchangeable elements. If some of them are, the framework referred to is of a different nature—sensitive sometimes on the writing level, where recurrences and displacements try to be free of all causal

From *Review* 72 (Winter 1972):32–34. Reprinted by permission of the author.

fixedness, but especially on the level of meaning where the opening for combinatory art is more insistent and imperative. The reader's option, his personal montage of the elements in the tale, will in each case be the book he has chosen to read.

What Chicken Tastes Like

62: A Model Kit is the inevitable step forward in Cortázar's development. And it is as lean as *Hopscotch* was fat. The reader had to work to get through *Hopscotch;* and although the reward was certainly commensurate with the effort, the more rigid and disciplined selectivity exercised by the author in his *62: A Model Kit* provides an infinitely more relaxing and less tedious reading. The key distinction between *Hopscotch* and *62: A Model Kit* is that in the former Cortázar's allegiance was to content, in the latter he is more interested in the concept, a concept which though equally philosophical, scientific, and incorporeal, is above all literary. To describe what he is writing about, however, is a little bit like trying to write what chicken tastes like or, to use an example I believe was Cortázar's, like explaining the color brown to a blind man.

Begin with Dèscartes's *Cogito, ergo sum* and the acceptance that the one thing that cannot be doubted is doubt itself. Proceed along with Descartes's use of Saint Anselm's "proof" (that our ability to conceive of an Infinite Being is evidence that such a being exists) to reach the conclusion that since God exists then reality exists because God would not deceive inquisitive, rational man's mind through perceptions that are illusions. Continue, then, through the existentialists who share in common, at least, the concept that the major problem is human existence, that reason is incapable of explaining the enigmas of the universe and that all men who confront the problem of life share a common anguish through their inability to resolve these paradoxes. Then accompany Sartre through the next step in which man, recognizing the futility of his efforts to resolve the paradoxes, accepting only proof of his own existence (again: *Cogito, ergo sum*), perceives himself as utterly alone and the universe as absurd. It is this aloneness, then, that permits him the *freedom* (a key word in Cortázar's lexicon) to choose, to reject, to behave howsoever he may wish without dependency, obligation, justification, acceptance, with the understanding that the emotional price he must pay for that freedom will be the anguish and despair of aloneness while celebrating (silently, one might hope) the intellectual processes which brought him there. Then, from Chapter 99 of *Hopscotch,* add the startling evidence that

> . . . the hygienic retreat of a Descartes appears partial and even insignificant to us today, because at this very moment there is a Mr. Wilcox in Cleveland who with electrodes and other apparatus is proving that thought and an electromagnetic circuit are the same thing. . . . Add to that the fact that a Swede has

just put forth a very impressive theory on cerebral chemistry. Thinking is the result of the interaction of certain acids. . . . *Acido, ergo sum.* . . . You can see then how the *cogito,* that Human Operation *par excellence,* is nowadays located in a rather vague region, somewhere between electromagnetism and chemistry, and probably not as different as we used to think from things like an aurora borealis or a picture taken with infra-red rays.

Given all of the above, then interject those extraordinary superstitions and intuitions about *déjà vues,* other realities, and "other sides" which one can find explained with such suspicious rationality in Carlos Castaneda's books, *The Teachings of Don Juan: A Yaqui Way of Knowledge* and its sequel, *A Separate Reality: Further Conversations with Don Juan,* and couple this with that unspoken, rampant paranoia all existentialists seem heir to. (Why else would they insist so on identifying the reality behind their random fate if not because they felt they were being pursued by some insidious conspiracy after all?) Blend in a pinch of Zen (although, God knows, the search for *satori* remains, the interest, really, is more in its language and its uses since the attempt is to duplicate the manner of Zen anecdotes where the most apparently trivial exchanges—punctuated by blows—reveal themselves to be of the most sublime and profound Zen nature) and let simmer in the back of the mind until only a thick, heavy residue of anguish remains: as in *62: A Model Kit.*

> But *beneath it all* I know that everything is false, that I'm already far away from what just happened to me and that, as on so many other occasions, it comes down to this useless desire to understand, missing, perhaps, the obscure call or signal of the thing itself, the uneasiness I'm left with, the instantaneous display of another order where memories, potentials, and signals break out to form a flash of unity which breaks up at the very instant it drags and pulls me out of myself. Now all of this has left me with just one kind of curiousity—the old human topic: deciphering. And the rest of it, a tightening at the mouth of the stomach, the dark certainty that around there somewhere, not with this dialectical simplification, a road begins and goes on.

It is from this residue of anguish that Cortázar must distill his literature—without depending upon any of the traditional literary or linguistic forms.

Again, from *Hopscotch* about Morelli:

> . . . one would have to recognize that this book was before anything else a literary undertaking, precisely because it was set forth as the destruction of literary forms. . . .

And again:

> Language means residence in a reality, living in a reality. Even if it's true that the language we use betrays us . . . wanting to free it from its taboos isn't enough. We have to relive it, not reanimate it.

CONTENT AND CONCEPT

Let me return for one final time to my distinction between *Hopscotch* and *62: A Model Kit:* the distinction between content and concept. Cortázar's concept has always been, I believe, to write a book that takes place less on the printed page than in the reader's mind. He states in *Hopscotch* that the novel that interests him is

> . . . not one that places characters in a situation, but rather one that puts the situation in the characters. By means of this the latter cease to be characters and become people. There is a kind of extrapolation through which they jump out at us, or we at them. Kafka's K. has the same name as his reader, or vice versa.

He also says:

> . . . I wonder whether someday I will ever succeed in making it felt that the true character and the only one that interests me is the reader, to the degree in which something of what I write ought to contribute to his mutation, displacement, alienation, transportation.

Obviously the content of *62: A Model Kit* is fascinating or else there wouldn't be any point in going through all of this: but for me, the more satisfying interest lies in the author himself. It is Cortázar's search that is so important because he is searching for a *collective* reality that we are all searching for—and he seems closer to finding it than anybody else.

Postmodernist Collage and Montage in
A Manual for Manuel

SANTIAGO JUAN-NAVARRO

In his last novel, *A Manual for Manuel,* Julio Cortázar explores one of the central paradoxes of postmodernist aesthetics: how to create an oppositional literature within an increasingly relativistic sociocultural context. As do many other contemporary Latin American writers, Cortázar addresses the intellectual's commitment within a climate of political change and philosophical skepticism. He seeks a compromise between the aesthetically and politically committed narrative form that could result in an alternative to the extreme contingency of contemporary thought, striving to maintain that difficult balance. On the one hand, he effectively avoids the usual tendency of political literature toward realism; on the other, he tries to escape the narcissism that characterizes many antirealist currents in contemporary fiction.

Three theoretical points of reference allow us to understand Cortázar's late work within the context of postmodern thought: the metahistorians' revision of historical production, the debate regarding the possibility of an aesthetic alternative to global hegemonic culture, and the emergence of self-conscious historical fictions as part of the postmodern literary mainstream. These three conceptualizations of postmodern theory and practice are well exemplified by the works of Hayden White, Fredric Jameson, and Linda Hutcheon, respectively.

Of all the revisionist philosophers of history, White has exerted the greatest influence—at least among literary critics—because of his tropological approach to historiography. Throughout his essays, White dismantles the empirical pretensions of traditional history and shows the formal similarities between the discourse of history and that of fiction. His primary object of study is "the status of the historical narrative, considered purely as a verbal artifact." By means of a minute analysis of the strategies of emplotment and figuration in historical narrative, White attempts to reveal the inevitable ideological mediations present in the writing of history.

This essay is published here for the first time by permission of the author.

Similarly, Cortázar's literary production of the 1970s and early 80s (until his death in 1984) reflects on narrative theory. Occasionally, the superimposition of historical and fictional levels shapes the structural pattern of his works. He tends to present official history as a mere simulacrum, a cultural artifice created on the basis of social needs and political pressures. Confronted by these monolithic visions of reality, he proposes an alternative epistemology characterized by the plurality and flexibility of its discursive forms. Although he never denies the existence of the past—indeed, he recurrently reflects on it—Cortázar suggests that our access to that past can only be channeled through other texts, which are by their very nature incomplete and limited. Within his consideration of the essentially narrative character of both historical and novelistic works, Cortázar mirrors at the level of fiction the postulates developed by the metahistorians in the philosophy of history.

Historical relativism as posed in Cortázar's works implies not a renunciation of representation but a radical problematization of its practices. Unlike the exclusively reflexive experiments of many novels of the 1960s, his political metafictions refocus literary self-consciousness back onto the historical world. Opposed to the critical pessimism of many postmodernist thinkers, Cortázar integrates historical revisionism into a program of social transformation. For him, epistemological skepticism and self-consciousness are two essential components in a program that seeks the transformations of the existing forms of representation in both history and fiction.

In his desire to democratize access to the past, Cortázar constructs a flexible and open narrative that requires the active participation of the reader both in the process of textual reconstruction and through his or her moral commitment to the message of change the work proposes. This effort to unveil the inherent contradictions within hegemonic cultural practices and simultaneously to place them at the service of a radical political agenda may be seen as a response to the cultural impasse of postmodernism, as theorized by leftist critics such as Fredric Jameson. In his analysis of postmodern society, Jameson expresses an apocalyptic view in which images and simulacra have displaced reality itself. In the face of the all-powerful capacity of the system to co-opt all kinds of insurgency, Jameson questions the possibility of an effective oppositional alternative to this state of affairs.[2] In what follows, Cortázar's *A Manual for Manuel* is analyzed as a conclusive example of such a possibility.

A third perspective in the postmodernist debate is provided by Linda Hutcheon. In her two major works on this topic (*A Poetics of Postmodernism* and *The Politics of Postmodernism*), Hutcheon proposes the term "historiographic metafiction" to describe what she considers to be the most representative form of postmodernist narrative. The works that she ascribes to this fictional mode respond to a paradoxical impulse: they purport to be self-referential, but they are presented as ultimately subject to history. In reflecting on themselves and on their own process of production and reception, these works initially convey the false impression that the literary work enjoys fictional and linguistic autonomy, a mirage that the text itself dispels. Likewise, the inclusion of historical characters and situations within the fictional context of these works aims at undermining the pretensions of objectivity and empiricism traditionally held by historiography. No matter how self-referential and reflexive they might seem, these works ultimately assert their subjection to history, a history that is depicted as equally incapable of escaping from the limitations of all cultural constructions.

Another aspect of Hutcheon's postmodern view of narrative developed fully in *A Manual for Manuel* refers to the use and abuse of intertextual and paratextual heterogeneous discourses. As in Hutcheon's analysis, intertextuality in Cortázar's novel is not limited to an occasional reference to other texts of the literary and the historiographic traditions but extends to mass culture. This hybridization of genres and multiple discursive practices tends to problematize the referent in conventional forms of representation and ultimately aims at establishing the textual nature of our experience of the world. Whereas according to the epistemology of realism, the referent was a prelinguistic reality ("the total objective process of life,"[3] for historiographic metafictions such as *A Manual for Manuel* every referent is itself always textual and thus mediated by other texts. In contrast with the apocalyptic dismissal of the referent),[4] these works claim that it has not disappeared but has, in fact, ceased to be simple and unproblematic. It has become unstable and textual. This "textualization" of the referent also implies a questioning of the human subject as a knower of an objective and passive world. Hutcheon associates this subject with the Western bourgeois white individual male subject who has always obtained power by masking himself as eternal, universal, and humanist. In contrast to this subject's pretensions of objectivity and common sense, historiographic metafiction affirms that any enunciative act is always mediated and therefore serves particular interests.

The dominant concerns among these three conceptualizations of postmodernism can be explored in most of Cortázar's late work (after the publication of *A Manual for Manuel* in 1973). The focus of his early fiction was on pure literature rather than on sociohistorical phenomena. Whenever historical motifs were present, they were treated obliquely, or employed to consolidate an aestheticist worldview in the line of international modernism. Cortázar began to write political fiction and essays regularly only after his firsthand discovery of revolutionary Cuba.[5] In *A Manual for Manuel* Cortázar examines this shift in both his life and his work. Apart from the minor inconsistencies pointed to by critics and by Cortázar himself, *A Manual for Manuel* is a crucial piece of Cortázar's oeuvre. Without this work it would be difficult to understand his political and literary evolution. In the following pages, I will discuss one of the most striking aspects of the novel in relation to historiographic metafiction and to postmodernism in general: the use of collage and montage discourse to communicate a fragmentary view of Latin America in the early 1970s.

Cortázar regularly employed narrative fragmentation and juxtaposition in many of his works. In book-collages such as *La vuelta al dia en ochenta mundos* (1967) and *Ultimo Round* (1969) (selections from both volumes appear in *Around the Day in Eighty Worlds* [1986]), he combines different visual materials (drawings, pictures, and graphs) with various literary genres (poetry, essay, and short fiction). The result is a melange of artistic and literary forms that challenges the notion of the text as a rigid artifact. This combination of the visual and the verbal is also apparent in works as unclassifiable as his illustrated collection of poems *Salvo el crepúsculo* (1984; *Save Twilight* [1997]); the visionary *Prosa del observatorio* (1972), which merges mysticism, science, architecture, and photography into a flowing poetic prose; and the art "anthology" *Territorios* (1978), in which the narrative texts maintain an active dialogue with the works of several Latin American visual artists.

In addition to the amalgamation of distinctive discourses, Cortázar's works tend to parallel techniques of film montage, in that they are organized in fragmented segments and narrated from multiple perspectives. Some of his earliest stories are composed on the basis of interwoven levels that offer the reader various perspectives and suggest original syntheses.[6] The influence of cinema can also be studied on thematic and symbolic levels, to the extent that Cortázar occasionally employs references to movies and film metaphors to mirror the inner workings of his own writing.

In *A Manual for Manuel,* Cortázar freely uses the expressive possibilities of both collage and montage to convey his aesthetic and political vision. Even though modernist writers had already mastered and refined most of these possibilities, Cortázar imbues *A Manual for Manuel* with a new sense of political immediacy that has to be understood in the highly politicized context of Latin America during the 1970s. The importance of collage and montage is noticeable in the novel's plot structure, narrative techniques, and ideology. The plot of *A Manual for Manuel* revolves around the activities of a revolutionary group of Latin American expatriates. While living in Paris, they carry out an intricate plan ("La Joda"; [The Screwery]) to kidnap an international undercover agent. Throughout the book, members of the group are making a scrapbook of newspaper clippings to preserve memories of their day for Manuel, the infant son of one of the revolutionaries. It becomes progressively clear that Manuel's scrapbook is in fact the novel we are reading, a novel in which the narrative alternates with various documentary materials. Aside from this journalistic collage, *A Manual for Manuel* is organized in narrative segments through which it is impossible to establish a stable narrative authority. The impression is that of a series of fragments that, as in film montage, require final assembly by the viewer-reader.

Along with the fragmented plot and literary techniques, the novel presents a similarly scattered vision of Latin American reality in the early 1970s. Famous political events are interspersed with seemingly trivial news without a definite hierarchy or even a rigorous chronological order. From the novel emerges a lesser-known version of history that favors discontinuity and fragmentation over organic and totalizing perspectives.

Cortázar's experiments with these forms seek to articulate the playfulness of cubist experiments, to spotlight mass media's preoccupation with the here and now, and to communicate a political message about the relationship between the Latin American intellectual and historical reality. The following sections describe the two major forms of narrative heterogeneity and fragmentation in *A Manual for Manuel:* on the one hand, the insertion of newspaper clippings in the novel (paratextual collage) and, on the other, the division of the novel into narrative segments and multiple perspectives to be "assembled" by the reader (montage).

I

In *A Manual for Manuel* the paratextual materials consist mostly of newspaper clippings that are contemporary to the period in which the novel was written. These paratexts can be divided into three major areas: (1) repression under Latin American military rule, (2) acts of armed resistance against that repression, and (3) eccentric news and advertisements. As the authorial-narrative voice of the prologue points out, the clippings were randomly incorporated as the novel was written (1969–1972). They attempt to offer an almost day-to-day chronicle of events in Latin America during these years—"la historia de nuestros días" [or the history of our own times].[7] The only clippings that openly and admittedly attempt to manipulate the reader's opinion are those at the novel's end, when Cortázar directs the reader's attention toward the international web of repression and especially the role of the United States government within it. An analysis of their content reveals that although the clippings do not directly refer to some of the most significant political events of these years, they convey the major trends of Latin American society during the late 1960s and early 70s.

The novel's paratexts provide detailed information about human rights violations in Central America, Argentina, Brazil, the Soviet Union, and Vietnam. The portrayal of Latin American political life focuses on events that occurred under Argentine military rule, paradoxically known as the "Revolución argentina" (1966–1973). Among the events mentioned are General Onganía's coup d'état (*MM,* 106), the imposition of military values on civil society (*MM,* 123), the popular struggle and uprisings during this period (*MM,* 304, 305), the increasingly high foreign debt (*MM,* 309), the government's servility toward the United States (*MM,* 333), waste in military spending (*MM,* 335), and the torture and inhuman treatment of political prisoners (*MM,* 373–84). Even those articles concerning Western countries

(France and the United States) are somehow related to the situation in Latin America.[8] In fact, military repression—initiated during Onganía's and Levingston's presidencies and further intensified during Videla's and Galtieri's regimes—utilized many of the techniques established by the French counterinsurgence in Algeria and the United States Army in Vietnam.[9] These international connections are dramatically revealed by the incorporation of impersonal statistics in the paratexts. By alluding to the participation of French security forces in the repression of Third World liberation movements, Cortázar seeks to destroy the image of France and other Western countries as the custodians of international peace and democracy. The novel's criticism of the repressive role of the United States goes even further in the final four articles, in which United States intelligence services and armed forces are depicted as being directly responsible for political repression, especially in Latin America and Southeast Asia. In the first of these clippings, United States interventionism in Latin America is established by means of a chart showing the number of United States military assistants in the region. The next two paratexts are reproduced in parallel columns. On one side are testimonies given by political prisoners tortured in Argentine prisons, and on the other, the testimony of United States soldiers who participated in torture sessions in Vietnam. The last clipping in the series is another chart, this one showing the number of Latin American officers trained in the United States. The source for both charts is the United States Department of Defense. Although the conclusion makes no explicit accusations, its implications cannot be clearer: the United States government finances political repression in Latin America and trains its executioners; the struggle against state terrorism goes hand in hand with the fight against U.S. imperialism.

In addressing this situation of generalized state terrorism, the novel justifies revolutionary violence. On both the textual and paratextual levels, *A Manual for Manuel* contemplates the urban guerrilla movements' final moments of splendor, before their rapid decline. Many of the articles specifically cite the guerrilla activity in Argentina (*MM*, 154, 186–87, 304), Uruguay (*MM*, 80, 219, 322), Brazil (*MM*, 96, 204, 299), Mexico (*MM*, 318), and Bolivia (*MM*, 310). In most cases, they describe kidnappings carried out by the extreme left. Such kidnappings were used as a means of attracting international attention and obtaining either the liberation of political prisoners or money to finance their activities.

The political strategies of these radical movements were based initially on the principles of *foquismo,* the theory of guerrilla warfare begun during the Cuban revolution, refined by Ernesto "Che" Guevara, and popularized by the French philosopher Régis Debray. *Foquismo* was based on the assumption that the revolutionary process was a spontaneous and dynamic one. Therefore, for a revolution to occur, no certain, specific objective conditions must be met; rather, the process itself will create them. *Foquismo* theory originally advocated the establishment of an operative base—a *foco*—in a remote region (preferably in the mountains) that would act as a stimulant and catalyst for mass revolution.[10] This idea began to lose credibility after Che Guevara's failed Bolivian expedition (1967) but survived nevertheless under different forms. In most cases the rural headquarters were replaced by urban centers, and in this way large cities became the operative hubs of activity for many guerrilla movements.[11] In South America *foquismo* theory was put into practice by several armed groups in Argentina, Uruguay, Venezuela, Bolivia, Colombia, and Perú during the 1960s and 70s. Most of these urban guerrilla movements were crushed by police, the army, and paramilitary groups during the mid 70s, as was the case in Argentina. In Venezuela and Uruguay, these armed organizations were integrated into the political mainstream as legal parties, while in Colombia and Perú they continued on the path of armed struggle.

In the years after 1972, Argentina's political panorama would rapidly and radically change, with guerrilla groups playing a comparatively insignificant role. In light of this, along with the book's specific subject matter and its precise, pragmatic goals, it is not surprising that Cortázar tried to have his novel published as quickly as possible.[12] *A Manual for Manuel* was in press by the end of 1972, but its actual publication was delayed until spring of 1973. It was finally released only a few days after the Peronist candidate Héctor Cámpora won the March elections. Cortázar's anxiety about the novel's urgent publication can be understood in relation to the crucial political changes that were taking place during those years, including, among others, the possibility of a political normalization in Argentina, the increasing suppression of guerrilla warfare, and the announcement of the withdrawal of U.S. troops from Vietnam. Had Cortázar spent a long time making stylistic changes and working out various inconsistencies, *A Manual for Manuel* could have lost its impact, which was wholly dependent on the timeliness of its release. A return to democracy in Argentina might have lessened the applicability of many issues raised by the novel. The dying urban guerrilla movements may have also lessened the impact of a novel whose plot centers around the activities of one of these groups. Finally, regarding the issue of U.S. interventionism, the final phase in Cortázar's writing of *A Manual for Manuel* coincides with the beginning of peace talks with the Vietcong. The withdrawal of troops from Vietnam could have been viewed as the first step toward a new era of moderation in U.S. expansionist policy.[13]

A final group of newspaper clippings consists of advertisements and stray news items. Among those included are articles about a sordid homosexual crime (*MM*, 321), a boxing match narrated in an unintelligible language, a robbery committed by a sociology student (*MM*, 26), the revolt and escape of young girls at a boarding school (*MM*, 107), and a surrealistic advertisement of sleeping bags (*MM*, 319).

What is the significance of Cortázar's apparently random inclusion of journalistic documents in *A Manual for Manuel?* Why are advertisements and sports chronicles placed next to political news? As is characteristic of the collage technique, Cortázar refuses to create a comprehensive vision into which all these events might be integrated. Instead, he opts for an imperfect juxtaposition of reality jolts. Unlike the decontextualization of collage in modernist painting,[14] *A Manual for Manuel* creates a recontextualization of the paratexts. Headlines preserve the original information, which in turn acquires new meanings within the novel's network of relationships.

Sometimes the paratexts "comment" on each other without any direct participation by the characters or the narrator. Such is the case in the previously mentioned clippings about United States military aid to Latin American countries. Whether isolated or preserved in their original context (for example, the United States Department of Defense reports), these clippings present a harsh statistical reality. However, because they are placed directly before and immediately after the confessions of tortured militants and North American torturers in Vietnam, they acquire a new meaning colored by the emotional value of these interviews. Similarly, the guerrilla violence is not directly justified by a political speech, but rather through another clipping in which the widow of a Tupamaro guerrilla fighter explains the circumstances in which armed insurgence originates: It is very important to realize that hunger-violence, misery-violence, oppression-violence, underdevelopment-violence, torture-violence lead to kidnapping-violence, terrorism-violence, guerrilla-violence (*MM,* 324). As for the most surrealistic clippings, their random inclusion serves several different purposes. By means of them, Cortázar criticizes the alienating effects of advertising, cautions the reader about manipulation by the mass media, destroys the illusion of freedom of choice in a consumer society, and more important, introduce some comic relief into the novel's political debate.

In addition to the interactions among paratexts, we also need to consider the text-paratext relationship. The clippings are not aimlessly inserted into the novel; rather, they maintain an active dialogue with the central narrative. Thus members of the Joda translate the news from the French press, all the while commenting on its content in a tone that oscillates between irony and indignation. These commentaries tend to underscore the characteristic features of each clipping, while at the same time justifying their inclusion in terms of documentary relevance (as happens with the political chronicles and the human rights reports) or for their ludic value (as is the case of the advertisements and the more absurd articles).

But the true significance of the novel can be appreciated only by centering on its declared goal. Unlike Cortázar's previous works, *A Manual for Manuel* is a novel with a straightforward and practical purpose. It is the result of an immediate historical reality and seeks to affect the very same context from which it arises. To that end, *A Manual for Manuel* must first educate the reader in terms of a "reality" that is often manipulated by the mass media. The postscript added to the novel's prologue attacks what it calls "the worldwide massage of the mass media." The indignation of the narrator (easily identifiable with Cortázar) results from the media's disproportionate coverage of the terrorist shootings at the 1972 Munich Olympic Games and their virtual oversight of events simultaneously occurring in Trelew, Argentina.[15] International press agencies cover the Third World only when events there affect more powerful nations. Instead of informing, newspapers, radio, and television frequently make access to information even more difficult.[16] In Latin American countries, especially during the period when *A Manual for Manuel* was published, this access was further hindered by censorship and, in many European countries and the United States, by the lack of interest in news of the non-Western world. When this information is finally offered, it is short-lived and goes practically unnoticed among the endless stream of other newspaper articles.

In *A Manual for Manuel,* Cortázar seeks to counter this transient nature of the news. As D'Haen points out, "when the documentary materials become part of a work of literature, they are estranged from their natural sphere and instead of possessing the ephemerality of a newspaper article—read today and forgotten tomorrow—they are embedded into a work of art which is supposedly eternal and which demands a different and increased kind of attention from the reader. As a result, the horror of the events described is arrested and emphasized."[17] By including newspaper clippings in the text, Cortázar seeks, therefore, to utilize two different genres—journalism and the novel—for his own purposes. On one hand, he exploits the urgent sense of "here and now" normally attributed to the press; on the other, he takes advantage of a different medium, that of novelistic discourse, to stress his political message.

The reader's political response to the novel is also activated through the paratextual emphasis on the conditions of injustice and repression suffered by the "Third World." By incorporating detailed descriptions of torture and human rights violations in Latin America and Vietnam, Cortázar seeks to incite the reader's reaction against these situations. Although *A Manual for Manuel* does not offer specific solutions to the current state of affairs (nor does it claim to do so), it does establish the need for corrective action. Cortázar himself referred to the novel's power when he wrote that he was seeking to create "an unexpected boomerang," that is, a reverberating effect on the very sociohistorical context from which the work sprang.

The critics' rejection of *A Manual for Manuel* has been based repeatedly on the great contradiction it apparently contains: the novel questions the validity of mass media to convey truth (and even suggests that the media manufacture that "reality") while simultaneously utilizing their legitimizing influence (Pope; McCraken; Solotorevsky). This blatant paradox is not, however, unique to *A Manual for Manuel,* nor does it invalidate the book's political message. Rather, Cortázar's use of the media must be understood in the context of postmodernism's counterhegemonic position: "Today, there is no area of language exterior to bourgeois ideology: our language comes from it, returns to it, remains locked within it. The only possible answer is neither confrontation nor destruction but only theft: to fragment the old texts of culture, of science, of literature, and to disseminate and disguise the fragments in the same way that we disguise stolen merchandise."[18] Through the use and manipulation of documentation, postmodernist historical fiction seeks to undermine the hegemonic values that documentation has traditionally served. Instead of endorsing a particular interpretation of reality, the documentary apparatus of these novels plays a problematizing role. On the one hand, it emphasizes the discursive—and therefore mediated—value of all representations. On the other, it denaturalizes the normalizing function of the document. This transgressive use of documentation suggests the need to adapt contemporary oppositional practices to a new literary and historiographic context, one in which the great master narratives yield to a fragmentary and ex-centric view of reality.

A Manual for Manuel constitutes an extreme case, in which the components of political affirmation and communicative immediacy go well beyond those of most postmodernist novels. This characteristic explains why the subjective epistemology that distinguishes historiographic metafiction, although always present, frequently becomes less prominent in the novel. One of the novel's objectives is to protest a situation of injustice and to disseminate the political uprisings in Argentina in the 1960s and 1970s, a series of events that, too often, go unnoticed. To that aim the author employs all available strategies, even those the media utilize to overlook the situation, in a critical manner. The journalistic paratexts are subject to the scrutinizing eyes of the book's characters and, ultimately, to the analytical observations of the reader. Whereas traditional historiography and literary realism used empiricist documentation "to support linear theories of historical development,"[19] Cortázar uses it extensively to problematize the organic worldviews at both the historiographical and literary levels.

The main problem Cortázar faces is how to preserve political immediacy without sacrificing the experimental and ludic character of his works. In order to solve this dilemma he employs the fragmentation that characterizes collage. The document is presented in all its integrity within a certain context—the novel—that is both political and playful. Instead of serving principally as visual stimuli (as in modernist collage), the paratextual clippings preserve their documentary and informative value, while at the same time gaining new significance through their incorporation into the novel's syntagmatic axis. It is precisely this syntagmatic level of fragmentation that is analyzed in the following section.

II

Although utilizing some of the strategies of modernist collage, *A Manual for Manuel* goes beyond the simultaneity and juxtaposition of the actual technique. The novel's educational and moral character demands incorporation of the paratextual "reality jolts" into a mobile and dynamic whole. The realization of a final synthesis—a distinguishing feature in film montage—is, however, problematic in this novel, as it is in all postmodernist works. *A Manual for Manuel* allegorizes the difficulty of achieving such a synthesis and suggests that the realm where it actually takes place is located not in the text but rather in the consciousness of its future readers.

In *A Manual for Manuel*, Cortázar extends his experiments in fragmentation still further. This fragmentation is employed on two main levels: (1) division into disjointed units, and (2) dispersion of the narrative voice. The novel is organized into a large number of narrative segments with practically no transition linking them. On many occasions, the segments are left unfinished and/or consist of equally incomplete dialogues or narratives. On others, they begin in medias res, without informing the reader of the background or context in which they occur. Their sense of discontinuity is enhanced because no clear narrative agency exists: rather, several voices follow—or are superimposed onto—one another, without any explanatory commentary or transition.[20] Two characters share the principal narrative role: *el que te dije* (the-one-I-told-you) and Andrés. The-one-I-told-you is the initial chronicler of the Joda.[21] Although occasionally interacting with the other characters, he is usually withdrawn from the main action, preoccupied by the recording of events in an endless series of notes that he will never be able to organize. A sharp criticism of the methodology and goals of conventional historiography emerges from the novel's portrayal of this character. Like the conservative historian, the-one-I-told-you tries to keep an objective record of the events with minimal ideological interference. To that end, he accumulates a chaotic pile of index cards and scraps of paper that he tries to organize according to the rules of causality and logical taxonomy: "Why that mania for going around slicing things up as if they were a salami? One slice of Screwery, another of personal history, you remind me of the-one-I-told-you with his organizational problems, the poor guy doesn't understand and would like to understand, he's a kind of Linnaeus or Ameghino of the Screwery" (*MM*, 242). Through other characters and narrators the novel also mocks the neutrality the-one-I-told-you tries so hard to maintain: "That neutrality had led him from the beginning to hold himself as if in profile, an operation that is always risky in narrative matters—and let us not call it historical, which is the same thing" (*MM*, 6)

The novel's ambiguous end implies either the death of the-one-I-told-you or simply his inability to complete the narrative project. Consequently, Andrés is left to organize the notes in a more or less coherent way (*MM*, 6), but he will be able to do so only after a violent break with his past. Only by means of his own personal acts of sexual and political transgression will Andrés emerge regenerated and willing to assume his narrative role. In fact, the novel suggests that radical transgression and political engagement are prerequisites to writing in postmodern society. However, Andrés does not completely rewrite the materials he inherits. Sometimes he allows the story to be told from the perspective of the-one-I-told-you (*MM*, 20–23), Ludmilla (*MM*, 239), or Francine (*MM*, 290–91). During these moments, Andrés assumes the simpler role of a regular character, and the absence of markers indicating the shift in perspective contributes to the novel's sense of fragmentation.[22]

What are the consequences of this entangled web of multifarious narratives and limited narrators? Above all, the novel professes to be a collective creation that questions all sources of knowledge. History in *A Manual for Manuel* is really a group of stories, a multifaceted conglomerate that can be approached only from multiple points of view. The novel offers a chain of limited interpreters of fragmentary texts that resist closure, giving the impression of a polyphonic, fluid, and heterogeneous discourse.

In addition to the aspect of multiple perspectivism, cinematic influence is manifested through film metaphors that reveal the novel's mechanisms of production. The metafictional center of *A Manual for Manuel,* its dominant *mise en abyme,* is Andrés's cinematic dream. By means of this obsessive metaphor, Cortázar figuratively presents a synthesis of his own aesthetic and political evolution, an explanation of the novel's inner workings, and a complete theory as to how the novel should be read.

In his recurring dream, Andrés is in a motion-picture theater watching a Fritz Lang mystery film. In the room are two perpendicular screens. Although Andrés tries to watch the film from several locations, there is always something between him and the screens. While shifting seats, Andrés is beckoned by a waiter—someone, a Cuban, wants to see him. As he enters the dark parlor where this mysterious character awaits him, "la escena se corta" [the scene is cut] (*MM*, 100). When Andrés leaves the room, he feels transformed. Now he has a mission to carry out. His meeting with the Cuban appears to have changed his outlook. He feels as if he were acting simultaneously in and outside of the film. He is both the film and a spectator of the film:

> . . . while I was coming back to the theater I could feel the total weight of all this I'm breaking into segments now in order to explain it, even though it's only partial. A little as if only thanks to that act I was to fulfill could I come to know what the Cuban has told me, a completely absurd reversal of causality as you can see. We have the workings of the thriller but I will fulfill it and enjoy it at the same time, the detective story I'm writing and living simultaneously. (*MM,* 101)

Andrés's dream clearly allegorizes his—and Cortázar's—"confuso y atormentado itinerario" [confused and tormented path], (*MM*, 3), to which the novel alludes in the prologue.[23] This effective metaphor portrays Andrés's ideological ambivalence at the beginning of the novel. The two screens suggest what initially seem to be two incompatible alternatives: the artist's engagement with art and his or her engagement with history. Although details of the meeting with the mysterious stranger are never revealed, the encounter clearly refers to the impact of the Cuban revolution on Cortázar's artistic and public personae.

The Cuban's message is not revealed until the final pages of the novel. Up to that point, Andrés refers to the meeting as a gap in his memory, a black hole. When he finally decides to join the Joda—that is, to actively participate in the revolutionary struggle—the veil covering this incident is lifted and we discover that the message is summarized in an expression that alludes to Andrés's awakening to history, and to revolution:

> . . . I catch a glimpse of the antenna and reconstruct the sequence, I look at the man who looks at me from the chair slowly rocking, I see my dream as if I'm finally dreaming it and so simple, so idiotic, so clear, so obvious, it was so perfectly foreseeable that tonight and here I should remember all of a sudden that the dream was nothing more than that, that the Cuban was looking at me and saying only two words to me: *Wake up.* (*MM,* 359)

Aside from its obvious allegorical meaning, Andrés's dream has a specular value. Throughout it, the novel comments on all aspects of its internal structure (story line, theme, form, and structure). In this precise metaphor lie some of the most important keys to understanding not only *A Manual for Manuel* but also Cortázar's political evolution.

Until this point we have examined the importance of this metaphor in terms of the story line, the most obvious aspect, as well as the one most frequently discussed by critics. But Andrés's dream also mirrors the novel's aesthetic qualities, and in relation to the topic under discussion, it reflects the basic conflict between the principles of postmodern collage and montage that dictate the structural pattern of *A Manual for Manuel.* On the one hand, the dream dramatizes the tension between the will to preserve the diversity of forms and ideas contained in the novel and the search for a synthesis that could transcend them, thus making them politically effective. On the other hand, it also suggests that this utopian synthesis can be achieved only through critical reading.

Through this specular metaphor Cortázar re-creates and complements the theory of reading that he had developed up to this point. In previous fictional works and essays he had outlined a poetics that called on active reader participation. According to this poetics, the meaning of a work is considered never an essence but rather an act, the result of the interaction between the reader and the text. In several short stories, as well as in *Hopscotch,* Cortázar condemns the codes of realism, which allow for a passive and complacent attitude from the reader. Instead, he proposes a participatory aesthetics in which the reader must collaborate with the author in the production of meaning. By projecting their consciousness onto the text, they are able to discover aspects of their inner world that they had hitherto ignored. From this approach, reading has a crucial cognitive value, since it allows us to expand our knowledge of the world and of ourselves.[24]

This formalist and psychological theory of reading, similar to the one proposed by reader-response critics during the 1970s, is complemented in *A Manual for Manuel* by the unique focus on politics. The novel's potential is aimed not only at the reader's self-knowledge but also at his or her transformation into a militant reader, one able to implement specific changes in his or her sociohistorical context. From this point of view, it is not simply coincidence that critics have drawn on Bertolt Brecht's theories to explain the underlying aesthetic and political codes in *A Manual for Manuel*.[25] Like Cortázar, Brecht was interested in communicating politically with his audience, without having to minimize his aesthetic aspirations. Brecht also based his literary theory on an admitted antirealism and was involved in a longstanding polemic with social realist theoreticians. However, this antirealism implied not a rejection of mimesis in his works but rather an investigation into its nature. Because both Cortázar and Brecht search for an art that is able to strip phenomena from the mark of normality, their works tend to defamiliarize everything we, the readers, accept noncritically as natural.

Among all the elements of Brecht's dramatic theory, his "alienation effect" plays perhaps the greatest role in understanding the "awakening" of Cortázar's protagonist. Although distancing and defamiliarizing techniques were not unusual in the literary tradition, Brecht developed a whole theory of drama around them and applied them to political goals. According to Brecht, bourgeois ideology masks its own contradictions and limitations, thus creating a pathological sense of normality. In his view, art should liberate the spectator from the passiveness bred by the established patterns of thought. To that end, he proposed to undermine everything that we would conventionally consider normal and acceptable.

Although Andrés's position in the dream is that of one of Cortázar's archetypal readers, the scene is pervaded by the Brechtian conception of revolutionary art. Andrés's initial situation is that of a passive spectator without a clear social position. There are two screens in the theater, and he alternatively contemplates each without comprehending the action of the Fritz Lang film being shown.[26] His condition at the beginning of the dream is hardly different from that of the main characters in two of Cortázar's most famous short stories, "Instructions for John Howell" and "Continuity of Parks." In "Instructions" a spectator is invited to participate in the play (a simple melodrama) he is watching, exposing his personal life as he transgresses his assigned role. In "Continuity" a reader is implicated in a deadly manner in the events of the novel he is reading. However, what in the stories constitutes an attack on forms of realistic illusionism and reader passivity acquires, in *A Manual for Manuel,* political overtones. Cortázar's active spectator becomes here a militant activist, who is called on to participate along with the author, narrators, and characters in the transformation of historical reality.

In *A Manual for Manuel,* this call to political action is expressed symbolically through the meeting with the Cuban. As the novel's end reveals, the Cuban admonishes Andrés's previous blindness and inaction ("Despertáte" [Wake up]). As a result of this meeting, Andrés undergoes a transformation, since he is now aware of the alienation he has experienced thus far and of the need for active participation in the political reality in which he lives. From this moment on, he becomes conscious of a schism ("soy doble," [I'm double]), which is also one of the steps in the Brechtian learning process. In Brecht's epic drama the spectator's awareness of his or her own alienation is followed by his or her critical involvement in the action. Such involvement is characterized by a double impulse of participation and withdrawal. To activate the spectator's critical capacity, the work must make him or her continuously aware of the play's own dramatic condition, its "artificiality." In this way, the spectator is alienated from the action and is no longer influenced by the illusionistic emotionalism essential to Aristotelian drama. In this phase of the dream, Andrés's schism is presented not as something exterior to his experiential realm but rather as his self-awareness of living simultaneously as both creator and spectator—"someone who went to the movies and someone caught up in a typical movie plot" (*MM,* 101). It is precisely at this moment that the character begins to perceive the possibility of achieving a synthesis. Amid the fragmentary perspective of collage and montage, an underlying whole begins to emerge: "While I was coming back to the theater I could feel the total weight of all this I'm breaking into segments now in order to explain it, even though it's only partial" (*MM,* 101). The last phase in this process of learning refers to the revolutionary praxis beyond the text's limits, to the spectator's transformation into the creator of his or her own work: "We have the workings of the thriller but I will fulfill it and enjoy it at the same time, the detective story I'm writing and living simultaneously" (*MM,* 101).

As in the epic drama, *A Manual for Manuel* depicts the process of learning that leads to sociohistorical engagement. The metaphor of Andrés's dream points, therefore, to the transformation of the character from a passive consumer into an active agent of social change. This goal is achieved only after the character becomes aware of his own alienation. In depicting this process, the novel utilizes a broad range of specular images that extend from initial fragmentation and total detachment toward a progressive involvement with the social body. Through Andrés's apprenticeship in both perception and social action, Cortázar again suggests an integration of literary and political activism. Andrés accepts the task of organizing the novel's narrative material only after embracing the human community, symbolized by his participation in the Joda. His involvement in political action is thus one of the prerequisites for the creation of *A Manual for Manuel.* The final synthesis, however, is not in his hands but in those of the critical reader, who will likewise have to respond to the novel's ethical and aesthetic demands.

The book's epilogue presents the penultimate step in the synthesis required from the reader. In a morgue, Lonstein, the novel's most ex-centric character, washes the lifeless body of a revolutionary killed in the police raid that wipes out the Joda. In this last narrative segment, the realms of collage and montage intersect to emphasize again the ideological message of *A Manual for Manuel.* As the text itself suggests, this final scene is also the last entry in the scrapbook that the characters have made for Manuel.[27] By means of a metalepsis, the structural levels of the text (that of the characters) and the paratexts (that of the news collected by these characters) converge to form a single entity. In this way, the text seems to insinuate that the manual created for Manuel by the characters is in fact the novel we have just read, which is, in its turn, part of Latin American reality, "that vast book that we can write among all and for all."[28]

The use of this metalepsis also implies a final connection between the techniques of collage and montage, as well as between an aesthetic and political program. The fragmentation that results from the use of both techniques leaves a trail of blank spaces, of kaleidoscopic arrangements that cannot be resolved within the physical limits of the text. Indeed, this last clipping of Manuel's manual is also the final frame of Cortázar's film-novel, whose assembly will be produced in the reader's consciousness. In a scene that evokes visions of the famous photograph of Che Guevara's dead body, *A Manual for Manuel* reflects on its leitmotifs for the last time. The narrator, probably Andrés, refers to the morgue as that place where "all marks of history will be washed away" (*MM, 389*). The scene portrayed in the epilogue summarizes the paradoxical concept of history that characterizes *A Manual for Manuel* and postmodern historiographic metafiction in general. Primarily, history continues to be the "permanent catastrophe" that Cortázar envisioned in most of his works. To the Hegelian view of history as an organic progress toward perfection, Cortázar opposes a destructive process that leaves its traces on the individual. This situation of oppression and injustice calls for a discourse able, on the one hand, to avoid the erasure of memory and, on the other, to correct such a situation when it does occur. That this rewriting of history stems from the encounter with Lonstein, the embodiment of playfulness in the novel, reinforces Cortázar's recurrently expressed view that a revolutionary work should not forget the spirit of play and experimentation that makes any work truly revolutionary. This search for a synthesis between revolutionary action and play, ethics and aesthetics, dominates Andrés's journey throughout the novel and pervades both the collage of newspaper clippings and the montage of disjointed narrative segments.

Cortázar's historical vision is paradoxical in its quest to attain a difficult synthesis between historical relativism and political affirmation, between antiorganicism and socialism. As a consequence of the equalization of the fictional segments and the documentary paratext, the truthfulness of the novel's political message must be questioned. At the end of the novel, Lonstein exclaims, "They're going to think we made it all up" (*MM*, 389). Indeed, *A Manual for Manuel* is the result, among other things, of Cortázar's creative invention. However, what critics have seen as a blatant inconsistency, a dead end that hinders the interpretation of the novel is, in reality, one of its most redeeming factors. The work's historical relativism is part of the self-criticism that Cortázar deems necessary in both literature and politics. Acceptance of an organic and totalizing historical discourse would have been incompatible with the simultaneous processes of political condemnation and epistemological subjectivism that characterize this novel in particular and postmodernist fiction in general.

Through this paradoxical vision of the relationship between history and literature, the novel affirms the need for records, recognizes the sheer difficulty of recording a gruesome past before its traces are erased and forgotten, and simultaneously warns against the conversion of this record into a new dogma. This need has been and still remains particularly urgent in Argentina, where previous decades have witnessed one of the most spectacular attempts at institutionalizing national oblivion. The "disappearance" of thousands of citizens has been followed by the military's attempt to seal the historical archive by granting general amnesty for most crimes committed during the "Dirty War." Cortázar's attempt to establish a corrective historiography is subject to the verbal limitations and ideological implications inherent in all historiographic works. The historian, the chronicler, and the novelist are always mediators between external reality and the textual realm. Their work is always influenced by both the rhetorical conventions of their discourse and their own ideology (White, ix). In this sense, Cortázar's novel is caught in the dilemma of all oppositional works in the postmodern era: how can we make political statements in a time of growing skepticism, and make them effectively? How can we reconstruct the past if the materials needed for such reconstruction are tinged with prejudices and ideology? The novel does not provide an explicit solution to these problems. It favors neither the denial of relativism and self-criticism nor the refusal of historicity and political commitment. It merely states the inevitability of these polarities, as well as the need for their future articulation. The collage of newspaper clippings and the montage of multiple perspectives contribute to the creation of a heterogeneous and kaleidoscopic space, whose resolution is projected into a utopian future, the realm of the messianic Manuel, *el hombre nuevo*, the ideal reader.

Notes

1. Hayden White, *Metahistory: The Original Imagination in Nineteenth-Century Europe* (Baltimore: Johns Hopkins University Press, 1973), 82.

2. Fredric Jameson, *Postmodernism, or the Cultural Logic of Late Capitalism* (Durham, N.C.: Duke University Press, 1991), 48–49, 54.

3. Georg Lukacs, "Art and Objective Truth", in *Writer and Critic and Other Essays,* ed. and trans. Arthur D. Khan (New York: Grosset & Dunlap, 1971), 41.

4. Jean Baudrillard, *Cultura y simulacro*, Trans. Antoni Vicens and Pedro Rovira (Barcelona: Kairós 1978), 11.

5. As he has repeatedly declared in autobiographical essays and interviews, his visit to Cuba in 1962 changed the direction of his career. In Cuba, Cortázar saw the collective struggle of people to achieve the radical transformation of experience that his characters were blindly seeking. In his interview with Omar Prego, Cortázar confessed that before this visit he held a political stance, but only on a private level. (Omar Prego, *La fascinación de las palabras: Conversaciones con Julio Cortázar* [Barcelona: Muchnik, 1985] 127). The Cuban revolution had a cathartic effect on him: "La Revolución Cubana me despertó a la realidad de América Latina: fue cuando, de una indignación meramente intelectual, pasé a decirme: 'hay que hacer algo' " The Cuban revolution woke me up to the reality of Latin America: it was then that I progressed from a merely intellectual indignation to telling myself: "Something has to be done" (Ernesto Gonzalez Bermejo, *Conversaciones con Julio Cortázar* [Barcelona: Edhasa, 1978] 132). For a description of the impact of the Cuban revolution on Cortázar, see also his open letter to Fernández Retamar (Julio Cortázar, *Último round* [Mexico: Siglo XXI, 1969], 265–80).

6. See Jaime Alazraki "From Bestiary to Glenda: Pushing the Short Story to Its Utmost Limits," *Review of Contemporary Fiction* 3, no. 3 (Fall 1983): 94–99 and "Los últimos cuentos de Julio Cortázar," *Revista Iberoamericana* 130–31 (Jan-June 1985): 21–46.

7. Julio Cortázar, *A Manual for Manuel*, English Trans. Gregory Rabassa (New York: Pantheon, 1978),3.

8. Two of the clippings, for example, allude to French police violence (*MM*, 383, 386).

9. Phil Gunson, et al., *The Dictionary of Contemporary Politics of South America* (New York: Macmillan Publishing Co., 1989), 96.

10. Timothy P. Wicham-Crowley, *Guerillas and Revolution in Latin America: A Comparative Study of Insurgents and Regimes Since 1956.* (Princeton, N.J.: Princeton University Press 1992), 313.

11. Robert Moss, *Urban Guerillas: The New Face of Political Violence* (London: Temple Smith, 1982), 159.

12. The dated nature of the political situation depicted in the novel accounts for Cortázar's interest in having it published as promptly as possible. The historical events cited in the clippings or mentioned in the characters' conversations together form a chronicle of the novel's immediate present. As he explains in his "Corrección de pruebas en la alta montaña"— written immediately before the novel's publication—*A Manual for Manuel* was completed in fall 1972, after two years of work.

13. However, later events did not affect the book's relevance. On the contrary, as the English edition acknowledges, they reinforced and even strengthened it. In Argentina a new, even more violent military regime (1976–1983) rose to power; in Nicaragua a guerilla movement led to revolution (1979); and the U.S. government continued its support of repressive activities in Central and South America. See Tom J. Farer, *The Grand Strategy of the United States in Latin America* (New Brunswick, N.J.: Transaction Book, 1988) for a discussion of U.S. interventionism in Latin America and human rights violations during the 1970s. U.S. government and corporate aid to the coup against Chilean president Salvador Allende in 1973 is also well documented (Gunson et al., 5).

14. Marjorie Perloff, "The Invention of Collage," in *Collage,* ed. Jaimine Parisier Plottel (New York: New York Literary Forum, 1983) 5–47.

15. As noted, in August 1973 a group of political prisoners were executed by their own guards. *A Manual for Manuel* does not comment on these facts, it just lists the words "Trelew"

and "Munich" side by side, so that the reader must make the connection and come to his or her conclusion concerning media manipulation.

16.   However, Cortázar does not reject the media per se but rather the alienation they cause. Indeed, he uses popular and mass culture for his own ends. The potential value that Cortázar attributes to the media as well as the need for the Latin American intellectual to use it to his or her benefit is evidenced by his use of the press in *Libro de Manuel* and of comic strips in *Fantomas*.

17.   Theo D'Haen, *Text to Reader: A Communicative Approach to Fowles, Barth, Cortázar and Boon* (Amsterdam: John Benjamins, 1983), 92.

18.   Ihab Hassan, *The Right Promethean Fire: Imagination, Science and Cultural Change* (Urbana: University of Illinois Press, 1982), 17.

19.   Barbara Foley, *Telling the Truth: The Theory and Practice of Documentary Fiction* (Ithaca, N.Y.: Cornell University Press, 1986), 221.

20.   Jonathan Titler has used the term "schizoid narration" to refer to the novel's heterogeneity of perspectives in *Narrative Irony in the Contemporary Spanish-American Novel* (Ithaca, N.Y.: Cornell University Press, 1984), 188.

21.   At the very beginning of the narrative segment that follows the prologue, the narrator (Andrés) refers to the-one-I-told-you as the first narrator who tries to record the history of the Joda: "Otherwise, it was as if the-one-I-told-you had intended to recount some things, for he had gathered together a considerable amount of notes and clippings waiting, it would seem, for them to end up all falling into place without too much loss" (*MM*, 6).

22.   Another narrative agency present is the voice that sets the novel in motion. The opening segment is delivered by a voice that announces the novel's subject and the circumstances surrounding its writing. This narrative voice—clearly related to the author's—reflects on some of the values and limitations of *A Manual for Manuel* and helps place the novel in the context of its production.

23.   Although obvious, Andrés's and Cortázar's processes of growing historical consciousness are identified and established in the novel's prologue: "This man is dreaming something I had dreamed in a like manner during the years when I was just beginning to write, and as happens so many times in my incomprehensible writer's trade, only much later did I realize that the dream was also part of the book and that it contained the key to that merging of activities which until then had been unlike" (*MM*, 3).

24.   See Santiago Juan-Navarro, "77 ó 99 / modelos para desarmar: claves para una lectura morelliana de 'Continuidad de los parques' de Julio Cortázar," *Hispanic Journal* 13, no. 2 (1992): 241–49, "Un tal Morelli: teoría y práctica de la lectura en *Rayuela*," *Revista Canadiense de Estudios Hispánicos* 16, no. 2 (1992): 235–52; and "El espectador se rebela: 'Instrucciones para John Howell' de Julio Cortázar o la estética de la subversión," *MIFLC Review* (1991):148–58.

25.   See Theo D'Haen *Text to Reader. . .*, and Linda Hutcheon, *A Poetics of Postmodernism: History, Theory, Fiction* (New York: Routledge, 1988).

26.   Given the political nature and avant-gardism of *A Manual for Manuel*, the reference to Fritz Lang is especially relevant. As Parkinson Zamora has suggested, Fritz Lang was a member of the German avant-garde movement in film that confronted problems that, in a historical and political sense, were similar to issues Cortázar dealt with in his novel. Both Lang and Cortázar are artists who seek to harmonize aesthetic innovation and political content. Both also wrote in a period in which the rise of fascism was seen as an increasing threat to their respective countries: "By alluding to Lang, Cortázar allies his novel to a tradition of formal experimental and politically committed art. . . . He also allies his work to a highly problematic historical and national context in which artistic commitment was both difficult and essential, as Cortázar feels it to be in contemporary Latin America as well". Lois Parkinson Zamora, "Movement and Stasis, Film and Photo: Temporal Structures in the Recent Fiction of Julio Cortázar," *Review of Contemporary Fiction* 3, no. 3 (Fall 1983): 59.

27.   The previous segment, in which members of the Joda discuss the making of Manuel's manual, ends with Andrés passing on to Patricio a final clipping to be included in the album. According to Andrés, this clipping "begins with a pitcher of water" (*MM*, 388). Similarly, the final scene begins with these words: "Lonstein slowly filled the water pitcher and put it on one of the empty tables" (*MM*, 389).

28.   Julio Cortázar, *Argentina: Años de alambradas culturales* (Barcelona: Muchnik, 1984), 107.

Selected Bibliography

◆

JULIO CORTÁZAR'S WORKS IN ENGLISH TRANSLATION

End of Game and Other Stories. Trans. Paul Blackburn. New York: Pantheon Books, 1967. Selections from *Bestiario, Final del juego,* and *Las armas secretas.* Successive reprints published as *Blow-Up and Other Stories* (New York: Collier Books, 1968).

The Winners. Trans. Elaine Karrigan. London: Souvenir Press, 1965.

Hopscotch. Trans. Gregory Rabassa. New York: Pantheon Books, 1966.

Cronopios and Famas. Trans. Paul Blackburn. New York: Pantheon Books, 1969.

62: A Model Kit. Trans. Gregory Rabassa. New York: Pantheon Books, 1972.

All Fires the Fire and Other Stories. Trans. Suzanne Jill Levine. New York: Pantheon Books, 1973.

A Manual for Manuel. Trans. Gregory Rabassa. New York: Pantheon Books, 1978.

A Change of Light and Other Stories. Trans. Gregory Rabassa. New York: Alfred Knopf, 1980. It includes stories originally collected in two separate volume—*Octaedro* (1974) and *Alguien que anda por ahí* (1977).

We Love Glenda So Much and Other Stories. Trans. Gregory Rabassa. New York: Alfred A. Knopf, 1983.

A Certain Lucas. Trans. Gregory Rabassa. New York: Alfred A. Knopf, 1984.

Around the Day in Eighty Worlds. Trans. Thomas Christensen. San Francisco: North Point Press, 1986. Includes texts originally collected in two separate volumes—*La vuelta al día en ochenta mundos* (1967) and *Último round* (1969).

Unreasonable Hours (Deshoras.) Trans. Alberto Manguel. Toronto: Coach House Press, 1995.

Save Twilight; Selected Poems (Salvo el crepásculo, 1984), Trans. Stephen Kessler. San Francisco: City Lights Books, 1997.

CRITICAL BIBLIOGRAPHY

For the most complete critical bibliography on Cortázar's works, see Sarah de Mundo Lo, *Julio Cortázar, His Works and His Critics: A Bibliography* (Urbana, Ill.: Albatross, 1985). In the present bibliography only selected book-length studies and special issues of university journals published in English are included.

Book-length Studies

Alazraki, Jaime, and Ivar Ivask, eds. *The Final Island: The Fiction of Julio Cortázar*. Norman: University of Oklahoma Press, 1978.

Boldy, Stephen. *The Novels of Julio Cortázar*. Cambridge University Press, 1980.

Brody, Robert. *Julio Cortázar: Rayuela* (Critical Guides to Spanish Texts Series). London: Grant & Cutler Ltd. (In assoc. with Tamesis Books Ltd.), 1976.

D'Haen, Theodor Louis, *Text to Reader: A Communicative Approach to Fowles, Barth, Cortázar, and Boon*. Amsterdam: John Benjamins, 1983. (on *A Manual for Manuel*).

Gale Research Company (Publishers), *Short Story Criticism*, Vol. 7: Julio Cortázar (Detroit: Gale Research, 1991), 47–97.

Garfield, Evelyn Picon. *Julio Cortázar*. New York: Frederick Ungar, 1975.

Hernández del Castillo, Ana. *Keats, Poe, and the Shaping of Cortázar's Mythopoesis* (Purdue University Monographs in Romance Languages). Amsterdam: John Benjamins B.V., 1981.

King, Sarah E. *The Magical and the Monstrous: Two Faces of the Child Figure in the Fiction of Julio Cortázar and José Donoso*. New York: Garland Publishing, 1992.

Peavler, Terry J. *Julio Cortázar*. Boston: Twayne Publishers, 1990.

Yovanovich, Gordana. *Julio Cortázar's Character Mosaic; Reading the Longer Fiction*. Toronto: University of Toronto Press, 1991.

Special Issues of Literary Journals

Books Abroad; An International Literary Quarterly (University of Oklahoma, Norman, Oklahoma), Vol. 50, No. 3, Summer 1976.

Review 72 (Focus on Julio Cortázar) (Winter 1972).

The Review of Contemporary Fiction (Elmwood Park, Illinois), 3, no. 3 (Fall 1983).

Point of Contact (University of Syracuse, Syracuse, New York) 4, no. 1 (Fall/Winter 1994).

Index

♦

activism, for "disappeared," 2
Adiós Robinson y otras piezas breves, 3
adulthood, 124–32
"After Lunch." *See* "Después del almuerzo"
(After Lunch)
Alazraki, Jaime: "From *Bestiary* to *Glenda:*
Pushing the Short Story to Its Limits,"
133–40; Introduction, 1–18
Albatross (publisher), 3
Alfaguara Publishers, 3
alienation, 186
"All Fires the Fire," 133
Anales de Buenos Aires, Los, 39
Antonioni, Michelangelo: *Blow-up* (movie),
147–48; on image of reality, 151; *Red
Desert* (movie), 149
"Apocalypse at Solentiname," 102–4
Apocalyptic vision, in "Perseguidor, El," 92–111
Argentina, 2; "desaparecidos" in, 104; dis-
satisfaction with, 8; exile from, 70;
political violence in, 139; politics in,
6–7 , 8–9, 177–80. *See also* Buenos
Aires; Cortázar, Julio; politics
Argentinian, meaning of, 53–54
Arias, Mercedes, letters to, 6, 7
Armas secretas, Las (Secret Weapons), 9–10,
34, 137
Around the Day in Eighty Worlds, 1, 124–25,
128
art: politics and, 100; totalitarianism in,
104–5
"Art and Revolution in the Fiction of Julio
Cortázar" (Zamora), 92–114
artist, struggle of, 146–47
artistic consciousness, 96

artistic imagination, apocalyptic vision and, 92
autobiography, 1, 75; in "Apocalypse at
Solentiname," 102; childhood elements
in writings and, 117–18. *See also* childhood; children
*Autonautas de la cosmopista, Los (The Autonauts
of the Cosmohighway or An Atemporal
Journey Paris-Marseille),* 23, 69
"Axolotl," 135, 143, 150

"Babas del diablo, Las," 144 (*see also* "Blow-
up")
Babilonia, Aureliano, 87
Bachmann, Susan M., 96
Banfield, childhood in, 117, 118, 119–24
baroque, in writing, 75
Barrie, J. M., 117
Barth, John, 99
Basualdo, Ana, 14
Benedetti, Mario, 14
Bergson, Henri, 111
Bermejo, Ernesto, interview with, 116
Bernárdez, Aurora: marriage to, 9;
"Perseguidor, El" ("The Pursuer") and,
10
Bestiario (Bestiary), 4–5, 8, 9, 10, 34,
38–39, 43, 135; images in, 39
"Bestiary" (story), 116, 117, 120, 123
Bibliography (Mundo Lo), 10, 15
bibliography of works, 3
Biblioteca Personal (series), 5
biographical tradition, 1
Blackburn, Paul, 80, 81
"Blow-Up: The Forms of an Esthetic Itiner-
ary" (Grossvogel), 144–54

The Volume Author

♦

Jaime Alazraki was born in Argentina in 1934 and is professor of Latin American literature at Columbia University in New York. Among his most important books are *La prosa narrativa de Jorge Luis Borges* (1967, 1974, 1983), *Versiones, inversiones, reversiones: El espejo como modelo estructural del relato en los cuentos de Borges* (1977), and *Borges and the Kabbalah and Other Essays on His Fiction and Poetry* (1988), and he has edited the volume on Borges for G. K. Hall's Critical Essays on World Literature series. On Julio Cortázar's work he has written *En busca del unicornio: Los cuentos de Julio Cortázar* (1983) and *Hacia Cortázar: Aproximaciones a su obra* (1994). Alazraki is the co-editor of a collection of essays *The Final Island: The Fiction of Julio Cortázar* (1978) and the editor of the following editions of Cortázar's writings: *Rayuela* (Caracas, 1980), *Final del juego* (Madrid, 1995), and *Obra crítica/2* (Madrid, 1994).

The General Editor

◆

Robert Lecker is professor of English at McGill University in Montreal. He received his Ph.D. from York University. Professor Lecker is the author of numerous critical studies, including *On the Line* (1982), *Robert Kroetch* (1986), *An Other I* (1988), and *Making It Real: The Canonization of English-Canadian Literature* (1995). He is the editor of the critical journal *Essays on Canadian Writing* and of many collections of critical essays, the most recent of which is *Canadian Canons: Essays in Literary Value* (1991). He is the founding and current general editor of Twayne's Masterwork Studies and the editor of the Twayne World Authors Series on Canadian writers. He is also the general editor of G. K. Hall's Critical Essays on World Literature series.